Armchair Advice

"You will need to don a coat of arms in order to get out of here," it said. "It is hard to depart this region if you aren't suitably armed, and you have only two arms. There's a coat hanging behind you. Don that, and you should be all right."

I looked behind me, and almost leaped out of my shoes. There was a mass of arms almost touching me. But I realized that this was no ordinary situation, so I nerved myself and took hold of the mass. The arms were linked, forming a clumsy kind of jacket. I put this on over my shoulders. It was heavy, but not uncomfortable. "Thank you," I told the armchair.

I moved on in the direction I hoped was out, but the brush and foliage closed in so thickly that it seemed impossible to proceed. Then my coat of arms began to react. The arms writhed and reached out all around me, grabbing branches, nettles, thorns, spikes, and unidentified obstacles and pushing, bending, twisting, shoving, and hauling them out of my way. I walked forward, into the opening cleared in this fashion, and soon was beyond the otherwise impenetrable thicket.

"Thank you, coat of arms," I said gratefully, glancing down. But now my coat was merely woven of sticks and twigs.

I was baffled for a moment, then realized what had happened: the coat had lost its special magic. That meant I was out of the Region of Madness.

TOR BOOKS BY PIERS ANTHONY

Alien Plot
Anthonology
But What of Earth?
Demons Don't Dream
Geis of the Gargoyle
Ghost
Harpy Thyme
Hasan
Isle of Woman
Letters to Jenny
Prostho Plus
Race Against Time
Shade of the Tree
Shame of Man
Steppe
Triple Detente

WITH ROBERT E. MARGROFF:

Dragon's Gold
Serpent's Silver
Chimaera's Copper
Mouvar's Magic
Orc's Opal
The E.S.P. Worm
The Ring

WITH FRANCES HALL:

Pretender

WITH RICHARD GILLIAM:

Tales from the Great Turtle (Anthology)

GEIS OF THE GARGOYLE

PIERS ANTHONY

TOR®
fantasy

A TOM DOHERTY ASSOCIATES BOOK
NEW YORK

GEIS OF THE GARGOYLE

Cover art by Darrell K. Sweet

A Tor Book
Published by Tom Doherty Associates, Inc.
175 Fifth Avenue
New York, NY 10010

Tor® is a registered trademark of Tom Doherty Associates, Inc.

ISBN: 0-812-53485-9
Library of Congress Card Catalog Number: 94-41006

First edition: February 1995
First mass market edition: February 1996

Printed in the United States of America

0 9 8 7 6 5 4 3 2 1

Contents

1.	GARY GAR	1
2.	GOOD MAGICIAN	17
3.	IRIS	32
4.	SURPRISE	49
5.	HIATUS	71
6.	MADNESS	88
7.	RUINS	108
8.	ANIMATION	130
9.	HINGE	147
10.	KEYSTONE	167
11.	INTERFACE	187
12.	DISCOVERY	203
13.	FUTURE	222
14.	PAST	244
15.	LOVE	263
16.	DREAM	287
17.	HARNESS	306
18.	RETURN	333
	AUTHOR'S NOTE	338

1
GARY GAR

The demoness formed into smoke, and then into an insidiously lovely (if you like that type) human-style woman. Her face was unutterably fair, her hair flowed like honey, her bosom was so full and well-formed that it was probably sinful just to look at it, and the rest of her was moreso. But there was something odd about her apparel.

She eyed the creature sitting in the dry riverbed, who was about as opposite from her as it was possible to be. "My, you're an ugly customer," she remarked.

"Thank you," the thing replied gruffly.

"You can speak!" she said, surprised.

"Only when I make the effort."

She walked around it. Her dainty delicate feet did not quite touch the ground, but the ground here was so scabbed and messy that this was just as well. She peered closely at every detail. "You have a face like a cross between a lion and an ape, with the worst features of each, and with an extremely big mouth formed into a perpetual O. You have a grotesque compact body with an inane tail and four big clumsy feet. And you have a pair of really ugly stumpy leathery wings. Overall I can't imagine a worse-looking creature."

"Thank you. You, in contrast, are unconscionably aesthetic."

"I'm what?" she asked, frowning.

"Disgustingly pretty."

"Oh. Thank you."

"My statement was not a compliment."

"Well, neither was mine! I have just three questions to ask of you, monster."

"Then will you go away?"

She shook a fine firm finger. "Answer mine, then I'll answer yours, you refugee from a horror house. What are you?"

"I am a gargoyle."

"Who are you?"

"Gary Gar."

"And what are you doing, Gary Gargoyle?"

"I am performing according to my geis."

"What's a gaysh?"

"Forget it, demoness! You promised to answer mine after three of yours."

She frowned prettily. "Very well, Gary Garble. Ask your stupid question." A large mug appeared in her hand. "Would you like a drink from Ein Stein first?"

"What's tha—" he started to ask, but caught himself almost barely in time. She was trying to trick him into wasting his stupid question. "No. I don't know what that is, so I won't risk it."

"Too bad," she said. "One drink from this would have made you Xanth's smartest creature, capable of concluding that Eeee equals Emcee squared." The mug disappeared.

"I can live without that conclusion," he said. "Who are you?"

She fidgeted, beginning to lose definition. "That's awkward to answer."

"Well, make the effort, smokeface."

Her features reformed, lovelier than before. "I'm D. Mentia, but that's only a half-truth."

"What's the other half of the truth?"

"I'm the alter ego of the Demoness Metria. She did something disgusting, so I'm sailing out on my own."

"What did she do?"

"She got married, got half a soul, and fell in love, in that order. Now she's so nice I can't stand her."

"Do demons marry?"

"Forget it, gargle. I answered three already. Now it's my turn again. What's a gaysh?"

"A misspelling of geis."

"How can you tell it's misspelled when I'm speaking it?"

"I am long familiar with the word. You're pronouncing it as it sounds."

She grimaced. "Sorry about that. So what is it?"

"An obligation of honor."

"What does an ugly character like you know about a fair concept like honor?"

"That's your fourth question. Mine first: Why are you wearing a skirt upside and a blouse downside?"

Mentia glanced down at herself. The clothing faded out, leaving a body so barely luscious that any ordinary man who spied it would freak out in half a moment. "That's hard to explain."

"Make another effort, bareface," Gary said, looking slightly bored though her face was the least of her bareness.

"Well, my better nature—that is, D. Metria—has a certain problem with words. For example she would say you really don't look properly volant, and you would say—"

"Properly what?"

"And she would say feathers, uplift, flapping, sky, winging—"

"Flightworthy?"

"And she would say Whatever, crossly."

"That's what *volant* means?"

"Uh-uh, Garfield. I answered three. What's this about honor?"

Gary sighed. It was a good effort, because his stone body was mostly hollow. "From time vaguely memorial on, my family of gargoyles has been in charge of this river, the Swan Knee, which flows from drear Mundania into Xanth, as you can see." He gestured with a wing. Sure enough, to the north the dry channel wound unhappily through truly dreary terrain. The line where the magic of Xanth took effect was marked by increasingly magical vegetation, such as shoe trees, lady slippers, and acorn trees. The Mundane equivalents were sadly deficient. "Normally the water flows south, and it has been our geis to guarantee its purity, so that Xanth is not stained by Mundanian contaminants. Normally the water was mostly clean, so this was no problem, but in recent decades it has become sullied, until it was virtually sludge. It was awful, cleaning it up! But now there's a drought, and there's no water at all, which is worse yet. I hope that when the rains return, and the flow resumes, that it will be cleaner, so that it doesn't leave such a foul taste in my mouth. But regardless, I will do it, because my line is honor bound to guarantee the quality of this water. No wading swans will get their knees dirty in *this* river."

"Now that's interesting," Mentia said, looking about as bored as he had been when she had lost her clothing. "But why are you wasting your time here, when you could get the job done without all that fuss?"

Now the gargoyle began to show some feeling. "What do you mean, wasting my time? This is my *job*, demoness."

"So it's your job. But why not do it the easy way?"

"Because it's the only way I know." He paused, counting. "That's three questions I've answered. My turn. What's this easy way?"

"How should I know, spoutface?"

"You don't know how?"

"That's right, garnishee."

Gary paused, realizing that two of his questions were already gone, by her slightly crazy rules. He had already failed to learn why her clothing had been confused, and he didn't want to fail to learn how to do his job the easy way. So he phrased his question carefully. "What gives you the idea that there is an easy way to do my job?"

Mentia shrugged, making ripples all across her front and down her arms. "There has to be, because if you went to ask the Good Magician about it, he would have the answer."

The Good Magician! He had never thought of that. But he realized that this was not a wise course for him. "I couldn't go to ask him, because the moment it rains, the river will resume its flow, and I shall have to be here to clarify it. Anyway, I understand he's extremely grumpy. And I don't know the way there."

"Why don't you make a dam, so the water can't pass until you return to process it? And what's so bad about grumpiness, if it frees you from a lifetime's geis? And why not ask me to show you the way there?"

Three more questions. Gary pondered, then answered them. "I could make such a dam. A few minutes of grumpiness seem a bargain, when I think of it that way. And I won't ask you to show me the way there because you're a demoness who surely has mischief in mind."

She considered that. "It's your turn for questions. Why don't you ask me if I mean to lead you astray?"

He became interested. "Do you?"

"No."

"Why not?"

"Because I have a defect of demonly character: I'm slightly crazy. That's why my clothing was mixed up." Her blouse and skirt reappeared, correctly placed. "I share this with my better half: I like to be entertained, and you promise to be entertaining. I don't care about you personally, of course, but I hate being bored."

That seemed to be a fair answer. So Gary gambled and asked the expected question: "Will you guide me safely to the Good Magician's castle?"

"Yes."

"Very well. I shall make the dam."

He got to work. There were some wallflowers not far distant, and he was able to transplant several to the river bed. But there was a problem: they needed water in order to flower, and he had none.

"Well, find some water lilies or water melons or water cress," Mentia suggested impatiently. Her body was aimed away from him, but this didn't matter because her head was now on backwards; she had gotten confused again.

"There aren't any in sight," he pointed out. "I know only the plants that are in sight, because I have been bound to my post in the river for the past century or so."

"Oh for illness sake!" she exclaimed. "I'll find some." Her lower section fuzzed and formed into a peculiar wheeled vehicle.

"What's that?" Gary asked, surprised.

"Haven't you seen a snit before?" Then a dirty noise pooped out of the thing's tailpipe, its wheels spun, and it zoomed away at magical speed. She was departing in a snit.

Then it zoomed backward, just as rapidly, coming to park just under his nose. "Just be thankful it isn't a snot," the demoness said, and was gone again.

Gary was duly thankful. He had not had a lot of experience with demons, but this one seemed tolerable despite being rather too pretty for his taste.

Soon she was back, bearing a boxlike object. "That doesn't look like a water plant," Gary said dubiously.

"Naturally not," she agreed, setting it in the river bed beside some of the rocklike pillows there. "It's a closet."

"What good is a closet? We need water."

"A water closet," she clarified. She opened the door, and a flood of bright blue liquid poured out.

"That's polluted!" Gary cried. He jumped down and placed himself in the path of the flow. He sucked up the water, then spouted it out. "Oh—it's water color."

"Whatever," she agreed. "It will do, won't it?"

He considered, tasting more of the water as it changed to red and then to green. Already some of it was sinking into the ground around the wallflowers, and they were growing. "Yes, as long as it doesn't flow away from here."

"So make another little damn."

"A what?"

"To divert the curse."

In a short moment he figured it out. A dam to divert the course of the flow. Mentia might be her self's worse half, but she did seem to suffer from a bit of her better half's problem with vocabulary. He hastily scraped dirt and rocks across the path of the stream, causing it to puddle. That left it nowhere to flow but into the ground around the flowers. These responded by developing blue, red, green and other colored walls, depending on the color of the water. The walls walled off the main riverbed. The job was done.

"Let's be off," the demoness said, floating up. She had resumed her full human form, and was correctly garbed.

But Gary hesitated. "I'm not sure this is appropriate."

She floated over him, becoming even more lovely in her moderate pique. "Why not, garlic?"

"Because my powers of flight are limited. I weigh considerable, being lithic."

"Being what?"

"Being made mostly of stone, so I can fly only when aided by a steep slope or a gale-force breeze. I shall have to proceed along the ground."

"So why not proceed, garnet? That doesn't mean *I* have to be landbound."

"I think it does."

"Why, garland?"

"Because from down here I think I can see your panties."

She exploded into roiling smoke. Flames licked around the roils. Her voice emerged, tinged with soot. "You aren't supposed to look, garget!"

"I didn't look. But I suspect that if I did—"

"Oh." The cloud sank to the ground, coalescing into her luscious human form—this time in red jeans. "Point made, garden. I'll walk when you do. Thanks for not looking."

"Thanks for getting my name straight."

She paused, fuzzing briefly before firming again. "Got it, Gary Gar." She glanced speculatively at him. "It occurs to me you're not quite as stupid as you look."

"I don't look stupid, I look properly grotesque. It occurs to me that you're not quite as careless as you seem."

"You know, if you were less ugly, I could almost be tempted to think about possibly starting to get to like you."

"If you were less pretty, I might be tempted not to dislike you."

Once more she fuzzed. "You like ugly!" she exclaimed. "How fitting!"

"I'm a gargoyle. We're the ugliest creatures in Xanth, and righteously proud of it."

"What about the ogres?"

Gary pondered. "I suppose you could call them ugly, if you dislike that type," he concluded grudgingly.

"Maybe we'll encounter some along the way, and see." Then she thought of something else. "You're no more human than I am. Why should you care about panties?"

"I don't. But you evidently do."

"Well, when I emulate the human form there are codes of conduct to be observed, or the emulation is imperfect. But that does give me a notion." She fuzzed, and reappeared as a female gargoyle, horrendously ugly. "How do you like me now, Gary?"

He studied her. "I wish you were real. I'd be glad to spout water with you."

"Ha! You mean I can tempt you in this form, and endlessly frustrate you? This promises to be entertaining after all."

"Let's be on our way," he said shortly.

"On down the riverbed," she said. "It will take us south to the gulf."

"But I can't swim," he protested. "I would sink right to the bottom."

"Then we won't enter the water. We'll proceed along the shore. Except—" She broke off, evidently waiting for his query.

"Except what?" he dutifully inquired.

"Except for the whatever. You'll have trouble navigating that." Then she brightened. "But maybe I can figure out a way. Onward!"

"Onward," he agreed, determined not to oblige her by asking again.

They set off down the riverbed, bound by bound, using their little wings to steer the bounds and keep them within bounds. It was the gargoyle way.

Before long the dry riverbanks changed color, turning yellow. Gary paused. "What's the matter with the ground?"

Mentia looked. "Nothing. It's just doing its thing."

"But it's all sickly yellow!"

"No it isn't." She raked a claw across the dirt. Golden coins rolled down into the channel. "This bank is pay dirt. And there's a mint." She pointed to a plant with odd oblong greenbacked leaves and round golden flowers with serrated edges. "This is the bank where the money comes from, is all."

"Money? What good is it?"

"No good that I know of. But I understand they love it in Mundania."

"They do?"

"They say that the love of money is the root of all evil."

She looked at the mint's roots, which did look bad, if not actually evil.

"But doesn't that mean that they think it's bad?"

"No, Mundania is such an awful place that they must love evil."

Gary nodded. "That does make sense."

"Pennies and cents," she agreed.

They bounded on. They came to a sign:

WHEN PASSING THIS BOG   BEWARE OF THE DOG

"I don't see any bog," Gary said.

"I don't see any dog either. But maybe it doesn't matter; that's just doggerel."

A new kind of tree appeared along the bank. There was the sound of barking. "Dogwoods," Mentia explained. "They're harmless if you don't try to rub against their bark, which is worse than their bite."

But then real dogs appeared. "I thought Xanth had no dogs," Gary said.

"This is close to the border; a pack must have crossed over, and the dogs haven't yet had time to turn magic. It happens."

The dogs converged, growling. "They don't seem to be friendly," Gary remarked.

"Who cares? They can't hurt us. I'm a demoness and you're mostly mythic."

"Lithic."

"Whatever." So they bounded on, ignoring the dogs. But the animals pursued doggedly.

It got worse. Ahead was a solid line of canines. It was impossible to bound through them. So they stopped before the large female in the center. "Who are you and what do you want?" Gary asked, hardly expecting an answer.

"I am Dogma," she replied. "I want your dog tags."

"We don't have anything like that."

"Then we'll have to eat you."

"Just because we don't have something you want?" he asked incredulously.

"I'm a real bitch," she reminded him.

"Then we'll just have to fight you," Gary said with regret, for he was a peaceful creature. "Have you ever been chomped by stone teeth?"

Dogma reconsidered. "I'm really not dogmatic. Just what kind of a monster are you?" she demanded.

"I'm a gargoyle. I purify the water coming along this river, but I'm trying to find a better way to do it."

"Doggone it," she complained. "Why didn't you say so? We thought you were pretending to be a dog."

"Why would anyone want to be a dog?" Mentia demanded.

Dogma turned to the others. "Let them go, dogfaces," she growled. "We don't have a problem with gargoyles, and we don't want our river to get spoiled. The swans would go away."

The dogs looked disgusted, but gave way, and the two moved on down the river channel. But they had hardly cleared the dog region before they encountered worse.

"More dogs?" Gary asked, seeing the creatures approaching.

"No. Wolves."

"What's the difference? Aren't wolves just wild dogs?"

"Not in Xanth."

They stopped as the wolves closed in. "What do you creatures want?" Gary demanded. He was getting impatient with these delays; at this rate it would be hard to accomplish his business with the Good Magician and return before nightfall.

"We are the Wolf clan," the lead female said, changing to human form. "I am Virginia Wolf."

"You—werewolves!" Gary exclaimed, surprised.

"We still *are* wolves," she said. "We were wolves yesterday and will be so tomorrow."

"I mean you change form," he said, flustered.

She looked around. "We do? Where?"

"Right here."

"Here, there, everywhere; what's the difference where wolves are?" More wolves were assuming human form.

"I mean you're magical. You're not true wolves."

Virginia shook her head. "Never cry wolf," she cautioned him.

"She's teasing you," Mentia said.

Gary was catching on to that. "I'm the gargoyle who purifies the Swan Knee water. I want to get a better way to honor my geis from the Good Magician."

"We suspected as much," she said. "Otherwise the dog pack wouldn't have let you through. But you know you have a long road to run."

"I do? How far is it?"

"Several days plus the Gap Chasm."

"The what?"

"You don't know about the Gap Chasm?"

"I've never been south of the border," he said, nettled. "What's this about a gap?"

"It's a big crevice across Xanth," she explained. "It used to have a forget spell on it, so nobody remembered it, but most folk know about it now. You look too heavy to fly far, so maybe you can't get there from here."

Gary turned to Mentia. "You didn't tell me about this!" he said accusingly.

"That wouldn't have been entertaining," she retorted.

"And what's this about several days?"

"You didn't ask."

"I'll never get this done before it rains!"

"That's why you built the dam."

She had him there. "Still, if I can't cross the chasm—"

"I have an idea how to do that."

He was frustrated, but decided to go ahead. Maybe it was still possible. The notion of returning to his dry riverbed to wait for more Mundane sludge to come through was appealing less, for some reason. "So will you let us through?" he asked Virginia.

"We might as well. We don't want dirty water either. It would mess up our apparel."

"Your apparel?" he asked blankly.

"We are underwear wolves," she explained. "We're training to crowd out the regular monsters under children's beds, and get a cushier life-style."

He realized belatedly that what he had taken for a specialized costume on their human forms was actually underclothing. In fact Virginia was wearing panties. It was a good thing he wasn't human, or he would have freaked out, because that was the magic of panties.

They resumed their bounding. They made good time, but the distance stretched farther, and night caught them.

"Do gargoyles sleep?" Mentia inquired.

"Only when we're bored."

"Are you bored?"

"No." Frustrated, but not bored.

"So let's keep moving. I know the way."

Gary was glad to do that. They bounded on through the darkness. There were surely predators of the night, but they evidently elected to leave the demoness and the gargoyle alone. The result was that as morning came, they were just arriving at what looked like a stall fashioned into a house.

"What is this?" Gary asked.

"A stall fashioned into a house."

"I mean what are we doing here?"

"Arriving."

Demons could get exasperating on occasion. "Is this going to help us cross the chasm?"

"No."

"Then why are we—?"

"The occupants may help, however," she clarified. "Houses don't seem to care much about chasms, but the centaurs do."

The door opened. A winged centaur filly about nine years old peered out. "Eeeek," she screamed. "An incredibly ugly monster!"

"Oh be quiet, Cynthia," the demoness snapped. "It's only me, Mentia, Metria's worse aspect."

"But Metria's safely married and no longer doing mischief abroad," the filly protested.

"I know. It's disgusting. That's why *I'm* abroad." Mentia assumed human form. "A demon broad. Tell Chex I could use a favor."

In a moment a mature winged centaur emerged, tying her damp hair back; she must have been interrupted as she washed it. "Metria has a split personality?" she inquired.

"Emotional havoc can do that," Mentia said. "I couldn't stand her half-souled loving attitude, so I fissioned off. Now I'm in charge of the mischief. But I got distracted by this ugly brute, so I'm guiding him to the Good Magician's castle. But the Gap Chasm's in the way, and he's too solid to fly, so—"

Chex gazed at Gary. "Why you're a gargoyle, aren't you?" she asked. "We seldom see your kind here."

"That's because most of us are purifying the waters flowing in from Mundania, according to our geis," he explained. "But now if I can find a better way—"

"Of course," she agreed immediately. Centaurs, he remembered, were very bright. "And you need to fly across the Gap Chasm. I can certainly help you to do that."

"You can?" he asked, amazed. "But my weight—"

She turned and flicked him with her tail. Suddenly he felt light-headed and light-bodied. He flapped his wings experimentally, and sailed into the air. She had made him so light that he was able to fly!

"Thank you," Mentia said. "Some day I shall fail to do you mischief, when I have the chance."

Chex smiled. "That seems a fair bargain. We do need clean water. In any event, we winged monsters have to help each other."

Mentia rose into the air. "I knew that," she said. Then, to Gary: "Move it, monster. You don't want to be over the chasm when her magic wears off."

"Just how big is this crevice?" he asked.

"You'll see."

They flew south as the sun made a nest of colors to the east and lifted itself out of the clouds. Suddenly an enormous chasm opened out below. It was so wide and deep that a few of the pink morning clouds were nestling within it. Gary could not see to its base; that was still shrouded in night. But he felt new urgency to get across it; already he was feeling heavier.

They landed beyond the Gap on what the demoness assured him was an enchanted path: only folk on legitimate business could use it, and while they were on it, they would be protected from monsters.

"But *I'm* a monster!" he protested.

"You have to be a nice monster for now. Can you stand it?"

"I was never a nasty monster. Just an ugly one."

"So you'll have no problem. We'll soon reach the castle."

"It will be good to get this done with."

She glanced sidelong at him. "There's a detail or two I may not have mentioned."

"The last detail or two related to the distance and the Gap Chasm. I hope these aren't as bad."

"No, not as bad," she said, smiling. "Worse."

"Worse! Why didn't you tell me, you crazy creature?"

"Thank you. I thought it would be more interesting this way. You see, you don't just walk into the Good Magician's castle. You have to struggle past three challenges. That's because he doesn't like to be disturbed by folk who aren't serious."

"If I had known that—"

"To be sure," she agreed so sweetly that flakes of crystallized sugar formed on her surfaces.

He tried to get a grip on his unruly emotion. "What's the other detail?"

"The Good Magician charges."

"Charges?"

"One year's service for each Question he Answers."

"One year!" he cried, outraged. "That's ridiculous!"

"To be sure," she agreed even more sweetly. Cloying syrup oozed from her pores. "Well, this path leads right to it, so you can't get lost. I have to be going now, to realign with my better half. Bye."

"Now just a long moment!" he said.

But she had already faded out.

2

GOOD MAGICIAN

Gary gazed at the castle. It looked ordinary, being pretty much like his mental image. There were walls and turrets and pennants and the rest of the usual. But it differed in one significant respect: the moat was dry. The drought must have affected this region too. That was sad. No castle was worth much without water.

D. Mentia had said that there would be three challenges. She was slightly crazy, but she seemed to have been truthful when she wasn't omitting key details. So he would be prepared.

There seemed to be a drawbridge to the side. He bounded toward it, because that was surely better than descending into the caked gunk at the bottom of the defunct moat.

The vegetation closed in with thick brambles. His stone hide couldn't be hurt by brambles any more than by the bites of dogs, but he didn't like getting his finish scratched, so he followed the path that offered. It curved away from the castle, but surely would return to find the drawbridge. It took him into a small forest of cane of all colors, a rather pretty scene.

He came to a glade. There an armored warrior was laboring to harvest some of the canes, looking somewhat tired and sweaty. Perhaps it was someone doing a service for the Good Magician. Maybe he could learn more about this situation.

Gary bounded to a halt. "Hello, sir warrior," he said politely. He understood that human folk liked to be given titles, and since it cost him nothing to humor their foibles, he did so.

The figure paused and turned to him. "Don't 'sir' *me!*" it snapped. "I'm not a man."

Gary was somewhat set back. "I apologize," he said contritely. "I took you for human."

"I *am* human," she said, straightening into a warlike pose. He saw that her metallic armor was curved in front in a manner reminiscent of Mentia's decolletage, when the demoness remembered to have one. This did suggest the figure was female. "I'm Hannah Barbarian, and if you were a smart-mouthed man I'd cut off three of your legs as readily as I do these hurry canes."

"Hurry canes?"

"They are used as walking canes," she said aggressively. "But they make you rush. I'm sure they're useful, but they're hard to hang on to." Indeed, the one she had just cut was whipping around as if trying to escape her grip, and the trussed bundle of them was hopping on the ground, eager to go somewhere.

"Perhaps I could help you accomplish your task," Gary said.

This seemed to make her angrier. "I don't need any male's help! Now get out of here before I forget myself and practice something feministic on you." The cane in her hand whirled menacingly.

Gary hastily bounded on. He had heard that human females were sweet and soft, but evidently he had been misinformed. Perhaps this was another detail the demoness hadn't mentioned.

The path curved around and brought him to the drawbridge. Two young human men stood before it. Gary bounded to another stop. "Hello," he said, carefully omitting the "sir" so as not to annoy anyone.

The two eyed him sourly. "Hello yourself," one said sharply. "You are a horrendously ugly creature," the other said candidly.

"Thank you," Gary replied. He realized that humans liked compliments, so he offered one in return: "You're not exactly handsome yourself." He was stretching a point, as the man was far from the gargoyle standard of ugliness, but social nicety seemed to require it.

The second man grimaced. "Perhaps we should introduce ourselves. I am Frank. He is Curt."

"I am Gary," Gary said.

"That is not the most original name," Frank said directly.

"He's an animal," Curt said brusquely.

"All true," Gary agreed innocently. "Now if you will step aside, I would like to cross that drawbridge."

"Not a chance," Curt said tersely.

"I must inform you straightforwardly that we are here to prevent you from trespassing," Frank said openly.

"But I need to see the Good Magician," Gary said perplexedly.

"Tough," Curt said shortly.

"Perhaps you don't understand," Frank said forthrightly. "This is a challenge."

"Oh," Gary said naively. "I hadn't realized."

"Perhaps because you are not very intelligent," Frank said boldly.

"You're ignorant," Curt said bluntly.

"I surely am," Gary agreed, bemused. He realized that these two had a job to do, and that his own job was to get them out of his way. He could simply barge on through, knocking them into the stinking muck of the moat, but though his hide was stone, his heart was soft, and he couldn't bring himself to do that. So he turned away, pondering alternatives.

"What a clod," Curt remarked gruffly.

"They do not produce challengers the way they used to," Frank agreed freely.

Gary wandered on around the moat. The path gave up after a few paces, evidently tired. Gary had to stop lest he step on some T-shaped plants grouped in conic formations, bearing what looked like peas. He picked a ripe pea and put it in his mouth. It turned instantly to fluid. It was tea! These were tea peas.

However, this didn't help him cross the moat. He still didn't want to wade through the muck, so he turned his tail on the tea-pea patch and returned to the drawbridge. "Are you sure you won't let me cross peaceably?" he inquired artlessly.

"Absolutely," Curt replied abruptly.

"It is not in our job description," Frank replied openly.

Gary still didn't want to act in a nasty manner, so he followed the path back to the cane. There was a wind rising there now, with gusts becoming quite stiff. The canes swayed, looking as if they wished they could hurry elsewhere.

Hannah was worse off. Her militantly coifed hair was getting blown all askew, and her amazonian skirt was flapping so badly as to show her stiff knees. She did not look particularly pleased.

"Hello," Gary said hesitantly.

She whirled on him, a struggling cane in each hand. "You again? What do you want?"

"Nothing," he said cautiously. "It's just that I discovered a patch of tea peas. Maybe if you drank some of them you would feel better."

Hannah paused in mid-whirl. "Maybe you're right, monster. I am thoroughly thirsty from this windy work. Where is that patch?"

"Down this path to the drawbridge, and turn right. You can't miss it."

She eyed him. "Where are you going now?"

Gary shrugged. "I don't seem to have what it takes to get into the Good Magician's castle, so perhaps I'll go home, if I can find the way. But I'm still willing to help you gather some cane, if there is any way I can be useful."

"You're not exactly a typical male," she remarked.

"I haven't had much practice," he confessed. "I have worked alone all my life."

Hannah seemed almost unmilitant for half an instant, though this was probably a misinterpretation of her mood. "I know the feeling. Stick around, gargoyle. Maybe I will accept your help, after I take some tea." She marched off along the path.

Gary shrugged and followed. He was hoping that he would figure out some way to cross the moat, because he didn't like giving up, and also was not unduly eager to try to cross the larger ditch known as the Gap Chasm without having something to show for his excursion.

Hannah came into sight of the drawbridge. There were Frank and Curt.

"Look!" Curt cried briefly. "A tart!"

"That is one messed-up girl," Frank said in an up-front manner. "She's wearing a ridiculous military outfit, carrying some kind of clumsy stick, and her hair resembles a dismembered mop."

"Now there's a pair of typical jacks," Hannah exclaimed. "How fortunate that I was already angry." She strode forward, wielding her cane. "I never did take any guff from cartoon characters."

"What's up, sweetie?" Curt inquired in a sexist way.

"You intrigue us, darling," Frank said. "I wonder whether under that metallic skirt you wear a pair of—"

Then Hannah caught up to them. There were two thunks and a sudden splash, as of bags of rocks falling into mud. It was all over in an eye-blink, and by the time Gary finished blinking, the barbarian woman was on her way to the pea patch and the drawbridge was empty.

Gary realized that he had inadvertently made an opportunity for himself. Hannah, who was not particularly soft-hearted about obnoxious men, had done the job Gary had shied away from. So he might as well cross the draw-bridge while he had the chance.

But as he bounded to it, another figure appeared. It looked human, but was faintly glowing. And it barred the way. "Are you another challenge?" Gary inquired as he came to a stop.

"I am indeed! I am Fiera. My talent is the control of fire." She lifted her hands, tossing a ball of fire between them. "If you try to pass, I will burn you."

"Fire," he said, impressed. "I've never met anyone who wasn't a salamander who could do that."

"My brother Fiero's just as hot as I am, and together we are even hotter," she said proudly. "We're Xanth's hottest act."

Gary couldn't be hurt by fire any more than by thorns or teeth, but he didn't want to have to dump a nice human woman like Fiera into the muck, so he retreated. This time he found a path circling the moat in the other direction. In a moment it debouched into a little circle of glassy stones. In the middle of the circle was a big feather. He picked it up so that it wouldn't get stepped on, for it was a pretty feather. Then he wasn't sure what to do with it, because it could get blown into the path again and get stepped on after he left. So he tucked it into the rock wool between his horns for safekeeping. When he found someone who appreciated pretty feathers, he would give it to that person.

Then he saw that one of the glassy stones had fallen out of the circle, perhaps having been blown over by the wind. He tried to move it back into place with his paws, but it splashed. Astonished, he jumped back—and it sagged and started slopping onto the ground. It was actually a container of water!

He couldn't just let it pour out. After all there was a

drought, and water was precious. So he returned and tried to shape it up with his paws, but it still slopped. The sides of it were bendy, and there was a hole in the top, so that as it sat it sagged, and as it sagged it flowed. It was probably his fault; he must have inadvertently knocked it over, and now it was no longer tight. What to do?

He put his mouth to the edge and caught the side of it between his teeth. He bit down gently, only hard enough to be able to catch hold and pull it up. That stopped the leaking. But the moment he tried to let go, it sagged again. He couldn't let it go without ruining it.

Maybe Fiera would know what to do. She was part of this situation, after all. So he set his teeth carefully into the rock and slowly dragged it down the path, making sure that no more water spilled.

"What are you doing with that quartz?" Fiera demanded when he reached the drawbridge.

"Quartz?" he asked blankly. As he did so, his teeth let go of the rock, and it began to sag and leak again. He snapped at it, trying to stop the spillage, but couldn't get a proper hold.

"Yes, you have quartz of water," she said, alarmed. "That's worse than pintz of water."

"Yes, the water's leaking, and I wondered if you know how to stop it," he said, nipping again for the edge, and missing again. The feather fell from his head and landed in the water.

Then something odd happened. The quill pointed up and squirted water. A jet of it shot up, making an arc toward the woman.

"EEEEK!!" Fiera screamed, falling back. "A Fountain Pen!!" She was so upset that she managed double exclamation points. Her pert posterior landed on the wooden drawbridge and set it afire. But the quill pen kept fountaining, drawing from the quartz. Trying to escape it, she scrambled to her feet and charged past him in a fiery flash.

"I'm sorry!" Gary cried, starting to bound after her. But she was already out of sight, and the pen was still squirting. He had to turn back and pull out the feather, getting roundly squirted in the snoot. The jet stopped when he got the feather clear of the water.

He looked around. The planks of the bridge were still burning around the seat-shaped spot where Fiera had landed. She must have lost control of her fire for a moment. He could put it out, but he would have to use the rest of the water in the quartz, and he wasn't willing to do that. So he dragged the half-full rock back to the stone circle. Now he was able to prop it up without leaking. He hoped it would heal in time. He had certainly made a mess of things.

When he returned to the drawbridge he saw that the fire had burned itself out. But the remaining planks were charred, and he doubted that they would support his weight. He realized that he could have crossed, and won the challenge, if he had just been willing to use up the rest of the water. But he was a stone creature, and he had an affinity with stone, and just couldn't mistreat the quartz like that. He was obviously not the type of creature the Good Magician wanted to see.

Still, there was not much to be gained by departing at this stage. He might as well plow onward. Even if the Magician wasn't going to let him in.

He considered the moat again. Now he saw that the muck in the bottom was filled with fish. They must have been stranded by the drought. That was no good. He didn't want to squish them underfoot, of course, but neither did he want to let them suffer longer. They needed water, and plenty of it.

Perhaps this was what the quartz rocks were for: to refill the moat when it got dry. But there weren't enough of them to do the job. He needed to find some other way.

He lay down beside the moat and put his head over the edge. "I want to help you, but you will have to help me," he said. "Do any of you fish know where I can find enough water to fill this moat?"

One big fish wriggled a bit in the muck. "Scales," it gasped.

"What do your scales have to do with water?" Gary asked, perplexed.

"Balance," it gasped.

"Balance?" He was no more enlightened. But the fish had gasped its last gasp; it had no further strength for dialogue. It was surely very uncomfortable for a fish to be out of water, and talking made it worse.

Still, this suggested that there was water to be had somewhere. All he had to do was find it. At least he could help the fish before he departed.

He bounded back along the path. He discovered another fork leading from the glade in the cane grove. The wind was still strong, but he was too heavy to be much affected. He followed the new path.

It led to a small mountain. On the top of the mountain was a big stone, precariously balanced. It was a wonder the wind didn't blow it off its perch, so that it crashed downward crushing all before it.

Balance. The fish had said that. This must relate. But what did it mean?

He looked around—and spied another mountain, with another boulder. More balancing. But he still didn't know how any of this could help.

He bounded between the two mountains, hoping for some clue. He saw that the sunlight fell across this region in a checkered pattern, interrupted by the shadows of the mountains and stones. Halfway between the balanced rocks was a square that seemed to have been etched into the ground by the pattern of sunbeam and shadow. He wasn't sure how it had happened, because normally shadows did not stay still very long. But this was a fairly magical region, and with magic almost anything was possible. There must be some significance.

A checkered region between the balanced rocks. Checks and balances? The scales of a balance?

Scales. Now he saw markings around the square, as if

something was being measured. He followed the marks, and found a single fish scale. He peered at it. There seemed to be words: RAIN CHECK.

Suddenly he didn't care about scales, checks, or balances. This related to rain, and rain was what he wanted. Maybe it was an amulet or other magic device to summon rain. He picked it up with his teeth and carried it away.

The wind was blowing more fiercely than ever, but Gary flowed on through it. He reached the moat and dropped the rain check in. "Rain!" he cried.

Suddenly the wind whipped into a storm. Mist formed, thickening over the moat. From beyond the horizon came a cloud, borne along by the fierce wind. Gary gazed at it. He knew that cloud! That was Fracto Cumulo Nimbus, who loved to float by and withhold rain at critical times. That was one reason for the drought. Fracto must be magically bound by a geis of his own, to honor the rain check when it was invoked. Thus the scale between the balances, there for Gary to find—if he could. He had more or less blundered across it, but had at least recognized it when he spied it.

Now Fracto was over the castle and the moat, boiling into a frenzy. The bottom fell out, and water gushed out of the cloud. The moat began to fill.

The big fish swam up. "Thank you," it said, no longer gasping. "You saved us!"

"You're welcome," Gary replied. "I hate to see any creature suffering. I'm surprised there are so many of you in such a small section of water."

"It's not normally this crowded," the fish confessed. "We're here for the playoffs."

"Playoffs?"

"This isn't generally known, dryside," the fish said. "But we of the wetside have a secret passion for baseball. We play it all the time. In fact we have twenty thousand leagues under the sea. We gathered here for the Xanth championship series—and got caught by the drought. We are extremely fortunate that you managed to abate it."

"Yes, now you can swim back to the sea," Gary agreed.

"By no means. Now we can finish the series. We've been tortured by our inability to complete it and determine the winning teams. Ah, I think the moat is full enough now; it's time for me to go o-fish-iate. Thank you and good-bye. I'll send Naia." The fish swam away.

Gary hardly had time to consider what to do next before another kind of fish swam up: a mermaid. "Hi, winged monster. I'm Naia Naiad, wearing my tail for this occasion." She twisted, showing him a piece of tail. "The big fish told me to guide you across the moat, so you can make your appointment with the Good Magician."

"My appointment?"

"Everyone who gets past the challenges gets to see him. Didn't you know?"

"But I didn't get past them!" he protested.

She shrugged. "You must have. Well, come on, hero."

Bemused again, he stepped into the water, which was now almost to the top of the moat. He sank to the bottom, being denser than any water. It was cloudy, because of the stirring of the mud, but the naiad swam close enough so that he could keep her tail in sight. In fact sometimes he saw more than her tail, as she looped around to check on him; but since he wasn't human those parts didn't much concern him. It did occur to him, however, that such creatures must be very good at feeding their babies.

Naia led him to the far bank. He couldn't bound very well underwater, but he made sufficient progress by slowly flapping his wings instead. He climbed out, shook his body and wings dry, and turned back to thank her, but she was gone. The surface of the moat was rippling as the storm eased; the fish were already into their playoffs.

He bounded to the inner side of the drawbridge, and to the castle gate. It opened as he got there, admitting him. A human young woman of about twenty stood there. "Hello," she said, looking past him.

"Hello. I am Gary Gargoyle. I am not sure I—"

"Oh, yes; we were expecting you. I'm Wira, the Good Magician's daughter-in-law. Come in."

"Well, I'm still a bit wet, as you can see, and—"

"I can't see, but I know what gargoyles look like. I'm sure a few drops of water won't hurt. Mother Gorgon wants to talk to you." She set off down the inner hall.

He bounded cautiously after her. His state of bemusement seemed to have become chronic. "Who? Your mother?"

"My husband Hugo's mother. She's very nice, but her gaze turns people to stone, or it did before she had Humfrey make her face invisible and replace it with an illusion of her face. She says she has an affinity for stoned creatures, so she came here for this occasion."

The business about an invisible illusionary face was beyond him, so he fixed on something simple. "I am a stone creature, yes."

They came to a nice inner chamber with stone walls and stone furniture. He felt quite comfortable. Within it stood an older human woman. "So nice to meet you, Gary Gargoyle," she said. "I am the Gorgon. We must talk."

"As you wish," he agreed. "But I'm not sure I should be here. I didn't—"

"You handled the challenges in your own compassionate fashion. You are a good creature, worthy of the Good Magician's Answer. But are you aware that there is a payment in service required?"

"I learned that along the way," he admitted ruefully. "I think I don't have the time. You see, when it rains in Mundania, and the Swan Knee River starts flowing again, the dam will soon overflow, and I must be there to honor my geis."

"That is part of what I wanted to talk to you about. A year will not do, for you; you have a responsibility elsewhere. Instead, the Magician will settle for a single service of lesser duration, if that is satisfactory to you."

Gary began to realize that his mission might be possible after all. "If I can return in time, then it's all right."

"But it is an unusual service, and you may not wish to perform it," she said. "That's why I had to talk to you first. The Magician's Answer is one thing, but the terms of the service are another. If you are not willing to do it, your meeting with Humfrey is pointless."

"I'm willing, so long as it is brief. What is it?"

"To tutor a precocious human child."

"But I don't know anything about humans, and less about their children," he protested.

"Precisely. And this one is no ordinary child. She will be extremely difficult to handle."

"I'm a winged monster! She'd think I was going to eat her! There must be a hundred better tutors for her."

"Apparently there is only one who can do the job in the manner it needs to be done. I confess that my husband's dictations don't always make sense to me at the time, but he is invariably correct. We need you for this."

Gary struggled, but could not come up with a suitable argument against this. His soft heart was betraying him again. "If she really needs my help—"

"She really does. But there is more."

There always did seem to be more. "What more?" he asked warily.

"You will have to be transformed to human form for the duration."

"Human form!" he cried, appalled.

"I realize that this is a considerable sacrifice for you, but it will be temporary. Magician Trent will transform you, and transform you back after the service is complete."

"I suppose if it is temporary, I can stand it," he agreed grudgingly. But privately he was wondering whether he ever should have listened to D. Mentia, who had gotten him into a crazy fix.

"There is more," she said, with that tone.

"Are you trying to dissuade me from this?"

"No. I very much hope you will accept it. But fairness

requires that you be warned. In human form you will not be as competent as you are naturally, and your flesh will not be stone. Your normal reflexes may lead you into mischief, such as assuming that thorns won't hurt or that dragon bites won't damage your flesh. You will need Magician-caliber protection until you change back."

"But if you have a Magician for this, why can't *he* tutor the child?"

"Not he. She. She absolutely refuses to baby-sit a child alone. Perhaps she has reason; she is ninety-three years old."

"But that's doddering, for a human! Flesh ages so much more quickly than stone."

"She will be youthened to an effective age of about twenty-three. That's prime, for a human female."

Gary shrugged. "Then I don't see the problem."

"There could be a personality conflict. She is said to be not the easiest person to get along with."

Gary strained his stony memory for what it knew about human Sorceresses. Only one bad name emerged. "Just so long as it isn't the Sorceress Iris. She is said to be impossible for anybody but her family to stand for more than two moments."

The Gorgon merely looked at him. Her illusion face looked soberingly real.

Oh, no!

After a time he bowed to the inevitable. "Maybe if the service really is brief . . ."

"It should be. I repeat, my husband's dictates can seem peculiar, but there's always a rationale. It is quite possible that you will be glad of this experience, once it is over."

"I shall hang on to that hope," he said ruefully.

"Excellent. Now it is time to see Humfrey."

"I will take him there," Wira said. Gary had forgotten she was there.

He followed the young woman up endlessly winding stairways until they reached an obscure chamber buried deep within the castle. A gnomish man sat at a desk, poring over a monstrous tome. This was the Good Magician Humfrey; it could be no other. He looked about a hundred years old.

"Father Humfrey, here is Gary Gargoyle," Wira said.

"Well, let's hear your Question," the gnome grumped.

"How can I more readily purify the water?"

"Get a philter." The face returned to the tome.

"But—"

"Now don't try to argue with him." Wira said urgently. "That only makes him grumpier."

"But I have no idea where—"

"Ask Hiatus," Humfrey said without looking up from the page.

"Who is Interruption?" Gary asked as Wira guided him back down the tortuous stairway.

"Hiatus. He's Lacuna's twin brother. He grows noses and things on surfaces. He must know where the philter is."

"But how can I find it, when I have to tutor this child?" he asked plaintively.

"Take her with you!" the Good Magician's annoyed voice floated after them.

"I suppose I can do that," Gary agreed. "But this still seems perplexingly confused."

"Things usually work out in the end," Wira said reassuringly "Somehow. Even if coincidence, chance, and common sense have to be inordinately strained."

Gary hoped that was the case. Once more he wished that the demoness had left him alone. His life had been simple; now it was unduly complicated. But he also had to admit that it had been boring, and now it was interesting.

3
IRIS

Gary found himself outside the castle, with no idea where to go next. In the confusion of the Good Magician's grudging bits of Answer, Gary had forgotten to get lesser information he needed. Such as how to find Magician Trent or the Sorceress Iris.

He gazed at the moat and the mixed terrain beyond. Would he have to find his way out as deviously as he had found his way in? And then search for the people he needed? It was all so confused.

"You look extremely perplexed," someone said behind him. "I love that in a creature."

Gary didn't bother to look, because he recognized the voice. "Shape up or ship out, Mentia," he said gruffly.

A small ragged brown cloud drifted into his field of vision. "How did you know I was out of shape?" the demoness asked, disgruntled.

"I don't care about your physical shape," he said. "I just mean that if you're not here to help, I don't want to bother with you. I have enough problems already, thanks to your interference."

"My interference!" the cloud said, forming into a huge smoky exclamation point. "Is this the thanks I get for trying to help you?"

"You want thanks? Here it is. Thank you for not smoking in my presence."

The smoke solidified into the demoness' supposedly natural human aspect. "Are you really annoyed with me?" she asked, looking woebegone.

Gary knew it was an act, but fell for it anyway. "I guess not. I know you thought you were trying to help me. But now I'm stuck not knowing where to go, and not only am I far from my river, I owe the Good Magician a Service. I wish I'd never met you."

Mentia sighed. "I guess it was sort of crazy to think you'd be grateful. But I'm a crazy creature. Maybe I should help you some more."

"No!" he cried, alarmed.

"Not even if I showed you how to find Magician Trent?"

"Not even—" He paused. "You'd do that?"

"And the Sorceress Iris too," she said sweetly. "If that would make you feel good about me."

"Why should you care how I feel about you?"

"I shouldn't. But I'm a bit crazy, as you know. I'm not a bad creature, and you're an interesting one. So maybe I'll get you clear of your confusion."

Gary didn't trust this, but seemed to have no viable alternative. "Agreed, then. Show me how to find Trent."

She paused to consider, her feet not quite touching the ground. "The old folk are down in the Brain Coral's Pool, waiting for you. So we'll have to go there."

"What kind of pool?"

"Oh, you don't know about that? I thought you gargoyles knew all about water."

"We purify running water," he said, slightly aggrieved. "We ignore pools."

"This pool is not to be ignored. The Brain Coral is a weird inanimate entity who likes to collect things, such as living creatures, which it keeps in suspended animation in its deep subterranean pool. Once every decade or so it lets a creature out, if there's really good reason, and that creature is exactly the same age as it was when it went in, even if it's been there for several centuries. Of course in the Time of No Magic, back in the year ten-forty-three, fifty-one years ago, everything got messed up and some captives escaped; it was decades before the Brain Coral completed its inventory and knew exactly who was gone." Mentia shrugged in sections, like a moving caterpillar, her head, shoulders, breasts, midsection, pelvis, thighs, legs, and feet taking their turns. The effect would have been interesting, had Gary been a human male. "By then it was a bit too late, of course. But there's still good stuff in those dark waters, and right now Magician Trent and Sorceress Iris are there."

"They are *in* the pool? In suspended animation?"

"Of course. Do you think they want to wait in the regular realm, getting older every moment? Iris already has too much of a problem in that respect."

"She does? What's wrong with getting older? Doesn't everyone do it?"

"Every non-demon, I suppose." This time Mentia's right side shrugged in one direction, and her left side in the other direction. Gary did find that interesting, especially when her eyes passed each other on the return trip, overshooting the mark. "But Iris is ninety-three years old. That's ancient and doddering, for the average human being."

"But Magician Trent must be old too, so they're even."

"Ninety-seven, technically. But he was youthened to about twenty-five last year, and is now one handsome hunk of human. Why should he mess with a woman of great-grandmotherly physical age?"

"That makes a difference?"

"To a human, yes. The man can be as old as he wants, but the woman has to be young, or she's a waste. That's the way it is, with human folk. So she'll take a youth potion to knock about seventy years off her physical age; that's her reward for helping you. After that, who knows what she may be up to. She's a long-suppressed woman." Mentia's clothing turned transparent for an instant, showing a flash of her considerably curved outer contours.

Gary shook his head. "You claim to be a little bit crazy, Mentia, but you don't seem any worse than regular humans are."

The demoness, caught by surprise by the compliment, flushed. The contents of her head melted into red fluid and drained down the pipes of her neck, leaving a hollow translucent shell. The fluid gurgled through her body, and pooled in her feet, which swelled voluminously. Then, gradually, her head filled again, the fluid rising from the bottom to the top, until it was complete and she resumed normal activity. "Thank you," she said when her lips were full again.

Gary realized that for all Mentia's disclaimers, she did care at least a little what other creatures thought of her. That didn't seem to be too much of a fault. "How old are you, Mentia?"

"A hundred and ninety-three, but who's counting? It doesn't matter for demons." She inhaled, and her bosom became magnificent and burst out of its halter. Gary was no judge of such things, of course, but he suspected that a human man would find her attractive. "Or one year, depending how you count it; I haven't gone out on my own as Metria's alter ego all that long."

That seemed like a fair dual answer. "So this ninety-three-year-old ancient old woman, youthened to her twenties, is assigned to help me on my mission," Gary said, somewhat dispiritedly. "I suppose I had better get on with it."

"That's what I was up to. I can pop to the pool just like that, but you can't. You need a physical conveyance. Can you sing?"

That must be her craziness showing again. "No."

"Too bad. We could have had you ride a diggle. They

carry folk through rock for a song." She pondered, her body fuzzing out as she lost focus. "Maybe a figgle."

"A what?"

"That's another subspecies of vole. All it wants is a fig. So you don't give a fig."

More craziness! "You don't give it what it wants?"

"Yes. Because when it gets its fig, it eats it and goes home to snooze."

"So why not promise it a fig after it has helped you?"

"It doesn't work that way. Figgles don't plan for the future. They want to know *now*."

"But you can't give it the fig now."

She smiled. "You are catching on, stoneface."

"So we can't use a figgle."

"Yes we can."

He knew she was teasing him, but he was stuck for it, so he asked the obvious question: "How?"

"By telling it what we aren't giving it."

"I don't understand."

"Well, you're only a stone animal. Now I'll summon a figgle for us to ride."

She was crazy, all right! But what else was there?

Mentia put two fingers to her mouth, inhaled to just short of bursting, and blew a piercing whistle that made his stone ears craze. There followed a rumbling in the ground, and in two moments and half an instant the worm-like snout of a huge nether creature poked from the soil. "Ffiigg?" the sloppy mouth inquired.

"Well, we're not giving you a shoe," Mentia retorted. "But if you take us to the Brain Coral's Pool, who knows what we might give you?"

The figgle cogitated in vermicular fashion, its thoughts evidently twisting deviously. "Ffiigg?" it repeated.

Gary was starting to begin to think about catching on. "We're not giving you a castle," he said.

Mentia stepped onto the creature's broadly rounded back, her solidly fleshed thighs straddling it. Gary did the same, as well as he could, straddling it with four legs. The creature was so solid that this did not feel as precarious as it looked.

"Go poool," the creature said. "Then ffigg?"

"We're not giving you a parasol," Mentia said.

The creature's snout angled down and plunged into the earth as if it were water. The body followed sinuously. Gary wondered whether he should be alarmed, but before he could come to a conclusion they were descending through the ground. There was only the faintest sensation, as of dirty fog sliding by. But after most of a moment the fog thickened, becoming more like sludge. "Get your mouth in gear," Mentia said. "And don't repeat anything; that confuses it."

Oh. "We're not giving you a purple rock," Gary said, and the sludge thinned around them. He did not care to discover what happened when the figgle got confused deep in the ground.

"Or a green pair of socks," Mentia added.

Gary warmed to this. "We're not giving you the talent of conjuring things from the Void," he said when the ground around them began to solidify again.

"Or Stanley Steamer's birthday, which happens to be Dismember two-four," Mentia said.

So it went. The figgle seemed to be satisfied as long as they reassured it that they weren't giving it something other than a fig; that suggested by implication that they might give it a fig. The fact that there was an almost infinite number of things that weren't figs didn't seem to matter; the figgle's strength was not intelligence. So they mentioned shoes and ships and sealing wax, and cabbages and kings, and apples and ideas, as well as acorns and mountains and pictures of things best left undescribed. Through it all, the figgle plowed on down through earth, rock, and whatever.

Well before they had run out of things not to give the figgle, they arrived at the Brain Coral's Pool. They were sliding through layers of rock when the environment abruptly became thin, and Gary realized with a start that this was because it was air. There was a flat cave floor, and beyond it a deep dark cave pool fed by a slow lazy river. The walls and water glowed faintly, so that there was no problem seeing. It was a rather pretty region, though of course to a gargoyle any place with plenty of flowing water was appealing.

"Now we have to give our steed the whatever," Mentia announced.

"Yes, it's time," Gary agreed. "Give it the fig."

"Ffigg!" the figgle exclaimed, coiling with eagerness.

The demoness writhed, emulating the figgle. "Me? I don't have a fig. Don't you have one?"

"Ffigg!" the creature said hungrily.

"Of course I don't! How could I have known I would need a fig?"

"FFIGG!" The very rock shuddered with the urgency of it, and the surface of the pool rippled nervously.

"Well, you had better find one quickly," Mentia remarked in a rare flash of sanity, "because a figgle's patience grows short when payoff time is delayed."

So it appeared. "What happens if the figgle doesn't get a—whatever?"

"Oh, I wouldn't recommend finding out." Indeed, the creature was thrashing around with increasing force, and since part of it was anchored in the rock, the whole cave was shaking. Gary had heard of earthquakes, and was catching a glimmer of what caused them.

But what could they do? They had no fig.

A chunk of stone fell from the ceiling and splashed into the water. Cracks were opening in the stone floor. The walls were blurry, not because of any problem with Gary's vision, but because they were vibrating so violently.

Then desperation gave Gary wit. "Mentia—you're a demoness!" he exclaimed.

Her mouth drew down into a pout that became so large it made her face pear-shaped. "You noticed."

"You can assume any form you wish," he continued.

"I thought that had become evident." Her head expanded until it was like a watermelon, and the rest of her body shrank so that only little arms and legs projected from the giant fruit.

"And you can't be hurt by mortals."

"Not physically," she agreed. "Or mentally, now that I think of it. However, a mortal can hurt a demon emotionally, if she's stupid enough to get half a soul."

"So become a fig!" he said.

The watermelon's eyes expanded in surprise. Then the entire big juicy fruit shrank into a little dried fruit.

Gary reached out with a forepaw and picked it up. "Here is your fig," he said to the writhing figgle. "I'm giving you a fig."

The creature snapped up the fig and dived into the wall so quickly that anything as long as an instant would have been lost in the shuffle. Suddenly Gary stood alone in a quiet cave. And he knew that one thing he would never say hereafter was "I don't give a fig." He had learned the consequence.

Now he had to find Magician Trent and Sorceress Iris. That should not be difficult, as he understood that both were human beings. He walked along the ledge beside the pool. No person, whether of animal or human shape, seemed to be in the vicinity.

Then he remembered that the things were stored *in* the pool, in suspended animation. That explained why it was so quiet here outside the pool. He would have to go down into it to find the folk he needed.

He found a shallow place and stepped carefully into the water. The pool was neither cold nor hot; it seemed to be perfectly neutral. Of course it didn't matter to him, because he was made of stone, but it probably made a difference for those stored within it. They wouldn't want to be shivering with cold for hundreds of years.

He continued down until the water was over his head. That didn't matter either; he didn't need to breathe. He wondered how the flesh creatures managed, though.

Now he saw something. It seemed to be a wooden structure. Maybe it was an office. But as he came to it he saw that it was just a collection of boards piled somewhat haphazardly together. Gary was no neatness freak, but it did seem that these would take up less space if carefully piled, so he might as well do that before moving on.

He took hold of a board. "Hey!" the board protested.

Startled, Gary paused. "Did you talk to me?" he asked.

"Do you see any other ugly stone monster idiots in the vicinity?" the board demanded in a warped tone. "What do you think you're doing?"

"I was just going to pile you more neatly, so you wouldn't be scattered around," Gary explained.

"Well, I'll thank you knot to interfere with our board meeting," it said. "We want to get our business done before we season, you know."

"Sorry," Gary said, and quickly moved on. He had not realized that boards talked, or that they had meetings, and was a bit embarrassed for his ignorance.

He came to a man reading a book. Maybe he would know where Magician Trent was. "I say, may I interrupt you a moment?" Gary inquired cautiously.

"I wish you would," the man said without raising his face. His voice was somewhat muffled.

"I am looking for Magician Trent, who I understand is in this pool somewhere. Could you direct me to his location?"

"Love to. But I can't."

"Can't?"

The man lifted his face. The book came up with it, covering his eyes. "My nose is stuck in this book, and I can't see around it."

That did seem to be a predicament. "Can I help you remove it?" Gary inquired solicitously.

"No. My nose would come off my face if you pulled the book away. Unless you know where there's some solvent?"

"I don't know, but I'll see if I can find some." Gary looked around, and saw a tree deeper in the water, growing as if on land. There were many signs of activity around it, though at the moment nothing was actually moving. So he approached it. "Do you happen to have any solvent?" he inquired.

"Of course I have solvent," the tree retorted. "I'm an industree. It's one of the things needed in construction and manufacture."

Soon Gary had plucked a can of solvent from one of the industree's twigs. He put a drop on the book attached to the man's nose, and it came free. "Oh, thank you, stranger," the man said. "It has been a bore, not being able to turn the page." He reburied his face in the book so firmly that Gary realized that it wouldn't be long before his nose got stuck again. The man hadn't even noticed that Gary was not a human being.

He returned to the industree. "Can you tell me where—"

"The first sample was free," the tree told him severely. "You will have to pay the going rate for anything more. Do you think I'm in business for my health?"

Gary hadn't realized that the industree was in business at all. Embarrassed again, he retreated. This was certainly a strange region! Apparently not all the things in it were suspended, because he had had no trouble talking with several, even if they hadn't proved to be very helpful.

Gary walked on. He heard music, so he went toward the source. It turned out to be a harpy with very stiff erect tailfeathers; she was reaching back and plinking them with her claws so as to generate a nice tune.

It occurred to Gary that if a human man hadn't helped him, and an inanimate board hadn't, and a tree hadn't, maybe an animal type of creature would. But he knew that harpies were perverse, so this might require some finesse.

He approached the harpy. "That's awful music," he told her gruffly.

"Why thank you!" she screeched, flattered. "I'm a harpychord, and I love to annoy folk."

"You are surely succeeding. And I know you'll never tell me where Magician Trent is."

"Yes, I'll never tell you to look twenty paces to your left," she screeched, plinking a few more notes.

"A curse on you, you miserable creature," he said, and turned to his left. The harpy really had appreciated his comment on her music, so had answered his question in the only way she could, without soiling her reputation: negatively.

Twenty paces later he came to a handsome young man snoozing against a pillow bush. He remembered that Magician Trent had been rejuvenated, so this could be him. He did not want to disturb the Magician, but he didn't have much choice. "Magician Trent?" he inquired hesitantly.

The man woke. "Yes. Are you lost? Just settle down anywhere you're comfortable; the moment you relax, you'll tune out, and years or centuries will pass in an instant."

"No, I was lost, but now I'm found. That is, I found you. I am Gary Gargoyle."

"Hello Gary Gargoyle," the Magician responded politely. "You were looking for me?"

"The Good Magician didn't tell you?"

"Humfrey never wastes information if he can help it. What did he tell you?"

"Actually he did not tell me much. But others in the castle explained, I think."

"And what did they explain?" the Magician inquired patiently.

Gary grimaced. "That you would transform me into manform for this quest. That I would have to baby-sit a difficult human child."

"Ah, yes, Surprise. She will be a handful."

"And that the Sorceress Iris would come with me."

The Magician nodded. "Now it comes together. Iris did want to go on a quest where she could be useful. This must be it. We shall have to notify her."

Gary was amazed. "The Good Magician told you nothing about me? You have to take this all on faith?"

Magician Trent smiled. He had a warm smile, and it was reassuring. "I have known Humfrey a long time. I understand his ways. This is his way. Come; we shall rouse my wife." He got lithely to his feet and walked deeper into the depths of the pool.

Bemused, Gary followed. Trent led him to a weird kind of chamber. It seemed to have been fashioned from old cooked cereal. "She is of advanced years," the Magician remarked, glancing back. "She prefers a soft residence. This is her mushroom."

Now Gary recognized the configuration: a room made of mush. Probably it was pretty soft throughout.

Inside the mushroom was a mushbed, and on the bed lay a distressingly ancient old woman, sleeping. "Iris," the Magician said, "your quest has come."

The crone's eyes flickered open. "Is it morning?" she asked sleepily.

"Who knows?" Magician Trent said, smiling faintly. "Your quest is here."

Then another strange thing happened. The three of them were abruptly no longer in a room of mush under dim waters, but in the receiving chamber of an elegant palace. Rather, Gary and the Magician were; the hag had been replaced by an elegant queen of moderately middling age for her species. He knew she was a queen, because she wore a crown as well as a sumptuous ornately bejeweled royal gown.

The Queen looked around. "But where is the Quest person?" she inquired, a royal frown crossing her noble features.

"Allow me to introduce Gary Gargoyle," Magician Trent said, gesturing to Gary.

The Queen looked at Gary, blinking. "But I can't stand gargoyles!" she protested. "They're horrible dank stony grotesque monsters."

"And this," the Magician continued grandly, "is Queen

Emeritus Iris, Sorceress of Illusion. All that you behold at the moment is her work."

Gary was amazed. He knew of illusion, but this was so much more than he had imagined that it was daunting. The withered old harridan was making all this? It seemed so real!

"Pleased to meet you, gargoyle, I'm sure," the Queen said, seeming not sure at all.

"Likewise, your majesty," Gary said with similar conviction.

"Of course I am to transform him to manform for the occasion," Trent added. Iris looked relieved. "And Humfrey left me some youth elixir to delete seventy years from your physical age, my dear, when the time came. It has come."

Iris looked delighted. "I will be twenty-three again!"

"I wish I didn't have to be transformed," Gary said. "But at least I can return to my natural shape after the quest is done."

"I assure you that such transformation will improve your—um, that is, that you will get used to it," Iris said, evidently making an effort to be polite.

"I have the impression you don't very much like me," Gary said. "I assure you that the feeling is mu—"

"Impressions are transitory," Trent said quickly. "It is wise not to judge by anything other than direct experience."

Iris nodded. "I apologize for being prejudiced, Gary Gargoyle. I had a bad experience some time ago, with which a gargoyle was associated, but actually the creature didn't do anything, and anyway I'm sure you're not like that."

"I hope I'm not," Gary said cautiously.

"Just what is the quest?" Iris inquired.

"I have to tutor a child."

"A child of merfolk?" she asked. "I understand that gargoyles know something of water."

"It is the little daughter of Grundy Golem and Rapunzel," Trent explained. "A tyke they call Surprise."

"I didn't realize that they had a baby delivered," Iris said. "It must have been after my time."

"Yes, it was," Trent agreed. "She was delivered to them a year and a half ago."

"A squalling baby!" Iris said with distaste. "What kind of tutoring could a gargoyle give her? Swimming lessons?"

"She is six years old," Trent said.

She turned to him. "Are you teasing me, Magician? I distinctly heard you say she was delivered a year and a half ago."

"Delivered at the age of five years," he explained.

Both Gary and Iris stared at him. So great was the Sorceress' shock that the illusion palace developed fuzziness.

"But that is not the most remarkable thing about her," Trent continued blithely. "She has an impossible talent."

"Nothing is impossible," Iris said, getting a faltering grip on her manner and her illusion. "Except that any person have more than a single talent."

"She seems to possess an indefinite number of talents," Trent said.

"How can you know this?" she demanded. "It must be illusion."

"I met her in the course of my own quest, when I was helping Gloha Goblin-Harpy find her ideal husband."

"Oh, is there a male flying goblin?" she asked. "I thought she was unique."

"There is now. I converted him from an invisible giant."

"She married a giant? However did they come together?"

"That is a story for another tome. This story is about a remarkable child who I think will be a handful like none other. Why she should require the special attention of a gargoyle I have no notion, but I suspect it will be an adventure finding out."

Iris sighed. "I should have known there would be a stiff

price for youthening. But I would give half my soul to be
young again in body, and this seems to fall within that
range. Let's get on with it."

"As you wish, my dear. First let me transform Gary
Gargoyle, since this is his quest."

"Oh, I'm satisfied to wait," Gary said, being as uneager
to change his form as the Sorceress was to change hers.
But even as he spoke, something truly awful happened to
him.

He found himself standing on his two hind legs, while
his front legs changed their orientation, becoming shorter
and far less sturdy. His head diminished and his teeth
shrank into tiny dull pegs, almost useless for combat. His
forepaws became weak fleshy digits with pale flat nails.
And his wings, O horrors, disappeared entirely. He felt naked. But he wasn't; there was a cloth covering hanging on
his torso.

Iris surveyed him. "Well, that's an improvement. He
makes a halfway handsome young man." She turned to
Trent. "Now it's my turn."

"To be sure." Trent handed her a vial containing a clear
liquid. "Drink and be merry, my dear."

She almost snatched it and put it to her lips, gulping it
down. Then she stood there, unchanged.

"Perhaps we should dispense with the illusion for the
nonce," Trent suggested.

"Oh. Yes," she agreed.

Then the mushroom reappeared around them, and the
water of the pool. But the shriveled old woman was gone.
Now there stood a woman in the most vibrant flush of human youth. The effect was diminished somewhat by her
clothing, which hung on her body in some places and was
stretched painfully tight in others.

"Perhaps you should change your dress," Trent suggested with three-quarters of a smile.

Iris looked down at herself. "Yes. Out with you both
while I see to some alterations."

"Oh, we have no objection if you prefer to strip now and remake your outfit," Trent said.

"Out!" she cried.

"Women tend to be unreasonable for no particular reason," Magician Trent remarked as they stepped out and heard the mushdoor slam closed behind them with a squishy sound.

But Gary had problems of his own. The moment he took a two-legged step he lost his balance. He wasn't used to this vertical positioning.

Trent steadied him with a hand. "You can do it," he said reassuringly. "Most of my transformations have no trouble; the ways of their bodies are inherent. But you have had your natural form for centuries, so may be a bit set in your ways. Emulate me." He strode a few steps, turned, and strode back.

Gary started a stride, tilted over, caught himself, and veered off the other way. But in a few steps he began to get the hang of it. It was after all possible to walk this way, however awkward it seemed.

"Soon you will not even notice the difference," the Magician reassured him. "But your intellectual adjustment may be more difficult. You have human form now, but your spirit remains gargoyle."

Already Gary was learning. He found that he did best when he simply let his body handle motion, instead of trying to dictate to it. The human form required constant balancing, but seemed to have inherent mechanisms to accomplish this. He also found that he had to be careful of the clothing, which tended to snag on things in ways that stone fur did not. He would have preferred simply to remove the clothing and be natural, as before, but realized that this was not the human way. All human beings he had seen were dressed, and though parts of their flesh showed, the central torsos seldom did.

The mushdoor opened and Iris emerged. Now her clothing fit, being tight around her narrow waist, loose around her upper torso, and flaring around her slender legs. Gary was of course no judge of human anatomy, but he suspected that she was now a reasonably aesthetic example of her species.

"You look ravishing, my dear," Magician Trent said politely. "Youth becomes you."

"Thank you," Iris said, and smiled at him. She looked nice when she did that, for a human. Even her hair, which had been whitish and straggly before, when not enhanced by illusion, was now a rich reddish brown, and it flopped in loose curls about her shoulders.

"Now I think you must be on your way," the Magician said. "We do not know what time constraints are in operation."

Iris looked as if she might wish to linger in the pool somewhat longer, but did not argue. "How do we find the golem residence?" she asked him.

"I'm sure the demoness will be able to locate it, once you are on the surface." He turned to Gary. "And you should be able to summon the demoness by speaking her name. She seems to be interested in you, so will probably appear."

"But we aren't on the surface," Gary said, using his funny human mouth for the first time. "We'll need to find another figgle."

"A figgle!" Iris exclaimed. "I wouldn't want to mount one of those oversized worms."

"There should be an easier way," Trent said. "I believe that Brain Coral has a private freight elevator to ship freed creatures up in." He lifted his chin. "Coral?"

A golden glow appeared before them. It was in the form of a path leading away.

Trent smiled. "Follow the yellow slick road," he suggested.

"Yes, we had better," Iris agreed. "Come on, gargoyle man. We have a quest to get out of the way."

Gary shrugged, using his human shoulders, and followed her. He still wasn't sure that this quest was a good notion, but he seemed to be stuck for it.

4
SURPRISE

The path led up out of the pool and across the dry cave floor. Neither Gary nor Iris dripped as they emerged from the water; they were dry. Gary realized that the pool was magical in several ways.

But as he walked through air instead of water, the slight change in environment eroded his orientation, and he began to stumble. He half fell into Iris.

"What's the matter with you?" she demanded sharply. "Are you trying to paw me?"

"If I had my paws, I wouldn't be stumbling," Gary said, embarrassed.

"Oh, that's right, you're as new to human form as I am to youth," she said. "And you are an animal, so pawing has no meaning for you."

"Should it?" he asked, perplexed.

"Just follow the path and try to stay steady."

In two or perhaps three moments Gary adjusted to the different feel of balancing in air, and was able to walk without stumbling.

"You might try swinging your hands," Iris suggested.

"Swinging my hands?"

"It helps you balance when you walk."

He moved his hands in circles as he took another step, but it didn't seem to help.

"Like this," she said, and strode briskly forward, her arms pumping vigorously.

He tried it, but suffered worse problems than before.

"Opposite sides, dummy," she snapped.

"Opposite?" he asked blankly. This was all very confusing. When he walked four footed, one hind leg came forward and landed before the forefoot on that side took off.

"Here." She sounded exasperated. She came to stand behind him, putting her hands on his human elbows. "This foot, that hand." She pushed at his left leg with hers, and shoved his right elbow forward.

Gary tried it, putting the left foot ahead and bracing himself to retain his balance.

"Now the other two," she said, shoving at his right leg and left elbow. "And swing back your arm on the opposite side. This time don't stop; just keep going."

"I'll fall," he said, wary of this awkward combination of moves.

"No you won't. Try it."

He tried it, and got all fouled up. He began to fall, and she was entangled with him. She braced her legs between his and looped her arms around his chest, hauling him back to upright. They swayed precariously together before steadying.

"You were right," she gasped. "You tried to fall."

But now that he was steady, he became aware of something else. "Your front is soft."

She let go of him and stepped back. "This isn't working. Don't you coordinate your limbs when you walk four footed? I don't see why you should have so much trouble."

"Yes. I have a four-beat gait when I walk, two-beat when I trot, three-beat when I canter—"

"Two-beat!" she cried. "That's it! Move your arms as if you're trotting."

He tried it—and suddenly he was beautifully in balance. "So human folk trot when they're walking," he said, amazed. "But what do they do when they're trotting?"

"They still trot," she said.

"Then what about cantering?"

"They remain hot to trot," she said firmly.

"They have no other gaits? Surely when they gallop—"

"No! They trot at any speed. They've got permanent trots." Then she looked surprised, but did not amend her statement.

"The trots," he agreed. "It seems so limited." But it did work for him. He found he was able to go at any speed, using the same opposite-side arm-leg coordination. She had solved his problem. "Thank you."

"You're welcome," she said.

They moved with greater ease along the glowing path. Soon they came to a blank wall. The path had dead-ended in a squared-off cave. "What now?" Gary asked.

"We must have to do something." Iris examined the wall. There were several glowing spots on it. She touched the lowest one.

There was a grinding clank behind them. Startled, Gary turned. Suddenly the floor gave way. Gary and Iris, both alarmed by the sensation of falling, grabbed on to each other for support. Now her softness was jammed against his front, but he didn't object, because their balance together did seem to be better than it was apart.

The floor was still falling. But so were the walls. The two of them seemed to be in a plunging cage. There was even a wall behind them now, where one hadn't been before. It had a window, and through the window they could see a dimly lighted wall zooming upward.

Then the chamber slowed, and they felt heavy. It clanked to a halt, and the windowed wall split in half and the halves parted and separated and slid into the walls on either side, leaving them standing in another dead-end cave.

They pushed away from each other and stepped back along the passage. But there was no glowing path. "This does not seem like the surface," Iris remarked.

There was a rumbling roar, as of some enormously gigantic huge big animal sounding defiance. The walls shook.

"We went down," Gary said. "It must be deep." He really did not feel like remaining here long, especially while not in his natural stone body.

"Do you think I touched the wrong spot?"

Gary was privately gratified that the Sorceress was as doubtful in this situation as he was. "Maybe if the bottom glow made it go down, the top one would make it go up."

They returned to the dead end. Iris touched the top glow. This time Gary saw what happened. The two halves of the wall came out from the sides and clanked together. Then the newly formed cage lifted, carrying them up with it. They were being elevated.

The cage quickly got up speed, and they saw the dim lights plunging downward beyond the little window. Sometimes there seemed to be holes in the wall, and he realized that these could be other passages. There were many levels to this cave. Then the cage slowed, and stopped moving, and the walls parted.

This time there was an open landscape beyond, with trees. They had reached the surface.

They stepped out. The walls clanked behind them. Gary turned—and there was the blank wall of a cliff. It was part of a mountain. There was no sign of any chamber or elevator. Truly, the ways of the nether realm were marvelous.

"We must be somewhere south of the Gap Chasm," Iris said, looking around. "And east of Castle Roogna. But I have no idea where the golem residence is. I fear I wasn't paying much attention to routine things during my dotage."

"Your dotage?"

"I was old and feeble and querulous of mind at age ninety-three. Now I have shed seventy years, and my wits are close about me. I can appreciate how much I was missing. So maybe it is time to summon your demoness friend, and see whether she will help us."

Gary nodded. "D. Mentia," he called. "Are you there?"

A cloud of purple smoke formed. "Who wants to know?" it inquired.

"Oh, let it be, Mentia," Gary said. "You got me into this, so you should help me see it through."

The cloud solidified into the familiar shape of the slightly crazy demoness. "But you know what you got *me* into? Worm intestines. They were interesting. I've never been digested before."

"Have we met before?" Iris asked.

"I doubt it. I've only existed for less than a year, as a half-separate entity, and I don't recognize your face anyway."

"I am the Sorceress Iris."

"I doubt that too. She's an old and feeble crone, neglectful of what's what in her dotage."

"Rejuvenated to a vigorous twenty-three," Iris clarified. "Here is what I used to look like." Her appearance changed to that of the ancient old woman.

"Oh, sure, I'd recognize that old hag anywhere! But you almost never looked that way."

"Because I used my illusion to look more like this," Iris said evenly, reverting to her real appearance. "Now I don't have to. I am reveling in my newfound youth. So are you going to show us the way to the Grundy Golem residence?"

Mentia considered. "Why should I?"

"Because it's bound to be interesting," Gary said.

"Good point. Very well, follow me." The demoness walked roughly west, passing through a tree.

"Oh, great," Iris said sourly.

"She's a bit crazy," Gary explained. Then he called to

the demoness. "Mentia, if you want us to be interesting, you will have to show us a route we can use."

The demoness reappeared, close. "Oh." She put her feet to the ground and walked around the tree.

There was a faint path there. They walked west, past innocuous trees and shrubs. Gary spied a breadfruit tree, and felt a strange sensation. It was a kind of distress below the midpoint of his new body. His fleshy innards burbled.

"You must be hungry," Iris remarked.

"Hungry?"

"When did you last eat?"

"Gargoyles don't eat. We're made of stone."

"Not any more." She stepped off the path and plucked a loaf of bread from the tree. Then she took another pace and took a butternut from a butternut tree. "Bread and butter. Try it."

Still he hesitated, not knowing what to do with the things she brought him. "Oh, for pity's sake," she said. "It seems I have to show you how to eat, too."

"Yes."

She took a slice of bread from the loaf and squeezed the butternut so that butter spread across the surface of the bread. Then she put the edge of the slice to her mouth and bit into it. She wrinkled her nose. "Needs something," she decided. She looked around until she spied an orange egg on the ground. "Good—a marma nested here. Here's what the marma laid." She picked up the egg and squeezed some of its orange onto the slice. Then she took another bite. "Yes, this is good."

Then she set up a second slice similarly for Gary. "Just bite and chew," she said.

Gary took the bread and bit into it. To his surprise, the weird combination did taste good. He chewed a mouthful, swallowed it, and took another. Eating was all right.

Soon they had finished the loaf and the butternut and the orange marma laid. "I forgot how hungry the young healthy folk get," Iris said, wiping her face.

"I never knew how hungry flesh folk get," Gary agreed.

They finished with some fluid from a leaning beerbarrel tree; someone had kindly provided it with a spigot, and there were some mugwumps nearby with pretty mugs. The stuff was dusky colored and it foamed, but it tasted good and Gary drank several mugsful. After that he felt better than ever, if somewhat unsteady.

They resumed their trek. But before long there was a growl. "That sounds like a dragon," Iris said, her tone hinting that she was not completely pleased.

"Of course it's a dragon," Mentia said. "Whose path do you think this is?"

"This is mischief," Iris muttered.

"I'll go first, and it will break ish teesh—its teeth on my body," Gary suggested.

"You are forgetting that you are no longer a stone animal, but a flesh man," Iris said. "And I am no longer a leathery husk, but a plump young chick. We have a problem."

Gary's thinking had become somewhat fuzzy for some reason, but he realized that she was right. The dragon would want to eat them both. "Maybe we should gesh— get off its path."

"Too late," Mentia said cheerfully. "Here comes the dragon."

"Why didn't you tell us this was a dragon path before? Iris demanded.

"You didn't ask."

"That makes so much sense it can't be the reason."

"You're right. I'm too crazy to have a straight reason."

Meanwhile the dragon was charging down on them. Gary wasn't sure what kind it was—smoker, steamer, or fire breather—because wisps of smoke hovered around its mouth, and jets of steam hissed from its ears, and there was fire in its eyes. Its huge foreclaws gouged divots, and its great mouth was cranking open to chomp the first victim—which happened to be Mentia.

Of course that didn't work. The teeth passed right

through the demoness without effect. "What are you trying to do?" she inquired, breathing on her nails.

The dragon made a fiery snort of disgust, realizing her nature, and oriented on the second morsel, which was Iris.

Then a giant serpent replaced the young woman. Huge and green, it lifted its enormous head and bared its sword-like teeth. Its mouth was just about big enough to take in the dragon's whole head. "What is the meaning of thiss?" it hissed.

The dragon blanched, and its fire went out. "Ssorry, naga," it hissed back apologetically. Then it quickly turned tail, and was gone in three-quarters of an instant.

"But you aren't of the naga folk," Gary protested, somewhat confused.

Iris reappeared as the serpent vanished. "How was the dragon to know that? It saw a woman transform into a serpent, as the naga do. I think its conclusion was reasonable."

Her illusion had done it! "You saved us," he said weakly.

"Well, I wasn't going to let the thing chomp us," she said. "What's the use of going on a quest if you just get eaten?"

Gary realized that there might be advantages to having the Sorceress along. Her power of illusion could be as good a defense as real weapons, if the enemy did not know the difference.

They walked on, but another threat developed: a hungry roc bird spied them as they crossed a flat plain. It folded its wings and dived toward them. But a boulder appeared around them. Gary was inside it, yet it looked real. The roc blinked, twitched its beak, and sheered off, thinking it had gotten confused.

"Birds are not phenomenally smart," Iris observed.

Gary understood that, but still, had he been a roc, he would have sheered off too, because that boulder was so realistic. Still, he wondered what would happen if some creature called her bluff, and charged on through the veil of illusion.

They continued, entering a deep valley. In its center was a chasm, an arm or maybe a leg of the great Gap Chasm, which had offshoots extending far afield. "How are we to get across this?" Gary asked as they approached the brink. He was feeling less dizzy now, which was just as well, because it would not have been good to lose his balance and fall into the depths of the cleft.

"There must be a bridge somewhere," Iris said. "Is that right, demoness?"

Mentia appeared. "Sure, right beyond that copse to the north."

But then another threat appeared. This was a truly ferocious creature, with the head of a serpent, body of a lion, cloven hooves, and a formidable stinger. It bayed as it spied them, making a hideous noise.

"There's the Blatant Beaste," Mentia remarked, interested. "It has a thousand tongues, and it doesn't let anything stand in its way, not even a naga or a boulder. I wonder what kind of illusion will help you now?"

"We shall see," Iris said. She looked around. "I see that this chasm offshoot is highly irregular."

"That is the nature of gap radiations," Gary agreed, watching the beast nervously. He had never been much concerned about such creatures when he was stone, but now in this feeble flesh manform he felt extremely insecure.

"Let's get beyond that jag," she said.

"Won't it just skirt the edge, as we do, and get at us with only a small delay?"

"Perhaps not."

They walked quickly around the jag, putting its depth between them and the monster. Then they turned to look back. Gary was surprised. He had evidently misjudged the position of the jag, because they had not after all gotten beyond it. "We had better move farther over," he said.

"No, this will do," Iris decided.

"But—"

"Trust me, stone beast."

Gary did not trust her judgment, but since it didn't make a lot of difference anyway, he settled down with her to wait for the arrival of the Blatant Beaste. This was horrible, because of its noise. It really did seem to have a mouthful of tongues, and all of them were shaping piercing screams. It was definitely intending mayhem.

It charged right toward them. Gary gazed desperately around, trying to find something that this puny human body could use as a weapon, but there was only level dirt leading up to the edge of the chasm to the side.

The Beaste's screams became deafening. It was only three bounds and ten paces from them, and there was nothing to stop it, not even an illusion wall. Yet Iris seemed unconcerned. In fact, she even lifted her spread hand, put her thumb to her nose, and waggled her fingers at the creature.

The Blatant Beaste became, if anything, even more baleful. It picked up speed, charging straight across the level sand.

And suddenly dropped out of sight. There were only the continuing sounds of its screams rising from under the ground.

Then Iris banished her illusion. The jag of the chasm reappeared, right where Gary had first thought it was. She had covered it with the image of sand, and the Beaste had been fooled and plunged headlong in.

"Blatant Beastes aren't very smart either," the Sorceress remarked as she resumed walking north.

Gary hadn't been any smarter, he realized. It hadn't occurred to him that illusion could cover up something that wasn't there, as well as making something appear. She had made an illusion chasm to the side and concealed the real one.

As Gary walked, he found that he was uncomfortable in the midsection again, but this time he wasn't hungry, so he tried to ignore it.

Soon they reached the bridge and crossed over. The track continued wending generally west. Apparently they had gotten beyond the dragon path and were now on a more established route.

"I recognize this now!" Iris exclaimed. "It's one of the enchanted paths."

"Yes, we intersected the enchanted network at the bridge," Mentia said.

"And here I was worrying about staving off more monsters. Why didn't you tell us?"

Mentia shrugged. Her shoulders misjudged the range and went on up over her head before she thought to draw them back down into place again. "Why didn't you ask?"

Iris decided to ignore that. "And just where along this is the golem residence?"

"Just north of the Gap Chasm. They live in a club house."

"North of the Gap!" But again, she hadn't actually asked. Gary had assumed, as Iris evidently had, that it was south. Had they struggled to avoid monsters when they might have taken a more direct route and avoided them entirely? Gary made a mental note not to take the demoness on faith; it wasn't worth it.

Meanwhile, Gary's discomfort of the midsection hadn't eased. Maybe his soft human body was just getting tired.

They came to a campsite. "We might as well stop here," Iris said. "The day is getting late."

"Yes," Gary said.

She glanced at him. "You look uncomfortable."

"I am. But I'm not hungry."

Iris considered. "You haven't been a flesh creature before? You didn't have to eat?"

"Yes, I didn't."

"Then maybe I can guess what else you didn't have to do. You had better go to that toiletree over there and do it."

"Do what?" he asked. "I really don't feel up to anything very energetic."

"Precisely. Just go there and maybe you will figure it out." Then she thought of something else. "But maybe you should take off your clothes before you do."

"What has my clothing to do with it?"

She shrugged, and her shoulders stayed in proper place. "Maybe you will have to find out on your own."

So Gary went to the toiletree, stepped behind it, and pulled off his awkward clothing. He still felt quite uncomfortable.

Then he saw something floating by. It seemed to be a dot. It was followed by a second dot, and then a third dot.

• • •

"Are you feeling better now?" Iris inquired as he rejoined her in the main section of the camp.

"Much better." And he did. But the curious thing was that he couldn't remember what had happened by the toiletree. He had seen the three floating dots, and then he was here, dressed and in good order. Apparently those dots had made him forget about whatever happened, if anything had happened.

"Then you must have seen the ellipsis," she said.

"The ellipsis?"

"The three dots. They cover up anything that's unmentionable, such as stork summoning or natural functions. That makes it possible for us to live without perpetually blushing."

That explained it. But now Gary was hungry again. Fortunately there was a pie tree growing at the camp, with many kinds of pies, and there were milkweeds too. They had everything they needed.

As the sun set, they made piles of pillows and blankets harvested fresh from their bushes, and settled down for the night. Gary had never seen the purpose of pillows before, but now that he was flesh he took great comfort in them. He lay relaxed—and found himself in a weird other realm.

"Yo!" he cried, startled.

"What now?" Iris asked sleepily from her bed nearby.

"I was somewhere else, and everything was in fragments and confused."

"Oh. You were dreaming."

"Dreaming?"

"It's what living folk do when they sleep."

"But I was seeing things, and doing things. I was awake."

"You were awake in your dream, but asleep in real life. When you dream, your soul enters the gourd realm and you get the dreams they make for you. Just forget them when you wake."

"Forget them? You mean they don't matter?"

"Not in ways we need to remember. So you can ignore anything that happens while you are sleeping. Most live creatures do."

That was a relief. Gary settled back down on his bed of pillows, and if he dreamed again, he didn't remember. It was possible to get along, as a flesh creature, once he learned the knack of it.

#

"What was that?" Gary asked, alarmed.

"What was what?"

"That hurtling whatever that just went by."

"Oh, that. Just a time break," Iris explained. "It's so we don't have to go into boring detail all the time. It's like the ellipsis, only moreso."

"Oh." He relaxed. He realized that he had seen similar things before, but hadn't paid attention. Now that he was in vulnerable flesh form, every detail bothered him until he knew it was safe.

They ate breakfast, used up another ellipsis or two, and resumed their trek. The Demoness Mentia wasn't in evidence; apparently she was quickly bored when things were dull, so faded out. Gary was satisfied to leave her out, now that they had a safe path to follow.

They intersected a path heading north, and followed it up to the invisible bridge across the Gap Chasm. Iris used it without hesitation, so Gary did too, though it looked like nothing at all, and it took them right across the yawning gulf. That surprised him; then he realized that even the Gap Chasm might get bored and sleepy when nothing much was happening, so yawning was natural.

At last they came to the golems' club house. But the club was lying on the ground. The family seemed to have moved into a more conventional home recently. There it was: a small cottage industree. It looked like a cross between the industree he had seen before, and a big cheese.

Gary approached the treetrunk and knocked on the door there. In a moment a tiny woman with very long hair opened it. "Stranger, we don't mean to be unfriendly, but this region isn't safe for visitors," she said, looking worried.

"I am Gary Gargoyle in manform," he said. "And this is the Sorceress Iris in youthform. The Good Magician sent us to—to tutor Surprise."

"Oh, you're the one!" the little woman exclaimed. "Oh, wonderful! We just can't handle her any more. She's out of control. I'm her mother, Rapunzel. Here she is." She reached back inside the tree and brought forth a small bundle.

"But—" But his protest was stifled, because there in his hands was the bundle. It seemed to be a tiny little girl. The door to the house was closed.

"But she's so small," Iris said, almost as doubtful about this as Gary was.

"Surprise!" the tot exclaimed. Her tiny eyes crossed. Suddenly she was full normal six-year-old little girl sized, being awkwardly held by Gary's arms. She kissed him on the cheek. "Do you like me?"

"Why, I don't know," Gary said as he carefully set her down. "Are you likable?"

"Sure, when I want to be. Are you going to be interesting or dull?"

"I have no idea."

"That's interesting," Surprise decided. "Let's go."

"But we can't just take you from your family," he protested. "We have to talk to your parents first." Then he became aware that she wasn't standing before him any more. "Where are you?"

There was a giggle from somewhere. He looked around, and Iris looked around, but they couldn't spy the source of the giggle. So Gary knocked on the door again.

The door opened. "Yes?" Rapunzel asked, as if they hadn't just met.

"We seem to have lost your daughter," Gary said, embarrassed.

"Oh, that's all right. We lose her all the time. It's one of her talents."

"One of her—?"

"She can't be found when she doesn't want to be found," Rapunzel explained. "She has a number of ways to get lost."

"But then how can we find her?"

"You'll just have to make her want to be found. Do you have anything that might interest her?"

Gary was blank, but Iris came to the rescue. "I can make very interesting illusions."

Surprise reappeared. "You can? Let me see!"

A miniature replica of the golems' cottage tree appeared in the air before the Sorceress, complete with tiny figures of the four of them. It looked extremely realistic.

"Gee!" the child exclaimed. "I like it." Her eyes crossed. And before her appeared an even smaller replica, with even tinier figures.

Iris gaped. "But I'm the only one who can do this kind of illusion," she protested.

"I'm sorry," Surprise said, and her replica vanished.

"She just does anything she wants to," Rapunzel said. "We love her, but we can't handle her. When she knocked over our club house in a fit of super-strength, we gave up and petitioned the Good Magician for relief. He said he would send a tutor. We're certainly glad to see you! Bring her back when she's under control." She closed the door again.

"But—" Gary began helplessly. But he realized it was futile; this was his Service to the Good Magician, and he would have to try to perform it. Despite his complete incompetence. The little girl did not seem to be mean spirited, just wild.

"And I'm supposed to help," Iris said morosely. "Can youth be worth it?"

"Youth!" Surprise exclaimed, crossing her eyes. Suddenly Iris was her apparent age: six. Her clothing was piled around her, as it had not shrunk to fit—and in any event it wouldn't have fit, because the proportions were different.

Iris took only half an instant to realize what had happened. "Surprise, restore me this instant!" she said severely.

"Okay," the little girl said contritely. Iris reappeared in full size. But now her collapsed clothing was bunched around her midsection, leaving her top bare. Gary had not seen a grown woman's top exposed, since assuming manform, and he found it interesting.

"Gary, look away!" Iris screamed. "Surprise, restore my clothing too."

Gary started to turn away, obedient to the voice of command, but before he completed the effort the Sorceress' clothing jumped into proper place, making it unnecessary.

"Why didn't you just clothe yourself with illusion?" he asked as she adjusted herself.

"I didn't think of it," she confessed. "But this needs to be dealt with." She addressed the child. "Surprise, you must not fool with other people. It's not nice."

"Why?" Surprise asked, her cute little brow furrowing in perplexity.

"I told you: it's not nice. Promise not to do it again."

Surprise frowned. "But it's fun."

Gary realized that there was a problem, reasoning with a child. He remembered how young gargoyles were disciplined. "Because if you do it again," he said firmly, "the Sorceress will make the illusion of a monster that looks like a—" He hesitated, not certain what would properly scare a human child. He grasped at a straw. "Like a big stone gargoyle."

Iris obliged by conjuring the illusion of a creature that looked just like Gary himself, before his transformation. He had to admire it; he had not realized what a fine specimen he was.

Surprise stared at the gargoyle, daunted. Then she summoned her childish courage. "Aw, that doesn't scare—"

The gargoyle opened its ponderous mottled marble mouth and spewed forth a splash of water.

"Eeeeeek!" Surprise screamed, vanquished. "I promise! Please, no cold baths!"

The gargoyle vanished. "That's nice," Iris said graciously. She shot a glance of gratitude at Gary for his help. It was slowly becoming muddily clear why the two of them had been selected to handle this mission. They had just worked together to pass the first hurdle in bringing the wild child under control.

But what was he supposed to tutor Surprise about? He doubted that she needed to know how to purify water, and she certainly wouldn't have the patience to sit still for a century spouting fluid from her mouth. His expertise was in no discipline that related well to the needs of a human child.

Yet it was widely believed that the Good Magician never gave a wrong Answer, however farfetched or irrelevant it might seem initially. Gary had to hope that this was not the exception.

"Now we had better go somewhere," Iris said. "I don't think this child's folks want her back until she has been, um, properly tutored."

"The Good Magician said to take her with me on my quest to find a philter," Gary said. "So we might as well get started."

"A philter?" Iris inquired. "What for?"

"To purify all the water of Xanth, so that there won't be any more pollution from Mundania."

Iris glanced significantly at Surprise. "Maybe someone could find or make that philter for you."

"What's a filter?" Surprise asked.

"Then again, maybe not," Iris concluded.

"The Good Magician also said that Hiatus would know where it was, I think."

"Hiatus? The brother of Lacuna?" she asked sharply. "I remember those two mischievous tots! They were completely empty of responsibility; it was just one lapse after another. Do you know what they did at the wedding of Humfrey and the Gorgon?"

"No," Gary admitted. "Was it interesting?"

"It was outrageous. They used their talents to entirely disrupt the ceremony. They—"

"Gee," the child said, interested.

Iris glanced again at Surprise, and evidently changed her mind. Gary understood why: the child was too apt to imitate any talent anyone mentioned. "Well, that's irrelevant. No doubt Hiatus has matured some in the interim. It has been a number of years. We shall have to enlist his assistance in your quest."

"Yes. But I don't know where to find him."

"He's probably at Castle Zombie. If not, the Zombie Master or Millie the Ghost will know where to find him."

"There's a ghost among the zombies?" Gary asked.

"A ghost!" Surprise exclaimed. Her eyes crossed. A human-sized translucent spook appeared before the three of them, with dark holes for eyes and a boo-shaped mouth.

Iris paused. "Harmless," she murmured. "Ignore it."

The ghost actually seemed as surprised by them as they were by it. In a moment it floated away, somewhat out of sorts. Gary realized that this was probably the best course, when feasible: to ignore Surprise's magic tricks. "Castle Zombie?"

"I know where it is. But it's a long walk from here. I wish we had a carpet to ride there."

"Carpet!" the child said, and a carpet appeared, with several socks on it.

Iris looked at it. "Where did this come from?"

"Mundania," Surprise said.

"The talent of summoning things from Mundania," Iris said, pretending a calmness she probably didn't feel. "A rug, with whatever happened to be on it. This surely explains why Mundanes are always losing their socks. But this isn't what I was thinking of, dear."

"Oh." The carpet and socks vanished. "What did you mean?"

"Why a magic carpet, of course." Then Iris caught herself. "But don't—"

"Magic carpet!" Surprise exclaimed brightly as her eyes crossed. A carpet appeared, floating at about knee level.

"Can we trust it?" Gary asked warily.

Iris peered closely at it. "This seems to be the Good Magician's carpet; I recognize it. It is quite trustworthy. But we should return it—after we're done with it." She sat on the edge of the carpet, and it bowed down a bit with her weight, then firmed in place. She lifted her legs, swung them onto the carpet, and tucked her skirt closely around them. "Get on. I'll hold you, Surprise."

Gary climbed onto the back of the carpet and drew up his knees in the manner Iris had. His impulse had been to crouch on it, gargoyle style, but this human form just wasn't suited for that. The little girl sat on the woman's lap, approximately, and Iris held her in place with her arms.

"Carpet, rise slowly," Iris commanded it. The carpet responded, lifting somewhat in the manner of the elevator, until it floated above the trees. Gary wondered what it would have done if she hadn't cautioned it to be slow. They might have slid off the back as it zoomed forward.

"Carpet, proceed in moderate manner to Castle Zombie," Iris said. And the carpet turned and moved smoothly south.

Gary had never been partial to heights, because a bad fall could crack stone, but discovered that he felt secure on the carpet. Its magic held him in place without confining him, so there was no danger of falling off. He saw the trees passing below, and then the Gap Chasm, and then more trees, with crisscrossing paths through the forest and occasional fields. Xanth was interesting, viewed from above. He tried to spy where they had walked before, but couldn't see the invisible bridge, and wasn't sure which particular trails were the ones. He couldn't even be sure which particular jag from the Gap they had crossed, after dumping the Blatant Beaste. But it was fun looking.

Before long a castle came into view ahead. It looked somewhat slimy, and its stones were greenish, and its moat was clogged with gook. Obviously this was Castle Zombie.

They landed before the drawbridge and got off. "Carpet, go home," Iris told it, and the carpet took off smoothly without riders, spiraled into the sky, and headed northeast. "That was a useful thing to summon," Iris informed Surprise. "When all your magic is that helpful to others, you will be ready to go home."

"But I was starting to get bored," Surprise said, pouting.

Gary realized that the ride had been more chancy than it had felt. If she had done some mischief, such as summoning a basilisk to join them on the rug, it would have become dangerously interesting. This adventure probably had most of its complications still ahead.

Iris took the child's hand and marched forward across the decrepit planking of the drawbridge. Gary hesitated, uncertain whether it would support the weight of stone. Iris glanced back, saw him—and abruptly the drawbridge assumed the look of a fine stout iron and stone bridge. He knew it was illusion, but it helped. He followed them across.

A zombie guard challenged them at the portcullis. "Whoo?" he demanded, moving his rotting arms to bring a rotting spear into play.

"Gee," Surprise said, thrilled. "A real zombie."

"Let me handle this, dear," Iris murmured quickly. Then, to the guard: "Queen Emeritus Sorceress Iris to see Millie the Ghost."

In a moment a surprisingly appealing older woman came out. "Iris?" she asked. "You don't look like—"

"Like this, Millie?" Iris asked, clothing herself with illusion so as to appear her real age.

"Iris!" Millie exclaimed. "It *is* you! What a wonderful surprise. I thought you had gone to a fade-out party."

"I did, along with Magician Trent, Bink, Chameleon, Crombie, and Jewel the Nymph. But there was a complication."

"There must have been," Millie said. "Come in, and we'll catch up on everything. Who is your friend? And you have a child with you, too!"

They joined Millie, who was clearly no ghost, in her nice apartment, which was free of the rot elsewhere in the castle. Surprise played with a zombie werewolf, changing forms herself to match him. That seemed to be as good a diversion as any, so Gary and Iris studiously ignored it.

Iris quickly explained about how their fade-out party, which had been intended to see them fade gracefully from the current Xanth scene so it wouldn't be cluttered by too many old folk, had been postponed. Gloha Goblin-Harpy was on a quest in search of a suitable husband, she being the only crossbreed of her kind, so Magician Trent had been designated to help and protect her until she found her man. Since ninety-six was too old for adventure, he had been youthened, and his subsequent story of that adventure had convinced her to try it too. So now she was performing her service for the youthening by helping Gary Gargoyle tutor Surprise. "But we need to consult with Hiatus," she concluded. "We hoped he would be here."

"Oh, he is," Millie said somewhat sadly. "But he lacks ambition in life. Something is missing; there's no continuity. I'm not sure how much help he will be to you."

Iris pursed her lips. "The Good Magician's ploys act in devious ways," she said. "Do you suppose that we represent some kind of encouragement for him?"

"I wonder," Millie said, turning hopeful. "I really fear there is no cure for him, but it would be wonderful if he were to take an interest in marrying and having grandchildren, the way his sister Lacuna did, after suffering emptiness in her life. At least you can talk with him."

"At least we can," Iris agreed. Gary wondered what Hiatus' problem was, and hoped it wouldn't make it impossible for him to help them find the philter.

Millie sent a zombie to call Hiatus. Soon he appeared: a tousle-haired man nearing forty, looking morose. Millie introduced the others, except for Surprise, who was conjuring miniature zombie animals and setting them to running around the floor; by mutual silent consent they let her be. "Perhaps you should tell them your story, dear," Millie suggested in a kindly tone.

"Are they interested?" Hiatus asked listlessly.

Gary knew that the man would never be of any use in the quest if they didn't understand his problem. "Yes."

So Hiatus sat in the remaining chair and began to speak.

5
HIATUS

I was a wild child, and my twin sister Lacuna was mischievous, and together we drove our mother wild. She
was Millie the Ghost, who was a ghost no more but
preferred that title to "Zombie." None of us were zombies,
of course, but she was the wife and we were the children
of the Zombie Master, so folk tended to assume that we
had at least some zombie ooze in us. The truth was that
Millie was one of Xanth's most lovely women, or had
been before my sister and I wore her down. We were a severe interruption to the steady course of her current life,
and we disrupted whatever we encountered.

Lacuna's talent was to form print on anything, such as
walls or blankets or even to superimpose it on existing
print, changing the text of a printed page. Of course her
print faded out when she lost her concentration, doing no
harm, but it could be quite mischievous on occasion. Such
as when she made the words KICK ME form on the rear end
of a fat man as he bent to pick up a heavy rock, in the
presence of a literal-minded zombie. My talent was to
grow temporary organs on various surfaces, such as eyes,

ears, or noses, on windows, treetrunks, or rocks. I never quite understood why some adults got so upset when one of my noses sprouted and sniffed audibly as they walked by, or when one of my eyes formed on the ceiling or floor and peered down a lady's blouse or up under her skirt and winked. It was just good clean fun. But somehow Lacuna and I were not too popular at formal occasions like weddings or funerals. Today I can appreciate why—but today I am considerably more experienced and responsible than I was as a child.

I don't remember exactly what it was I did on the particular day I'm thinking of, but I'm sure in retrospect that my mother was justified in screeching me out of the house and slamming the door. I was then eleven or twelve years old, and thought that all Xanth owed me entertainment. Outraged by her overreaction to an innocent prank, I decided to run away from home. So I called Doofus, our zombie dragon, and climbed on his back and told him to gallop as far away as he could. Doofus wasn't smart—few zombies are, because their heads are filled mostly with disgusting goo—but his legs and back were strong, so he galloped off in the direction he happened to be facing at the time, which was sloppily southeast. I didn't care; I just wanted to get so far away that I could never be found.

But after a time Doofus began to slow. "What, are you getting tired already?" I demanded. He just snorted some soggy smoke. I realized that he was under standing orders not to go too far from Castle Zombie, so as he approached the limit of his territory, he lost momentum. I could not override those orders, for they had been impressed on him by my father the Zombie Master himself, and all zombies owed their ultimate allegiance to him. Doofus obeyed me only so long as my directives did not conflict with those that were more deeply entrenched.

Finally the dragon stopped entirely. Disgusted, I got off him. "All right, go home then, you rotten creature!" I yelled. He obeyed immediately, and galloped off in the approximate direction of home.

I was left alone in a strange forest. I looked around, my anger fading into something like apprehension. I knew that strange places were dangerous. All I saw were trees, and some rocks and rolls, each rock rolling around and banging into things so that there was a series of loud sounds as each roll rocked with the vibrations. Well, that was better than nothing; I went to grab one of the rolls, being hungry. But its rock got in my way, threatening to squish my fingers, and I had to leave the roll alone.

I heard some music, and hoped that there might be some people there. But when I made my way through the forest, I discovered that the music was coming from another collection of rocks. Or rather from the way they were being eaten; a very nice-looking animal was grazing on them, probably a dear, and with each bite the rocks popped, making attractive music. But I wasn't sure I was ready to eat pop rocks, however tasty they might be to the dear.

So I set my face in the direction it was facing and began to march straight ahead. I wasn't sure where I was going, but I was surely going somewhere.

"Child," a woman's voice called me. I paused, orienting on the sound. There was a woman standing by a spreading acorn tree. She wore a brown dress and seemed adult.

At this point my bravado had just about expired. I wanted very much to have an excuse to go back home, or, failing that, to find another home where someone like my mother would feed me and give me a safe place to sleep and take care of me. Of course I couldn't admit that, even to myself, but it may have influenced my reaction.

I went to her. "I—I—could you tell me where the nearest human village is?" I asked politely. "I seem to be—be—"

"Lost?" she inquired gently.

I nodded, abashed.

"How did you come to this region?" she asked me, with that tone of unconscious authority that comes naturally to all adults.

Naturally I had to answer. "I rode my pet zombie dragon. But he went home."

"Perhaps you should go home also," she suggested, with more of that inherent authority, making it somehow seem reasonable.

"I, uh, suppose," I agreed reluctantly.

"Where is your home?"

"I, uh, live at—at Castle Zombie," I faltered, preferring to remain anonymous.

"Oh, you must be the Zombie Master's little boy," she said brightly.

"I'm not little," I protested bravely. "I'm eleven."

She gave me a glance that made me feel nine without actually insulting me. "Of course. What is your name?"

"Hi." Then, as she continued to gaze at me, I realized that my answer was incomplete. "Atus," I added.

"Hiatus," she repeated. "Don't you have a sister?"

"Lacuna," I agreed. "Our names mean the same thing: a gap or a missing part. Our parents thought that was cute."

"That was very clever of them. I am Desiree Dryad."

I remembered my rudimentary manners. "Pleased to meet you, Ms. Dryad."

She nodded. "Well, Hiatus, are you ready to go home?"

I scuffled my feet. "I guess."

"I happen to know a nice magic path that will take you there before nightfall. I think you would not care to remain in this forest at night."

I was uncomfortably aware of that. "I guess I'd better take it."

Desiree eyed me again. "But I think not without some food. I wouldn't want your mother to think I had sent you home hungry. I have some hybiscuits and finger and toe matoes." She stepped around the tree and returned in a moment with a plate of these things: exactly the kind of wholesome food I really wasn't much keen on eating. But I knew better than to protest, because that's a sure way to make adults get even more set in their ways, so I reached for the plate.

"But first you had better go to that toiletree and clean up," she said firmly.

"Oh. Yes." I went to the tree and cleaned up. Then I took the plate from her and ate the healthy food, and it was surprisingly good once I got into it, even if I would have preferred dragon steak and chocolate milkweed juice.

I did try to wheedle some, though, in my naive childish cunning. "I'm thirsty!" I exclaimed. "Do you have some tsoda popka or beerbarrel tree juice?" I knew she wouldn't let me have those, but might compromise on flavored milkweed.

"No, Hiatus," she replied gently. "Just some excellent water in the little spring there." She gestured to a pleasant depression I hadn't noticed before, where a spot of clear water showed.

Oh. There was no help for it but to go and glug some straight unadorned flavorless water. Actually it wasn't bad; I hadn't realized that truly fresh water could quench thirst so well.

I burped and returned to Desiree, wiping my wet mouth on my sleeve. "I guess I better go now," I said. "Where's the path?"

She frowned. "There might be a more polite way to ask a favor," she remarked to no one in particular.

I realized that she meant something. "Huh?"

She made a moue. "Don't you usually say 'please'?"

Oh, that. I obeyed the adult protocol. "Please show me where the path is," I said formally.

She smiled exactly as if she meant it; adults are good at that. "Of course. It is right that way." She gestured.

I peered, but all I saw was a tangle of brush. "Where?"

She was silent, and after a moment I realized that this was a hint that I had used the wrong phrasing. Adults were funny about such things. "I mean, please show me more clearly where the path is, Ms. Dryad."

She smiled again, turning, and I realized that though I

was a boy and she was a woman, she was no taller than
I was, and she probably weighed less. That surprised me,
because adults had always seemed by definition to be
larger than children. "It is concealed by foliage, as most
private paths are. If you walk directly between those two
laurel trees you will find it, and once you are on it you
will see it clearly. But be careful not to stray from it until
you get in sight of your castle, because the moment you
step off it you will not be able to see it again."

"Oh, an invisible path!" I exclaimed, delighted.

"In a manner of speaking," she agreed, seeming to find
something amusing. "We prefer to think of it as being visible to those who appreciate nature."

I was about to protest that I appreciated nature, but then
I realized that she probably meant things like dull vegetables and plain water. "Thank you," I said somewhat doubtfully, because it sure didn't look like any path there.

"Perhaps I should lead you there," Desiree said.

"Gee, yes!" I agreed immediately.

She walked in the direction she had indicated, and I
followed. I marveled again at her smallness, because she
certainly had that adult woman way of walking. It's as if
their bones are more bendy. When we reached the two laurel trees, suddenly there before us was a nice little path,
winding on through the forest. I blinked, wondering how
I could have missed it before.

Desiree turned, and saw my confusion. "If you step
back a pace, it will disappear," she said.

I stepped back, and the brush closed in, leaving no path
in sight. "Oh, it's magic," I said, catching on.

"What we call situational magic," she agreed. Adults always had complicated words for simple things. "I think
you would have had trouble seeing it even when on it, if
I were not showing you. So it would be better not to be
tempted by things like lollipop plants just off the path.
Those can be mischief."

"Yeah," I agreed, impressed. "I sure better not get off it
till I'm home."

"Yes, you certainly had better not do that," she agreed. I realized that she was correcting my speech, in the maddeningly oblique way adults had. But she had fed me and shown me the way home, so I had to forgive her her adultish ways.

"Thanks, Ms. Dryad," I said, about to go. "I know I'm just a kid, but I do like the favor. You're a nice woman, for a grown-up."

A curious ripple of emotions crossed her face. Maybe she realized that I was making a real effort to be proper by adult definitions. That I wasn't a bad boy, just an ordinary kid, crude around the edges but gradually getting polished.

"Hiatus, what are your hopes for the future?" she inquired.

"Oh, that's easy," I said with enthusiasm. "I'll grow up and get famous, growing big eyes and ears and noses on everything in sight, and everybody will be amazed."

"That is an interesting ambition," she agreed. "But what of romance?"

"Huh? I mean, what's that?"

"Normally boys grow up and get interested in girls, and marry them and form families of their own. Have you no such ambition?"

"Oh, sure, I guess," I agreed, catching her drift. Girls were always more interested in the mushy stuff than boys were. My sister was stupid in the same way. "I'll marry the most beautiful girl in Xanth and let her do the housework."

"That is all?" Something concerned her, but I couldn't tell what.

"Naw, I'll be out growing big noses on trees and things, making them sneeze," I said.

"On trees!"

"Sure. Trees look real funny with noses. It's real fun to grow a Mundane elephant nose on a tree. Get it? A trunk on a trunk." I had to laugh at my cleverness.

For some reason she seemed annoyed, but she didn't make anything of it. "What about your wife?"

"Her? I dunno. I guess she'll do what women do. You know, laundry, cooking, sewing, making beds, sweeping dust, all that dull stuff they like."

Desiree still seemed to have some kind of subtle problem. "Are you sure they like it?"

"Well, maybe not, but who cares? Mom never complains."

Desiree considered. "As I recall, your mother was a ghost for eight hundred years. Perhaps she had her fill of freedom, so was glad to be mortal again, even if it meant tolerating dull routine. But do you ever thank her for what she does for you?"

"Huh?"

The dryad seemed to come to a decision. "Perhaps it would be better if you did not marry," she remarked irrelevantly. "Better for womankind."

I shrugged. "I'll find someone, 'cause I'll be handsome and they'll all want to marry me," I said confidently.

"Perhaps so," she agreed. But then she contradicted herself. "And perhaps not."

"Huh?"

Desiree faced me squarely. "Child, look at me," she said. "Look deep into my eyes, and at my hair, and at the rest of me."

Curious, I did as she bid me. I met her gaze. And something happened.

Her eyes were green and as deep as the spring I had drunk from, like two grassy pools. I felt myself drifting into them, now swimming, now floating, now sinking, just getting encompassed by the way of them. Her hair was brownish red, with leaves on it, like a tree in autumn. It was as if I stood within a quiet magic forest, just looking at her. It was wonderful in a way I had never before appreciated.

"When you are a man," she said with quiet conviction, "you will never see a girl as fair."

And I realized that she was fair, and more than fair; she was the most beautiful creature I could ever have imagined. Strange that I hadn't noticed that before, but maybe it was as it was with the magic path: I couldn't see it until she showed me. There was simply nothing in all Xanth that could possibly be as lovely as this maiden of the forest. I had known that dryads were pretty creatures, but never actually experienced it. Now I knew completely and forever.

She moved her tiny hands, and they were like delicate leaves fluttering in the breeze. She made a little turn, and for the first time I saw just how slender yet well-formed her body was. I had never thought to notice any such thing before in my life. She lifted her arms above her head and swayed in the wind, and it was as if she were a graceful fern or a slender tree, yielding to the force of the air and returning to equilibrium as it passed.

She came to a halt and met my gaze again. "And what have you to say now, Hiatus?" she inquired gently.

"Oh, when I'm a man I'll have a girl just like you!" I swore.

"I doubt it." She smiled, a bit sadly it seemed. "But you will remember me, for the rest of your life." Then she walked away from me.

I started to follow her, suddenly unwilling to let her out of my sight. What a transformation there had been! She had seemed like an ordinary woman, and now she was more lovely and precious than anything I could dream of. But she walked around the tree where I had first seen her, and behind the trunk—and did not appear on the other side. I ran there, and around the tree, but she was gone.

"Desiree!" I cried, suddenly desolate. "Where are you?" But already I realized that she was a magic creature, a dryad, a nymph of the wood, and would appear only at her desire, not mine. She was through with me.

So I returned to the two laurels, and the path reappeared. I took one look back at Desiree's tree, marking its exact place, then set my face firmly toward home.

The magic path led me promptly to Castle Zombie. There may have been lollipops growing beside it, but I never noticed them; I was still bemused by the vision of the girl in the wood. How gorgeous she had so suddenly been! Never again would I encounter a dryad without remembering.

I stepped off the path and walked to the castle. Then I thought to verify the location of the path, so I could follow it back on another day. But I couldn't find it, though I must have crossed and recrossed it several times. Like the dryad, it was gone. There was nothing to do except return to the castle and make what I could of the rest of my life.

Next day I searched for the path again, trying to track my own footprints back, but there was nothing. I realized that it was foolish to seek something magical; a mortal could never find such a thing without the help of a magic creature. Yet I kept trying, day after day, until finally my heart realized what my mind did, and I gave up the effort. But for some time thereafter I cried myself to sleep.

I don't know why it didn't occur to me to find my way directly to the dryad's tree by my original route; perhaps there was a spell on me to make me miss the obvious. But that may not have been feasible anyway, because I really hadn't paid attention when trying to run away from home; Doofus Dragon had taken me. He had found his way home, but was too stupid to find his way anywhere else; he would be as likely to take me in the opposite direction, and I would hardly know the difference. So I suffered at home, and told no one, not even my twin sister Lacuna. Who, after all, would understand? I didn't understand myself; all I knew was that I wanted to see Desiree again. I didn't know why, or what I would say to her; I just wanted to be with her, even if she fed me more finger matoes. In fact I found that I had developed a taste for them, and for unadulterated spring water, especially from green grassy pools. And for the sight of acorn trees in their autumn colors.

For Desiree was a dryad, a nymph associated with a tree. She resembled the things of the forest, and her hair surely changed color with the seasons. I had known about dryads, of course, but now I cared. One might wonder why I didn't seek some other dryad, and the answer is that not all trees have dryads; they are relatively scarce. In any event, it was only this one dryad I wanted to be with, no other.

In fact I was in love, but too young to know it. Desiree had fascinated me, in the nicest possible way; she had shown me her beauty, and I was destined to remember her, as she had said, for the rest of my life.

Time passed, and I became a man. I was, as I had expected, handsome, and the girls did flock around me. But the memory of the girl in the wood made all of them uninteresting. Not one of them came close to matching Desiree. None of them possessed that first wild beauty that only I could see. It was as if the dryad's face was superimposed on the face of any girl I saw, a model for comparison representing perfection, and in each case the mortal face deviated and was imperfect. The same was true of their bodies; all seemed gross and unfinished, like sculptures that had been done by an unskilled artisan. They turned me off. So while I would have liked to marry, I just could not; I did not even want to touch any ordinary girl.

As time passed, my mother and sister became concerned. My mother tried to be delicate about her concern, but my sister Lacuna was blunt: a line of print appeared on the table before me. DON'T YOU LIKE GIRLS?

That was the question. "I like one girl," I told them. "I just can't find her."

Then they had the story from me. My mother was appalled. "A dryad! How could you?"

"I didn't know it was going to happen," I said. "She was just a woman to me, an adult, treating me like a child. She asked me what I was going to do with my life when I grew up, and I told her, and she flashed her beauty at me and vanished."

"You told her about your low opinion of women," my sister said accusingly. "That all we're good for us to wash dishes and clean house."

"Well, sure. It's true, isn't it?"

Millie and Lacuna exchanged a glance that was almost two and a half glances long. Then my sister resumed. "So she decided that maybe you weren't going to be Xanth's gift to womankind, so you shouldn't marry, so she saw to it that you wouldn't. And you aren't."

I began to understand. Desiree was, for all her nymphly nature, a woman. "Then I guess I'm doomed to bachelorhood," I said. "Because there isn't any mortal woman I want to marry." But by this point I wished that Desiree had never looked at me that way, flashing her loveliness. She had, indeed, doomed any future romance I might otherwise have had. No mortal woman would have to suffer through my attitude.

Millie sighed. "There seems to be no help for it. You will simply have to find her."

How much I would like to do that! "But how? I can't find the path!"

"And it's no good searching for every acorn tree in Xanth," Lacuna said. "You could go right by it and never see her, because she wouldn't show herself."

"But I looked carefully at her tree," I protested. "I would know it if I saw it. And I know the general area. It's southeast of here, the distance Doofus can go in a run."

"Then perhaps there is a chance. Ride Doofus there, then grow some ears and eyes and make them tell you what they have heard and seen."

"I never thought of that!" I exclaimed.

"Because she didn't want you to," Lacuna said. "She wanted you to remember her, but not where she was. But now time has passed and the peripheral magic is wearing off, so you have a notion. But she still may not show herself if you do locate her tree."

"If I found the tree, I'd just go there and beg her to join me," I said. "She'd have to listen."

"And if she didn't," Lacuna said wickedly, "you could threaten to chop down her tree."

I felt as if a shaft had pierced my heart. "Oh, no, I could never do that! I could never hurt her. I love her!"

"I didn't say to *do* it," she retorted. "I said to threaten to. To make her appear."

"I couldn't even threaten her," I said, still feeling pained.

"Very well, no threats," Millie said decisively. "But you can at least try to locate the tree. Maybe she'll appear when you ask her to. She doesn't sound like a bad sort; indeed, I rather understand her attitude. If you locate her and apologize, perhaps she'll relent." She focused on me, frowning. "But you have to understand that a dryad can't leave her tree, normally. She has to be in it or near it. So if you want to be with Desiree, and if she's willing, you will have to stay there too."

"I don't care where I am, so long as it's with her," I said.

So we organized the search, and I rode Doofus southeast as far as he could go. The region began to look familiar. I got excited, thinking my quest was going to be successful. But then came disaster. Something none of us had anticipated.

The dryad's tree was in a region of high magic. In fact it was not far from the Region of Madness, where there was so much magic that things went crazy. I discovered that the madness had expanded, or shifted, perhaps because of a change in the prevailing winds, and now the dryad's section of forest was within it. I knew better, but such was my desire for Desiree that I entered the fringe of madness, hoping to find her. Naturally I got hopelessly lost and fouled up. I encountered a limb-bow, which looked like a branch of a tree with ribbons. In fact all the branches of all the trees here were like ribbons tied into huge bows. They seemed harmless, until they started to untie themselves and reach for me; then I ran back the way I had come.

But I was lost; the more I ran, the less familiar things seemed. So I forced myself to pause, because I was after all no longer a child. I decided to grow an ear on a boulder, and an eye, so that I could inquire the way out and the eye could look in the proper direction. But to my horror I discovered that I could not grow either ear or eye; instead the rock formed a vile purple excrescence with waving green tentacles. What was the matter? This had never happened to me before.

Then I heard a voice. It sounded rather wooden, but this was after all a forest. I went toward it, and discovered a man standing under a chair, addressing an empty glade. "Meeting will come to order," he was saying firmly. "Meeting will come to order."

I didn't want to interrupt the meeting, but there just wasn't any meeting here. So I entered the glade and approached the man, hoping he could advise me on the best way out of here. Then I stopped so suddenly I almost fell on my face, for this was no ordinary man. He was not standing under a chair; his top *was* a chair. The chair was there instead of his head. I tried to back away.

But he saw me. "I told you to come to order," he snapped, one of the rungs of his head making an emphatic pop as it snapped.

"Uh, sorry," I said, hastily sitting on a stump. "Who are you?"

"I am the chairman, of course," he said. "Now that you are here, the meeting is in session."

"But I was only looking for the way out," I said.

"The exit is that way," he said, pointing. "Meeting adjourned."

I got up and started in the direction, more than eager to get out. "Thank you."

"Wait!" the chairman called. "Have you paid the stumpage fee?"

I paused, uncertain what would happen if I didn't. "The what?"

"You sat on a stump. There is a stumpage fee, of course."

I didn't care to argue. What would a stump want?

Surely not anything human. I checked my pockets, and found a twig that must have snagged when I was charging heedlessly through the brush, and had broken off. I brought it out and tossed it toward the stump. "Here it is," I said. Then I turned and ran out of the glade, and the chairman did not challenge me again.

But I was not yet out of the woods. I almost stumbled over another chair. But this was no ordinary chair; it was made out of human arms. "You must be related to the chairman," I said, trying to edge around it.

"Of course I am," it said. "I am going to attend the meeting."

It occurred to me that it was odd to have such a chair talk. But of course the chairman had talked too, so it must be all right. "The meeting is in that glade behind me," I said.

"Thank you." The armchair wiggled the fingers on those of its arms that pointed down, and finger-walked toward the glade. But then it paused. "Are you by any chance trying to get out of here?" it asked.

"Yes," I said. "How did you know?"

"No offense, but you are such a peculiar creature that I knew you didn't belong here. But since you were courteous enough to help me on my way, I will help you on yours. You will need to don a coat of arms in order to get out of here."

"A coat of arms?" I asked blankly.

"Yes. It is hard to depart this region if you aren't suitably armed, and you have only two arms. There's a coat hanging behind you; don that and you should be all right."

I looked behind me, and almost leaped out of my shoes. There was a mass of arms almost touching me.

But I realized that this was no ordinary situation. So I nerved myself, and took hold of the mass. The arms were linked, forming a clumsy kind of jacket. I put this on over my shoulders. It was heavy, but not uncomfortable. "Thank you," I told the armchair.

I moved on in the direction I hoped was out. But the

brush and foliage closed in so thickly that it seemed impossible to proceed. Then my coat of arms began to react. The arms writhed and reached out all around me, grabbing branches, nettles, thorns, spikes, and unidentified obstacles and pushing, bending, twisting, shoving, and hauling them out of my way. I walked forward, into the opening cleared in this fashion, and soon was beyond the otherwise impenetrable thicket.

"Thank you, coat of arms," I said gratefully, glancing down. But now my coat was merely woven of sticks and twigs.

I was baffled for a moment, then realized what had happened: the coat had lost its special magic. That meant that I was out of the Region of Madness. The coat of arms had given up its animation to get me through.

I took it off, being careful not to damage anything. "I shall do for you what you did for me," I said. "I shall return you to your environment." Then I heaved it back the way I had come.

I saw it fall to the ground. But as it landed, it changed—to a mass of human legs. It was now a coat of legs. Maybe the wind had shifted inside the madness, bringing a different flavor of magic. One leg kicked up in what looked like a wave; then the coat ran on into the thicket.

So I had managed to win clear of the madness. But it was clear that I had been fortunate. I knew better than to enter it again. The mad things within it might not be as friendly next time.

So I could not reach Desiree. That grieved me, but I knew when I was beaten. With heavy heart I faced back toward home.

And so it remained for some time, as I was resigned to being a bachelor the rest of my life. Until my sister went to see the Good Magician Humfrey, and got retroactively married and with a family. She had become rather dowdy in her thirties, but now she was busy and happy. "Hi, I have a great idea!" she told me. "Why don't you go see the Good Magician and ask him how to find Desiree Dryad?"

"But he charges a year's service," I protested. "It's an awful nuisance just to get in to see him. And his Answers are so cryptic you wish you hadn't bothered."

"But he's always right," she said.

She had a point. So I went to see Humfrey. It was indeed a nuisance getting in, and he didn't even give me an Answer. He just told me to go home and wait for my quest, which would serve in lieu of my year's service.

"What quest?" I asked.

"Surprise," he said. And he would say no more. So here I wait, disgruntled and unsatisfied, waiting for the surprise. I don't suppose you know what it could be?

6

MADNESS

"Surprise!" Surprise exclaimed, suddenly taking note of the discussion.

"That does seem to be the answer," Gary said. "The Good Magician told you to wait for your quest, and you thought he meant it would be a surprise. Instead it is this child, named Surprise, who is with us. I must tutor her as I pursue my own quest. So come with us, and we will try to unravel the Good Magician's mystery."

Hiatus shook his head, bemused. "A child! This *is* a surprise. But it must be so."

"And it must be that Desiree knows where to find the philter," Iris said. "So we will help you find her, and she will help us find it. Meanwhile, we'll all help Surprise learn self-control, teaching her what is needful."

"Needle!" the child cried, her eyes crossing. A slew or two of needles appeared, piling up on the floor in the shape of an evergreen tree. They smelled fresh, and trailed green threads.

"Yes dear, pine needles," Iris said, carefully pulling

some of them out of the hem of her skirt. "However, the word was 'needful,' not 'needle.' "

"Oh." The needles disappeared.

"Why can't the child be tutored at home?" Hiatus asked.

" 'Cause I'm out of control," Surprise said happily. "So I get to go on a venture."

"An adventure, yes," Iris agreed warily. "Now perhaps we should be off, before someone gets bored."

"Board!" Surprise exclaimed, and the boards of the board meeting appeared on the floor. On the back of one of them was printed the word EDUCATION, and on another board was ROOM AND. The others said CIRCUIT, ACROSS THE, and SURF. It seemed to be a convoluted discussion.

"Exactly," Gary said. They had to keep things interesting, or the child would make them become so in her own fashion.

Hiatus, at first evincing astonishment, was starting to catch on. But he surely did not yet understand the whole of it, because all Surprise had done recently was conjure things. "Yes, let's go."

"But I thought you would like to visit for a while," Millie protested.

"We would," Iris said. "But it's not S A F E."

"Essay effee!" Surprise cried, her eyes crossing. A scroll appeared, on which was written an essay consisting entirely of the word "EFFEE," repeated endlessly.

Now Millie pursed her lips, appreciating the possible awkwardness of the child's continuing presence. "But if you really must be going—"

"We must," Hiatus agreed.

They bundled out of the castle. They were now a party of four, and their adventure could not be delayed.

"I wouldn't think of complaining," Iris remarked as they rode their beasts, "but I can't say I truly enjoy being on a zombie cameleopard. Some crossbreeds are weirder than others."

"Crossbreed!" Surprise exclaimed. Suddenly she was a

merchild, her tail making riding awkward. So she became a harpy chick, but her bird's legs weren't much of an improvement. So she became a reverse naga child, with the head of a snake and the legs of a human being. It seemed that her current talent was the ability to assume the form of any human crossbreed, real or imagined.

"I believe your regular form will prove to be more comfortable, dear," Iris said mildly.

The child's regular form reappeared.

Gary agreed with Iris about the awkwardness of their steeds, but did not care to make an issue of it. After all, the Zombie Master was trying to be nice by providing them with transportation to the Region of Madness, so they wouldn't wear themselves out walking.

"Why not?" Hiatus inquired from his zombie unicorn. "They behave well, and they get the job done."

"But they're a bit icky. I'm getting ick on the seat of my skirt. I wish we could dehydrate them a bit."

"Dehydrate!" Surprise exclaimed from her zombie werecat steed, crossing her eyes. Suddenly the creature dried up. Unfortunately, since it was mostly made of viscous ick, this meant that it shriveled into bones and powder and became useless.

"Ixnay, dear," Iris said quickly. Gary was impressed with her emotional control. She had not wanted to take care of a child, but was doing a fine job, considering the severe challenge of it. He had not wanted to associate with her, but was coming to realize that she was invaluable. "It's not nice to dry up the zombies. They don't like it. You had better ride with me." She hauled the little girl up on the cameleopard.

"But I saw that child do conjuring," Hiatus said. "She can't be doing other magic."

"Um, maybe best not to mention—" Gary started.

"Other magic!" Surprise exclaimed. She became a girl-sized teddy bear.

"But that's Prince Dolph's talent of self-transformation," Hiatus said. "She can't do that!"

"Maybe you had better change back, dear," Iris said gently. "You wouldn't want to get stuck in that form, now would you?" And the girl changed back.

"She can do surprising things," Gary explained quietly. "We try not to encourage it, because—"

"Change something else?" Surprise inquired. She looked at a nearby pillow bush, and the pillows became stones and sank to the ground.

"But this can't be!" Hiatus protested in vain. "Nobody has multiple talents!"

"Nobody has *controlled* multiple talents," Iris clarified. "Surprise has uncontrolled talents. We need to make her learn how to bring them under control."

Meanwhile, Surprise looked cross-eyed at the pillow-stones, and they became invisible. Hiatus managed to control his gape, realizing that it was true. Surprise had wild talents.

"I've never seen anything like this," Hiatus said. "Such varied talents! She's a little Sorceress."

"Sorceress!" the child echoed. Her hair changed color and quality, matching Iris'.

After a bit, Hiatus recovered enough to explore the matter. "She does seem to have some control," he said. "Surprise, can you cut any of that corn?" For they were now passing a field where corn, wheat, oats, and barley grew.

"I wouldn't—" Iris started.

"Sure!" Surprise cried, her eyes crossing. The entire field of plants fell flat; all of them had been invisibly cut down.

"You're a cereal killer," Hiatus said, amazed anew. "Can you even transform—"

"That's enough!" Iris cried, alarmed for excellent reason.

"Sure," Surprise said. A bunny that was watching them abruptly turned to stone.

Hiatus, who wasn't strong mentally, opened his mouth to say more. But Gary cut in before him. "Can you muffle him?" he asked Surprise.

"Sure." Her eyes crossed, and a muffler appeared on Hiatus' head, effectively silencing him. Then the child, bored, dropped off to sleep, in the manner only the young could manage.

Gary and Iris were finally able to relax somewhat.

"You know, I craved youth and adventure and romance," Iris remarked. "I got the youth, and am getting the adventure, but not of precisely the type I had envisioned."

"Romance?" Gary asked. "What's that?"

"That's when a boy and girl get together and find each other intriguing," she said, sending him an intriguing glance.

Gary, however, being ignorant of the matter, let the glance fly right past him without effect. "I thought old married human folk didn't do any of that."

"True," she said. "And my marriage to Magician Trent was political rather than romantic. He never loved me, he just wanted me under control, so he married me." She frowned. "It was an effective tactic. We just barely managed to summon the stork that brought our daughter Irene. I always knew I had missed something vital."

"I know exactly how that is," Hiatus said.

"So now that I'm young again, and on an adventure, I mean to make up for what I missed before. This is my significant opportunity."

"But aren't you still married to Magician Trent?" Gary asked. "I mean, even if it isn't romantic, doesn't your kind disapprove of any other associations?"

"I married Trent when I was forty-one years old," she said grimly. "Of course I made myself look like this." Suddenly she was clothed in illusion, and had the appearance of a splendidly curvaceous human woman of about thirty years' age, with a golden crown and gem-studded robe somewhat open in front to reveal the top halves of very full breasts.

Gary found the outfit interesting; he could identify the gems as striped diamonds, green rubies, blue emeralds, firewater opals, and other more exotic stones. "Fascinating," he remarked, staring.

"Thank you," Iris said, inhaling. The robe fell farther open. Unfortunately that caused the intriguing stones to be harder to see; there was too much dull flesh in the way. "But now I am twenty-three, and in that sense won't be married for another eighteen years. I consider myself free to seek romance." She darted another glance at him, but this one also missed its mark.

Then there was a swirl of smoke before them. "Anything interesting happening?" it inquired.

"Nothing at all, Mentia," Gary said immediately.

"I can tell when you're fibbing, gargoyle," the demoness said, assuming her usual shape.

"Demoness!" Surprise exclaimed, awakening, and turned into swirling smoke.

"Stop that!" Iris cried, distraught.

Even Mentia paused for a moment, her shape distorting as she forgot to focus. "You have a demon child?"

Surprise's smoke became a smaller replica of Mentia. "Tee-hee!" she laughed.

"Just wild talents," Iris said. "You wouldn't be interested."

Mentia got back into shape. "Can you do this?" she asked the child, making one eye small and the other huge.

Surprise matched the expression, after first crossing her eyes.

"How about this?" The demoness swelled to twice her normal size, but retained her proportions.

Surprise swelled to four times her size, matching the demoness perfectly. Now there were two voluptuous human female figures floating above the path.

"Um—" Iris began.

"Oh come on, I'm not going to hurt her," Mentia said, frowning, and the figure beside her frowned similarly. "We're just having fun. We'll rejoin you in a while."

"Maybe it's all right," Gary murmured. "Especially since we can't stop them."

Iris was quick on the uptake. "Very well. Be back in an hour." That put her effectively in control of the situation: she had Given Permission.

"Come on, Surprise," Mentia said. "Let's go sail over the mountaintop." She zoomed away, and the duplicate figure followed, giggling.

Iris turned to the others. "This is even chancier than I thought. If that child gets lost or hurt, we'll be responsible."

"I know," Gary said. "But until we figure out a way to get her under control, we have no choice but to play along. At least this will keep the child entertained for an hour, and maybe after that she'll be tired enough to sleep."

"I see your problem," Hiatus said. "That child's a real handful."

"Just as you and your sister were, in your day," Iris said grimly.

"I know. I really regret that, in retrospect. We both made up for it by becoming vacuously dull adults, however."

Meanwhile Gary had been looking around. "I think we have a problem," he said. "Are we getting lost?"

Iris looked. "No, we're just passing through a tall cornfield. We'll be beyond it in a moment."

"But it seems like a puzzle," Gary said.

"It's not corn—it's maize," Hiatus said. "We should have gone around it."

"Maize!" Iris exclaimed. "You're right. We're lost in its puzzle." Indeed, they seemed to be stuck in a confusing array of paths between rows of corn that looped around, leading nowhere.

"I can find the way through," Hiatus said. "I'll grow eyes on all the stalks, and they'll spy the way out." He rode around, and wherever he passed, eyes appeared. "And noses, to sniff the way out," he added, and noses also sprouted. "And mouths, to tell us the way out."

Soon his ploy was effective. "Out, out," said a mouth, and they went to it, and then to the next out-mouth, ignoring those that said "No way, no way." It seemed that the organs Hiatus grew were able to communicate with each other, perhaps in some sniffing or blinking code, so the mouths knew.

It didn't take long to emerge from the maize. "I must admit, Hiatus, your talent has its uses," Iris said.

"It is my hope to do enough useful things to make up for the mischievous ones I did as a child," Hiatus said.

"That's probably impossible," she said. "But a worthy ambition."

They rode on, making better time now that they didn't have to be watching Surprise. Because of this, they soon approached the Region of Madness. Gary could tell, because the terrain ahead became weird. The trees had green trunks and brown leaves, and the forest animals seemed to be rooted to the ground.

Hiatus gazed at that and gulped. "That's the madness, all right. It's different from when I was here last, but I suppose it does keep changing. I—I really don't feel much like trying to go in there."

"I am not exactly sanguine about it either," Iris said. "Particularly not with a wild child like Surprise."

"Suddenly I grasp something I didn't quite understand," Hiatus said. "Her talents aren't uncontrolled—*she* is."

"Precisely. She seems to be able to do what she chooses, but she's a child. She doesn't see the point in behaving perfectly. We have to persuade her that there is a point. That's why Gary was assigned to tutor her."

"And I still have no idea how," Gary said. "It's bad enough being in manform, and that confusion makes it worse."

"Manform?" Hiatus asked.

"Remember, I'm a stone gargoyle. Magician Trent transformed me for this quest, and I think won't transform me back until I complete it. So I really have to accomplish it."

"A gargoyle," Hiatus echoed. "Iris told me, but I forgot. We are an unusual group indeed!"

"With an impossible mission," Iris said. "I think Humfrey overreached himself on this one."

Two clouds of smoke appeared before them. "We're baaack!" the larger one said.

"It was fuuun," the smaller one said.

"It is just as well that you returned before we entered the Region of Madness," Iris said.

"Oh, do you have to go there?" the larger magic cloud asked, shaping into Mentia.

"It's a mean place," the smaller magic cloud said, two eyelike swirls crossing before it shaped into Surprise. "We didn't dare go in."

So there was a region the demoness avoided. Gary made a mental note, in case the information should ever be useful.

"It's where Desiree Dryad is," Iris said. "We have to find her."

"You'll get lost," the demoness said. "Everything's weird in there."

"How well I know," Hiatus said. "But how can we find her if we don't go in?"

Mentia considered. "You might ask the fringe dwellers."

"The what?" Gary asked.

"Richard and Janet," Surprise said. "We met them. They're nice."

"They are human beings?" Iris asked uncertainly.

"Sure," the child said. "They live right next to the madness, and sometimes the wind changes and sweeps it across them, so they know what it's like."

Gary exchanged two glances with Iris and Hiatus. "Maybe they'll know something useful," he said.

Both Iris and Hiatus looked relieved. "Yes, let's consult first with them," Iris said.

They turned the zombie animals and traveled beside the madness, rather than into it. But the boundary wasn't smooth; filaments of madness reached out from it, and there were cracks extending into it. They stayed suitably clear, because any stray breeze could mischievously move the madness across them. They could see plants turning weird as the filaments passed them.

They came to a giant gourd, rotting at the edges. "That's a hypnogourd!" Hiatus exclaimed, stopping before its giant peephole, shielding his eyes. "A zombie gourd. I didn't know there was one here."

"Why not?" Iris asked, shielding her own eyes so that she couldn't get locked into its spell. "With mad magic anything can happen."

"That's right—it must have grown in the madness, and then the madness retreated a bit, and left the gourd out here. I must tell my father when I return home, because he can use it to travel."

"Travel?" Gary asked. As a stone gargoyle he hadn't worried about gourds, but now he took the cue from the others, and did not look directly at the peephole.

"A person can walk into one, and walk out another one on the far side of Xanth, if he knows the route through," Hiatus explained. "My father marks routes so he can use them safely."

"But I thought it was the dream realm, inside the gourd," Gary said. "That people couldn't enter them physically."

"They can when the gourds are big enough," Hiatus assured him. "But it's not smart to do it without a marked route, because the dream realm is, well, it's a lot like the madness. Anything can happen."

There was a rattle near their feet. Then a snake appeared, biting the leg of the cameleopard. The creature leaped, shaking off the snake, which quickly slithered into the gourd.

"Oh, now I've lost my steed," Iris said, irritated.

But the cameleopard did not collapse. Instead it seemed to be healthier than before. "Oh, it's one of those," Hiatus said. "Its bite cures zombies. They hate that."

"Instead of killing zombies, it makes them alive?" Gary asked, amazed.

"Why, I know someone who would love to be bitten,"

Iris said. "Zora Zombie. She's almost alive as it is. I must tell her before I return to the caves. Her husband Xavier will be pleased too."

"A zombie married a live man?" Gary asked.

"Well, Zora wasn't very far gone," Iris explained. "And she's remarkably well preserved for her condition."

They moved on, leaving the giant gourd behind. Iris' cameleopard was stepping along with renewed vigor, being now completely alive. Gary was sure Iris appreciated the fact that it was no longer icky.

As the day waned, they reached the house where Richard and Janet lived. It was a neat cottage surrounded by clusters of toadstools and flowers. "Why those are irises!" Iris exclaimed, delighted. "And really fancy ones, too!"

They dismounted and approached the cottage. "Hey, folks, come on out!" Mentia called, appearing.

A man appeared in the doorway. "Oh, it's the lady demon again," he said. "And the demon child."

"And some real live folk too," Surprise said, turning smoky and floating up to join Mentia.

A woman joined the man in the doorway. Then both stepped out. "Hello," the man said. "I'm Richard, and this is my wife Janet. We're from Mundania, originally, but we like it better here. Are you native folk?"

"Yes," Iris said, stepping forward. "I am the Sorceress Iris, and these are Gary and Hiatus. We don't mean to bother you, but we thought you might help us locate something. We understand you know something about what's behind the veil of madness."

"We really haven't been in Xanth long," Janet protested. "Only a year or so—it's hard to remember exactly. I couldn't see very well at first, and I haven't traveled. So I'm afraid I won't be of much help."

"I haven't traveled either," Richard said. "Only far enough to explore the immediate surroundings, and to meet Janet. But I have talked with folk who travel through, and exchanged stories with them. Perhaps I will have heard of something useful to you."

"We are looking for Desiree Dryad," Gary said. "She's a tree nymph. We hope she will know where to find a philter."

Janet brightened. "Oh, yes, we met her not long ago, when the madness shifted away from her tree."

"We try to stay clear of the madness," Richard explained. "It's weird in there."

"Weird!" a voice exclaimed as two clouds of smoke appeared, one smaller than the other.

"Oh, the madness is returning!" Janet said, alarmed.

"No, those are the other two members of our party," Iris said, grimacing. "They're already weird." She addressed the clouds. "Mentia. Surprise. Shape up for a formal introduction."

The woman form and girl form took form for the form-al introduction. "I'm the Demoness Mentia. I'm a little crazy."

"I'm Surprise Golem. I'm out of control."

"So nice to meet you formally," Janet said doubtfully.

"Would you like something to eat?" Richard asked. "All we have at the moment are orangeberries, but they are tasty." He stepped into the house and brought out a bowl of orange berries.

"I want an icecream berry," Surprise said.

"I would find some if I could," Richard said—then stared. For the child was holding a chocolate-shelled icecream berry, and licking it with gusto.

Gary was coming to appreciate the uses of diplomacy. "Perhaps the others would like some icecream berries too," he suggested.

"Oh, sure," Surprise said. Her eyes crossed. Suddenly the bowl Richard held was filled with chocolate-covered icecream berries.

"She can change one fruit to another!" Richard said, surprised.

"Among other things," Gary agreed. "We had better eat these before they melt."

They did so. Each berry was a different flavor under the chocolate, but all were good.

"You inquired about Desiree Dryad," Richard said. "Her tree is within range when the madness shifts away. But most of the time it's in the madness. She's not happy about that."

"What does it do to her?" Hiatus asked with restraint. He was surely excited about this, but afraid to hope too much.

"Nothing to her directly," Janet said. "But it affects her tree, and therefore her, indirectly. It gives her tree square roots, and they don't work well, so the tree suffers. If it weren't for the occasional periods of un-madness, that tree might have died by now."

"Died!" Hiatus cried, anguished.

Richard and Janet looked perplexed. "He met Desiree before the madness came," Iris explained. "He loves her but can't reach her, because of the madness."

"But tree nymphs don't usually marry ordinary men," Richard said. "They just like to tease them, if they show themselves at all. They don't like adults. They relate best to children."

"Children!" Surprise exclaimed. Her eyes crossed. But for once nothing happened; she was already a child.

"But how could you talk to Desiree, if she won't meet adults?" Gary asked.

"We're somewhat childlike about Xanth," Janet said, blushing. "It is taking us time to believe much of what we see. We didn't know Desiree was different, until she told us."

"I think she was a bit lonely, after the madness," Richard said. "Disoriented, maybe. When she saw how little we knew, she was glad to talk. But her tree is suffering. We wish we could help her, but we'd just get lost in the madness. So we visit only when it clears."

"When it comes here, we hide in the house and hardly move," Janet said. "Fortunately it usually doesn't stay long. Usually we can sleep through it, though our dreams are weird."

"It sounds as if the madness is constantly changing," Gary said. "What makes it move?"

"The wind, mostly," Richard said. "A storm will blow it across, and then the wind from the opposite direction can clear it. So we're very careful about the weather."

"Sometimes we wish we could control the weather," Janet said. "But of course no one can do that."

"Weather!" Surprise said. Suddenly there was a swirl of cloud above her head. It expanded into a tiny storm, with little lightning jags that struck the ground and made stray dry leaves jump. Then it rained over a small area.

"I see I still have things to learn about Xanth," Richard said. "I had somehow gotten the notion that each person had only a single talent."

Iris smiled, somewhat wanly. "That's a notion quite a number of us had. It seems to be a general rule but not an absolute one, as is the case with the non-repetition of talents. Talents do repeat on occasion, and now it seems that they can also come in bunches. Surprise seems to have just one talent at a time, but that can be almost anything she chooses. We are trying to encourage her to use her magic wisely, rather than for mere fun and mischief, but so far with imperfect success."

Gary had a notion. "Suppose Surprise made a storm to blow the madness away from Desiree's tree?"

"I'm not sure that would be wise," Richard said. "Storms are unpredictable. It could more madness in, or get you trapped in it when you thought it was clear. And the effect wouldn't last."

"Unless she could exert a more thorough control of the elements of the weather," Hiatus said. "To change the actual climate here, so that the madness would stay away."

Iris shook her head as she glanced at the child, who was inspecting the irises. Sure enough, one of them had sprouted an eye, making it an eye-ris. It was not wise to let the child get bored. "She would never have the patience. Her attention span is very brief. She's a little tomboy."

"Boy!" Surprise exclaimed, overhearing part of it. And suddenly she was a cross-eyed little boy.

Richard whistled soundlessly. "That is one remarkable child!"

"Understatement of the month," Iris muttered. "I think we had better move on before she causes more mischief here. We'll have to brave the madness. What direction is Desiree's tree?"

"That way," Richard said, pointing. "But I wish you would reconsider about going into the madness."

"I know what you mean," Hiatus said. "But we seem not to have much choice. I'll grow some noses on the trees to point the way."

From each nearby trunk sprouted a human nose, or other projection, pointing the direction Richard had indicated. Gary had seen Hiatus' talent in operation before, but was impressed.

They looked around for their zombie steeds, but those had wandered away. "They wouldn't care to enter the madness anyway," Hiatus said. "Best just to let them go home."

"Come, child," Iris said briskly to the Surprise boy, who was searching out slugs and snails. When he ignored her, she put out a hand to catch his arm—but her hand passed right through his body. He had become intangible, in the manner of a demon.

"Oh, for pity's sake," Iris said. Suddenly a gargoyle appeared before the boy, opening its mouth as if to spew out clean water.

"I'm coming!" Surprise cried, back in her natural gender and solidity. Iris' illusion had frightened her into compliance. But Gary wondered how long that would be effective. They needed to find a better way to control the child.

They bid good-bye to Richard and Janet, and followed the noses. Surprise soon got bored with walking, and adapted her arms into wings. She flapped them vigorously until she lifted into the air, but then she was unsteady, so she tried to sprout a tail. Her clothing got in the way, so she landed, reverted her arms to normal, then stretched them far ahead so they could grab on to a sapling. After that she let them spring elastically short again, hauling her rapidly forward. But then she stumbled and fell, scraping her little knees, and let out a wail. It shaped itself into the cloudy image of a huge sea creature and swam away, jetting a gaseous fountain into the air.

"We need some healing elixir," Iris said in a matter-of-fact tone.

"I don't have any," Hiatus said.

Gary found a puddle of water. He scooped up a double handful. This was one thing his natural body couldn't do. "Please change this to healing elixir," he said to Surprise.

The child only glanced at it. But he felt a change in his hands; all their little abrasions had suddenly faded. He splashed some of the elixir onto the child's scraped knees, and they instantly healed.

"After this, just make yourself stronger," Iris suggested without any great store of sympathy.

"Gee, yes," Surprise agreed. She jumped up, her muscles suddenly stronger. "I see a funny bug," she said, looking ahead.

The others looked, but all they saw was a small tree some distance away. "Where?" Gary asked.

"On the top branch of that tree."

They walked to the tree. There on the top branch was a tiny bug.

"I hear a funny bird!"

"Where?" Gary asked again.

"Way up in the sky," she said, pointing.

They looked. After a moment a shape appeared, winging toward them. It was a bird, and as it passed overhead it fluted pleasantly, making an unusual melody.

"She strengthened her sight and hearing along with her muscles," Iris said, as if this were ordinary. Gary knew why; she was afraid that if she made anything of it, the child would do something even wilder.

They came to the edge of the madness. They could tell by the line of weirdness ahead. The trees had regular noses, mouths, or ears on them, but at the fringe of madness the projection looked like some kind of machine. There were even little wheels and pistons on it, moving. "What is that?" Gary inquired.

"It was supposed to be an ear," Hiatus said. "Now it's an engine."

"So it's an engine ear," Iris said impatiently. "Now are we plunging into this madness, or are we hesitating some more?"

Mentia appeared. "Are you actually going to do it?" she asked. "This should really be interesting."

"You lead the way, demoness," Iris said grimly. "We'll follow."

"No, you lead, and I'll follow," Mentia said. "I'm a little crazy, not a lot crazy."

"We'll go together," Gary said, suffering a fit of decision. He grabbed Mentia's hand with one of his, and Iris' hand with the other. After an additional flicker of hesitation, Mentia took Hiatus' hand, and Iris took Surprise's hand. The five of them stepped forward, linked.

Gary's breath caught. There was air, but it seemed different, the wrong color or sound. It was as if he were looking down from the bottom of a pool, or up from the top of a mountain. The landscape had a bulgy, curving shape, as if he were looking through the eye of a fish. When he took a step forward, it was as if he were zooming a long way, while hardly moving at all.

He turned to look at Mentia on his left. She looked composed. Since a person would have to be slightly crazy to be at ease in this madness, that made sense. He looked at Iris to his right. She was clothed in illusion, looking middle-aged, perhaps in the confusion forgetting that her physical form was now much younger.

They let go of each other's hands and looked at each

other. "This is different than it was before," Hiatus said. "Not as bad."

"Maybe it's the luck of the draw," Iris said uncertainly.

"Draw!" Surprise said, crossing her eyes. She picked up a thin stick and drew a figure in the dirt. It was of course a stick figure, with a balloon head.

"I wouldn't—" Hiatus began. But of course he was too late.

The stick figure jumped off the dirt, leaving the ground bare behind it.

Surprise drew a simple house, in the manner of her age: just a square with a door and windows and a peaked roof. She put her free hand to it and lifted it up. It was like a wire figure, two dimensional but firm. She drew an animal, with a boxlike body, four stick legs, a curl of a tail, and a round head with two ears sticking up. It bounded out of the picture and away, having height and length but no depth.

"Has her talent changed?" Hiatus asked.

"It's hard to tell," Gary said. "We didn't see that particular talent outside of the madness."

"We had better move on," Iris said. "Hiatus, grow some more noses so we can follow the direction."

Hiatus concentrated. Things appeared on the trees. "Those aren't noses!" Hiatus said.

"I had noticed," Iris said. "Nose hairs, perhaps?"

Hiatus went to inspect the nearest one. "This looks more like a root," he said. "I'll try again."

This time round flat green things appeared on the trunks.

"I think those are leaves," Gary said.

"Leave!" Surprise cried.

"Oh, no you don't!" Iris said, snatching the little girl's hand. But Gary saw that she would have been too late, if Surprise had used magic to depart; her eyes had already crossed. Instead of leaving, the girl had stayed. That suggested that her magic was fouled up, just as Hiatus' magic was.

"But I can't grow leaves on things," Hiatus said, dismayed.

"It seems you can now, in the madness," Mentia said. "It seems like a reasonable talent."

"But I've always grown ears, noses, mouths, and eyes," Hiatus said. "What will I do with leaves?"

"Leaves, leaves, leaves, who cares!" Iris snapped.

"Fleas fleas fleas!" Surprise cried. Suddenly there were cracks all through the ground where they stood.

"Those aren't fleas," Hiatus pointed out. "They're flaws."

"So her talent *is* changed," Gary said. "She tried for fleas and got flaws. The madness has changed our talents."

"What about yours?"

"I don't have one, in this form. In my natural form I'd probably be polluting water instead of purifying it."

"What about Mentia?"

"My talents are inherent," the demoness said. "I can still do the usual demonly things."

"But you don't seem crazy."

"Oh!" she said, appalled. "You're right. I'm perfectly sane. This is awful."

"Shall we get on with our journey?" Iris demanded impatiently. Then she forged ahead on her own.

"But maybe *she's* a little crazy, now," Hiatus muttered.

They proceeded through a region that wasn't as bad as they had feared, perhaps because this was actually the fringe of the Region of Madness, where the effects were not really intense. There was silence for a time as they passed through a field of deaf-o-dils, and then they had to dodge to avoid a group of hopping plants which turned out to be rabbit's foot ferns, and then they had to duck out of sight lest they be caught by a mad dentist who was determined to dent anything he could find. "The brassies must really hate him," Hiatus remarked as the sound of denting moved on beyond. "They're made of brass, and dents really spoil their appearance."

"They should hate this, too," Gary said. For now they

encountered several metal sheep who were grazing on ironwood leaves and twigs, and on ironweed. They were covered with steel wool.

At last they came to the dryad's tree. They could tell it was the right one because the roots and leaves that sprouted from treetrunks in lieu of ears and noses led right to it. There was a somewhat haggard nymph resting against the tree's base.

"Desiree!" Hiatus cried. "I have found her at last! See how beautiful she is!"

Gary, Iris, Mentia, and Surprise exchanged a combination of glances. Beautiful? The nymph was hardly that, in her present state.

"I think we have a problem," Iris murmured, and the others nodded agreement.

$\overline{7}$
RUINS

But Hiatus was already plunging ahead, and they had to follow. "Desiree!" he cried. "I have found you at last!"

The nymph saw him and tried to hide, but both she and the tree were so gaunt that there was no way. So she leaned against the twisted trunk and faced him with weak resignation. "Please pass on by, stranger," she said. "I have no dealings with adults."

"Don't you know me? I'm Hiatus."

Desiree looked blank. "I'm sorry, but I don't know you or your companions. Please go away, because I am very shy, I look awful, I don't have the strength to turn invisible, and I'm afraid you'll hurt my tree."

Iris stepped in. "Let me introduce myself. I'm the Sorceress Iris, with the power of illusion." She made the scene change, so that the forest seemed to become a vast grimy dump. "Oh, that's not what I meant," she said. The scene changed to a bleak plain. "Nor that! What's the matter with me? I wanted a nice meadow."

"Your talent is being fouled up by the madness, just as

the other talents are," Mentia said. "Try making a horrible scene."

"I'll make hell itself," Iris said. Heaven formed around them: a lovely place with sculptured cloudbanks and soft music in the background.

"What the Sorceress was about to say is that we are a party on a special quest," Mentia told the dryad. "Perhaps she can enable you to look as you once did."

"Don't bother with me," Desiree said. "Beautify my tree."

Iris focused on the tree. It worsened, becoming a rotting column. The nymph was a hideous crone. "Oops." Then the tree turned beautiful, with a rich brown trunk and enormously spreading crown of leaves. The nymph was radiantly lovely. Gary realized that Desiree was a reflection of her tree, prospering or suffering as it did, even when only in illusion. Now it was clear how anyone could have fallen instantly in love with her, for she was as pretty as the human form could be. He was a gargoyle, who hardly appreciated beauty, but maybe the madness was interfering with that, because the dryad definitely looked appealing.

"And what Hiatus is trying to say," Mentia continued with perfect sanity, "is that he was a child of eleven or twelve when he met you, twenty-seven years ago."

"Oh, then," Desiree said. "But now he is grown. That's different."

"You told me that I would never see a girl as lovely as you," Hiatus reminded her. "And I never have. So you are the one I want to marry."

"Marry!" Desiree exclaimed, appalled. "Dryads don't marry. Especially not mortals."

"But you—"

"I never promised to marry anyone," she said with all the firmness of her present appearance. "I merely said you would never see a mortal girl quite as fair."

Hiatus seemed somewhat discommoded. "But I thought—"

"She's right," Iris said. "Nowhere in your story of her

did she say that she had any intention of marrying you, or even of seeing you again. She was just teasing you."

"But—"

"Butt!" Surprise exclaimed, crossing her eyes. A bunch of balloonlike faces appeared and floated away. Her magic had been diverted upward by the madness. It occurred to Gary that this was probably just as well.

"It's what dryads do," Mentia said. "Just as demonesses do. Teasing foolish men is amusing, because they are so readily deluded by appearance. They don't care about substance at all."

"I do care about substance," Hiatus protested. "I want to hug her and kiss her and feel her substance against me."

"What about her personality?" Iris asked.

"Her what?"

"Point made," Mentia said. "Hiatus, I'm afraid your dream is as empty as your own personality. The dryad isn't interested in you."

"But there's no one else," he said plaintively. "She spoiled me for any mortal woman."

"As she intended to," Mentia agreed soberly.

"There must be some way," he said.

Mentia shrugged. "Is there some way?" she asked the dryad.

"No way," Desiree said.

"A way!" Surprise cried, making her expression. The dryad's tree glowed.

"What way?" Hiatus asked the child.

"Save her tree."

Mentia turned back to Desiree. "Would you marry Hiatus if he saved your tree?"

"I would do anything, no matter how awful, to save my tree," the dryad said. "Because without my tree, I will cease to exist."

"There you have it," Iris said with a third of a smile. "Save her tree, Hiatus, and she will do the awful thing of marrying you."

"Then I'll save her tree," he said enthusiastically. "How do I do that?"

"Make the madness go away," Desiree said. "Since the madness came, my tree has wilted and lost its leaves. Its roots have turned square. I'm afraid it will die if the madness doesn't go away soon."

"How do I do that?"

"I wish I knew," Desiree said sadly. "The madness has been expanding and taking up more territory than it used to. I saw it coming, but I hoped someone would stop it. Every year it was closer, until finally it got here, and my poor tree started suffering."

"Then it must be more than just the vagaries of the wind," Mentia said. "There must be more madness than there used to be."

"But the madness is merely the intensification of magic near where the magic dust emerges from the ground," Iris said. "It should dissipate as it gets carried away."

"Intensification?" Gary asked. "Shouldn't that mean you can do your magic better?"

"It should. But for some reason it doesn't. It just fouls things up."

"This doesn't seem to make much sense," Gary said.

Mentia nodded agreement. "Nothing makes much sense in the Region of Madness."

"Then I suppose we should just get on with the quest," Gary decided, ill at ease. He didn't like leaving the dryad to her fate, but saw no alternative.

"But we need Desiree's help for that," Hiatus reminded him. "Why else would the Good Magician have put us together?"

So Gary spoke to the dryad. "I need to find the philter. Do you know where it is?"

"Not exactly," she said. "I understand it's in the ruins, beyond a veil."

"In ruins!" Gary exclaimed. "I need a good philter, not a broken one."

"In *the* ruins, she said," Mentia clarified. "Beyond a vale."

"Veil," Desiree said.

Mentia frowned. "Whatever."

"Where are the ruins, then?"

"I used to know, before the madness changed everything," Desiree said.

"Then how can you help me?" Gary asked.

"I could show you the path to the fallen giant."

"What good would that do?"

"He may know where the ruins are. He blundered around a good deal before falling."

"Then show me the path to the giant."

"What deal will you make?"

"What do you mean, what deal?" he demanded, frustrated.

"If I help you, you should help me in return."

Oh. "What deal do you want?"

"Save my tree."

"I don't know how to save your tree! I can't make the madness go away."

Mentia stepped in again, rationally. "We do not know that Desiree's information will truly help you find the philter," she pointed out. "The giant may not remember where the ruins are, or we may not find the philter at the ruins. We simply have to take the effectiveness of her help on faith."

"Which makes it an even worse deal," Gary said.

"It is also true that you do not know how to save her tree," the sane demoness continued. "So you can not agree to do that. However, you can reasonably promise to try to find a way, just as she can reasonably give you information that may help your quest. This seems like a fair deal."

"Why so it does," Iris said. "You each *try* to help the other, without being certain of success."

Gary looked at the dryad. "Does that make sense to you?"

Desiree considered. "Are you an honorable man?"

"I'm not a man at all. I'm a gargoyle in manform."

"Oh, then it's all right. Gargoyles are very constant."

"But if Gary saves her tree, she won't marry me," Hiatus protested.

"Gary will try," Mentia said reasonably. "You will try. Whoever first succeeds will have his reward. And Desiree has two chances to survive."

"But—"

"If you fail and Gary succeeds, would you prefer to see her tree die rather than be saved his way?"

Hiatus looked stricken. "No, of course not. I want her and her tree to prosper, even if I don't."

The dryad glanced at him, surprised. The first faint flicker of maidenly interest crossed her face.

"Then I will undertake to try to find a way to save your tree," Gary said.

"The path is over there," she said, pointing.

"But that's just a tangle of nettles."

"I trust her," Hiatus said. He marched into the nettles— and through them without getting snagged. Meanwhile the second flicker of interest touched the dryad, as the illusion surrounding her faded and she and her tree turned gaunt again.

The others followed him, and lo, there was a path there. Gary was the last to go. "I'll try," he repeated. "I have no idea what will help, but I'll try to find it and bring it back to you."

"Thank you," she called, and her tree almost seemed to wave a branch, though that was probably just from a breeze.

After a suitably maddening trek they stumbled across the giant. That was because he was invisible, as most giants of Xanth were. He was lying on the ground, his huge outline roughly marked by the foliage that was starting to grow around him.

"Ahoy there, giant!" Mentia called. "Where is your head?"

"Over here," the giant responded.

The brush was so thick that they could not get through it, so they scrambled up onto the giant's leg and walked toward his distant head. Now they seemed to be floating, though they were as solid as ever, because they were half the height of the surrounding trees with only air showing beneath them. Actually it wasn't air, but giant flesh. It would have been scary if the leg weren't so solid to touch. The giant was enormously huge.

They reached the chest, which was rising and falling with the quakelike fluxes of his breath, and concluded that this was close enough. "Are you injured?" Iris asked.

"No, merely confused," the big head-shaped space replied with a gust of warm wind that smelled as if it had crossed a burning landfill on a bad day. "I can't find my way out of this madness, so I'm resting. I'm Jethro Giant."

"We're a party consisting of a demoness, a gargoyle, a child, a Sorceress, and an ordinary man," Iris said. "We're looking for the ruins."

"I lumbered through there," Jethro said. "Just follow my footprints back."

"Did you see a veil?" Mentia asked.

"It's not a vale, it's more like a plain. Will that do?"

"Not vale as in vole," she said precisely. "Veil as in maiden."

"Oh. No. No maidens there. It's too harsh for them."

"Aren't you going to try to make a deal?" Surprise asked.

"Deal?"

"For your information," Iris clarified, grimacing toward the little girl.

"Should I?" Jethro asked.

"The dryad did," Gary said. "We thought you would want us to find you a way out of here, or something like that."

"No, I will surely blunder my way out in due course, just as I blundered my way in," the giant said. "Once I have rested and have my brute strength back. I will wait until you are well clear, so I don't step on you."

"Thank you for that consideration," Mentia said. "But will you answer a question?"

"I will make the effort," Jethro said. "But my mind is not nearly as big or strong as my body or my breath, so I may be unable."

"Why are you so large?"

"Why all giants are large. That's part of the definition."

"I know that. But my better aspect Metria has been around for centuries, and on occasion she has encountered invisible giants. She spoke with one fifty years ago, and he was only a tenth your height. Are you a giant among giants?"

"Why no," Jethro said, sounding perplexed. "I am the same size as any other invisible giant, as far as I know. We can't see each other, of course, but we leave similar-sized footprints. I was a lad of about forty fifty years ago, and I was the same size as my friends then."

"You're ninety years old?" Iris asked, surprised. "When were you delivered?"

"In the year one thousand and one."

"That's when I was delivered! We're the same age."

The tremendous face must have been squinting. "No offense, Sorceress, but you don't look ninety-three. I would have guessed more like twenty-three. Or are you using illusion?"

"No, I have been rejuvenated. But now that Mentia mentions it, I too have had some concourse with giants, and I remember that when I was in my maidenly forties, they stood about ten times the height of a normal man. But you must be a hundred times a man's height. How do you explain this?"

"I must have continued to grow," Jethro said. "Now that you mention it, I do seem to remember that trees and houses have gotten smaller than they used to be. But normally giants don't increase much in size after they reach their maturity. This does seem odd."

"Extremely odd," Mentia agreed. "One of several odd things."

"There are others?" Gary asked.

"Some. For example, the centaurs used to be slower living than straight human folk, so they would take about four times as long to fade out from old age. But now they seem to age at the same rate. And sphinxes faded out centuries ago, but now they are back as if they had never been gone. These are curious matters to explain."

"You are right," Iris said. "I have lived long enough to remember. Things have changed."

"And the madness has expanded," Hiatus said. "Could that be related?"

"That's right," Mentia said. "The madness seems to have been expanding for some time, but not prior to this century. All these changes seem to have occurred recently. I wonder why?"

"If we could figure out why," Hiatus said, growing excited, "we might know how to reverse the madness."

"It would help to pinpoint the time of change," Iris said. "I think things were stable while I remained on the Isle of Illusion. But after I married Trent and moved to Castle Roogna, it was different. I never really thought about it until now."

"That is my impression," Mentia agreed. "My better half wasn't much concerned about giants because they were invisible, but each time she encountered one, it was bigger."

"Was there anything special that happened?" Gary asked. "I mean, something that might have affected the whole of Xanth, like the Time of No Magic, or—"

"The Time of No Magic!" Iris and Mentia exclaimed together.

"That must have been it," Jethro said. "That disrupted myriads of the old spells, and started the break up of the forget spell on the Gap Chasm so that now we can remember it. Who knows what else it did?"

"Who knows, indeed," Iris breathed. "All the men

stoned by the Gorgon returned to life and returned to their wives—" Her jaw dropped. "And thereafter her talent matured some more, and she started stoning females as well as males. We thought it was simply a matter of competence with age, but now I don't think so."

"But could the Time of No Magic cause the madness to expand?" Gary asked. "That seems farfetched."

"Not if there were some ancient spell holding the madness in check," Mentia said. "That the Time of No Magic wiped out, so that the mischief could spread. Since the madness is an effect of concentrated magic dust, that wider spread of dust could have had sundry effects, such as making the giants grow, or the centaurs to align with humans, or some talents like that of the Gorgon to intensify. It could have had scores of slews of smaller effects folk never really noticed. Because the changes happened gradually. The Time of No Magic was in the year one tenforty-three, fifty-one years ago, and those changes are still occurring. Who would notice a single year's change? But it seems it has been happening—and it may indeed represent the key to our dilemma."

"It may?" Gary asked. The demoness was now making so much sense that she was leaving him behind.

"You started getting overwhelmed by Mundane pollution in the water in that same period, Gary," Mentia said. "You need the philter so you can keep up. Your quest may be because of another consequence of the Time of No Magic."

It did make sense. "But the philter is only for water. How can we restore an unknown spell that confined the madness?"

"That is what we shall have to find out," Mentia said. "We shall have to hope that there is more in those ruins than your philter."

"They looked pretty bare to me," Jethro said. "But of course I wasn't looking carefully."

"We shall have to look carefully," Iris said. She faced the empty giant face. "Thank you for your valuable assistance in this matter, Jethro. You may have been far more help to us and to the Land of Xanth than any of us anticipated."

"Gee," the giant said, pleased.

They climbed down his arm and made it to the ground. Then they followed his huge tracks on into the heart of the madness. There were the usual weird effects and confusions, but Gary felt encouraged and knew that his companions did too.

But the day was late, and this was no region to try to traverse in the dark. So they found a reasonably sedate alcove formed by wallnuts, and foraged for pies and juices, and settled down for the evening.

Or at least they tried to. But this was the Region of Madness, and it couldn't leave them alone long. Surprise, tired from the day's events, wasn't bothered; she was floating just above the ground, sound asleep. But Gary and the others took longer to settle.

The trees took on alien forms and seemed to nudge quietly closer, extending hooked branches. Gary thought it was his imagination, until a branch tugged at his human-clothing sleeve. He knew that branch had not been that close before. But he didn't say anything, so as not to make a fuss about nothing. This was no tangle tree, and was probably harmless.

He removed his man-style shoes, which were pinching his human toes in the prescribed manner, and set them before him. They made two little sighs, and small gobs of vapor rose from them. "What is this?" he asked.

Hiatus glanced at him. "Those are the souls of your shoes, of course," he said. "They get uncomfortable with your weight on them all day, and only at night do they have a chance to relax. Let them be; they'll need their strength for tomorrow's trek."

"I didn't know shoes had souls," Gary said. "I thought only creatures had souls."

"Shoes are special," Hiatus assured him. "They have to work very hard."

"Actually, usually only human creatures have souls," Iris said. "Or part-human creatures, like harpies or centaurs. The shoes must get their souls from association."

"Only human-related creatures have souls?" Gary asked, troubled. "Then what about gargoyles?"

"Do you have any human derivation?"

"Not that I know of?"

"Then you must lack a soul."

"No, he must have a soul," Mentia said in her rational way. "Because his shoes do. They could not get souls from association if there were no source."

"Well, he is in human form," Iris said.

"Form alone does not count. We demons can assume any form we choose." She illustrated by becoming a toadstool, complete with a frog. The frog croaked with surprise and jumped off. "I'm supposed to be a toad," it said with disgust.

"The madness is interfering again," Iris said.

"Do demons have souls?" Gary asked.

"We *are* souls," Mentia said, resuming her normal form. "So we don't *have* souls. Not that we miss them."

"But what about your better half?"

The demoness grimaced. "She did get half a soul when she married, and suddenly she had love, conscience, loyalty, self-sacrifice, and all the better human traits. It was disgusting. That's why I had to split. I am her soulless remnant. I at least remain demonly pure."

"But if you are souls, shouldn't you have the good traits?" Gary asked, shrugging away another branch.

"No, all our energy is used just maintaining our existence," Mentia said. "We don't have any left over for those awkward things. You have to have a physical body before your soul can get into the mushy stuff."

"What about the human/demon crossbreeds?" Iris asked.

Mentia shrugged. "An argument can be made that they have two souls. Their demonly aspect is one, and their human aspect can have another. They might even be able to have two talents, because each soul can have its own talent."

Their eyes turned to the sleeping child. "I wonder," Iris murmured.

"No, she is not a demon," Mentia said. "I would know. She is just a child with wild talents. She will surely be less interesting when she gets them under control."

"But her family will be relieved," Gary said. This time he had to remove two branches that were plucking at his clothing. "Am I imagining it, or is this tree trying to grab me?"

"It is trying to snatch your clothing," Hiatus said. "Another has been trying to do the same thing to me, but I am discouraging it by growing warty excrescences on it. This twisted talent of mine still has its uses."

"Another has been trying for mine," Mentia said. "But without success, since I am in smoky form at the moment."

"Snatching clothing?" Iris asked. "Eeeek! One has taken my blouse! It was so slow I never noticed."

"It is dark enough so that we can't see you anyway," Hiatus said reassuringly.

"But now I shall have to clothe myself partly in illusion," she said, irritated. "And illusion isn't warm enough."

"I will try to find a blanket bush," Gary said. "A blanket should help you." Actually he was getting cold himself.

"I'll help," Iris said. A light flared, and Gary saw that she was carrying a lamp. It illuminated her slip-covered upper torso.

"You conjured a lamp?" Hiatus asked, surprised.

"No, this is illusion," Iris explained.

"An illusory lamp makes real light?" Gary asked, surprised in turn.

"The light is illusory too," she said. "Come on; let's find that blanket bush."

They stepped out by the illusory light, which spread

widely enough to prevent them from walking into trees or holes in the ground. Gary decided not to question the matter further. He was afraid that if he did, he would no longer be able to see clearly enough to pick his way past the sharp stones and sticks that lurked for his tender bare human feet.

There seemed to be no blanket or pillow bushes to be found. But Iris spied a low-lying cloud. "Maybe some of that will do," she said, going for it.

"But that's just mist," Gary protested.

"No, we haven't missed it yet. But it won't remain there long."

"Fog, I meant. Vapor. No substance."

"Not necessarily. Clouds can be solid enough to hold pools of water; only when they get tilted or shaken does it come down as rain. And this is in madness; that probably affects its nature." She reached the cloud and caught hold of its substance with her free hand. Then she set the lamp on her head so she could use both hands. A big puff of cloud stuff came away in her arms. "Yes, this will do just fine. Help me get enough, Gary."

Gary put forth his human hands and touched the cloud. It felt like fluffy cotton. He pulled, and an almost weightless chunk of it came away from the main mass.

He followed Iris back to the wall-nut tree. "I'll put mine on the ground, and we'll use yours for a cover," she said. "We can't let go, or it will float away."

"I got this for you," he said. "I will return for more for me."

"Don't be silly. You'll never find your way in the darkness. We'll share."

"But what about Hiatus and Mentia? Aren't they cold too?"

"I don't think so," she said. She lifted her lamp high, and he saw by its expanding light that Hiatus was now settled comfortably on a feather bed under Surprise, who was still sleeping while floating.

"Where did that come from?" he asked. "And where is Mentia?"

The bed opened a mouth on the side. "Don't be silly, gargoyle," it said.

The demoness had formed herself into the bed, he realized. Still, he had a question. "If your magic is messed up by the madness, how could you choose to do that?"

"By trying to turn myself into a block of concrete," the bed said. "Madness can be managed, when you understand it—and I, being a bit crazy normally, have not had much trouble relating to it, though I remain uncomfortably sane."

So Gary sat on the bottom puff of cloud, and found it quite comfortable. He lay back on it, and it was heavenly soft without yielding so far as to let him touch the ground. The cloud substance retained some of its daytime warmth, and he realized that it was probably better for this purpose than a blanket would have been.

Iris settled beside him and pulled the other fragment of vapor over them both. Her body was warm and soft too, and very close. "But—" he started.

"Oh, that's right—I left the light on," she said. The lamp disappeared, leaving them in darkness. "Comfy now?"

"But—you aren't wearing anything, I think."

"There's no need to maintain illusion clothing in darkness," she pointed out. "I will make a new illusion outfit in the morning, and perhaps use what remains of this cloud to fashion a new blouse."

"But your body is so close."

"Why so it is," she said as if surprised. "However, allow me to remind you that I no longer need illusion to make my ancient bones appear young. I am physically twenty-three years old, which I believe is about your human physical age. We match rather nicely, I think."

"Match? For what?"

"Well, we might start with a kiss on the ear," she said, suiting action to word.

Gary was so surprised he slid right out of the cloud cover and landed on the cool hard ground.

"Oh come *on*," Iris said, hauling him back between the layers. In the process her body got even closer than before.

"What are you trying to do?" he asked.

"Isn't it obvious? I'm trying to seduce you."

Gary was amazed. "To what?"

She laughed. "Aren't you interested?"

"No. I don't understand this at all."

There was a pause consisting of perhaps two and a half moments. "I have been so old so long that it is a real relief to be young again, in body," she finally said. "What use is it to be young if you can't enjoy the potentials of youth?"

"I don't know. What are the potentials of youth?"

There was another pause, not as long. "You perhaps hesitate to indulge with a married woman? Let me assure you that I will never tell. This is purely passing fun, a private diversion."

"Indulge in what?" he asked, baffled.

"In signaling the stork, you idiot!" she snapped.

He began to get a bit of her drift, possibly. "The stork? But for that I would need a female."

"What the bleep do you suppose I am? A wall-rus?"

"Why, you're human," he said, perplexed by her vehemence.

"Precisely. So what is your objection?"

"I am a gargoyle. I have no stork interest in any other species."

"For pity's sake! You are in human form at the moment."

Gary remembered that it was true. "Still, I am really a gargoyle, just as you are really an ancient hag. We have no human relationship."

This time the pause was so many moments long that he lost track. He drifted peacefully off to sleep. He assumed that Iris did the same.

* * *

In the morning they foraged for grapefruit and passion-fruit. The grapes were good, but Gary didn't eat the other. He remembered that the cloudbed he had shared with Iris rested on passion vines. That accounted for her attitude, he realized belatedly. He would try to avoid those in the future, so as to be able to get better sleep. It would have been nice had there been a girl gargoyle, though. Meanwhile Surprise conjured several livers, looked disgusted, and finally got what she wanted by *trying* to conjure the most loathsome liverworts she might imagine: she got a pun-kin pie and a honey-comb. She poured the honey on the pie and stuck the comb in her hair so it wouldn't flop around. Then she gobbled down the pie with an appetite that would have done credit to a goblin.

The Sorceress Iris seemed somewhat out of sorts. Gary realized that it might have been polite to pretend some sort of interest in her, of the sort that he presumed a human man his seeming age and health would have. But there was just no denying the fact that she was not a gargoyle.

"The follies of the human folk seldom cease to amuse demons," Mentia remarked as she glanced at the passion vines. "Would you like me to assume the shape of a gargoyle?"

"Of course not. We gargoyles never confuse any other creature for one of us. No others can hope to match our impressive ugliness."

"To be sure," the demoness agreed, still amused.

They followed the giant's footprints on into what seemed to be the very center of the Region of Madness, though Mentia explained that this could not be so, because the center was the Magic Dust Village. Nevertheless, the maddening effects remained, with the trees coming to resemble enormous sea monsters, and sometimes acting like them too. Iris had to use her illusion frequently to fend them off, and Hiatus was kept busy growing loathsome hairy excrescences on those branches that weren't daunted by the illusions. When both these measures failed, Mentia assumed the form of a tree-chomping huge-a-saur and crunched off their reaching limbs.

Still, they were glad when the jungle thinned somewhat, and they climbed through a moderate range of hills. The hills themselves resisted their passage, becoming mountainous and angling their slopes unexpectedly so as to cause the travelers to lurch into treetrunks or boulders and bash their own noses.

"I think I know of these hills," Mentia said. "They're called the Poke-a-nose."

At last they emerged onto a level plain. That was a relief, because their noses were pretty sore by this time. But they were wary, knowing that soon enough some new threat would materialize.

Here the trees were somewhat stunted, though the madness was frighteningly strong. Gary, who specialized in stone, discovered why: "There is hardly any place here for their roots to gain purchase. The ground is covered with chunks of stone."

"Doesn't stone underlie most land?" Hiatus asked.

"Deep down it does," Gary agreed. "But it is usually covered by layers of sand and soil, so that plants can get purchase. These seem to be artificially carved stones, perhaps parts of buildings that collapsed. Some seem to form ancient roads. So there just isn't much soil, and the plants can't make much progress. This is our fortune, because most of the plants here seem to be hostile."

"I wonder," Iris mused. "The trees and plants around Castle Roogna do their best to repel unfriendly strangers. But it isn't malice; they were instructed to do that, to protect the castle. They also did their best to encourage any Magician to remain there. So maybe we simply don't properly understand these particular plants." Then a nettle vine tried to curl around her ankle and yank her into the bed of nettles. "But I could be wrong," she said as an afterthought.

"Whatever they were in the past, they must be different

now," Hiatus said. "Because the madness changes everything."

Surprise found a stone in the general shape of a chair. She crossed her eyes, and it quivered and started walking. The child jumped up onto it and rode in style for a while, until a leg tripped on an irregularity in the ground and the animated chair toppled, dumping her out.

They continued to follow the giant's tracks. The stones in the ground became larger, and some rose up above the ground, presenting ragged silhouettes. "These are definitely artificial," Gary said. "I mean that they have been quarried and moved here. I begin to see the outlines of large buildings."

"Then we must have found the ruins," Mentia said. "Maybe our quest is almost done."

"That would be nice," Gary agreed doubtfully. "But finding the ruins is only one step. We have to find the philter. And we have to try to find a way to save Desiree's tree. I don't see either, yet."

Iris gazed ahead at the barren plain. "This is a wasteland, for sure. It seems to me that if the philter were here, it would be purifying water, and making an oasis or something. But all I see are more ruins."

Gary had to agree. But what could they do, except search the ruins as well as they could, hoping to find what they sought?

"Now that's odd," Mentia remarked, staring up at a particularly large stone set endwise in the ground.

The others looked too. Gary saw that it seemed to consist of two stones, connected at the top with a band of a different kind of stone. "Odd?" Hiatus said. "That's downright weird! Why prop two stones together like that?"

"To make an arch?" Iris suggested.

"Too narrow," Mentia said. "Far too narrow. Those stones are right together, so that no one can pass between them, let alone have anything useful here."

Surprise approached the stones. Then claws extended from her hands and she dug them into the stone and pulled herself up, climbing to the linked top. She inspected the connection. "Hinge!" she announced.

"A stone hinge?" Iris asked. "Ridiculous." But she reconsidered immediately. "Yet that does look like what it is. A hinge made of stone, connecting the two big stones."

"Why would a stone be hinged?" Hiatus asked. "It would take a giant or a pair of ogres to lift up one of these stones; they each are the size of small buildings."

"And neither giants nor ogres go in for fancy construction," Mentia said. "Only humans and termites do, as a rule, and termites don't ordinarily work in stone."

Gary considered the matter. "Gargoyles don't work stone," he said, "but we do appreciate it. I would say that this is one support for a fancy building. One stone is set deep into the ground, while the other rests on top of the ground; that second stone could be lifted to a horizontal position and connected to another stone column, here." He touched a nearby pillar. "Other stones could be lifted similarly, and form a solid roof for the building. I see columns appropriately placed all around."

"You do?" Hiatus asked. "I see nothing but lumps of broken stone."

"They are broken, but they are in a pattern. See, here is another hinged column, and there is one whose hinged stone has broken off. This city has been destroyed by time and weather, but it once contained some marvelous buildings."

The others shook their heads, not seeing it. But to Gary it was clear enough. He wished he could show them his vision of stone. But they weren't gargoyles.

They walked on through the ruins, but found nothing special. There might have been greatness here a long time ago, but it was forgotten now—and had been forgotten long before the madness overran it. And there was no philter they could find. They searched all day, but only succeeded in getting more tired and depressed. Even Surprise had become bored and passive.

In the center of the plain was a sodden pool. It was

overgrown with disreputable weeds that hissed at anyone who tried to dip water, but Hiatus grew some truly loathsome shapes on them, and they shut up. This was as good a place as any to camp for the night.

This time Iris did not try to bother Gary, to his relief. She did try to distract Hiatus, but Hiatus could think only of Desiree. She finally made herself a fancy pavilion of illusion and retired there with Surprise, who formed her own smaller pavilion within it.

Gary lay on his human back and stared up at the stars. He was familiar with the constellations, having contemplated them many times over the centuries. But tonight something was wrong; he didn't recognize any of them. Instead he saw a merman swimming through a field of grazing mice. The merman spied Gary watching and mouthed words at him: WHAT ARE YOU LOOKING UP HERE FOR, GARGOYLE?

"Where are the regular constellations?" Gary demanded.

"*We* are the regular constellations," the merman retorted angrily.

"Not where I came from."

"You are not where you came from, stone-heart." And the merman and mice glared. "You are from the dull side of the veil."

Gary thought about that, and concluded it was true. "This is the Region of Madness, so it figures that there are mad constellations."

"You got that right, man-rump."

"How long have you been here, fishtail?" Gary asked, responding in kind.

The merman mellowed insignificantly. Perhaps it had been some time since anyone had taken him seriously. "As long as the madness has reigned."

"Then you must have seen these ruins back when they were a magnificent stone city."

"How do you know about that?" the merman demanded.

"I'm a gargoyle. We admire stone. I wish I could see

this one as it was in its greatness. Perhaps there were gargoyles here."

"There were, along with all manner of other creatures. But it was doomed."

"I wonder whether they had the philter," Gary said musingly.

"The philter!" the merman exclaimed. "You're after that?"

"Yes, it's my quest. Do you know where it is?"

"Don't fetch it!" the merman cried, alarmed. "It's dangerous. Return to your own side of the veil."

"So it was here!" Gary exclaimed. "And it must still be here, because it isn't mortal the way flesh folk are. I must have it."

"Cease this disaster," the merman said. "I'll not help you recover that thing." And he swam away with such force that his tail stirred up the entire field of mice, and the scene blurred into blah.

But Gary now knew that his quest was not in vain. The philter was here among the ruins—if he could just find it.

8

ANIMATION

I n the morning the others were ready to give up the quest, except for Surprise, who was busily searching for colored pebbles, but Gary would have none of it. "I know the philter is here," he said.

"How do you know?" Iris asked disdainfully.

"The constellation told me."

"The what?"

"The merman constellation I saw in the sky last night. He saw the city before it was in ruins, and he said the philter was there. He told me not to fetch it."

"A talking constellation?" Hiatus asked.

"Remember, we are in madness," Mentia said. "These things happen."

Iris sighed. "So they do. I seem to remember Bink saying something about talking constellations. But they weren't trustworthy."

"Except that this one was trying to prevent me from finding the philter. So it must be where I *can* find it."

"Mad logic," Mentia said. "It will do. But how shall we find it, since we've already looked and failed?"

"The secret must be in the stone," Gary said. "I can read stone. I just need to find the right one."

"You mean an obelisk?" Iris asked. "Something with writing on it?"

"Not exactly. I merely need a stone that has seen things at the right time."

"What nonsense is this? Stones can't see anything!"

"Not the way we do," Gary said. "But they do see, and they can be read by gargoyles. But the process is slow, and meaningless if the stone hasn't seen what is needed."

"And what exactly is needed?" she demanded.

"The philter, of course. But it may be as hard to find a stone that has seen it as it is to find the philter itself. So I shall search for a stone that has seen the old city in its heyday. Maybe there will be a hint there."

"Now look," Iris said impatiently. "Hasn't every stone here been part of that city? So they all have seen it, haven't they?"

"But many faces of stone are turned inward; they see only what was inside the building, and perhaps only the back of whatever carpets were hung on those inner walls. The walls facing outward may see only alley streets or things piled up before them. I need a stone face that has seen the whole city, or enough of it to enable me to see it too."

"You to see it too?" she asked skeptically. "Because of this mysterious writing on it?"

"Oh, there would be no writing on it, unless some human person did that. I read the stone itself."

Iris threw up her hands. "I give up! This is beyond madness."

"I am not certain of that," Mentia said sensibly. "Gargoyles do know stone, as they know water, and Gary is speaking in the manner of one who knows whereof he speaks. Gary, just how do you read stone?"

"I look closely at it, and refocus my eyes until I can see the images behind the surface. Then I interpret them." He paused. "Oh, I am not sure I can do it in this human body! I keep forgetting its limitations."

"And its potentials," Iris muttered from the edge.

"The thing to do is to make the attempt," Mentia said seriously. "Then we shall know whether this is viable."

"But if I don't have a good stone, I won't learn anything useful," he protested.

"For testing your potential, useful information is not necessary. If you find you can read stone in this form, then we shall search out the most knowledgeable stone on the plain."

"Why yes!" he agreed. "You are remarkably sensible, Mentia."

She made a grimace that extended off the side of her face. "It is not by choice, gargoyle. Once we get this mission accomplished, we can leave this madness and I can revert to normal."

"You're a demoness," Hiatus said. "Why haven't you popped away already?"

The grimace floated entirely away from her face, leaving it without a mouth. Nevertheless, she spoke without difficulty. "Because the madness also reverses my natural irresponsibility. It would not be proper to desert you folk in your hour of need, so I am not doing it. I assure you that this attitude distresses me almost as much as my better half's acquisition of a conscience. I might as well have stayed with her."

"Conscience is madness to a demon," Gary agreed. "But I must say that I like you better this way, and am glad for your present company."

"But she's not even being seductive!" Iris said, annoyed.

"Exactly," he agreed.

"What a nuisance," Iris muttered.

"Nuisance!" Surprise said, her eyes crossing. She had found a handful of pretty colored pebbles. Now these floated up to form a pattern in the air.

"But that's not a nuisance," Iris said. "Those are nice stones."

"That is the nature of the nuisance," Mentia said. "Surprise suffers as I do, becoming more responsible. Borrow one of those little stones to test your ability, Gary."

"This one," Surprise said. A fragment of granite in the shape of a smiley face left the formation and jumped to his hand. "I like it."

So Gary held the stone and focused on it, seeking the message within it. His human eyes lost their focus, then recovered it in a different style. He read the patterns on the surface of the stone, evoking the rock pictures.

"Maybe if you cross your eyes," Surprise suggested.

"Nothing here but recent events," he said. "Because this is a chip from a larger piece, and before it chipped away all it saw was the other stone around it. Once it landed on the ground, it saw plants growing and bugs foraging, and the silhouette of the column from which it had fragmented. Nothing of interest to us."

"But you can read it!" Mentia said. "*That's* of interest to us."

"Why so I can," Gary agreed, startled. "So it is."

"So now we must find some stone that has seen something significant. That can pierce the veil of time."

"Yes. But there's a great deal of time and space to check. This may be slow and tedious."

"I've had enough of slow and tedious!" Iris snapped. "This whole adventure has been unconscionably dull. Can't we find a way to speed it up?"

Mentia looked thoughtful. "It occurs to me that we have a bottleneck. Gary is the only one of us who can read the rock pictures. If we could find a way to help him do it faster—"

"How?" Iris asked eagerly.

"I'm not sure. But I wonder whether it might be possible to animate the pictures Gary describes, so that we could all see them. Then we could all join in the search."

"Animate?" Hiatus asked. "But which of us has such magic?"

"Iris does," Mentia said. "Her enormous power of illusion can make anything appear."

"But my illusions don't make things actually exist," Iris said. "They are just as I see them, rightly or wrongly."

"But if Gary can give you a detailed enough description of what he sees, so that you can translate it to illusion, that should do the job. We know it isn't real—at least, not real today. But if we can in this manner see what has happened in the past, and where someone may have left the philter—"

"You are making sense," Iris said. "Very well. You find the perfect stone, and I'll try to relate closely enough to Gary so that I can readily translate his images to illusion. But remember: here in the madness my illusion tends to reverse, so I'll make some mistakes before I get the full hang of countering it."

Gary wasn't sure he liked this, but the notion did seem sensible, so he couldn't object.

"Let's practice on that pebble," Iris said. "You saw plants growing? What kind?"

Gary peered into the stone again and described the plants. At first completely different plants appeared, as Iris got caught by the madness, but she muttered a nasty word and tried again. In a moment similar plants were growing around them, in large size, because that was the way the small pebble had seen them. Then the bugs came by, assuming ever more precise detail as Gary corrected Iris' impressions.

"This is working," she said. "But I think not well enough. Let's see if we can get closer." She put a hand on his hand.

"But—"

"I'm not trying to vamp you, at the moment. I just think that I may be able to pick up some of your impressions from the reactions of your body, and that may help me get them right without as much verbal correction. I want to try to bypass my instincts, because they keep revising the images; maybe if I can attune more closely to yours, it will come out right. Illusion is my business; I'm good at it, when I can do it straight."

They continued to work on it, and to Gary's surprise she was right. She was more than good at it; she was a genius of illusion. The miscues became fewer and finally disappeared. Every part of what she showed was authentic in image, and was responsive to his corrections. When he described a day passing, the shadows moved across it as they had in life. When he described a season passing, the trees dropped their leaves and then sprouted new ones. When it rained, and temporary streams flowed, they appeared in the scene in fully animate manner. There were aspects of illusion he had not appreciated before, such as a thin screen that gave him a translucent map-image of the scene overlying the stone, without obscuring it. He no longer had to keep looking at the illusions to correct the errors; he focused entirely on the pebble, telling what he saw in a general way, and it took form around them complete with most of its details. Sometimes a tiny illusion image of Iris herself appeared, pointing to one aspect of the scene or another, so that he was able to direct her the right way. They were making an increasingly effective team. He had not liked Iris much, but now he was coming to appreciate her better; she could do good work when she made the effort.

As last he looked up, disconnecting himself from his reverie of the stone—but the illusion image remained in all its detail. "This is good," he said. "If we find the right stone, we can re-create history itself."

Iris smiled. "Yes, I think we can. You have a marvelous ability to fathom the secrets of stone."

Gary discovered that his tacit dislike of her was fading. She had clothed their surroundings with illusion, but left herself as she was: a well constructed young, mature human woman. He was beginning to see the appeal.

D. Mentia appeared. "They have found a good stone, we think," she announced. "It sits high enough to survey the entire plain, everything within the ring of hills. They are making scaffolding so you can get up to read it all."

"Oh, did they find fallen timbers for construction?" Iris asked as they set off for the site.

"No, Surprise made them, and nylon cord for the lashings. Hiatus has a notion how to construct such things, it seems."

"What is nylon?" Gary asked.

"It is something they make from stockings taken from nymphs," Mentia explained. "You know: NYmph plus LONg legs, one of their salient attributes. It's why they run so well, and have such attractive legs." She formed into a slender-legged nymph as she spoke. "Sometimes the stockings even run by themselves, but that is frowned on; folk prefer them without runs. The stockings are twisted up so tightly that they form a strong cord. They link them together, and have as long and supple a cord as is needed. I understand that if they squeeze the stockings together tightly enough, they form a tough, solid mass. All derived from that magic intended for the nymphly legs."

"Amazing. How do they catch the nymphs, to take their stockings?"

"I'm not sure. It must be hard to do, because normally they are able to run teasingly close but always just out of reach of the pursuing men. Only fauns can catch them regularly, and that's because the fauns are really their kind, and have goat feet to make them faster. The nymphs don't really try to get away from them. So maybe someone bribes fauns to get the stockings."

"I could use a pair of those stockings myself," Iris remarked. "So that I won't have to use illusion on my legs as I grow older. Is there anything similar for the upper portion of the body?"

But she didn't get an answer, because they had arrived at the site. There was the largest standing stone yet, towering despite being hinged. There was now scaffolding around it, and a wooden ladder, so that Gary could climb

to a wooden platform circling the top of the stone. They
had done a nice job.

"So tell them," Mentia murmured.

"How did you know what I was thinking?" Gary asked.

"Common sense, something I now have too much of. It
also tells me that folk are happier and more cooperative
when complimented on their achievements."

That hadn't occurred to him. But he was coming to respect her judgment as it existed here in the madness. So he
tried it. "Hiatus and Surprise, that is a very nice job you
have done. It will be ideal for my purpose."

The result was impressive. The man smiled so broadly
that his mouth threatened to emulate the demoness' trick
of extending beyond the limits of his face, and the child
sank blissfully backwards onto a small pink cloud shaped
like the number 9 which then floated gently in a circle. It
seemed that they did appreciate the compliment.

Gary realized that he had also inadvertently complimented the Sorceress Iris before about her facility with illusion, and she had complimented him about his ability
with stone, and he had felt quite positive thereafter and
disliked her less. This was an interesting form of magic,
that apparently the madness did not interfere with. He
would try to remember that, as magic that anyone could do
was rare.

It occurred to him that if the stone had been hinged to
be upright during its heyday, he might get most of what he
needed right at ground level, reading the second stone. But
that could wait, lest it seem that he did not properly appreciate the scaffold. So he climbed the ladder to the platform, and Iris followed. Soon all of them were up there,
enjoying it. Indeed, the view from up here was good; he
could see the entire plain without difficulty, and the ring
shape of the mountains was clear. Now he saw how many
of the standing stones there were; they were scattered
throughout the region more abundantly than he had realized while trying ineffectively to search the ground for the
philter. What a city this must have been!

Gary picked a spot on the stone at random and refocused his eyes. He found the range quickly, now that he had practiced with his human eyeballs, and the pictures leaped into sight. They were of the bleak surroundings, but those merely overlaid the earlier impressions. He plunged right through to the very first ones, when the stone was erected and shown the light of day on this site.

The first pictures were fragmentary, seeming to relate to the quarrying and shaping and moving of the stone. It took awhile for a stone picture to form, and when a person was in view only briefly, the image was blurred or ghostly. When a scene was steady, as was the case with features of the surrounding landscape, it became clear. In any event, the quarrying wasn't important; it was the living city he needed to see.

But the stone turned out to be a foundation; it was covered by other stones and by wood, so offered no good visions. Until it was abruptly uncovered by fleeting ghost figures, at the time the building was hinged down and deserted. Thereafter there was only the view that existed at present, only with most of the folded buildings still erect.

"This stone doesn't offer what we want," Gary said regretfully. "It was covered while the building was active, and must have been one of the last to be shut down, so that it didn't see the active city."

"Then we must find a better stone," Mentia said sensibly.

"But I hate to see all this work on the scaffolding wasted."

"We can move it," Hiatus said. "We made it to be readily taken apart and reassembled."

They dismounted from the platform and took it apart. Mentia had spied a double-hinged stone that seemed to start with a massive foundation, continue with a folded-down upper segment, and finish with a folded-up spire. "This wasn't a building," she said. "This was a steeple. It should have had a good view of the city from its point."

Gary agreed. They set up the scaffolding and climbed to

the platform, as before. Now he examined the blunt tip of the spire.

"Oh, my!" he breathed, awed.

"Tell me!" Iris said urgently. "Let me animate it." Her illusion screen appeared, ready to respond to his words and reactions.

Gary began talking. "I see a city being constructed, so vast it fills the entire plain within the ring of mountains, so new it shines in the sunlight, so intricate it is like nothing Xanth has known since. It is as if every building is a palace, and on the distant hills are castles linked by walls of such magnitude that they seem like mountains. . . ."

The illusion took shape, first on the screen between him and the surface of the stone, where he could readily correct it and amend it, then beyond, where everyone could see it. There was a murmur of awe that echoed his own as Hiatus, Surprise, and Mentia saw a wedge of the great city of the distant past take shape around them. It might be illusion, but it was patterned on the reality of long ago.

Gary walked slowly around the stone, reading the rock pictures as he did—and as he did, the illusion city spread out in other directions, as seen by the stone that faced that way. When he completed his circuit, there was a complete ancient city around them, maintained in illusion though Gary could no longer look at the images on the far side. Iris' talent provided a stability that his eyes alone lacked; she could hold the image once it had been evoked.

"Now the other three of us must search the city to see who has the philter and where he put it," Mentia murmured. "We will not be able to touch anything, but we can see everything. See, the illusion is three-dimensional; we can look at the far sides of buildings."

"Not if we stay up here, we can't," Hiatus said.

"Then we shall go down to the ground. But be cautious, because the illusion city is covering up the real things, and we can stumble into them. We must remain aware that what we see is not what is there today."

"Can you feel the way for us?" Hiatus asked. "Guide us so that we can look without stumbling and hurting ourselves?"

"Why yes; that's a good idea. I will become a fog and touch the ground ahead of you. I will make a green stripe where it is safe for you to walk."

There were the sounds of their descent to the ground. Then Gary and Iris were alone, working on the image. Gary was still examining it, concentrating on one detail and then another, and as he did so, Iris clarified the illusion image to match. The buildings which had been shown in general outline became more specific.

"These buildings are hollow!" Surprise cried from below.

"Oops," Gary said. "I should have realized that the stone can see only what is in its line of sight. Whatever was never in its sight remains blank."

"But once we have what this stone offers," Iris said, "we can go to other stones and get other views. We can make this city whole, in time."

"But if we take the time to do that, we won't be able to follow it forward in time, to see what happens to the philter."

"Let's save that until we actually spy the philter," she said. "Our first priority is to get the most complete replica of the city that we can, so that we don't miss anything."

She was right. So he worked to complete the description of this region as seen by this stone. Then the two of them went down to the ground and through the illusion, following a green stripe. Sure enough, the buildings were hollow—but it was comparatively easy to fill them in from the spot viewpoints of other stones. It was not necessary to climb them; for this limited purpose the ground views sufficed. It was merely necessary to find projections on the stones that had not been covered by paneling or paint. The views were limited, but adequate.

They worked in their separate fashions all day: Gary

reading one stone after another, Iris building the most phenomenal structure of illusion of her old/young life, Hiatus and Surprise eagerly searching every street and building that was sufficiently defined, and Mentia coordinating and guiding all of them. But by the end of the day they knew two things: they had not gotten even a glimmer of the philter, and they were ravenous.

"There aren't any people," Hiatus complained. "We can't see what they're doing, only what they've done."

Gary explained about the need for people to stay in the vicinity of the stone for long enough to make an impression. "Rock pictures usually aren't very good for animate creatures. I might evoke some if I concentrated on exceedingly fine definition, but that would take time and probably wouldn't be as good as the larger view is."

"Let's not bother with that for now," Mentia said. "When we find a really promising area, then we can do the fine focus. There's no point in wasting the effort randomly."

"I hate to shut down this magnificent restoration after we have made it," Gary said. "But we must rest and sleep."

"I can maintain it," Iris said.

"What, even while you sleep?" he asked, amazed.

"I told you I was good at illusion. Once I have crafted it, I can maintain it with minimal effort."

He shook his human head. "I think I never understood before the power of a Sorceress. I never imagined such a thing."

"Thank you."

"What are you mortals going to eat tonight?" Mentia asked. "We have already foraged for most of the berries and things that grew in this wasteland."

"Eat!" Surprise said, crossing her eyes. Suddenly a barrel of fish livers appeared. It smelled awful. The little girl stared at it, appalled. "But I tried to conjure a huge chocolate layer cake!" she said. "Not codfish! I hate cod liver oil!"

"Your magic got twisted again," Mentia said.

"I'll get rid of it!"

"No!" Mentia said. "Keep it. It is good food for you, and the next thing you conjure might be worse."

"Yuck!" Surprise cried in true child fashion.

The demoness turned to Iris. "Can you spare some illusion for this without losing the city?"

"Some," Iris agreed cautiously.

"Can you make these fish livers look, feel, and taste like chocolate layercake?"

"Yes, I can do that much." Iris glanced at the barrel, and it became a giant cake overflowing with chocolate icing. It looked and smelled as good as the fish livers were awful.

"Wow!" Surprise cried, delighted. "Your magic is pretty good."

"Thank you, dear," Iris said wryly.

Iris made an illusion pavilion for them all, under the shelter of stones that were hinged in an A formation. They gathered dry grass and leaves for beds, and these seemed to become downy mattresses. They slept in comfort, each in his or her own chamber.

At least Gary assumed that the others did. He found himself beset by a growing apprehension, not of something wrong or threatening, just confusing. His dreams got downright weird. He remembered the constellations that had become animated, and feared that they were doing it again. Fortunately the Sorceress' illusion dome shielded him from a view of the night sky, and prevented the constellation merman from seeing *him*. But the weirdness seeped in anyway.

In the morning they held another conference, and concluded that it was after all time to search out the finer detail. "What we really need are to talk to the people of this ancient hinge city," Mentia said.

"I dreamed I did," Hiatus said. "I asked a man what the city was called, and he said Hinge. He said that when they shut it down, they called it Un-Hinge. And that strangers called it Stone Hinge."

"I dreamed too," Iris said. "But all I saw were odd crossbreed species, like merchickens and micephants. I asked one about that, and it said it was because they couldn't avoid the love spring."

"I dreamed I was stultifyingly normal," Surprise said, scowling cutely.

"Fortunately demons don't dream," Mentia said. "But that animated constellation gives me the creeps."

That made Gary feel less secure. "I think something is affecting us all," he said.

"Well of course it is," Mentia said. "It's the extra wash of madness that flowed through in the night. It's getting to us."

So they found what seemed to be a significant spot in the city, where ancient metal tracks had crossed by a special stone building, and Gary and Iris concentrated on evoking whatever had been there. They were eager to get this job done before the madness infiltrated their bodies too deeply and affected more than their dreams.

But what Gary found was not a picture of a person or people. It was some sort of huge wagon or vehicle, linked to another like it. In fact there seemed to be a chain of them, each as big and blocky as the next. What could this be?

"A train of thought!" Surprise exclaimed, clapping her hands. "I want to ride on it."

"That is not the kind of train you can ride on," Mentia cautioned the child. But then, as the train took shape, she reconsidered. "However, here in the madness, maybe it is possible."

"It's an illusion train," Iris reminded them. "An image from the past. All we can do is look at it."

Nevertheless, as Gary explored its finer detail and Iris improved the picture, it seemed like a very real vehicle. There was an engine steaming in the distance at one end, seeming as hot as the Gap dragon, and a caboose at the other end, with a red light. In the middle was a chain of wheeled cars with lines of windows.

"This is just like the stories some travelers have told of Mundane trains," Iris said. "Trent mentioned seeing one, during his exile. Do you suppose that when such trains died, they went to the Region of Madness?"

"It seems possible," Mentia agreed. "The City of Hinge is a strange place, and so deserves strange vehicles. Perhaps such a train transported the philter somewhere."

"The philter!" Gary said. "Do you really think so?"

"More likely the train carried people to wherever the philter was," Hiatus said. "Or wherever else they wanted to go. I think some zombie animals would have been better for such transport, but they evidently had odd tastes."

Iris' mouth quirked. "Clearly so," she agreed. "Perhaps we can follow this train as it travels, and see if it passes the philter."

"I think I'll ride it," Mentia said. She floated up and toward the entrance steps at the end of the nearest car.

"Me too!" Surprise said, clapping her hands. She ran to the steps and scrambled up them.

"You can't do that!" Iris cried, dashing after the child.

"Nyaa, nyaa, you can't catch me!" Surprise called, running inside the car.

"We shall see about that!" Iris retorted grimly. She charged up the steps after the child.

Hiatus exchanged a heavy glance with Gary. "Of course we know this isn't possible," he said.

"But we had better see that those three females don't get into trouble," Gary agreed.

The two of them followed the others up the steps and into the long car. "This is sheer madness," Hiatus said.

"This is the place for it," Gary agreed.

Iris and Surprise were in the main compartment of the car. The child was running up and down the long central aisle, while Iris was sitting in one of the comfortable reclining chairs. She glanced back and saw them. "Sit down, men," she suggested. "If I can walk into one of my own illusions, why not you too?"

They joined her. "You know this is crazy," Gary said.

Mentia appeared. "This is a feature of joint imagination," she said. "I think the madness has lent substance to the Sorceress' illusion. Thus what we are experiencing is a partial truth."

There was a jerk that shook them all. "The train is moving!" Hiatus cried. "We must get off it!"

Iris shrugged. "Why? Since it's all imagination, why not go along for the ride?"

Hiatus looked surprised. "I suppose we can." He peered out the window. "The city is going by outside."

"This will make it easier to search the city," Iris said. "We might as well enjoy it."

They looked out the windows as the train of thought gathered speed. The buildings seemed to be moving back while the train was still, but Gary knew that was just another effect of illusion. Since, as Iris pointed out, it was all just imagination, it hardly mattered. But where did they think they were going?

Gary pondered this, as he watched the buildings thin out, to be replaced by trees and fields, with an occasional small lake. His quest was to find the philter. Would this train of thought take him there—if he thought it should? Once he had the philter, he wouldn't care how it had been achieved. So he concentrated on that: *philter, philter, philter*.

The train slowed. "We are arriving somewhere," Iris remarked.

Was this where the philter was? Gary kept up his thought, doing his best to train the train to respond.

The train squealed to a halt. "I believe we have arrived," Mentia said. "I am not at all sure we shall be comfortable with where we are. There is entirely too much madness here to suit me."

"Any time we get tired of it," Iris said, "I can simply abolish the illusion, and we will be back among the ruins."

"Perhaps," Mentia said grimly.

That bothered Gary, because Mentia was now their sanest member. But he did not want to leave the illusion until he had located the philter.

They got out of their chairs and walked in file toward the exit.

9

HINGE

Gary led the way out of the train, wary of what might lie outside. The illusion of the ancient city remained, but he wasn't sure whether they had actually traveled anywhere in reality. If they had, where had the train of thought taken them? Here in the madness, anything could be dangerous or non-existent, or both.

There was a small group of people gathered on the station platform. One of them evidently recognized him, for she stepped briskly forward. She was armed, and her hair was militantly coifed.

"Hannah Barbarian!" he exclaimed, dismayed. "What are you doing here?"

"My lord, surely you jest," she replied diffidently.

Could he be mistaken? She looked like the aggressive woman he had encountered at the Good Magician's castle, but she wasn't acting like her. "Am I confusing you with someone else?"

She smiled, which was another disconcerting thing. "My lord Gar the Good, you know I exist merely to serve your will. Let me help you down the step. You are surely fatigued after your wearisome travel." And she reached forth to take firm hold of his elbow, steadying him as he descended.

Gary got smart, realizing that this had to be an aspect of illusion or madness. "I confess I am a bit confused. Humor me. Your name is—?"

"Hanna the Handmaiden, of course, my lord, as it has ever been. I see you are in sore need of my ministrations."

It seemed better to play along with this illusion rather than challenge it. Maybe Sorceress Iris was having a bit of fun with him.

But Iris was the next off the train. "What is this?" she asked, startled.

"O Queen Iri, have you forgotten me?" Hanna asked. "I am handmaiden to my lord Gar the Good, loyal and sub-servient."

"Subservient?" Gary asked, surprised again.

"My lord, you tease me cruelly," Hanna said, looking woeful. "When was I ever other than your most humble and obedient servant?"

"I didn't conjure this image," Iris said, looking perplexed and faintly alarmed. "This madness is getting out of hand."

"Not for naught is she called Iri the Irate," Hanna murmured to Gary. Then, smiling brightly, to Iris: "My lady, I apologize most humbly for making you angry."

"I said mad, not angry," Iris said. But she seemed to have come to the same decision as Gary: to play along until she had a better notion what was happening.

Surprise appeared next. "And how good it is to see you again, Princess Supi the Super," Hanna said. "I pray your esteemed mother the Queen has not been wroth with you too."

The child, startled, changed color. She turned bright green. "Supi the Super?" she echoed. "I like it!"

Iris glanced back. "Dear, you had better change back before someone notices," she said guardedly.

Surprise changed to blue, then back to normal. "Super!" she repeated, smiling.

"My lord, do you encourage her in this?" Hanna inquired anxiously.

"Encourage her?" Gary said blankly. "How can I prevent her from doing whatever she chooses?"

"But you are her tutor, my lord. It is your prerogative to instruct her in all things mannerly and magical, so that she does not waste her powers."

"Waste her powers?" Gary was still having trouble orienting.

"You know as well as do we all that though Supi, being the sole heir to the crown of Xanth, has more magic than any other, she can invoke each aspect of it once and once only. Thus it is horrible to waste it frivolously, lest we need it for the final conjuration."

"Once only?" Gary asked, and saw that Iris was as surprised as he. "Can this be true?"

But the next person was descending from the train. This was Mentia.

"Ah, my lady Menti the Mentor," Hanna said. "And it is good to see you again, too."

"Mentor to what?" Iris asked, her voice carefully controlled.

"Why to Princess Supi, of course. For she is ever in need of attention, and you her mother are naturally often too busy to be bothered."

Iris frowned, but did not respond. Mentia, rationally quick on the uptake, merely nodded. "Certainly we take excellent care of the child," she agreed.

Now Hiatus appeared. Another person stepped from the background group. "My lord Hiat!" she cried. "I am so glad to see you safely home."

"Desiree!" he cried, astonished. For indeed it was she.

"Desi the Desolate," she agreed. "Surely you have not so soon forgotten the nymph you rescued from evil and befriended, and who now serves you in any way you allow?"

"But—" he started.

"We all have titles or descriptions, it seems," Gary told him. "We feel it best not to debate them."

"Descriptions?"

"Hiat the Hedonist," Hanna offered helpfully.

"I never called you that!" Desi protested. "I honor you as uncle of Princess Supi, closest in the royal descent after her, and a bold and handsome man."

Hiatus seemed stunned by this description, but not annoyed. He, too, was coming to realize that something odd was occurring here. "I am glad to be with you again, Desiree—I mean Desi."

"And now that the introductions have been accomplished," Iris said, "perhaps we should go where we are going."

"Why, to the palace, of course," Hanna said. "We know you all are tired after your sojourn abroad."

"Abroad?" Gary asked.

"To the very nonmagical extreme edge of Xanth, where the awful Mundanes threaten to overrun," Hanna said. "Surely a harrowing excursion."

"Very true," Iris agreed quickly. "And now we really must get home and rest for a time. Please convey us there by the simplest route."

"We have merely to cross the street," Hanna said. "How clever of my lady to express it so." But her sober expression suggested that she did not regard the Queen as all that clever.

So they followed Hanna out of the station and across the street, which was now being used by assorted crossbreeds. A small sphinx was hauling a wagon of fruit, and a clean harpy was sweeping the street by blowing the debris and dirt away by the force of her wingbeats. An ogre was scrubbing the palace windows, using an assortment of sponges mounted on long handles.

Gary was amazed. He had never heard of a sphinx serving as a beast of burden, or of a harpy cleaning anything up, or of an ogre being gentle with windows. These were illusion figures, of course, but usually illusions echoed the natures of the creatures they represented. He glanced at Iris.

"Don't look at me," she muttered. "None of these people or creatures are my handiwork."

Hiatus took note. "They aren't? Then who's making them?"

"How should I know?" she asked irritably. "I thought I was the only one with illusion of this caliber."

"Maybe they're real," Mentia said.

"No, they're illusion," Iris said. "Trust me to know my art. They just aren't mine."

"I knew Desi was too good to be true," Hiatus said morosely. "The real Desiree isn't interested in me."

"And the real Hannah is a militant feminist," Gary said. "Not at all like Hanna the Handmaiden."

"Something very strange is occurring," Mentia said. "It's a function of the increased madness, of course, but not of any type I have heard of."

"It's fun!" Surprise said.

Iris was thoughtful. "Actually, my husband Trent remarked how he entered the madness and encountered figures from his past in Mundania. They seemed real, and acted as they had when he knew them, but were actually animated by his companions in the quest he was on."

"Among whom was my better self Metria," Mentia agreed, remembering. "She became sober in the madness, as I have, and developed a taste for love. That was the mischief that drove me out—and now I am discovering aspects of it myself. So perhaps this is the normal course of madness, after all."

"But what of the people and creatures we aren't remembering or imagining?" Iris asked. "They aren't like those we may have known, other than in their appearance."

"That remains odd," the demoness agreed.

They reached the palace gate. Gary admired the fine stone structure, as it had a number of rare facets, including a self-cleaning panel of detergent stone. He would have liked to study it more closely, but didn't want to separate from the party.

The interior of the palace was of course palatial, with arched ceilings and spacious chambers. The group was guided up an elaborate spiraling stone stairway to the residential floor, where it seemed their apartments were clustered. Gary saw Desi take Hiatus to their suite, after guiding Iris and Surprise to theirs. Hanna showed Mentia to hers, then took Gary into his.

"I must massage your tired body, my lord," Hanna said solicitously. "I know how traveling wearies you beyond endurance."

"Actually I didn't travel that far," Gary said. "And the train was comfortable."

"First we must get these grimy clothes off you," she said, as if he hadn't spoken. He realized that as an illusion imitation person, she probably didn't have a lot of personality. But her hands seemed surprisingly solid as she drew off his jacket and then his shoes and trousers. He knew that illusion was remarkable stuff, but hadn't realized that it could be felt this solidly as well as seen and heard.

She made him lie on a stone pallet, and she pressed and kneaded his human shoulders and back. Suddenly he realized how tired he actually was, and how wonderfully relaxing this massage was. Hanna the Handmaiden was a maiden who really knew how to use her hands.

But he knew he could not afford to relax mentally. There were strange things here that could be dangerous, and he had a quest to pursue. He did not know how long this dreamlike illusion would persist, so he wanted to take advantage of it to locate the philter as soon as feasible.

"Hanna, exactly what is our relationship?" he inquired.

"Why my lord Gar, I am your ever-loyal and obedient servant," she replied as her competent hands moved on down his body. "I do anything you require of me."

"Why did you call me Gar the Good?"

"This is your description. Everyone knows that you are the best intentioned of all the few remaining humans in

Xanth, and that you have only the very most noble aspirations. That is why you were selected to tutor Supi the Super, that she not abuse her great magic powers and bring our cause to ruin."

"The others aren't well intentioned?"

"Oh, some are, but they lack discretion or temper or competence. Princess Supi is a wild child, and Queen Iri notorious for her angry outbursts. Menti does her best to pacify them both, but she is merely a demon nanny without authority. As for Lord Hiat the Hedonist—if there is any way of selfish indulgence he has not discovered, it is not for lack of trying." She paused as her hands kneaded his legs. "Though recently he has become sinister, which makes me nervous."

An illusion could be nervous? "How so?"

"He still supports the cause, but somehow his support seems measured, as if it springs less from the heart than from a schooled aspect of the mind. I do not trust him—or the dire effect he has on the Princess."

This was getting more interesting—and alarming. "What dire effect?"

"He keeps trying to tempt her with notions of pleasure for its own sake, and suggesting that she employ her power to gratify her appetites, such as for endless cake and eye scream, instead of saving them for the benefit of the cause. She, being but a child, is prone to pay attention. So far you have managed to counter that, my lord, but I fear you are losing ground."

"What is this cause?"

She laughed as she did his feet. "You have not teased me like this in ages, my lord! Playing the ignorant, when in fact you are our most knowledgeable remaining purebreed. It is the cause of preserving the nature and sanctity of Xanth, that it be neither overrun by brutish barbarians from Mundania nor depleted entirely of mankind. Surely there can be no more noble enterprise than this— yet success hangs by a thread. We need to be fully united in this ultimate endeavor, yet we are not—because of Lord

Hiat's subtle malignity. Was ever there a sadder state?" She finished his feet. "Now I am done, my lord, and shall garb you anew, that you be ready for the final effort."

Gary got off the table, feeling wonderfully refreshed. "Final effort?"

She brought him a fine cloth robe. "It is time to assemble the masterspell, securing Xanth for all future existence. After that it will not matter if our pitiful remnant of humankind is extinguished; Xanth as we knew it will endure."

Gary donned the robe. It fit him as if it had been made for him and worn to his contours. "There is a threat of extinction of our kind?" He did not think it expedient to mention that he was not actually a man.

She laughed, somewhat wanly. "As if you had not noticed that only this palace remains inhabited by full humans, in all the vasty city. When we are gone there will be only crossbreeds remaining, and they will not remain long, for they prefer concourse with the growing populations of their own kind. Xanth will have to be resettled by Mundanes—but at least they will not destroy it, once the masterspell is made."

"But what threat is there against us?" he asked. "Aren't we secure in this fine city?"

"Secure from all but ourselves," she said sadly. "Every time one of us is tempted to drink from the unprotected spring, that one is lost. After the masterspell is established it will not matter, but too many have not seen fit to wait."

"Unprotected spring?"

"The gargoyle must travel from spring to spring, there being no other willing to brave the madness. We must confine our drinking to the times she is present, lest we be ensorceled and forfeit our species' future."

Gary fixed on one word. "Gargoyle?"

"And now you claim not to remember gentle Gayle Goyle, who alone among her kind still serves the welfare of the city of Hinge? We could not endure without her."

Gary was so surprised and thrilled that he did not speak

for a moment. In that moment Hanna proceeded to a new mission. "I must go help the staff prepare the homecoming banquet, my lord. May you rest refreshed." Before he could protest, she opened the door and was gone.

The moment he was alone, he was not alone. Demoness Mentia appeared. "I thought she'd never go," she muttered. "Do you realize when this is?"

"There's a gargoyle in the city," he said, dazed.

"This is the year minus one thousand," she said. "This is before known human history. This is the last remnant of a twelve-hundred-year prehistoric human colony."

That got his attention. "The dawn of time? The unknown period of Xanth?"

"Exactly. When the stage was set for what we thought was the settlement of Xanth—the First Wave of human colonization. Which won't occur for another thousand years, but hey, who's counting? This is when it was all made possible."

"But there can't have been history before the dawn of history!" he protested.

"There was fantastic history. It merely was lost to later knowledge. Now we can discover it all."

"From an illusion replica? We are merely imagining it."

"I don't think so, Gary. If Iris knows illusion, I know reality, being a creature who is seldom bound by it. This city is not drawn from imagination, it is drawn from reality. It existed, and what we are experiencing now is how it was. We must learn all we can about it, because when we return to our own time, we will be the only ones who can tell this story."

"We aren't here to learn lost history," Gary protested. "We are here to find the philter."

"That, too," she agreed. "But there's one other thing one of those illusions let slip. Did you hear how Surprise can invoke a particular variant of magic only once?"

"Yes, I wondered about that," he agreed. "Can it be true? If so, we need have no concern about bringing her under control; she will soon enough have no magic requiring control."

"That may require some time, because it seems that she doesn't lose whole disciplines of magic, merely the spot variants. She has conjured many things, though we have seen her conjure no one thing twice. Still, it will definitely limit her. What I wonder is how can it be mere illusions who tell us this? If they're not real, they should not know anything. If they're animations of the distant past, they shouldn't know about the present. Yet I have the feeling that they do know, and that this *is* what limits Surprise. But I don't know whether to discuss it with her mother."

"You don't mean Rapunzel? She's not in this scene."

"Queen Iri." Mentia paused, then knocked her head with the heel of her hand, and some dottle flew out her opposite ear. "I mean Iris. I'm getting into the part despite myself. I was thinking that a mother would not want to hear about such a liability in her child. But I suppose Iris can handle it."

"But we don't know that it's true. We should find out."

"Yes." Mentia hovered in place for a stretched-out moment, evidently ill at ease. "But I'm her governess. I don't want to break the poor child's heart by establishing such a thing."

"You want me to do it?" Gary asked, disturbed for no good reason.

"You're her tutor. It's your job to teach her things."

He realized that in the framework of this episode, that was true. It was his job to educate the child. In fact it was true in the present, too, because he had agreed to be her tutor. He had not done a very good job of it so far. "Then I had better do it," he agreed.

"Great! Go to their room and do it." Mentia faded out, clearly relieved even when her image was fuzzy.

Gary gathered up his gumption and stepped out of the room. He walked down the hall to the Queen & Princess suite. He knocked on the door.

After a moment Iris opened it. She too had changed

clothing, and was in a gown that revealed about as much of her upper torso as when she had tried to tempt him. He found the flesh more interesting now than he had before. "Yes, Gar the Good," she said, smiling.

"I come on serious business," he said. "I fear that Surprise can invoke particular magic only once."

"That's what the local folk claim," she agreed. "We had better verify it, though." She opened the door wider to admit him. "I'm not sure how she will react."

Gary realized that a severely disappointed or disturbed child could evoke wild magic indeed, if she tried to deny such a limitation. He needed to find a circumspect way to address the matter.

Surprise was sleeping. She was on a princess-sized bed and looking angelic. Gary felt guilty for what he was about to do. But it did have to be done.

He didn't want to wake her, but he suspected that her sleep was lighter than it seemed. So he addressed the bed: "So can you repeat magic?" he inquired conversationally.

An eye opened in the footboard and stared at him. Then it formed into a mouth. "Can't you see the Princess is sleeping?" the mouth asked irritably.

Gary glanced at Iris, who shook her head No. It wasn't her illusion. "I shall be happy to talk to you instead, Eyesore," he said. "All I want to know is whether what the foolish illusion maiden said is true. All you have to do to put her in her place is re-form your eye."

The mouth became an ear. "Eh?" the ear said. "I'm hardwood of hearing."

"Form the eye again."

The ear shifted into the eye, which gazed placidly at him. Then it pursed its lids into a kind of mouth. "Like this, you mean," it observed.

Gary exchanged half a glance with Iris. "That's very good," he said. But it occurred to him that any magic had a certain duration, and this might be part of a single magic series rather than a repetition. "Can you erase yourself entirely, then reappear?"

The eye blinked out. Nothing remained but the polished grain of the wood. Then the eye reappeared.

"Well, that does look like a repetition to me," Gary said with mixed feelings.

"Ixnay," Iris murmured. "That's illusion."

And she knew illusion when she saw it. Different magic. "I mean a real eye," Gary said.

The illusion eye vanished. There was a pause. Then the grain of the wood curled into the shape of an eye.

"That is not the same," Gary said.

The air stirred by the footboard. Fog appeared, twisting into the shape of an eye.

"Not the same," Gary repeated. A heavy certainty was infusing him. She was demonstrating a remarkable variety of similar effects, but once a particular magic was abolished, it was not reappearing.

The fog dissipated in demonly fashion. Then an eyeball popped into existence. In a moment it was clothed by upper and lower eyelids.

"Not the same," Gary said once more. "I am very much afraid we have our answer."

Surprise burst into tears. The tears flew out in an expanding sphere, soaking everything in the room including Gary and Iris. They were hot and salty.

Iris went to the bed to comfort the child. "I'm so sorry, dear. But we had to know."

"You must conserve your magic," Gary said. "To save it for when you really need it. You have enough to last you for a lifetime, if you are careful. Just don't waste it."

Surprise looked miserable. For the first time she understood her limit. She had just matured enormously, but by the most painful route.

He turned and left the chamber, depressed. He had done his job as tutor. He had broken the heart of a child.

Mentia reappeared as he entered his own suite. "She will be no problem when she returns home," she said. "She will no longer use magic wildly."

"I might as well have beaten her."

"You might as well have," Mentia agreed. Her eyes were reddening. "I'm sorry I asked you to do that."

"It had to be done." But now his own vision was blurring.

"Demons don't cry," she remarked, apropos of nothing.

"Neither do gargoyles."

Then they were standing together, holding each other, crying. What else was there to do?

Later, Hanna returned. She had changed her dress and was resplendent in a full evening gown that destroyed any remaining vestige of militarism she might ever have had. "Dinner is served," she said.

Gary gaped at her. He was beginning to appreciate the appeal of human females. The way her unbound hair spread out like a little cloak, and curled around the architecture of her shoulders and chest, and the way the very act of breathing caused her contours to shift configuration—

"Am I uncomfortable to perceive?" Hanna inquired after a moment.

"By no means," Gary said hastily. "I was merely surprised by the change."

"Perhaps I will change again for you later," she murmured. Then she turned and walked from the room, in the process demonstrating the manner in which her hindside contours shifted also. That was another type of thing he had not noticed in any woman before. Their forms were actually more intriguing than he would have credited, when closely inspected.

She paused, half turning in a graceful manner. "Are you coming, Lord Gar?"

Bemused, he followed. He had never suspected that Hannah Barbarian had any such aspect. Human beings were constantly surprising him, and interesting him increasingly.

The others joined him in the hall. Iris and Surprise were subdued but stable, in well-fitted queenly and princessly robes, and Mentia was demurely but quite attractively garbed. Gary was aware that as a demoness she could assume any form she wished, but she had a role to play and she was playing it perfectly. She was the child's governess, so was quite prim and proper, yet by no means devoid of aesthetic appeal. In simpler terms, she looked great, for a human, which she of course was not. Hiatus was now in a tailored suit whose upturned collar and descending tails looked elegant; he was suddenly a broodingly handsome man.

The banquet hall had been decorated for the occasion. Ornate carpets carpeted the walls, and plush rugs were rugged on the floor. An enormous table was in the center, garlanded with blue and green roses, with places set for five.

"Oh, but I must not be at the table," modest Menti protested.

"Nonsense," Iris said. "You must make sure the Princess behaves. Do you think I wish to bother doing it myself?"

Also, Gary realized, it was best to keep their small party close together. Maybe the illusion folk were their friends, but maybe they weren't. Mentia, the most sensible and responsible person among them, needed to be kept close. Iris had evidently not forgotten that this was madness, and what seemed pleasant could become otherwise in a hurry.

The five of them sat around a giant oval table, while Desi and Hanna served them with a series of fancy courses. There was white whine in elegant goblets fashioned in the shape of the heads of little goblins. There was head and tail lettuce. There was pumpernickel bread in the form of shoes and coins, with butterflies waiting to spread themselves on it. There were purple stakes cut from the juiciest portions of the stakeout trees. And quickly at the end there was hasty pudding.

When the illusion maidens were out of the room, Gary grabbed the chance to talk to Iris. "What are we really eating?" he asked.

"Stale squash pie and hard water," she replied with a grimace.

He had suspected as much. He preferred the illusion.

After the meal the maidens cleared the table. "Do you wish your usual entertainment?" Hanna inquired.

"By all means," Hiatus said before the others could work up a sufficient degree of caution.

Hanna and Desi jumped up onto the table and began dancing. First one took the stage, as it were, and then the other. Their feet were bare, and their skirts flared as they turned, showing their delicate but healthy lower legs. In fact when they spun more rapidly, some of their upper legs showed also. Gary found the sight increasingly intriguing. The angle of view was such that it should soon be possible to see their—

"Enough of this nonsense," Iris snapped. "Is there nothing better to be seen?"

"Yes, as the dance progresses," Desi said, pausing. "When we remove our costumes, piece by piece."

"That isn't what I mean," Iris said with increasing ire. "I'm sure no one cares about costumes."

"Speak for yourself, Queen Iris," Hiatus said. "I find the view delightful, and shall be happy to see the rest of it. Yea, even to their wicked panties."

There was a faint flush in the air after his utterance of the provocative word. The child's eyes grew large.

Iris glanced angrily around at the others. "Who else wants to witness this sorry spectacle?"

Surprise clapped her little hands gleefully. "I do!" She seemed just about ready to scramble onto the table herself.

"But that would not be princessly," Mentia cautioned her.

"Oh pooh! Why do I have to be princessly? I want to dance and throw my clothes away and show my—"

"Princess!" Menti said sharply.

Supi realized that she had gone too far. She subsided.

"Who else?" Iris asked grimly.

Gary would have liked to see the rest of the dance, because he was coming to appreciate the pleasures of the human form. But he realized that if he voted to see the dance, that would make a majority, and he did not want to embarrass Iris. So he practiced his diplomacy. "What are the alternatives?"

The two maidens considered. "Why, we could tell a story," Desi said. "But usually the menfolk have preferred to see us dance, and then—"

"Never mind what then!" Iris snapped. "What kind of story?"

"We have numerous tales of dragons and damsels," Hanna said. "Of course those usually end sadly."

"What about history?" Mentia asked.

"History?" Both maidens looked perplexed.

"The story of humankind in Xanth leading up to this point," Iris said.

Suddenly Gary saw her purpose. They were here to locate the philter, and to do that they needed to understand the history of this ancient city. They were getting distracted into entertainment instead. It was time to orient on their quest. "Yes, the story of the city of Hinge," he said.

"But that's so dull!" Hanna protested.

"Dancing and dragons are much more interesting," Desi said.

"Yes!" Surprise agreed eagerly.

"History," Iris said firmly.

"Pictures!" Surprise said.

"Animate it," Mentia suggested. "From the beginning, in summary, skipping the dull parts."

"From the Demon Xanth on," Gary agreed.

The two maidens shrugged together. Then a picture formed around them, occupying the center of the table. It was of a desolate peninsula. "Way back in the time of minus four thousand years, give or take ten thousand or so, before the Xanth chronology proper commenced, the Demon X(A/N)th arrived in this dreary and isolated place," Hanna's voice said from somewhere within the scene. "He settled into the rock beneath and lost himself in contemplation. His thoughts percolated through the caverns and made them very strange." The picture showed a huge demon seated on a boulder deep underground, his head propped on one hand, surrounded by wiggling snakelike thoughts.

"He was oblivious to his surroundings," Desi's voice said. "He did not move for thousands of years. But there was a fringe effect: his magic slowly spread outward from his body, suffusing the rock, causing the denizens of that region to become magical. Nickelpedes, voles, and rock dragons developed. Then the magic rock welled upward and reached the surface." The scene showed a volcano spewing out hot stone. "Then the creatures and plants of the surface became magical." There were sea serpents in the water and tangle trees on land.

"Around the year minus twenty-two hundred a colony of human folk arrived from what was later to be called Mundania," Hanna's voice resumed. The picture showed a ragged group of men and woman with their clinging children. "They lacked magic, so had a hard time at first." In the picture a serpent slithered out of a lake, encountered a man, stared him in the eye until the petrifaction spell took hold, breathed slimy vapor on him, then swallowed him whole. "But their children delivered in Xanth arrived with magic talents, and that helped." A huge serpent lifted its head to stare down a child, but the little boy made his head swell until it was far too large for the serpent to swallow, and the reptile had to give up in disgust.

"So for several hundred years human folk migrated to the magic land, preferring it once they learned how to survive in it," Desi's voice said. "They moved to the area of greatest magic, now known as the Region of Madness, and their descendants became very talented magically. Indeed, there were a number of full Magicians and Sorceresses. Not all of these were nice people; one known as the Sea Hag was finally banished from human society, and she disappeared for several millennia. But most remained to contribute to the welfare of the main colony."

"However," Hanna's voice said, "this influx was not necessarily peaceful. Life in Xanth, for those who learned to stay clear of dragons and similar creatures, became relatively easy, because food could be conjured or simply plucked from obliging trees." The picture showed a woman harvesting a fresh cherry pie from a cherry pie tree. "So the folk of Xanth soon became moderately gentle." The people of the picture relaxed under pleasant trees.

"But the incoming Mundanes were hungry, violent, and often cruel," Desi said. In the picture tough men with swords drove the relaxing folk away and took over the trees—which they then chopped down. "Of course those with magic could stop them, but often they preferred to retreat rather than fight. So they went to the hinterlands, driven away by their barbarian neighbors."

"Such as my ancestors," Hanna's voice said disapprovingly. "Then Xanth became an island." The picture showed the sea extending an arm across the top to cut it off. "We aren't sure whether the Demon $X(A/N)^{th}$ arranged it so as to have more privacy, or whether it was coincidence. That cut off the inflow of pure humans and other Mundane creatures. Peace was restored."

However, it turned out the folk of Xanth were concerned that it might not always remain an island, and when it returned to peninsula status there would be more brutal invasions, worse because of the longer period without danger. They felt it would be foolish simply to ignore the matter and hope for the best; their children or grandchildren might pay a hideous price. It might happen even if Xanth remained an island forever, because Mundanes might use boats to cross to it. So they gathered together and pondered ways to protect themselves from invasion.

Yet there was a problem while Xanth remained an island, too. The human population was diminishing. At first no one realized that this was happening, and then the reason for it was not clear. But finally they understood: mankind was fissioning off into crossbreed species. There were numerous magic springs, including those with love elixir. Any human who drank from one of these fell passionately into love with the first creature of the opposite sex he or she saw, and proceeded to summon the stork with that creature. The storks, being literal-minded creatures, delivered babies split evenly between the two species. When those babies grew up, they preferred crossbreeds like themselves, and so magically new breeds appeared. Some humans changed size or form somewhat even without crossbreeding. At this time there appeared the first harpies, merfolk, naga, sphinxes, fauns, nymphs, ogres, goblins, elves, fairies, werefolk, and other crossbreeds and variants. All derived at least in part from human stock, but many preferred not to admit that their lineage had been debased by such a connection and became the enemies of pure human folk.

Some human communities were able to make deals with gargoyles to purify their water so that no more of them were lost. (Gary was jolted back into self-awareness at this point in the historical narration.) But sometimes there were misunderstandings or disagreements, and the gargoyles would move on. At other times foolish young humans would deliberately drink from love springs, thinking themselves invulnerable to their effects. Some did it on dares. Whatever the reason, their later offspring were lost to the core human species. As time passed, the human population slowly but steadily shrank.

Finally the remaining humans realized that they had to address this problem. They decided to collect the remnant of their pure human folk and live in a completely protected region, so that there would be no further fissioning. But they remained concerned about the other threat, of invasion from Mundania, for they saw that the water was slowly retreating in the north. In time there would once more be a land connection, and the brute Mundanes would charge savagely down again, overrunning Xanth and overwhelming the magic humans already there. Yet they did not want to prevent *all* immigration, because they desperately needed new pure human stock to replace what had been lost to crossbreeding. How could they address the problems of too much and too little at the same time?

From this dilemma came an answer that was to change the future history of Xanth. They decided to devise a mixed rampart of illusion and confusion to wall off Xanth from Mundania, working from a special city in the one place this could be done: the Region of Madness. Because only here was there magic of such intensity as to be able to power the special device they contemplated. There should be few other species in this region, and in any event they would make sure to have a gargoyle to protect their water supply. They would wall the city in, so that their foolish young could not readily go outside to imbibe mischief, and dangerous creatures outside could not enter. For there were indeed dangers here, of more than the mortal kind. It was an act of special courage for the community of mankind to come here.

Thus came to be the greatest and most special city in all the history of Xanth: Stone Hinge.

The picture faded. "But we see you are tired and sleepy," Hanna said. "We must let you retire now, and continue this history another time."

Gary was satisfied to agree. He found the story fascinating, especially the parts concerning gargoyles, but he needed to have some human sleep and time to ponder it all before he would be ready for much more. He saw that the others had a similar sentiment.

So by common consent they departed the banquet hall and went upstairs to their chambers. Surprise was already asleep; Mentia had to carry her.

Gary entered his suite and before he knew it he was asleep on the bed. He was hardly aware of Hanna helping him to get there. His human body had a need of rest that his real body had not.

10
KEYSTONE

In the morning Gary woke refreshed. But there was someone in the bed with him. Perplexed, he lifted away the cover to discover it was Hanna the Handmaiden. Not only was she sound asleep, she had lost her nightclothes. He hadn't realized that she lacked a place to sleep; he would have given her the bed if she had asked for it. He was accustomed to sleeping on the ground, though the human body required some cushioning that his natural body did not.

He got up carefully so as not to disturb her, and tended to the various inconveniences of the fleshy human condition. But he did wonder passingly how an illusion could be sleeping. Surely she should simply fade into nothingness when not conscious—if she had any true consciousness at all. And even if she did, why should she be in his bed? She must have her own place to sleep, if she required sleep.

Then he realized with a pang of guilt that she must have given him her own room. That was why she now lacked a private place. That explained why the chamber was so nice. He would have to apologize for unwittingly displacing her.

Dressed and ready for the day, he stood gazing at her. She was certainly an aesthetic creature by human standards, with a torso reminiscent of a sandglass, fine long dark tresses, firmly fleshed legs, and fine facial features. She made him think, oddly, of flying storks—many of them.

"Now there is an artful pose," Mentia remarked, appearing beside him. "Whoever is crafting her seems to know what he's doing."

"Crafting her?" Gary asked blankly.

"You don't think illusions generate themselves, do you? Someone is projecting likenesses of Hanna and Desi, and he's pretty good at it. Of course he can't animate them both at once."

"He can't? But they were both with us last night."

"Didn't you notice how they took turns dancing and talking? Only one at a time was truly animate, while the other was on autopilot."

"On what?"

"A term derived from pilot fish who are good at navigation. They can do it in their sleep. A sleeping fish may be moving, but is not responsive to others. That's the way the alternate maiden is. Right now Desi is active, seducing Hiatus, so Hanna is on standby mode." She glanced sidelong at him, her eyes gravitating to the side of her face so that her head did not have to turn. "It might be interesting if you were to accept her seduction now, to see what would happen. Possibly your hand would pass right through her body, or maybe the touch would wake her. That is, attract the attention of her master to you, so that he would animate her. Perhaps Desi would have to turn off in the midst of her activity."

"Seduction?"

Mentia laughed. "And you did not realize, as you did not with Iris. Because you are a gargoyle. But since we are in serious business here, with possible danger, I had better educate you. A human woman never exposes any portion of her body between the elbows, knees, and neck accidentally. Not when a man is present. The more she shows, the more interested in his reaction she is." Her eyes moved back to the front of her face. "I would judge that Illusion Hanna is about as interested in yours as she can be, because that is what we demons term X-rated. Not even any panties."

"Well, of course I wouldn't have looked, if there were panties!" Gary said righteously. "I know the human convention."

"Perhaps not enough of it. Panties represent the limit of what an unrelated male is supposed not to see. What Hanna is showing you now is beyond that limit."

"I don't understand."

She smiled, perhaps a bit wistfully. "Innocence is such precious stuff," she said irrelevantly. "For now, just accept my word: Hanna is extremely interested in you."

"But how can an illusion be interested in anything?"

"Ah, there's the rub," she said, lifting a hand to rub her face, which rubbed out at that spot. So for the moment she was missing half an eye. "Illusions have no consciousness and therefore no will. It simply means that whoever is crafting Hanna wishes to seduce you, being ignorant of your true nature. Perhaps it is some magically talented female who admires your looks."

"A woman like Iris?"

"There's another rub," she said, rubbing out the rest of the eye. "Iris is the Sorceress of Illusion, and is unique among human women in the nature and magnitude of her talent. There is no other human woman like her. But there may be some other kind of female with a similar, though surely not identical, talent of illusion. She may like you, but realize that you would not be interested in her true form, so she tries to seduce you by means of a human illusion."

"This could not be Iris herself?"

"It could be, but I am almost sure it isn't. At this mo-

ment Iris is sleeping, which means that her illusions are on
auto. Now I realize that this does not exclude Hanna, who
is on auto now. But it doesn't explain Desi, who is intrigu-
ingly active. Unless Lord Hiat is made of sterner stuff than
I judge, he will very shortly be discovering exactly how
far an illusion can go. I also have seen that Iris denies
crafting these particular illusions, as she denies crafting
last night's banquet, and I have no reason to doubt her
word in this respect. She is privately quite curious and annoyed at this rival illusion, which does seem to approach
her own in power and finesse. So I think Iris is innocent,
apart from the fact that she evinces no interest in Hiatus,
who is a pretty dull fellow whom she knew as an obnoxious child."

"Then who could it be?"

"Or *what* could it be. I fear we are encountering something mindboggling, and the only reason it isn't boggling
our minds is that we have next to no notion of its nature."

"Then what should we do?"

"Play along until we do get boggled."

"But I'm not here to get boggled! I'm here to find the
philter."

"And we are here to help you, albeit with our own di-
verse purposes also in mind. And in that helpful spirit, I
suggest that you not do anything foolish, such as trying to
break up this massive structure of illusion, because not
only would that be likely to mess up your quest, it could
be dangerous in its own right. We need to understand better the nature of the entity with whom we are interacting
before we do anything bold or devious."

There was as usual very good sense in what she said.
"So we play along, and stay alert," he said.

"And try not to let on about what we learn," she agreed.
"I consider it safe to talk candidly with you now only because I verified that the entity's attention is elsewhere at
the moment."

Hanna stirred. Gary and Mentia exchanged a hasty

glance, and she made a zip-mouth gesture, her mouth becoming a zipper. Then she faded.

So either Hiatus' seduction was complete, or it had halted for some reason. Hanna was returning to animation. And what should he do now?

He decided that it would be safer to take the initiative than to let her take it. "Ah, you are awake," he said warmly. "I was glad to see you sleep so well, after everything you did yesterday. Now we can go to breakfast."

Hanna seemed a trifle out of sorts. "Yes, of course," she said after a moment. She got out of bed, spreading her bare legs in his direction. When Gary politely averted his gaze, she made a little exclamation of modesty. "Oh! I am inadvertently indecent! Thank you for not looking." Panties appeared (he saw them by peripheral vision), and then a prim day dress formed around her.

They stepped out into the hall. Hiatus was already there, looking uncomfortable. "What's the matter?" Gary asked.

Hiatus shook his head. "If she had only been real, I would have done it," he muttered. "But I know the real Desiree would never be like that. Not without marriage."

But before they could join the others and go down for another presumably sumptuous meal, there was an odd wavering in the scene. "Oops," Hanna said. "A storm is coming."

Mentia appeared. "Something strange just—oh, I see you noticed."

"Hanna says a storm is coming," Gary told her.

Hiatus shrugged. "A storm shouldn't bother a stone edifice much."

"A madness storm," Hanna clarified. "We shall have to go into defensive mode. Hurry; we can't stay in the building." She led the way down the stairs almost at a run.

"I'll wake Iris and Surprise," Mentia said, popping out.

Gary and Hiatus followed Hanna out of the palace. There was the ogre tromping up. "The others will be out in a moment," Hanna told him. "You can start now."

The ogre went to the outer wall of the castle and

pounded a fist against a stone panel. The stone shook with the impact, and the whole palace shuddered. There were clicking sounds throughout.

Iris and Surprise emerged, following a bouncing ball. The ball took one last bounce, then sprouted arms and legs. In a moment a body filled in. "Everyone's out except Desi," Mentia announced.

Then Desi appeared. "I am here," she said.

Gary glanced covertly at Hanna. She was standing still, with no expression. She was, as Mentia had pointed out, on autopilot. There was only one presence, with alternating presentations.

He looked at the real people. Iris seemed understandably harried, but the child was unusually quiet. Probably the realization of the limit of her talent still depressed her. She had thought she could do anything, without limit, and now knew that she could do anything only once. Perhaps Gary had accomplished his tutoring with that discovery, and Surprise was now ready to go home. Once they found the philter.

The ogre pulled at the overhanging section of the palace roof. The roof separated, with widening cracks running up to the peak and radiating down from there. Then the ogre pushed up on the overhang, and the rest of the roof section hinged down toward the ground, the chamber beneath it collapsing into flatness. The other palace sections shut down similarly. They had thought that it would require a pair of ogres to fold these stones, but perhaps this was an especially strong one. Or one ogre sufficed for a palace that was in large part illusion.

Gary glanced again at the illusion maidens, without being obvious, and saw that now both were unmoving. The animation was being focused on the ogre and the palace. So this spectacle, while impressive, was not as extensive as it looked—and of course most of the scene was illusion anyway.

Hanna came back to life. "We must go to the center circle," she said. "There we will be safe."

They followed her away from the folding palace, along an avenue lined by large stone buildings being similarly compacted. The whole vast city was being reduced to a series of folded stones. But Gary saw that all the other ogres working on other buildings followed exactly the pattern of the ogre working on the palace; they were in lockstep, or perhaps lock image. More autopiloting. And they worked only when Hanna was walking in a straight line, neither speaking nor gesturing.

So the illusion had limits, as Mentia had explained. But who was directing it? For what purpose? This had started out as Iris' image of the ancient city, based on Gary's reading of the rock pictures. Now another party was contributing. But why? And what danger might there be?

Meanwhile signs of the coming storm were growing. Winds were tugging at distant pennants, and dust was stirring into clouds, obscuring the more distant buildings. There was a faint keening, getting louder. The sky was overcast and turning troubled.

In the center of the city was a clear region, and in the center of that was a round pool of clear water. Hanna relaxed. "We shall be safe from the storm here," she said.

"Howso?" Mentia asked. "The folded buildings may be able to withstand severe battering, but this is exposed."

"The battering is only partly physical," Desi said. "It is the madness that makes them vulnerable. See." She gestured, and they saw that one of the buildings had been missed. Either there weren't enough ogres for them all, or each ogre had several buildings to do and this one hadn't been done yet.

The dusty wind swirled around the building—and the structure changed. Its stone turned translucent, and faintly pink. When a strong gust of wind pushed against it, the building gave way like a mound of gelatin.

"The madness changes things," Hanna said. "That's why we can't depend on the firmness of stone. The structure will revert to stone after the storm passes, but it may be deformed into some other shape, if it remains intact."

"And it may not be much fun for the people in that building," Iris said, wincing.

"True," Desi said. "They may lose their lives, or their sanity, in which case they will not return to normal after the storm."

"That still doesn't explain why it should be any better here," Iris said.

"This inner circle is safe," Hanna said. "Because the city of Hinge is so designed that the pattern of folded buildings generates a madness-free zone here. Magic within the circle is normal or below normal, depending on the strength of the storm."

"Then why not simply live in the circle?" Hiatus asked.

"Because when there is no storm, the level of magic within the circle is very low," Desi said. "Talents don't work. Ogres lose their strength. Crossbreeds get sick as their bodies try to separate into the components of their ancestry. Magic plants wilt or even die."

"In short, it's like Mundania," Mentia said. "A drear place of no magic."

"Yes," Hanna said. "And demons can't function at all."

Mentia winced. It was impressive: her entire face drew back, folding inward, so that her nose inverted and dragged her eyes and mouth along after it. "I won't stay here after the storm is gone," she said from the other side of her head.

"But if you go out during the storm," Desi said, "you will be overloaded with magic, and perhaps explode into a cloud of madness."

Gary looked around. "So this is why the city is hinged. So it can be shut down during madness storms, and readily restored after they pass."

"Yes," Hanna agreed. "We suffer very few losses during the storms, and these can be repaired. So we are able to work well at all other times. Stone Hinge protects us both with and without the madness."

"This is very clever," Iris said appreciatively.

"Do the individual buildings have similar effect?" Gary asked. "That is, reducing the madness?"

"Yes," Desi said. "They ease the effect of the ambient background madness. But their effect is limited. They can't withstand a storm when not folded down."

Iris glanced sharply at him. "How did you guess that?"

"I noticed that Mentia was reverting to normal. When I talked with her this morning, her eyes traveled around her face, and just now her face reversed itself. That's part of her regular craziness; she does such things without noticing. But when the madness is around us, she usually indulges in no such foolishness, not even unconsciously."

Hiatus nodded appreciatively. "Gary, you are smarter than the average—"

"The average young human man," Iris finished. She might have been a bit crazy in the madness, but was back to her sensible self here, as she had been in the palace. Hiatus had reverted to his somewhat vacant innocence, so had forgotten that they were trying not to speak of Gary's true nature.

"Isn't the average young man interested in shapely young women?" Hanna inquired.

"Yes, but sometimes a bit shy," Mentia said, covering for him much as Iris had. "Would you believe that there are some who could see a maiden in the altogether and not immediately think of the stork?"

"Yes," Iris said, somewhat sourly.

"I'm thirsty," Surprise said. She left Iris and ran to the pool. She was back to her normal impetuosity. Gary had thought that her good behavior stemmed from her discovery of the limit of her talent, but now he realized that the surrounding madness could also have accounted for it.

"Wait, dear!" Iris cried, pursuing her. "We don't know what kind of water that is. It might be enchanted, or poison."

"Actually it's a love spring," Desi said.

"A love spring!" Iris screeched. She made a grab for the

child, but was too late; Surprise had already plopped down beside the pool and put her face to the water.

"But it's the city supply," Hiatus said. "So it must be pure."

Gary touched a finger to the water. "Yes, this is pure," he agreed, excited.

Hanna looked sharply at him. "How do you know?"

Gary knew better than to give away his true nature. "I have a talent for reading water," he said. "I know when it is pure. This is exceptionally so."

Surprise lifted her face. "Yes, it's scrumshus, for water."

Hiatus stared at Hanna. "You were having a little fun with us, not telling us that this water is good."

"Yes," Desi said. "I have tried to have fun with you."

Hiatus grimaced. "There are different kinds of fun."

"This is a spring that is unaffected by the madness around it?" Iris inquired doubtfully.

"Yes, it rises by the keystone on the island in the center," Hanna said.

"Keystone?" Surprise said.

"Don't do any magic, dear," Iris told her quickly.

"Yes, the keystone is in the very center of Hinge," Desi said. "As long as that's in place, all is well."

"Impossible," Gary said. "This water is too pure to have percolated directly from the depths."

Mentia looked at him sharply. "What are you suggesting?"

"I'm suggesting that there's a gargoyle involved."

"Oho! Let me check." Mentia walked across the water to the little island in the center. There was a fancy fountain there, from which water gushed into the pool. "Right," she called back after a moment. "There is a gargoyle here."

Gary dived into the water and swam in clumsy human manner to the island. The fountain had a high stone foundation surmounted by the fountain spout. He walked around it until he found a door. The door was closed, but opened outward when he tried it. Within, a short passage angled upward, curving. He walked its length, and finally saw what was in the center.

"Some keystone!" Gary exclaimed. But he was hardly displeased. He had confirmed what he expected, and in the process made a wonderful discovery.

It was a horrendous stone gargoyle, spouting water. A female. Gary gazed upon her hugely ugly countenance and stone contours, and was instantly in love.

"Easy, Gary," Mentia murmured. "Don't say anything we all might regret." She seemed quite sane and sober now.

She meant that he should not announce his own nature, lest the illusion folk of Hinge overhear. He wasn't sure why anyone else should care that he was a transformed gargoyle, but he respected the demoness' caution. He nodded.

The female gargoyle saw them. She closed her throat, shutting off the flow of clean water. "Hello, strangers," she said. "Are you real or illusion?"

"A bit of both," Mentia said quickly. "We are not necessarily what we appear to be. I, for example, appear human, but I am a demoness." She changed to the form of a striped green cloud for a moment, illustrating her nature, then re-formed as human. "But apart from that we are real, being two members of a party of five visiting the stone city of Hinge."

"That is a relief," the gargoyle said. "It's been so long since I've seen any but illusion folk." She twitched her whiskers. "I am Gayle Goyle."

"I am D. Mentia."

"And I am Gary Gar."

Gayle's eyes fastened on him. But before she spoke, Mentia did. "We prefer to leave it at that, for now. No further introduction is needed."

Gayle nodded, though her eyes had narrowed. "Perhaps that is best. But I would ask of you one favor. I dislike being fooled by illusions. Would you touch me, Gary, so that I can verify that you are tangible?"

"Gladly," Gary said. He stepped forward and put one human flesh hand on one of her stone lion paws.

The touch sent a thrill through him. Not only was she real, she was desirable by the standard of his species. And he knew that she recognized his nature through his touch, for gargoyles did know their own. And he knew she liked him.

Do not let them know your nature.

She had spoken to him in his mind! He hadn't realized that gargoyles could do that. But of course it had been centuries since he had encountered another of his species. He might have forgotten.

It is this intense magic that enhances my nature. Do not trust the illusions.

Hanna appeared. "Ah, there you are. Meeting the gargoyle."

Gary removed his hand, reluctantly. "Yes. I wanted to be sure she—it wasn't more illusion."

"To be sure the water really is pure," Mentia added.

"The two of you would not be standing apart from each other if this spring retained its original nature," Hanna said with a smile.

"Love elixir doesn't affect demons," Mentia said a bit primly.

"This spring might. There is very strong magic here."

Now Gary became aware of it: an aura like that of the madness, but worse. He had been so interested in the gargoyle that he hadn't realized that part of the magic of their touch stemmed from this.

"But you said this was a safe circle," Mentia said.

"Strictly speaking, it's a safe torus," Hanna said. "Are you conversant with the principle of a magnifying glass?"

"Oh, you mean the magic disk that sets fire to things?" Mentia asked.

"The same. Its magic focuses the light of the sun into a very small, hot center. But it takes light away from the region around that center. So that region is in shadow. Similarly the center circle of Hinge takes magic from most of that area and puts it in the focus island. That makes the circle safe for most folk during storms, but the island is dangerous."

"Not for me," Gayle said. "It has little effect on animate stone, and I can purify what remains, purging myself."

The demoness looked at the illusion. "So you make your safe haven by dumping the extra magic where it doesn't hurt anyone," Mentia said.

"Yes. This is the keystone of our defense," Hanna said. "Gayle has been here for the past several thousand years, loyally purifying the water."

"Well, it's the geis of the gargoyle," Gayle said modestly. "Someone has to do it." She wiggled an ear. "Now if you don't mind, I must return to work, for the magic is building up. It is pretty strong here."

That was perhaps the understatement of the millennium! The strength of the magic here was appalling, and Gary knew that only the fact that he was a gargoyle himself and Mentia a demoness enabled them to survive it without going utterly mad. In fact, if he didn't get away from it soon, his human body would succumb anyway. He couldn't be sure what would become of him then. "By all means," Gary said. "I congratulate you on your constancy."

"Thank you." She sent one more glance his way, then opened her mouth wide and resumed spouting.

They walked out of the fountain enclosure and closed the door. Then Gary swam across the pool while Hanna and Mentia walked across it.

"What did you see?" Hiatus inquired.

"A gargoyle," Mentia replied, assuming gargoyle form. "Big and ugly, spouting water. Nothing to interest any of us." The form fuzzed slightly, as if not quite true.

"To be sure," Iris agreed. "So Gary was correct: that is what keeps this water pure. Otherwise it would be extremely risky for any of us to drink from it."

Gary emerged from the pool. He realized that he felt different. He was of course excited by the discovery of Gayle Goyle, but it was more than that. The magic had diminished. It had indeed been intense, and now was ordinary. But there was still something else.

"You swam in your clothing," Iris remarked tartly. "You're all wet."

Oh. That was it.

"Well, get out of those things," Iris said. "You'll catch new monia, which can proceed on into middle monia and even old monia if neglected."

"Yes, let's see you in the altogether," Mentia said, rolling her eyes right over the top of her head.

"We are already all together," Gary protested. He knew that human folk were supposed to be clothed.

"I will clothe you in illusion," Iris said. "You can strip off your wet things under it."

A barrel appeared around him. It wasn't real, for he could pass his hands right through it, but it looked solid. He stripped off his clothing beneath it. He had to admit that the clothing had become uncomfortable. In his natural state he never used clothing, so he tended to forget about it.

Iris stooped to pick up his fallen, sodden things. "No fair peeking!" Mentia said, her eyes stretching out from her face in the manner of a snail's.

The Sorceress turned her face away from the base of his barrel, frowning. It occurred to Gary that she might indeed have been about to peek. She was back to normal too, in this reduced magic circle, which meant she was looking for the excitement and irresponsibility of youth. Yet she also was acting like a mother who had raised a willful daughter, insisting that wet clothing be changed. If the madness increased, she would become more like the daughter and less like the mother. And perhaps the madness was increasing, because he could see that the storm was intensifying beyond the rim of the circle.

Indeed, a sharp gust of wind cut across the circle. It passed through his barrel as if it weren't there and chilled his flesh in toward the bone. He shivered, which he realized was his human body's reaction to the discomfort.

"Oh, you poor thing," Mentia said. "You need a warm

blanket." She dissolved into vapor, and the vapor formed into a bright polka dot blanket, and the blanket slowly sank toward the ground, then undulated sinuously and moved toward him. It came up under the barrel and wrapped itself around his cold bare torso. One fold of it tweaked his behind. He would have protested, but realized that the blanket really was comfortingly warm.

"Then we won't be needing the barrel," Iris said, disgruntled. The barrel vanished, leaving him in the blanket. "But we shall have to get this clothing dry."

"We have a sun screen," Hanna said. A small square screen appeared, glowing faintly. Desi picked it up and set it right at the edge of the safe circle.

"A sun screen?" Gary asked, perplexed.

"Where do you think the sun goes when it's not on duty?" Desi asked rhetorically. "It retires to its sun house constructed of sun blocks, and drinks sundaes from sun glasses. We borrowed the pattern of one of its screens, is all; the sun will never miss it."

"You can borrow things from the sun?" Hiatus asked, as surprised as the others.

"We illusions are not as limited in imagination or performance as are you non-illusion folk," Hanna said. "This is of course an illusion copy of the screen."

The blanket around Gary opened a mouth. "How can an illusion screen dry real clothing?"

"This is a pretty strong illusion," Desi said.

This made sense to Gary, who remembered how Iris' illusion lamp had made real light.

Iris shrugged and brought the clothing to the screen. She held up Gary's limp shirt, stretching it out flat.

The sun screen brightened. In fact it became so bright that it was difficult to look at it. So Gary looked at the shirt instead. Steam was rising from it.

Then Iris dropped it. "Oh!" she cried. "My hands are getting scorched!"

"Fortunately it's already dry," Hanna said, picking up

the shirt. "Come and put it on, Gary." She stood at the edge of the circle, holding the dry shirt up.

"And how can an illusion pick up a real object?" the blanket asked.

"We're pretty strong illusions, now, too," Desi said, picking up the undershorts. She held them before the sun screen, which brightened again.

Gary walked to Hanna. "Ooo," the blanket said. "That magic is strong at the fringe! In fact, it's dangerous. I tell you this in utterly sincere sanity."

"But the shirt is warm and dry," Hanna said, holding it out. "Let me put it on you."

Gary stood before her, with the blanket sliding down somewhat, and she set the shirt on him, passing it over one arm and then the other. Her hands were firm and gentle.

The shorts were dry. Desi brought them over. Hanna took them and helped put them on him. "This is weird," the blanket said, floating away.

Finally the trousers were ready. Gary insisted on putting them on himself. They were warm and dry too.

Mentia reformed in her usual image. "What is going on here?" she demanded. "How can you two illusions be physical? A stronger illusion is merely a clearer, more detailed one, not a physical thing."

"Note that we are standing near the fringe of the circle," Desi said. "The storm has intensified the magic, and it is now more powerful outside the circle than any normal person can handle. So strong that it even lends the semblance of substance to some illusions."

That seemed to make sense. But now Gary remembered how Hanna had massaged him in his room in the palace. Her hands had felt quite solid then. Also, the covers of his bed had been supported by her body when she was sleeping there in the morning. She might have been on autopilot, but shouldn't her substance have faded then? The illusions were capable of some solidity even when they weren't at the fringe of a storm.

Mentia went to stand at the fringe of the circle. She put

an arm out into the madness beyond. "It is stronger outside," she said soberly. "But not nearly as strong as in the gargoyle's chamber."

"Nothing matches that strength," Hanna said. "It, too, varies with the ambient magic, but it is always by far the strongest on the surface of Xanth. It enables the gargoyle to purify highly enchanted water. Thus we make a virtue of excess: the magic we don't want in the main circle helps provide the water that makes the circle safe."

Meanwhile Hiatus was gazing out at the city. "It is really strange out there," he said.

The others looked. Indeed it was strange. All the buildings were now affected by the madness. They had been compacted by the folding process, but were swaying and twisting in the winds of the storm. Their colors were shifting constantly, and some were stretching and bobbing as if pulled or banged by a giant unseen hand. Snow was flying in one section, mounding up on and around the structures, burying them in green, red, yellow, and plaid. Ice was forming in another, coating the stones so thickly that they scintillated. But elsewhere the swirling clouds seemed to be producing black and white sand, which outlined the sharp angles of the stones, making them stand out in stark relief.

The storm swept right up to the edge of the circle, but was unable to penetrate it. The stone structures seemed to be the pedestals supporting an invisible dome that arched over land, pool, and island, marked by the sudden change in the aspect of the storm. The rampaging winds formed themselves into a kind of funnel, broad at the top, narrow at the bottom—and the tip was right at the island. Within the funnel was the color of madness, too compelling even to look at for more than an instant, while outside it was the calm of the protected area.

"This construction truly is a wonder," Iris murmured appreciatively. "I never dreamed that such a city ever existed."

"Naturally not," Desi said. "Hinge is excluded from the

realm of dreams. Dreams are mad enough already, without being fouled up by storms of madness."

"How long do these storms last?" Hiatus asked.

"Not long," Hanna said. "This one is already waning."

"I don't see it raining," Hiatus said.

"You are so clever," Desi said, making an illusory effort to look appreciative. "The storm is diminishing."

"Oh."

"Soon we will be able to restore the city and return to more comfortable surroundings," Hanna said.

Something had been bothering Gary, and now it surfaced. "All this is interesting," he said. "But it is not accomplishing our purpose."

"What is your purpose?" Desi asked.

"We are looking for the philter."

Both illusions froze for a moment. Then both came back to life. "We thought you were interested in the history of Xanth," Hanna said.

"We are," Iris said. "But that is a means to an end. The end is the philter, which will free the gargoyles of their geis. We understand that the philter is somewhere in this city."

Hanna exchanged a glance with Desi. Both seemed disturbed. Gary wondered again how illusions could have feelings. He also noticed that though the two still alternated speech, they were now acting at the same time. The heightened magic at the edge of the circle was enhancing them in several ways.

"We wouldn't know about that," Desi said. "But maybe we can help you find out."

"How?" Gary asked eagerly.

Hanna met his gaze, her face serious. "You know that Desi and I are illusions. Our roles are limited. We can show you only what we know. If you want to know more, you must get seriously into your roles."

"What are you talking about?" Mentia asked from the circle's edge, very seriously.

"You have the roles, but you aren't truly into them," Desi said. "You are not living them."

"The roles," Hiatus said. "You mean like my being Hiat the Hedonist?"

"Yes," Hanna said. "A sinister man who argues self-interest but whose true loyalty is shrouded."

"And Iri the Irate," Iris said. "The imperious Queen."

"Menti the Mentor," Surprise said. "Loyal nanny for Supi the Super!"

"Governess, not nanny," Mentia said firmly.

"And Gar the Good," Gary said. "Though I can't see that I fit any such role."

"They are the ones who made the Xanth Interface," Desi said. "When you live their lives, perhaps you will have what you desire."

"Not so fast," Iris said. "Exactly where did you two illusions come from? Why are you here showing us around and explaining things?"

"We are animations of the madness," Hanna said. "Drawn from images of two who thought of you at the time we were formulated. We know you have a job to do, and we are here to help you do it."

"*What* job?" Iris demanded.

"That we are unable to explain," Desi said. "But it is surely important, or you would not have come here."

"We came here to find the philter," Gary repeated.

Both illusions shook their heads. "You may have thought you did, but there must have been a deeper purpose," Hanna said. "You must discover that purpose, and honor it."

Mentia was thoughtful. "You were assigned a job by the Good Magician, Gary. He always has some devious purpose in mind, and he almost never lets anyone else know about it. Maybe we do indeed have a mission we have not realized."

It did make obscure sense. "Then let's do what we have to do, to get it done," Gary said.

Both illusions smiled. "Do it when you return to the

palace," Desi suggested. "You may find it a significant experience." She darted a look at Hiatus, and Gary almost thought he saw stork wings propelling the look along. It was clear that she had not given up on Lord Hiat.

Then he glanced at Hanna, and definitely saw wings on her returning glance. But he wasn't interested, because he had found a gargoyle.

The storm passed, and soon the ogres were out again, unfolding the buildings. Nothing seemed to have come unhinged, and the city was returning to its former splendor. At least they now knew the reason for its odd construction.

It was time to return. Gary took a last, covert, longing look at the isle where Gayle Goyle was hidden. He intended to see her again, when he could manage it.

11

INTERFACE

A s they entered the palace, a rumble from Gar's human stomach reminded him that they hadn't eaten recently. The storm had distracted them as they were about to go to breakfast. "Let's go directly to the banquet hall," he suggested.

"Brilliant notion," Iri agreed without irony, which was unusual for her. "I'm famished."

"Brunch will be served presently," Hanna said. "Just take your seats." She and Desi bustled off into the kitchen.

The five of them sat around the huge table. Iri glanced significantly after the two illusions and spoke in a low tone. "Can we trust them?"

"No," Gar said, remembering Gayle Goyle's warning.

"I will spy on them," Menti said. "To make sure they are out of hearing." She vanished.

Gar shrugged, getting into his role of educated person. "It is not as if we are able to conceal our activity from the servants," he pointed out. "And why should we have any concern about their motives?"

Hiat's smile almost resembled a sneer. "Always the positive outlook, eh, Gar?" he remarked.

Gar concealed his irritation, lest he spoil his reputation. In some other setting he would have liked to present the man with an item he had once seen: a punching bag. This was an innocent paper sack that looked as if it contained something interesting, but when a person opened it, a boxing glove shot out and punched him in the snoot. "At any rate, it is best that we proceed with our business expeditiously. We shall need the servants' assistance, as we are unable to handle all the details ourselves. We are simply too few in number."

'It's that infernal crossbreeding," the Queen said, scowling. "There's absolutely no excuse for it, as the gargoyle is reliable and no elixir-pollution enters the city's water supply. The fools must be sneaking out of town and drinking carelessly. They think it's a myth, or that they're invulnerable, or they just don't care."

Hiat shrugged. "This is the nature of youth, to be wild and gambling and full of potent juices." He eyed Iri suggestively. "You look young yourself, cousin. Do you not feel the urge?"

Iri flushed angrily. "Your impertinence does not amuse us, cousin. Were your contribution not essential to the project, I would find a pretext to have you banished."

Hiat made a rather too windy mock sigh. "Ever the cantankerous royal presence. Is it such an imposition to suggest that on rare occasions you take half a moment to relax? That would surely improve your disposition."

Queen Iri merely glared at him. But Princess Supi evinced her amusement with a girlish giggle. It was fun to hear the adults cutting each other up verbally.

Menti reappeared. "Caution warning. Brunch is arriving." She settled into her place.

Hanna and Desi appeared with covered platters. These turned out to bear egg-ons lined with bake-ons and bake-offs, pot-a-toe puncakes, sinnerman toes, and red, yellow, and orange juice. Gar decided to accept it without question, suspecting that he wouldn't like the answer. Menti did not eat, but that wasn't noticeable because she was kept busy catering to the Princess. Hiat and Iri seemed to enjoy their repasts.

When they were done, Desi approached. "Are my lords and ladies ready to retire to the observatory for the day's tutoring session?"

"Certainly," Iri snapped. "Did you think we were about to go out bean harvesting?"

"I am sure they did not think that," Hiat said, his tone suggesting that only an idiot would have raised the issue. "It's past season for those has-beans."

The little princess tittered, and Lord Hiat favored her with a conspiratorial smile. It was clear that the two got along well, at the expense of other members of the group. The rogue relative and the child.

The observatory was a dome in the upper section of the palace, shaped like a giant eyeball. They could focus it on almost anything in the line of sight, and that turned out to be a fair amount of Xanth, because it was above the height of the city wall. They could see beyond the Region of Madness to the rocks and rills of normal Xanth, where harpies perched in trees, merfolk swam in rivers and lakes, and many other crossbreeds and variants disported themselves. But there were no straight human folk in view. They had crossbred their species out of existence in Xanth, except for the desultory remnant here in Stone Hinge.

Hanna appeared. "And here are my lord's notes," she said, opening a cabinet containing an assortment of scrolls.

"Thank you," Gar said gruffly. He addressed Supi. "Do you recall the essence of yesterday's lesson?"

"Not at all, master tutor," the child replied, smirking.

"Harrumph. Then we shall have to go over it again." He unrolled a scroll.

"I'd rather go harvest has-beans."

"Hush, child," Menti murmured. "Don't sass Lord Gar like that."

Supi turned a pair of eyes big with naughty innocence on her. "Then how *should* I sass him, nanny?"

"Governess," Menti said patiently.

"Perhaps I can offer a suggestion," Hiat said, his devious smile implying nothing proper.

"Perhaps you can stuff it up your nose," the Queen retorted.

"Harrumph," Gary repeated importantly. "I shall now review the lesson material."

The Princess opened her mouth for a sass, but it was intercepted by a glare from the Queen and had to be stifled. Supi made a face; evidently the sass had a bad taste when held too long in her dear little mouth. Hiat turned away, ostentatiously bored with the proceedings. Menti relaxed, seeing that the lesson was getting under way at last.

The lesson concerned the proper formulation of the spell for the Interface of Xanth. The artisans of the city of Hinge had been working on it for centuries, tediously perfecting its every trifling detail, and now at last it was ready to be invoked. It consisted of a thin veil of repulsion around the west, south, and east coasts of the peninsula of Xanth, so that no Mundanes would even think to cross into magic territory. In fact they would not even realize that they had turned away from it. They would just avoid it, satisfied that there was nothing there of interest. Or they might label it as some kind of void, a shivery sensation, a scare square or a shimmery circle. Those boats that managed to cross over into magic territory would be assumed to be lost in storms. It was good protection.

"Boooring," the Princess muttered, yawning. It was clear that she was not the most avid scholar, and that there was nothing here of interest to her either. It was as if she were surrounded by her own little repulsion veil.

The north side of Xanth, which was now rejoining the ugly mainland of Mundania because of the disappearance of the inlet of the sea, would be covered by a veil of slightly different texture: illusion. It would make it seem that Xanth remained an island, separated from the Mundane coast by shark-filled water. Sharks were the Mundane equivalent of small sea serpents. Real sea serpents could not be used because they were magical, and there was to be no hint of magic, lest some idiotic Mundane put one and one together and realize that magic existed. However, since it probably was not possible to eliminate the whiff of magic entirely, the spell would deflect its seeming position somewhat, so that the magic seemed to be off to Xanth's east, in the middle of the sea. It would generate another scary feeling—

"A brrr mood!" Supi exclaimed, forgetting her boredom for half an instant.

Better that response than a closed mind, Gar realized. "Yes, a brrr-mood triangle in the sea, to make Mundanes nervous about the region, without ever quite being able to fathom why. Very good, Supi."

"Brrr mood triangle," she repeated, pleased.

But since they did need to allow some access to Mundanes, because they were needed to replenish the human stock of Xanth, distressing as the prospect was, there would be one small section of apparent access. This would be at the northwestern tip of Xanth, as far from the rest of the peninsula as possible. It was hoped that this would give the Mundanes time to learn the ways of Xanth as they made their inept way on into it, and to have some children who would have magic talents, thus becoming true Xanth natives. By the time these new colonists got down to central Xanth, they might even be bearable. Many of them would of course be eaten by dragons along the way, which was another consolation.

"Dragonfood!" the Princess cried, clapping her little hands. "Chomp chomp!" She was beginning to get into the lesson.

But even this very limited access had to be restricted, because otherwise it would be like a pot with a hole in it: endless slop could pour through. Here was where the most sophisticated portion of the Interface was to come. It would neither repel nor delude intruders; it would instead displace them somewhat in time. Thus they would be confused when they entered Xanth, and probably would not manage to come through in force. This portion of the Interface, being small, would be hard to find, and deceptive in its effect.

"Deceptive?" Hiat inquired, becoming interested despite his disdain for the proceedings. "Folk merely pass through it. So time differs on the other side; how are they to know or care about the difference?"

Gar wondered about that himself. He perused the scroll. "Because its effect differs, depending on the side you start from," he said. "A Mundane crossing into Xanth has no control over the time in Xanth's history he enters. When he crosses back, he has no control over the time or place in Mundania he returns to. It seems random. So he is likely to be lost. He can't enter Xanth, return home, fetch his family or friends, and reenter Xanth where he left it. This makes Mundane intrusion in force difficult."

"But what about the Waves?" Menti asked.

"Oh be quiet, you ignorant nanny," Iri muttered. "There won't be any Waves for another thousand years."

"Governess," Menti said, chastened.

"Of course there could be groups of Mundanes crossing together," Gar said. "So that families can come to Xanth without getting split apart. But they can't cross back and forth without risking great confusion. It seems like a reasonable compromise to restrain Mundane entry without stopping it altogether."

"Still doesn't sound deceptive to me," Hiat grumbled.

But the answer was in the scroll: when natives of Xanth, with magic talents, crossed the Interface, they could go to any time or place in Mundania they wished, with certain restrictions. For example, there had to be a peninsula in that region of Mundania, because the Interface was attached to the peninsula of Xanth and had a natural affinity for the form. It was also necessary to pay attention to the sea near the Interface, which changed colors. When it was red, the crossing would be to a peninsula near a red sea or tide of Mundania. When it was black, it would be to a black sea. When green, a green sea, or maybe a green land by the sea.

"I want to go to a plaid sea!" Supi said.

"Don't get anachronistic," Iri said. "It will be three thousand years before plaid makes its impression on Xanth."

The child, daunted by the impossibly complicated word "anachronistic," which no one in her right mind could understand, settled back into good behavior.

Furthermore, the Interface would lock on to a Xanth native, and when that person returned to Xanth after an excursion anwhere/when in Mundania, he would be exactly where he left it, and exactly when he would have been had he spent the time in Xanth without crossing. So if he spent one day in Mundania, he would return one day later in Xanth. If he spent a year, he would return a year later. So crossing the Interface would not disrupt him or his associations in Xanth; it would be just as if he had visited another part of Xanth for that time. Unless for some devious reason he preferred to return at another time, in which case it was possible if he was lucky. The Interface, in short, would be kind to Xanthians.

"But where's the deception?" Hiat demanded. He seemed obsessed with the matter.

Gar delved into the scroll again. "Because it treats Xanthians differently from Mundanes," he said. "If a Xanthian crosses into Mundania, he will say that there is no problem going back—because there is none, for him. But if the Mundane then crosses to Xanth, and back, he may be totally lost in some other time or place."

"Oho!" Hiat said, liking it.

But as Gar read further, he discovered another aspect of the situation. Mundanes, it seemed, spoke many different languages. It wasn't clear why they hampered themselves in this manner, but the fact was that a Mundane from one section could rarely converse with one from another section. When a Xanthian entered Mundania, he too was unable to understand the speech. But when a Mundane entered Xanth, he spoke the common language of Xanth, being magically converted. So probably the deception would occur when a Mundane was in Xanth, talking to a native, who thought that it was safe to cross either way. The Mundane would then cross back—and wish he hadn't.

"Yes indeed," Hiat agreed. "A very nice feature, suitably treacherous." Queen Iri shot a dark glance at him, but he fended it off without effort.

The folk of Hinge had spent several centuries perfecting the details of the Interface. It had been endlessly complicated to work out and refine each aspect, with many false starts. For example, they had made and tested prototypes of the Interface, and had folk cross repeatedly back and forth, discovering the effects. They had thought that groups would cross close together, but when one "Mundane" member of a group hung back for a look at an interesting flower, he had landed in a sea of Mundane blue grass instead of the blue-skied region the others entered. So a special detail spell had to be devised that caused the Interface to recognize the various members of a Xanth party, and keep them together even if they weren't physically or temporally quite together. All in all, a great deal of parchment scroll was used up in the course of perfecting such details.

Now it was time to invoke the masterspell for the Interface, because if they lost one more person it would no longer be possible to do. Queen Iri would craft the illusion aspect, while Lord Hiat would craft the roots the Interface would grow to anchor itself securely, and the antennae it needed to sense those who passed through it. Demoness Menti would provide the demonly substance it needed, as well as popping back and forth to make sure it was being set up exactly right. She could do what the others could not: Check the actual location of the parts of the Interface all around Xanth as they formed. Princess Supi, though the littlest of the people, had the biggest magic; she would make the raw magic essence of the Interface, giving it strength to perform and endure forever and ever. Gar was the organizer, making sure that all the others were coordinated and that the spell was being crafted exactly right.

For it had to be done right, because once it was done, it was set, and could be changed only in multiples of a thousand years. This was to prevent idle tinkering after the installation. If they made any trifling mistake during the compilation of the spell, that error would be almost forever locked into the Interface, because there might never be another group capable of fixing it. If they made a big mistake, the work of centuries might turn out to be for nothing. This was the major reason why the education of the Princess was so important. She had the most powerful magic, but was the least responsible person. She was at once their greatest strength and weakness.

"So do you understand the importance of your participation, Princess?" Gar inquired sternly. "After we compile the Interface, our job is done and we can all relax. Then you can play all you want to, in whatever way you want to. But first we must save Xanth from possible Mundane invasion."

He expected resistance, but to his surprise the child agreed. "I can use each talent only once, so I want to make my magic count in the most important way," Supi said. "This is the way."

"But Princess," Hiat protested. "That will use up most of your magic. You will be left a shell of your former self, magically. All that will be left for you to do will be to grow up into a dull irritable adult like your mother. Don't you want to save your magic for your lifelong pleasure?"

"What the %%%% side are you on, cousin?!" Iri rapped, using one of the dreaded four-letter words that no child was supposed to hear. However, Gar realized that this was back in Xanth's Dark Prehistoric Age, before the Adult Conspiracy took firm hold. The primitive folk of that time simply didn't know any better. "Are you deliberately trying to subvert the effort of the centuries?"

"What side?" Supi asked, intrigued by the slight scorch

marks and vile-smelling smoke the forbidden word had left in its wake.

"No side, dear." Menti said, rolling her eyes right over her head. "My lady the Queen merely misspoke herself." She sent a properly subservient warning glance at Iri.

"I am on the side of enlightened self-interest and common sense," Lord Hiat said. "As for that word, %%—"

"My lord Hiat is being facetious," Gar said quickly. "That is, he is joking. Of course he supports the great and important effort we are making." He sent a challenging look at Hiat, who arranged to turn away just before it arrived, so that it bounced harmlessly off the back of his head.

But privately Gar wondered: Exactly what was with Lord Hiat, that he continually sought to distract Supi from her vital dedication to the project? The matter was complicated enough, without such interference.

"I'm confused," Supi said.

"You would not be, dear, if you could see it through my eyes," Iri said.

"Okay." Supi crossed her eyes.

"No!" Gar cried, but too late.

Queen Iri's eyes crossed, and for a moment she looked almost like the child. What was happening?

Then Supi spoke up again. "Oh, I do understand, now that I've seen through your eyes. You are trying to do the right thing, and to you it looks as if Lord Hiat isn't. But maybe he doesn't really mean it, you hope."

"Yes, dear," Iri agreed, looking both discomfited and impressed. "You did see through my eyes. But please don't use up any more of your magic frivolously."

"Gee, yes. It's a good thing I didn't use the talent of switching places with you."

"An excellent thing," Iri agreed quickly.

"In any event, we can't accomplish it today," Hiat said. "We must do it only at the height of a major magic storm."

"And we must be in the center of the magic focus," Gar

agreed. "Where the gargoyle is." Ah, wonderful thought: to visit her again.

"But now you must rest," Hanna said. "To be prepared for the supreme effort, when the time comes."

Gar was glad enough to agree. These tutoring sessions tended to be emotionally fatiguing, and actually the Princess already knew what she needed to. The moment another storm came, they would be ready to act.

They retired to their several chambers, from which they would emerge later for the evening banquet. His chamber had been cleaned during his absence; he saw the last rug bee departing from the spotless rug on the floor. Gar sought to lie down on his bed—but Hanna was there before him, having somehow lost her clothing again.

"Don't you have a bed of your own, handmaiden?" he asked her somewhat shortly. "If I have taken yours, I apologize, and will seek another place of repose."

"Why should I need one?" she asked in turn. "I'm an illusion."

"Then what are you doing on my bed?"

"I hope to help you relax."

"By making me signal the stork with you? I can relax better in your absence."

"No you can't. You're all tense and tight from the burden of the tutor session. You need help to relax fully."

"No I'm not. No I don't."

She sat up, her upper torso changing its outline as she did so. It did make him think of storks, and the notion was increasingly intriguing. After all, this was a human body; perhaps he should explore its potentials. "Yes you are. Yes you do."

Maybe it would be simplest just to oblige her. But several things made him wary. First, she was an illusion, which meant that her half of the activity would not be real, even if it should seem real to him. And how could it seem real, when he couldn't actually touch her? (But she had touched him more than once. That was another mystery. He was unsatisfied with the "strong magic" explanation, as the magic was of about normal level here.) Second, he was a gargoyle, and there was a gargoyle he would much prefer to be with, whether indulging in stork summoning or anything else. If only he had his natural stone body back! Third, he didn't trust her motive. Weren't there other ways she could help him relax? Why did she insist on this?

That region of doubt loomed larger as he pondered it. What did he know of these illusions anyway? Something had to be making them, and he was satisfied that it wasn't the Queen. If Iri wanted to seduce him right now, she would be here in her own young body. He did not want to play the illusions' game without understanding their purpose.

"Perhaps you are right," he said. "However, I prefer to relax in my own fashion. If you will not let me rest alone, I shall simply ignore you." He walked to the bed and lay down beside her, closing his eyes.

"Then I shall massage you," she decided. She put her hands on his shoulders and started kneading.

It felt good, very good. So he rolled over to let her do his back as well. But that reminded him of one of his questions. "How is it that you, an admitted illusion, can touch me, here where the magic is of normal level?"

She laughed. "You can touch me too, if I wish you to. We are in the Region of Madness, and though the palace reduces the power of magic somewhat so as not to discomfit you, we do draw on it for our purposes, such as fixing food and helping you. At the moment I am making only my hands solid, but I could with a special effort make most of my torso solid too, for a little while, if you should wish to clasp it."

That answered one of his questions, but not the others. So he tried another. "Why are you trying to seduce me?"

"I am merely trying to satisfy you. If a massage is all you wish, then that will suffice. But if you should change your mind, I am sure I can be all that you might wish."

That he doubted. But then his doubt wavered. She was

an illusion in human form; couldn't she assume some other form? Suppose she chose to resemble a gargoyle? But he did not want her to do that. He already knew the gargoyle he wanted to be with. And there was his third question. "A massage will do nicely, thank you. Who is crafting you?"

"Desi and I are merely your servants," she said, her hands moving down his back. "We wish only to—"

"For a moment step out of the role," he said. "You are helping us reanimate the distant past. What of the present?"

"We are animations of the ambient madness," she said. "We are here to help you—"

"So you said before. But I doubt that madness animates itself to please intruders. There must be some person animating you, directing your images and responses. Who is that person?"

"Some other person?" she asked, sounding bewildered.

"You are an illusion. You have no being of your own. You are merely an image, a voice, and a pair of hands being projected for my benefit. Who is projecting you?"

"I can not answer that, any more than you can say who is projecting you. I know my creator no more than you know yours."

Gar considered that, and realized that she had a point. Who among the living could know the true source of his life? So though he wasn't satisfied with her answer, he realized that she had found a refuge from his curiosity.

"We have learned much about the origin and purpose of the ancient stone city of Hinge," he said. "But this has not brought us closer to the completion of our mission."

"But surely it has," she protested as she worked in his legs. She was certainly good at this! "You have to come to understand a great deal. When you grasp it all, you will know the answer to your quest."

"Perhaps," he said, not entirely satisfied. He just wasn't quite comfortable with evasive illusions. But her hands were so soothing that he was soon asleep.

* * *

Several days later another storm came. They were ready. The five of them hurried out as the city hinged into its defensive configuration, going to the protected circle and its mad island. Gar had wanted to go there before, but every time he thought he had a chance to sneak out, one of the illusions happened by. He did not want to give away his nature, so could not go while they were watching. It was frustrating. But now there was reason, and he would see Gayle Goyle again.

The storm was fierce. They barely made it to the circle before the buildings sprouted stone tentacles and tried to grab them in the manner of tangle trees. It was all the ogres could do to get the buildings folded down into their secure formats.

Even the safe circle was highly charged. They could all feel the madness laying siege to them. This was a ferocious storm! What would it be like on the island?

"We must link hands and hold tight," Menti said grimly. "Supported by each other, we can survive the intense madness. But if anyone lets go, we shall be lost."

The others nodded, knowing it was true. They linked hands, forming a circle. Gar was between Menti and Iri, with Hiat and Supi completing it beyond them. The intangible pressure eased. It was as if they were stones, making their own protected space. The madness battered at their backs, but their faces were calm.

They came to the pool. "We can't swim while holding hands," Gar said.

"We won't have to," Menti said. "Supi, this is the occasion for that spot spell we discussed."

"Yes," the child said. She was neither mischievous nor childish now; she was as deadly serious as the others. She turned her head and glanced cross-eyed at the pool. "Done."

"This way," Iri said, stepping toward the water and bringing the others along with her.

They stepped on the water, and it was firm, like a

slightly yielding mat. They walked across, holding their circle.

When they reached the island they had to flatten the circle so as to enter the inner passage. Gar found himself pressed face to face against Iri, but there was nothing remotely seductive about it. Her face was tense, and her pupils oscillated from pinpoint to enormous, and back again, constantly. He suspected that his own were doing the same.

They entered the inner chamber. Gayle halted her spouting. "You are here," she said.

"You are at the center," Menti said. "We must surround you."

"But to do that we must break the circle," Gar said.

"Put your hands on me," Gayle said. "I am proof against the madness, and will secure you for this time."

They broke the circle cautiously, putting their hands on her and moving around her until she was the center of a new circle. Now the worst intensity of madness was at their faces, blasting outward like an intangible furnace. Gar knew that they would not be able to endure this long. But they didn't need to.

"Now I craft the illusion of the template." Queen Iri said. Within their circle appeared a vertical column, translucent, like a wall surrounding Gayle.

"Now I give it substance," Supi said, concentrating. The illusion became tangible, scintillating like a living thing. The madness diminished; it was being absorbed by the circular wall.

"Now I give it roots and antennae," Hiat said, and the wall became firmer below and more sensitive above.

"Now I give it demonly presence to guide it where it must go," Menti said, and the column took on further animation.

"And now I direct it to go out to surround Xanth itself," Gar said. "On the count of three, all of us will send it there." He paused, making sure they were ready. "One. Two. THREE."

The column expanded, leaping outward. It passed them and disappeared, but they could sense its progress because of its demonly awareness. In a moment there was a feeling of a shudder, and of settling.

"It is done," Menti said. "The Interface has been set in place."

"Yes," Gar agreed. "Now we must extricate ourselves as well as we can." For the madness, though much diminished by the energy absorbed by the Interface, remained intense.

"Must you go so soon?" Gayle asked wistfully.

"We must," Menti said. "We can not endure this madness long."

"But perhaps I can visit when the storm has passed," Gar said.

"That will be nice," Gayle said.

They shifted around, breaking and reforming their circle and wending their way deviously out to the lake. They crossed it and stood in the protected circle. The lessening of the intense magic was a relief.

The storm was fading. They stood and watched as it cleared, and the ogres unfolded the buildings. Then they returned to the palace. Gar knew that they had accomplished something truly significant, but he would need at least one good night's sleep and perhaps several days' reflection before he truly understood it.

12
DISCOVERY

I 'll just pop off to make sure the Interface is in good order," Menti said, vanishing.

"And the rest of you can simply relax," Desi said, taking Hiatus' hand. The two illusions had not accompanied them to the center of magic. Gary wondered whether they had taken advantage of the occasion to have a private dialogue, but suspected that they had simply faded out for the duration.

Gary retired to his room, fatigued by their recent magical effort. But as he sought to relax on his bed, Queen Iris appeared. "Sh," she said, putting her finger to her lips. "I want to talk with you while Desi's taken with Hiatus. Hanna is out of action now, isn't she?"

"I believe so," he agreed. "She's not here at the moment, and if she were, she'd be unanimated. They usually can't animate at the same time."

"I know. Except when the magic intensifies. So I'm using my own illusion to contact you."

Gary was surprised. "You're an illusion? I took you for real."

"Thank you." She stepped forward and held out one hand. He touched it—and passed through it. "But if you prefer, I can plant the illusion in my chamber, and come here in person."

"No need." He wasn't sure what she had in mind, and her illusion self was likely to mean less mischief.

"We have learned a lot, and I value it," Iris said. "I find it easy to identify with my current persona. But we have not accomplished our mission."

"That's right," Gary agreed. "We haven't located the philter."

"And I think we won't, as long as we depend on the two foreign illusions. They have done everything to help us learn about anything except that, and they have done it with such finesse that we haven't noticed."

"Yes!" he agreed, seeing it. "Hanna's been trying to distract me every night."

"And succeeding."

"No, there was no seduction."

"Succeeding in her mission of distracting your attention," Iris clarified. She looked thoughtful. "I'd like to know her technique."

"Persistence," he said. "You tried to seduce me only once, and stopped when I demurred. She merely gives me a massage, and tries again another day. She arranges to show me her fair bare body often, as if by accident."

"Oh, like this?" Iris inquired, her gown fading out.

Gary contemplated her nude torso. "Yes, like that. I must say, your body is even better formed than I thought."

"I enhanced it," she confessed. "My real body looks more like this." The elaborate contours simplified somewhat.

"Still, quite appealing, for a human," he said. "If I hadn't met Gayle . . ."

"Persistence," she said, her robe reappearing. "Thank you. But at the moment, I'm here on business. I want to accomplish our mission, and I think we shall need to divert the illusions in order to succeed." She paused, gazing at him thoughtfully. "Would it be too much to ask that you let Hanna do it?"

"You mean—?"

"To seduce you. So that her attention will be taken up while Menti and I do some serious searching of our own."

"You think you can find the philter?"

"I'm not sure. But I think we shall never find it if we continue to depend on those two illusions for information."

She had a point. "But what about right now? Desi is with Hiatus, and—"

"And she has influenced him in a sinister manner. Haven't you noticed? We can not trust him in this context."

She had another point. "I really don't care to—"

Mentia appeared. "There's a problem with the Interface," she announced tersely. "It—"

"Oops," Iris said. They both vanished.

Gary looked around. Hanna had appeared. "I've neglected you, my lord," she said, smiling with false cheer.

Gary hoped that Iris and Mentia had gotten clear in time to avoid detection. He would have liked to talk with them longer, but he did have the gist of their concerns, which he shared. They needed opportunity to search for the philter in this ancient context, and to check the Interface closely, without any participation by the two illusions from madness.

Evidently Desi had finished with Hiatus; once he was asleep, Hanna could concentrate on Gary. He needed to take up her attention, so that Iris and Mentia could take their search farther. But the thought of being seduced by Hanna simply did not appeal to him; it was Gayle he wanted to be with. Yet he did not want to betray his real nature by being open about that. Gayle herself had warned him not to.

He looked at the illusion. What was he to do?

"I know you are really worn after your effort," Hanna said, approaching him. "I know just how to relax you."

Her gown went translucent, then transparent, showing him the form that had become increasingly alluring despite his better understanding of her nature. He was becoming entirely too human for comfort.

She wanted to distract him, and he wanted to distract her. All he had to do was let her do it. But he lacked the desire, in a certain way. "I'm not sure—"

She stepped into him and kissed him on the mouth. Caught by surprise, and somewhat off balance, he grabbed on to her to steady himself. His hands landed on her narrow back and plump rear. Both were rather interesting in their fashions. She had said she could make herself as solid as she needed to be, and she was doing so now. The illusion of sight had been augmented by the illusion of touch. Maybe her body was a mere shell without innards, and her mind did not exist, but that did not seem to make much difference at the moment.

Yet it was her mouth that commanded his main attention. What an interesting sensation this firm pressure of lips on lips generated! He had never realized how nice it could be.

She drew back a bit. "Let me take off your robe," she murmured. Her hands went to it, drawing it clear of his shoulders and body. As she did this, he looked at the front of her body, realizing just how intriguing it was. He had thought he lacked the desire, but he had not really given it a proper chance. This was not an objectionable process at all. Let her do it? He would help her do it!

In a moment she had him bare, and was embracing him again. Now his interest was intensifying in the manner of a storm of madness. All his prior cautions faded like forgotten illusions. He just wanted to proceed with what she had in mind.

"Maybe on the bed," she murmured in his ear.

Go to the bed? He would have leaped out the window with her, if she suggested it now! He moved eagerly to the bed and flung himself down on it, with her.

Suddenly they had company. The Queen and governess had returned.

"Ixnay," Iris said.

"Get out of here, you nuisance," Gary retorted.

"Separate," Mentia said, tugging at him.

"Go away!" Hanna cried, seeming even more annoyed than Gary. "This isn't your business."

"Yes it is," Iris said, putting her hands on the handmaiden's bare shoulders. But her hands passed right through the seeming flesh without effect. Iris might or might not be illusion at the moment, but Hanna was. She could be touched only when and where she chose to be.

"Get away from her," Mentia told Gary. "She's definitely not for you."

"How would you know?" he demanded, struggling to free himself from her hold. "Demons don't love."

"That's why we can be rational about the matter. This pseudo-creature is deadly." Mentia hauled harder, with considerable strength.

"Begone!" Hanna screamed.

"So maybe I can't touch you most places," Iris said. "But I can stop you from touching him where it counts." She put her hands on the illusion's torso. They passed through, of course, and came to the edge of Gary's body. Now Gary could no longer feel Hanna's torso either. Hanna could make parts of her body seem solid, but not for one person only. As a result, there was nothing to hold him close, and Mentia was able to pull him away.

"****!" Hanna shrieked, making the air turn bilious. "Then feel *this*!" Her hands formed into large sharp claws, and her face sprouted long fangs. She leaped at Iris.

But Mentia popped away from Gary and appeared between Iris and Hanna. The claws sank into demon flesh, and caught there, as if embedded in a thick mat. "You can't hurt me, you horror," the demoness said. "But I may hurt you, if you don't let go. I'll break your nails." She reached for the claws, her hands forming into metallic pincers. "And pull your teeth." Her head became a giant pair of pliers.

"$$$$!" Hanna hissed, and vanished. The odor of the word was like burning garbage.

Gary had landed on the floor when Mentia quit her support, but he hardly felt it. "What's going on?" he demanded. "Why did you break it up, when I was doing exactly what you asked me to?"

"You explain," Mentia told Iris. "I must safeguard Surprise." She vanished.

"Because we learned the folly of our strategy," Iris said, coming to help him up. She was solid; this was the real Queen. "We almost did you great harm."

"Harm? I was just getting to like it!"

"To be sure," the Queen said, grimacing. "And had you been with me, you could have continued and had a grand experience. Maybe we'll get to that, another time. But we have learned that those two fetching illusions are in fact our deadly enemies, and now that we have caught on to that, we're apt to have real trouble."

Gary began to realize that the Queen and demoness had not just been making mischief. Actually, he might have suspected it when Hanna screamed the unprintable four-letter words and sprouted claws and fangs. She had then seemed more like the Hannah Barbarian he had known before. "So what was the harm she was about to do me?" he asked.

"She was going to steal your soul."

This was so unexpected that Gary was unable for a moment to assimilate it. "My what?"

Iris picked up his clothing and offered him some of it to put back on. "I realize what a shock this is to you. It shocked us, too, but when we discovered it, we knew we had to act immediately. The two things the illusions desire are substance and souls. They can get some substance from the madness; it seems that the magic is so thick within it that it can be distilled into temporary solidity. But it can't be distilled into the stuff of souls. So those are what they have to steal, if they ever hope to become real."

"But illusions *aren't* real!" Gary protested. "How can they even have desires?"

"True illusions can't have desires. But those two do desire substance and souls," she said. "Which of course is two more than the illusions I craft. That's why I was so long about coming to this conclusion; I assumed that all illusions were like mine, which are really part of me. But you see, I have substance and soul, so I don't miss them, and neither do my illusions. But illusions that lack these things are different, it turns out. Perhaps only in the Region of Madness can there be such illusions, but it is clear that they do exist here."

"But aren't they projected by someone?" Gary asked, still confused. "The way they alternate in speech and animation, except when in the strong madness—isn't that because that person can't focus on two animations at once?"

"They may be projected by someone who lacks a soul," she said. "In which case, Hanna was merely trying to collect your soul for her master or mistress. The consequence to you would be similar."

"Someone without a soul?"

She handed him another item of apparel. "There are a number of creatures without souls. It seems that most animals lack souls, and don't miss them. But all who have any human ancestry, such as the human/animal crossbreeds, do have souls, and value them. So there might be an intelligent unsouled animal, like a dragon, hiding here in the Region of Madness. It might eat us, but then our souls would be lost to it, because killing the host frees the soul. So it is being more careful. It wants to get our souls first; then it can safely eat us. Now that we have balked it, it may decide to eat us anyway. That's why a situation that has been polite may now become dangerous."

"A dragon—hiding in the madness?" he repeated, his appreciation of the danger growing. "Smart enough to craft illusions that emulate us and talk to us intelligently?"

"It's a frightening notion," she said. "But yes, that's what we think we're up against. A dragon—or something worse."

"Then we had better get out of here in a hurry!"

"I'm not sure that's wise." She gave him the last of his clothing.

"But if it's going to eat us—"

"We think it won't eat us as long as it has the hope of getting at least one soul. The soul is incalculably valuable to it, as it is to us. But if we leave the Region of Madness, it will lose us. It would probably rather eat us than let us go. So that's when it's most likely to attack physically. We don't dare try to leave until we know a good deal more about the nature of our enemy, and then we'll have to do it by surprise, so we can get clear before it realizes. But if we act as if we're staying, it will probably hold off. After all, it hasn't even tried for my soul yet, or Surprise's."

"Probably it would have to shut down the two female illusions entirely, and craft male illusions instead," Gary said.

"Yes. And it may know that females are less foolish than males, so can't be seduced as readily. It was a close call with you—and with Hiatus."

"What happened with him?"

"That's how we got the key. He's in love with Desiree, and Desi is a real temptation. But he knows she's just an image, and he wants the original. He was willing to go along with the image, to an extent, because males *are* foolish about nymphs and the like, but he didn't turn off his mind. And finally he got her to admit what she was really after."

"Why did she tell him?"

"Hiatus' role as Lord Hiat is a pretty devious character. He hinted that he might be more seducible if he knew Desi truly loved him. She said she could truly love him if she got a soul. That gave him the hint. He told Mentia, and she told me, and we realized what Hanna wanted from you."

"I never even thought of it," Gary said, shuddering with reaction. "She said she just wanted to help me relax."

"Yes, so you would let go of your soul more readily."

"How—how would she actually take my soul?"

"We're not sure. But we think that at the moment of the ellipsis of stork summoning, a person's soul is loosened. It's the desire to share with one's partner; the two souls wish to embrace even as the two bodies are doing. So that instant of generosity may allow an unscrupulous partner to snatch the soul. Once it's done, it's done; I think you would have a hard time getting it back."

"I think I owe you my deepest appreciation for interceding," Gary said, feeling weak in the human knees.

Iris smiled. She was surprisingly attractive that way. "Just do the same for me, if it is ever required."

"But you are forewarned. You will never let your soul be loose."

"This thing is smart, very smart. It is surely figuring out a new strategy even now. We may find that as tricky to grasp and oppose as we did this one. With its command of illusion, we will hardly know what is real and what isn't."

"That's another thing. If talents never repeat—"

"How can it have the same talent as I have? That has bothered me all along. Actually it's not quite true that talents never repeat; a person in one historical time may have a talent used by another person in another time. And the Curse Fiends, or Curse Friends as they call themselves, all seem to have the same talent of cursing. But I have never known of a Magician-caliber talent repeating. There have been close variants, though. Sometimes different talents can have similar effect. So I think this creature has a talent for illusion that may seem similar to mine, but differs in its mechanism. At any rate, it's an interesting situation. I have learned how to identify its illusions, which complement mine. If I deleted my illusions, Hinge would become a mere shadow of itself. I see no point in that, so I maintain them. I think that's best, until we know more about

our enemy. For one thing, it might assume that I would
shut down my illusions preparatory to departing."

"Maintain your illusions!" Gary agreed.

"So now we had better get together with the other members of our party, and decide what to do next."

"We should keep searching for the philter," Gary said.
"That's why we came, and why we would be expected to
stay. Once we find it—"

"The crunch will come," she said. "Because our enemy
will know we're done here. Good point."

They left Gary's room and went to the one where
Mentia and Surprise stayed. The other two were there, as
was Hiatus. "I understand I helped interrupt something,"
Hiatus said to Gary.

"Thank you," Gary said feelingly. "The Queen explained."

"Just as I have explained to Surprise," Mentia said.

The child turned to Gary. "How come you weren't explaining it to me, Tooter?"

"Tutor," Gary said. "I was—" He caught Iris' warning
glance. He couldn't tell a child what he had almost done
with Hanna. "I was getting dressed."

"Oh. I thought maybe you were getting 'duced by
Desi."

"Seduced by Hanna," Gary said before he caught himself. "I mean—oh, never mind. We have a serious situation
here. What are we going to do about it?"

"On top of that, we messed up with the Interface,"
Mentia said. "I was about to tell you, before the illusion
got hot for you. It was supposed to incorporate a filter el-
ement, so that the water passing through it from Mundania
isn't polluted. But that isn't there."

"Philter?" Gary asked.

"Filter. It's right there in the specs they worked out over
the centuries. We forgot to include it in our invocation.
Now the bad water comes right in."

Gary was stricken. "That's why the geis of the gargoyle
had to continue! It was supposed to be abated by the inclu-

sion of the filter—of the magic philter. How could we have overlooked that all-important detail?"

Desi appeared. "It's our fault," she said. "I am desolate because of it."

"Desi the Desolate," Hiatus said somewhat cynically. "What do you care that we made a mistake?"

"Because if Hanna and I hadn't been distracting you, you might not have made it," Desi said.

"Distraction!" Hiatus exclaimed. "You were trying to steal my soul!"

"I didn't realize it was so important to you," Desi said, sending him a desolate glance. "I never had a soul of my own." She looked so sad that Gary was almost tempted to try to console her—and she hadn't even been directing her effort at him. "I'll do anything to make it up to you." She put one hand to her dress.

"Not that!" Iris snapped. "If you really want to help, tell us how to fix that omission from the Interface."

"Why, of course," Desi said. "Just assign the gargoyles to the inflowing rivers."

"But that's what we came to end!" Gary protested. "I'm tired of—" Then he caught himself. "Of having to depend on gargoyles to do what should be automatic."

"I'm sorry for the gargoyles," Desi said. "But the Interface is permanent. It can only be fixed by being corrected and recompiled."

"Recompiled?"

"That's what you just did, in your roles as ancient folk. You compiled it and set it in place."

"And now we are at the three-thousandth anniversary of that compilation," Mentia said. "So we can fix it."

"You could recompile it," Desi said, "but there doesn't seem to be much point."

"Why not?"

"Because the reason you didn't include the filtration factor is that you lost the philter. Since you don't have that, you can't improve on the Interface as it stands. The outer and inner filters will have to remain as they are."

"Inner filter?" Iris asked sharply. "What is that?"

"The one that confines the madness to a small region," Desi explained. "With that filter in place, only ordinary magic can escape to the main part of Xanth."

"The expanding madness!" Hiatus exclaimed. "Because of the missing filter!"

"How," Iris asked firmly, "can we fix the inner filter? Patch it with more gargoyles?"

Desi laughed. "Of course not! For that you need a spot filtration spell. Then the Interface, thus patched, will be as good as it was supposed to be."

"Except that the gargoyles will be stuck forever doing a job they shouldn't have to do," Gary said dryly, which was unusual for his species.

"Who cares?" Desi asked. "They're only animals."

Iris spoke before Gary could. "We, as compassionate folk, do not care to subject any species, whether human, crossbreed, or animal, to unnecessary drudgery. We must fix the Interface."

Mentia had another angle. "That spot filtration spell that contains the madness—how durable is it?"

"Oh, that's no problem; it will last as long as the magic does."

"Until the magic stops," Iris said, sending a significant glance around. Gary realized that she was thinking of the Time of No Magic: that was what had terminated the spot spell the ancients had made, so that the madness started overrunning its boundary and making all manner of mischief in Xanth. That was the last piece in the mystery of the problem of the present—and the philter could fix it, too. They really had to find that thing!

"We must find the philter," Hiatus said. "We know it is here somewhere. Can you help us do that?"

"No," Desi said. "It is impossible to find the lost philter."

"Let's speak frankly," Iris said. "We are here to find the philter, and we do not intend to leave without it. Why do you say it is impossible to find?"

"You want to speak frankly?" Desi asked. "Then you shall have it. You can not find the philter, because the ancients whom you have just reprised could not find it. They patched the Interface by means of gargoyles and spell, and then folded down Hinge for the last time and went to regular Xanth, where they soon crossbred the last of their species to extinction. If they couldn't find it, then neither can you, three thousand years later."

"Nevertheless, we intend to find it," Gary said. Not only was this his determination, he now knew that it could be dangerous to suggest that they might be leaving at all soon. It was better to make it clear that they would be here for some time, so that the thing behind the illusions did not decide to eat them immediately. "If you illusions do not care to help us, we shall proceed without you."

"We shall be glad to help you try," Desi said. "But you are doomed to failure anyway, because we don't know where it is either. Nobody knows where it is, or if it still exists."

"It exists," Gary said.

Desi turned a disconcertingly intense gaze on him. "What makes you so sure?"

"Because the Good Magician Humfrey told me to get the philter, and he wouldn't have done that if it wasn't possible to get."

"Who is this Good Magician?"

"You don't know that? I thought everybody knew that."

"Not anyone who is an illusion confined to the Region of Madness."

Gary grew canny. "But you know of Hannah Barbarian, who is outside the madness, and of Desiree Dryad, who has spent most of her life outside it."

"We drew these images from your mind."

"You said you drew them from *their* minds, because they were thinking of us."

"We lied. We can't go beyond the madness, or be aware of anything beyond it, except through the minds of those who enter our region."

"How can an illusion lie?" Hiatus asked.

"We can do anything we find in your minds. The Sorceress Iris knows much of Xanth, and is apt at deception."

"You can read our minds?" Gary asked. "I don't believe it."

"Why don't you?" Desi asked.

"Because if you could, you would know my secret."

"We do know your secret."

"What secret is that?"

"That you are actually a gargoyle transformed into the shape of a man."

Gary saw that the others were as taken aback as he was. "You knew this from the first? Why didn't you say something?"

"What does it matter? It is easier to deceive someone who is practicing deception."

Iris pursed her lips. "She's right, you know. You were concentrating on not letting Hanna know your true nature, while she was concentrating on seducing you."

"But she should have known I wasn't interested!" he protested.

"But she also knew that you lacked experience with the human form," Desi said. "And soon enough she turned that ignorance to her advantage. Had your friends not interfered, she would have had your soul by now."

She was right. Gary was chagrined. The illusions had been outsmarting them all along.

"So why have you illusions been so helpful?" Hiatus asked. "Why didn't you just try to seduce us at the outset?" He glanced across to Surprise, concerned about the devious subject, but the child, bored, had fallen asleep in Iris' embrace.

"We did try," Desi said. "But you were too intent on your mission, and too busy trying to figure out what was what. So we had to put you somewhat at ease, and wait for our opportunities. We almost succeeded."

Right again. "But you won't succeed now," Gary said.

"Because we know what you want, and we won't give you any of our souls. So you might as well go away."

"No, you are interesting folk, the first we have seen in Hinge for some time. We shall continue to associate with you."

"Suppose we don't want you to?" Hiatus asked.

"We're illusions. You can't stop us."

"There is something wrong about this," Iris said. "You illusions had reason to associate with us before, but now you don't. You know you won't get our souls. You don't care whether we're interesting or boring. So you must have continuing reason to be near us. What is that reason?"

Desi shrugged. "I have no answer."

"Obviously whatever is crafting these illusions is interested in us," Gary said. "So it wants to use them to spy on us. What I don't understand is why it is interested."

"Perhaps we can work it out," Iris said. "Obviously it has been around a long time, because it knows how Hinge was when it was inhabited. It knows about the Interface. What could remain here three thousand years, unaffected by the madness, and still care what a small party of human folk is doing here?"

"I can think of one thing," Hiatus said.

"No," Desi said.

"You read it in my mind," Hiatus said. "And you don't want me to say it. So it must be right."

"What is it?" Iris asked, looking slightly nettled.

"The thing that is making these illusions must be the philter itself."

"The philter!" Iris and Gary said together, amazed:

"No!" Desi cried, and faded out.

"The philter," Hiatus said grimly. "That managed to avoid being incorporated in the Interface, and now wants to avoid being found. Because if we find it, we can recompile the Interface with the philter included, and free the gargoyles and confine the madness."

"But the philter is just a thing," Gary protested.

"No," Mentia said. "He's right. I see it now. The philter is a demon."

"A demon!" Gary was amazed again. "But—"

"Which explains something that bothered me," the demoness continued. "The ability of the illusions to become partly solid. They said it was because of the intensity of the magic, but they were also doing it here in the palace, where the level of magic is ordinary. Illusions can't turn solid, but demons can." She made a huge fist and banged it against the wall, solidly.

"A demon," Iris repeated. "That does make sense. We have been dealing not with two animate illusions, but with a single demon who animates first one and then the other." She pondered a moment. "But there are illusions too; the ogres unhinging the buildings, and the quality of the food served, and the decorations of this palace—I have not been crafting these appearances." She glanced at Mentia. "Can you do such illusions?"

"Doubtful," Mentia said. "I would have to spread my substance thin." She concentrated, and thinned, and a shape appeared across the room. It formed into an ogre. But it was translucent. "This is me," the ogre said. "Connected to the rest of me by an invisibly thin thread of my essence. As you see, it's not a really good show." Then the ogre solidified as the female figure faded out. "Unless I get myself all together." The ogre shifted back to female form.

"Then how could one demon handle the rather extensive distant illusions of the ogres in the city?" Iris asked.

"Maybe a screen," Hiatus suggested. "Can you make a screen with images on it, Mentia?"

"Like this?" A wisp of the demoness' substance curled out, spread out, and formed into a vertical screen. On it pictures formed, of buildings and ogres moving among them.

"Yes!" Gary agreed. "That looks just like the scene we saw outside."

"But my powers in this respect are limited," Mentia

said. "It divides my attention. And what about the food and beds and pillows here? I can emulate one bed at a time, but I can't change the taste of a whole banquet."

"I think," Iris said soberly, "that the demonly arts may account for some of the effects we have seen. But there must be some substantial illusion along with it, and it must be an extremely powerful demon."

"A demon like none we know," Mentia agreed. "Except—"

"The Demon $X(A/N)^{th}$," Iris breathed. "And he wouldn't bother. He leaves the creatures of Xanth alone."

"And he's a whole lot stronger than this demon of madness," Mentia said. "No, this is not $X(A/N)^{th}$. This is some considerably lesser demon. But a greater demon than any ordinary one, with a remarkable combination of powers."

"Because of the madness," Gary said. "It has spent thousands of years in the madness, gaining power. So it has learned illusion, or maybe has the power to make a screen surrounding us with fake illusion. And to pad stones to seem like beds. And to run one imitation person at a time, and make her seem a bit solid at times."

"And to read our minds," Iris said.

"Though that is probably the limit of its strength," Mentia said. "Most of its power is in illusion, and it can't match even me in physical manifestation. So it does a lot of illusion, guided by what it reads in our minds, and buttresses it by just a bit of substance."

"But why does it want our souls?" Hiatus asked. "When we thought we were dealing with mere illusions, their wish for souls to make them become real was understandable. But demons don't want souls."

"I am no longer so sure of that," Mentia said. "When my better half got a soul, she really annoyed me. But here with you folk, and when we are in the ambience of stronger magic and madness, I have been coming to appreciate the virtues of souls. Almost to envy you your qualities of love and conscience. If I had a soul I would become like you in such respects. And if the philter had a soul—"

"It might be able to become enough like a person to be freed of confinement to the Region of Madness," Iris said. "A soul would give it the independence it must crave. Maybe it doesn't realize the significance of conscience; it thinks that its power would be vastly magnified."

"Aren't we conjecturing too much?" Gary asked. "Why should there be a demon in the Interface?"

"The Interface is an extremely sophisticated spell," Mentia said. "To operate properly, it has to assess all things that pass through it, and treat them as they deserve. Living things, too, even people. Only a demon could do that reliably. A demon who could read minds enough to know what folk want without their telling it, and use illusion to see and shape aspects of the Interface and to define and confine the Region of Madness. There must be many specially talented demons bound to it. But one got away."

"But we didn't summon any demons when we compiled it."

"We didn't really compile it," Iris said. "We simply re-enacted what the ancients did. They knew what they were doing; we merely pantomimed. They could have summoned and bound demons into it. All except the one that sneaked out. By the time they realized what had happened, it was too late; they couldn't recompile for a thousand years, so had to patch it up here and there."

"And that worked well enough," Mentia said. "Until the Time of No Magic, when the inner spell dissipated. The main external Interface must contain mechanisms of restoration, so reappeared when the magic returned, and the gargoyles of course remained loyal. But the spot spell containing the madness was gone, and slowly the effects of that loss manifested. Now at last we know the whole truth."

"Now we know why the Good Magician sent us here," Iris said. "He wants us to deal with it."

"To save Xanth from madness," Hiatus agreed.

"And help ourselves in the process," Gary said.

They gazed at each other. "This," Mentia said soberly,

"may be the most important quest any of us have ever dreamed of."

"The most important quest anyone in Xanth ever undertook," Iris added. "And we're such a motley crew."

"And we don't even know what to do," Gary said.

The others nodded agreement.

13
FUTURE

S o we shall simply have to try again to find the philter, and incorporate it in a recompiled Interface," Iris concluded. "That will not only abate the Geis of the Gargoyle, it will enable us to leave the madness safely."

It occurred to Gary that finding the philter might not be any easier than it had been before, and incorporating it into the Interface might be still more difficult, if they could figure out how to do a recompilation for real instead of in emulation. But he did not want to be negative, so he remained silent.

"But we looked for it before," Hiatus said. "And got nowhere."

"On the contrary," Iris said. "We got here. We have made enormous strides in understanding and vision. So we must be on the right track. We must continue our search."

Gary had to agree with that. But he had a question of his own. "We looked everywhere we could think of before. Where else is there to look?"

"We looked everywhere in the present ruins," she said. "Now we have seen the history of the city of Hinge. We must look throughout that history. Somewhere along it we are bound to find the philter."

"But there is so much to search!" Hiatus said. "How can we possibly cover it all?"

Iris nodded. "We shall have to split up again, to multiply our efficiency. With five separate searches—"

"I don't think so," Mentia said. "Remember that the philter is aware of us, and is trying to stop us. We don't know the extent of its powers, but I am the only one of us who is proof against the mischief of a demon. It would be foolhardy to let it attack us individually."

"Um, fair point," Iris agreed. "But we do need to increase our efficiency of searching. I'm not sure how else to do it."

"Efficiency is no use if the philter picks us off individually," Hiatus said, looking around nervously.

"I hate to say it," Gary said. "But there is another consideration. The philter doesn't seem to be able to focus on two things at the same time. That is, when Desi is animate, Hanna is on autopilot, and vice versa."

Iris eyed him. "So you and Hiatus can't be seduced simultaneously. Can't you live with that?"

"If we remain in one party, the philter can easily watch us. But if we make several parties, it can watch only one at a time. Then the others can search without distraction."

"Now there's a point!" Mentia said.

Iris nodded. "A point indeed. So it seems we must take the risk for the sake of an additional benefit. Suppose we break up into two groups? Three would be better, though. Maybe you, Mentia, could search alone safely."

"I could, but I'm not sure the rest of you could make safe pairs. I should probably be with one of you."

Gary had an idea. "Gayle Goyle—if we stop drinking water from the pool for a while, she can go off duty. Maybe I could search with her. Because she's a gargoyle, I know I can trust her. And when I explain the situation to her, I'm sure she'll agree to help us."

"And she should have an excellent notion where the

philter might be," Mentia agreed. "Because she's been here for three thousand years."

"But only on the island in the pool, in the enclosure," Iris pointed out. "That's not a good place to see anything."

"Only illusions," Gary agreed ruefully. "Still, she's secure against the demon, because it can't pull her soul from stone, and a gargoyle in its natural state fears no other creature. Except maybe a roc bird that could pick up a gargoyle and drop it from a great height so that it cracks into pieces—which I'm sure this philter demon can't do."

Iris exchanged a glance with the others. "Seems viable to me, if she cares to help you search." She considered. "That leaves four of us to make two parties. We should have one strong person in each party."

"None of us are—" Hiatus began.

"In the sense of being able to handle the demon philter," Mentia said. "Perhaps I should accompany you, Hiatus."

"I'll do my best to protect you," Hiatus said.

Mentia made an obscure smile. "Thank you." Gary realized that it was the demoness who would protect the man.

"Which leaves me with Surprise," Iris said. "I can keep alert, and she has enough magic if it is required. Now where shall we spread out to search?"

"Since we have no idea where to look, maybe we should just follow our noses," Hiatus suggested.

"And meet here by evening," Iris agreed. "But Mentia—if you would, you might pop back and forth every so often, to make sure that none of the parties are in trouble. We don't know what the philter will be up to, but we can be fairly sure it doesn't want to be found."

"And if we see either of those two illusions again," Mentia said grimly, "remember that they aren't *just* illusions, and they aren't our friends."

"And that they are going to try to prevent us from finding the philter," Gary said. "And steal our souls. So that's not the time to push the search too hard. But if we can take up their attention for a while, the other two parties may be able to get through the standing illusions better."

"Yes," Iris agreed. "If we're smart, we can turn the situation to our advantage, and distract the philter instead of letting it distract us. But watch it; remember that it can read our minds, when one of its figures is close. So try not to think of what we're doing then."

"Which is one tricky order," Hiatus said. "But I know one way to do it. Think instead of how the figures may be there to try to destroy us."

"That should be effective," Iris said. "Thank you so much for giving us that lovely notion." She looked around, as nervous as any of them. But it was the way it had to be. Where were those two philter figures? Were they planning some special mischief, or was the philter merely resting?

They left the palace. Gary felt the intensity of magic increase as they stepped outside; Hanna and Desi had been right about that. But he could handle it, when there wasn't a madness storm.

He made his way to the charmed inner circle. Then he swam across the pond. In the middle of his swim, Hanna appeared. "What are you up to, Gary?" she inquired, walking on the water beside him.

He glanced up at her—and right up under her flaring skirt, along her legs, almost to her knees. He lost his swimming stroke. There had been a time when he wouldn't have noticed such a display, which display he suspected was not accidental. But he had been in this human form too long, and was reacting as it did. Only when he started to breathe water did he manage to yank his clinging eyeballs away from the sight. But now he couldn't answer, because he was too busy sputtering.

"You poor thing," she said solicitously, squatting before him. "Let me mop your face." A handkerchief appeared in her hand, and she dabbed at his watering eyes.

The odd thing was that it helped. In a moment his vision cleared, and he looked—straight between her slightly spread knees. And tried to breathe more water. Only sheer luck and some strategic shadow had prevented him from seeing her panties.

"My, you really have a problem," she remarked in dulcet fashion. "Perhaps you should get out of the pool before you drown."

"Just get out of my way!" he gasped, desperately resuming his forward motion.

Unfortunately she did not. She remained squatting on the water, and his face passed right through her flesh, heading for the darkest shadow. Only an emergency clamping of his eyelids prevented him from getting his eyeballs petrified. And of course that was her intention. As a creature mostly of illusion she couldn't do him much physical damage, or perhaps did not want to while there was any hope of stealing his soul, but she could threaten to freak out his mind. Maybe she thought that if he lost his mind, she would be able to get his soul. He wasn't absolutely sure she was wrong.

Yet he knew she did not really exist. She was an animation crafted by a cynical demon. Legs and panties meant nothing to her; they were merely presented to make mischief for him. So why was he taking it so seriously? The answer was that he shouldn't. She hadn't actually shown him anything critical, and whatever she had was not real anyway. After all, he had seen her whole bare body in the bed. Of course that was an important qualification; there had been no panties on it, so his brain hadn't gone into overload. Probably there weren't any on it now; it was all a bluff. Yet considering what Mentia had told him about such things—maybe now that he knew—such a sight would indeed freak him out.

He felt the slope of the center island coming up beneath him. He had made it across. So he put down his feet and opened his eyes, ready to wade out of the pool.

There stood Hanna, garbed only in pale blue panties.

Gary fell backwards in the water, stunned. He had been completely unprepared for such a frontal assault. His eyes were unable to tell the difference between illusion and reality.

Sputtering again, he realized that he had after all survived her worst, or maybe her next-to-worst. She had tried to make him drown, but he hadn't. He crawled up the slope and out of the pool, keeping his eyes peering down.

When he stood on the island and looked around, Hanna was gone. He had defeated her. He knew that if she showed him her panties again, he would be better able to handle it, now that he knew that such handling was possible. She knew it too. All repeated shocks could do was harden him to the sight. He was after all not a true man, so was probably less vulnerable than, say, Hiatus would be.

He tramped on inside, feeling the magic intensify around him. He hoped it would not take long to persuade Gayle to join him. He had of course suggested that he approach her not merely to make a third team, but because he really liked the idea of being with her. Too bad he wasn't in his natural form. But he had to admit that this human form had been useful so far despite its liabilities of soft flesh, hunger, and vulnerability to the sight of panties.

He saw the gargoyle. What a lovely creature she was, from her grotesque face to her reptilian wings! "Hello, Gayle Goyle," he said, suddenly shy.

She closed her mouth, cutting off the waterspout, and turned her head. "Why hello, Gary Gar. It's so nice to see you again, even in—" She broke off.

"It's all right," he said. "They know I'm a gargoyle, so I don't need to conceal it any more. I wish I had my natural body back."

"I wish you did too," she said. "What brings you here, Gary?"

"I—we are searching for the philter, and I wondered if you—if you would like to—that is—"

Gayle shook her head sadly. "I do not know where the philter is, Gary."

"If you would like to—to help me search for it. Because we need it. To abate the geis."

"But I must purify the water here."

"Why?" he asked. "There have been no people to drink

from it for thousands of years. The illusions don't need pure water. We have been using it, but we are merely visitors who won't drink from it while you're away from it."

"But the geis—"

"Applies to water flowing into Xanth from Mundania. What you are doing here is merely a service to the inhabitants of the stone city of Hinge, who are long gone. I think you are entitled to a break. And if we find the philter—"

"I hadn't thought of it that way," she said. "I suppose I can relax for a few hours." She moved on her pedestal, stretching her lovely muscles. "Yes, I will help you search, Gary Gar," she said. "But I want you to know it is mainly because I like you."

"I asked you mainly because I like you," he admitted.

"Come on. I will carry you out of the strong magic. Your present form is really not adequate to handle it, no offense."

"Oh, I agree! But when my quest is done, I will be transformed back to my natural shape. That is one reason I hope to conclude it quickly."

"I hope I can help you to conclude it quickly." She squatted down, and he climbed on her stone back between her wings and took hold of her mane. It was a joy to be so close to her.

She rose and bounded down the passage, carrying his slight weight easily. She emerged to the pool and leaped in. Of course she sank to the bottom, but he hung on, knowing that she would be across it and back in air very soon.

Indeed she was. "Now where were you thinking of looking?" she inquired as the water coursed off her sleek stone hide. "No, don't get off; I can readily carry you, and we can move more swiftly this way."

"I really have no idea," he confessed, glad to remain on her. "I had thought no further than gaining your company."

"Does it matter where we look?"

"Since I have no idea where the philter is, a random

search is probably as good as a planned one. The others of my party are searching similarly, elsewhere. Do you have any preference?"

"Actually, I do," she said shyly.

"What is it?"

"For three thousand years I have heard the trains of thought passing close by, and wondered where they go. I would like to follow one. Do you think there's any chance the philter could be where the trains live?"

"Why, I don't know," Gary said. "I think it could be there as readily as any other place. Perhaps more readily, because we did not search to the end of the line; we merely rode the train here and got off."

"Then let's intercept the next train, and follow it to its lair. There we can search."

"We don't need to follow it," Gary said grandly, suffering a flash of inspiration. "We can ride it there."

"Oooo, wonderful!" she cried, delighted.

They went to the station. Soon a train pulled in. On its broad front was a sign that said FUTURE.

Gary got off her. His clothing remained wet, but he knew it would dry in time. "We shall go to the future," he said.

The train ground to a massive halt. No one got off, so Gary led the way up the steps to a coach. Gayle bounded up after him. She was solid stone, but the train was metal, and did not even settle perceptibly under her weight. They entered the coach.

"Oh, I forgot; these are human seats," he said. "They won't do for you. Maybe we can find a coach made for gargoyles."

As they walked down through the coach, the train started moving, at first slowly, then more swiftly.

The second coach was much better. It was open in the center, with seats lining the sides that could be turned around to face out the broad windows. Gary took one, and Gayle lay beside him on the floor, quite comfortable.

The scenery had changed. The stones of Hinge were

gone; now there were fields, forests, rivers, mountains, and chasms passing in their separate splendors. When he looked out the other side, he saw that the train tracks were forming a large turn, for they curved before and after, and allowed nothing to make them deviate from it. Where there was a river, they crossed it with a bridge; where there was a mountain, they bored through it with a tunnel; where there was a forest, they cut a narrow swath through it. They were inflexible about their course.

Gayle was delighted. "Oh, it has been millennia since I have seen scenery like this! What a pleasure it is."

Gary had thought the sights routine. Now he looked again, appreciating them as she saw them. All of Xanth was open to exploration without limit. Suddenly he wanted to bound out into that scenery and range through it all, with Gayle beside him.

But he was in his human form. If he tried to bound out of the train, he would probably break a limb. So he had become a prisoner of another kind, in a limited body.

"When this is done, and I have my real body back, let's run together through all of this, until we have seen it all," he said.

"It's a date," she agreed.

They spied a billboard. WELCOME TO THE FUTURE

"We are arriving," Gary said.

Some buildings appeared. They were of stone, so it seemed they had circled back to Hinge. Had the train changed its mind about going to the future?

But these buildings differed from those they had seen before. They were sleeker and of odd architectural designs. Some had grown exceedingly tall, so that their tops scraped against the clouds. Others spread wide, with flying buttresses and projecting ledges, as if determined to cover as much ground as possible.

There was another big sign. HENCE—POPULATION MIXED

The train passed a large paved-over field where a house with a pointed dome and tubular foundations squatted.

There didn't seem to be any doors or windows in its sides. "What a peculiar structure," Gayle remarked.

"I wish we could tell what it houses," Gary said.

Hanna appeared, entering the car. "I shall be glad to oblige," she said. "That is the spaceship of thought, which will take you farther than this train of thought can. It is based here in the great future city of Stone Hence."

"Hence?" Gayle asked.

"All the ships start here and get themselves hence in a hurry," Hanna explained.

Gary wasn't pleased to see her. "We're not trying to travel far. We're trying to find your master the philter, and I doubt you have any intention of helping."

"Her master?" Gayle asked, perplexed.

"We have concluded that the philter is a demon who doesn't want to be found, and that it is using two images to divert us from finding it. So Hanna the Handmaiden is not our friend. Indeed, she has been trying to distract me all along."

"What did she do?" Gayle asked.

"When I swam across the pool to join you, she showed me her panties."

"But human girls aren't supposed to do that."

"Precisely. I almost drowned. If I had been a real man, I probably would have."

"No, I would have saved you," Hanna said.

"And taken my soul."

"Well, it might have come loose in the process."

"So it was the philter making the illusions," Gayle said. "I never realized."

"Because we didn't want you to," Hanna said.

Gary felt a thought bobbing just below the surface of his mind, and finally it worked its way up. "You mean Hanna was talking to you, before we came along?"

"No, the image was of a gargoyle," Gayle said. "I was lonely for company of my own kind. But I knew it wasn't real. That's why I asked to verify you. I was thrilled to discover you were real, even if you looked like a man."

"How did you know him for a gargoyle?" Hanna asked.

"Gargoyles know their own kind. His body was like illusion, but I felt the reality beneath. Just as I knew you were no gargoyle, I knew he was no man."

"And now you are helping him find the philter?"

"Yes." Gayle returned her gaze to the window, evidently losing interest in the figure.

"Do you know what they mean to do with the philter?"

"Use it to abate the geis of the gargoyle."

"But that will make it prisoner in the Interface."

Gayle shrugged. "We gargoyles have been prisoner of the geis ever since the philter defaulted on its purpose in existence. It is time to correct that situation."

Hanna frowned. "So you are no friend to the philter."

"I don't wish the philter any harm," Gayle said. "I'm just tired of having to do what it was supposed to."

"As am I," Gary said. "So it's time to set things right."

"I thought you gargoyles liked purifying water."

"We do," Gary said. "But we have had no time off from it. We would like to be free to explore sometimes."

"I have an idea," Gayle said. "Suppose your master the philter purifies the water of Xanth half the time, and we gargoyles do it the other half?"

"No," Hanna said.

"You won't meet us halfway?" Gary asked.

"No."

"One quarter of the way?" Gayle asked.

"No."

"Then how much of the way?" Gary asked.

"No part of the way. The philter isn't interested in being harnessed."

"Does that seem fair to you?" Gayle asked.

"What does fairness have to do with it?"

"Demons have no conscience," Gary said. "They don't care what's right or wrong, only what works for them."

Gayle was outraged. "You mean that for three thousand years I have loyally confined myself and purified the water of the pool of Stone Hinge, because my conscience told me to honor the geis, and the one for whom I was filling in doesn't care?"

"Exactly," Hanna said. "You have a problem with that?"

"Now I do," Gayle admitted. "I think I have been a fool."

"Well, you're an animal, and you have a soul," Hanna said. "All souled creatures are foolish."

"Then why do you want my soul?" Gary demanded. "Don't you know it would make you just as foolish?"

"No it wouldn't. I'm a demon. I know better."

Gary exchanged a glance with Gayle. "I'd almost like to give her a soul, so she'd find out," he said.

"Don't do it," Gayle said. "Demons don't necessarily react to souls the same way as others do."

"And this is a very hardened demon," Gary agreed. "It's not worth the risk. Some souled folk are pretty mean, I understand."

"Yes, there seem to be some degraded souls," Gayle agreed. "And surely any soul the philter got hold of would soon be degraded. So it mustn't have any of ours."

Hanna's eyes narrowed. "So it's like that," she said grimly.

"I think it always was like that," Gary said. "You watched Gayle doing your job for three thousand years, and you don't care. You have shown that you are not a worthy creature. So go away and let us continue our search."

"I will go when I choose to go," Hanna said. "And I choose to remain, for now. I will guide you through the future."

"Why should we pay any attention to you?" Gayle demanded. "Since we know you are trying to hinder us?"

"Because you won't be able to ignore me," Hanna said.

Both gargoyles laughed.

Then Gary's laugh was choked off as Hanna's dress went translucent, showing the fuzzy outline of her panties. He tried to close his eyes, but they refused to close. They were locked on to the almost vision, as if he were peering into the peephole of a hypnogourd.

After a moment Gayle realized that he had stalled out. Then she realized why. She bounded between him and Hanna, blocking his view. Then he was able to blink and clear his gaze. He had thought he would have less trouble with such sights, but realized he had misjudged the case. His human reactions were too strong.

Then Gayle stiffened. Her whole body became as rigid as the stone it was, making her like a statue. What had happened to her? Surely the sight of human panties wouldn't bother her, both because she was inhuman and female.

He needed to find out what Hanna was doing to freak out Gayle. But did he dare risk getting freaked out again himself? He realized he had to, because it was his fault Gayle was here.

He peered around her. There was the image of a pool of water. But it had a hole in it. In fact it was a water hole.

Oh, no! The hole was sucking in the water and making it vanish. That was the bad thing about it: the water around it tried to fill it in, and got consumed, until no water was left. That was an awful sight to a gargoyle, who lived to make good water available to others. Where would the gargoyles be if all the water disappeared into the water hole?

He stepped between Gayle and the image. He was in manform, so not quite as horrified as she was by the sight. Men were typically careless about water, though they needed it as much as any other creatures did.

When her gaze at the water was interrupted, Gayle relaxed. "Oh, that's horrible," she breathed. "I can't abide a water hole."

"No gargoyle can," Gary said.

The vision fuzzed. Hanna reappeared, fully clothed. "Had enough?" she asked.

Gary stifled an angry retort. "Maybe we should have a

truce," he suggested. "We'll be halfway civil to you if you are halfway civil to us."

"Agreed."

"But we won't give up our search for the philter."

"Even if you found it, you wouldn't know what to do with it," Hanna said. "So you might as well enjoy your tour of the future."

"We might as well," Gary agreed, less than pleased. He looked out the window again, and saw the funny building on the paved field. "But we haven't moved!" he said, surprised.

"Well, I was distracted," Hanna said. "I can't focus on too many things at once. That will change when I get a soul."

Gary remembered how Hanna and Desi had alternated speech and animation when they were together. He understood the principle. Hanna had been continuously active, so the outside illusion had frozen in place. But did this mean that the train and the scenery, and indeed the whole land of the future, was all an illusion crafted by the philter? If so, it was another distraction from their search.

But illusion could be penetrated. If he and Gayle kept alert, they might spy what they sought anyway. And there was one benefit: if they were taking up the philter's attention, then the other two searching parties were free of it, and would have a better chance. So Gary and Gayle might be accomplishing more than they seemed to be.

"So how does that building travel in space?" Gary asked as the train moved on by it.

"Watch."

They watched. In a moment smoke poured out from the base of the building. It rose into the air. Now it was apparent that fire was jutting out of its bottom, like a dragon in terrible trouble. To get away from that fire, the building was hauling itself ever higher. But the fire followed it, burning its tail. The building shot right up into the sky, the fire in relentless pursuit.

"And so the spaceship is off to Alpha Centauria," Hanna said. "And you can go there too, if you wish."

"A centaur named Alpha?" Gayle asked, impressed.

"A centaur world named Alpha."

"Not Xanth?"

"This is the future," Hanna said. "The magic has spread to other worlds. Now each species has its own world. The centaurs really appreciate that, because they never liked associating with ordinary creatures."

Gary had heard that. Centaurs were pretty snotty crossbreeds. But that made him realize something else. "There were no centaurs in Hinge. Where were they?"

"They did not appear until Hinge was deserted," Hanna said. "A few more fresh human beings straggled in with their horses, and inadvertently drank from a love spring. The centaurs don't speak of that; they are ashamed to admit that there is human stock in their lineage."

Gary had heard that too. He could understand their position. He didn't like to think that there was human influence hidden somewhere in his own ancestry, though the evidence of the souls was suggestive. "The Hinge spring?"

"Of course not!" Gayle said. "I kept it pure."

Oops. "Of course; how could I forget! So it was some unfiltered spring."

"Yes," Hanna agreed. "The early centaurs did come to Hinge and live there for a while, but in the end they preferred to avoid the madness storms and migrated south to Centaur Isle. It didn't matter, because there was no need for inhabitants in the madness region once the Interface had been established."

"Established without the philter," Gayle said.

"Which absence cost us gargoyles dearly," Gary said. "And is now costing the rest of Xanth more subtly. Poor Desiree!"

"Hiatus will take care of her stupid tree," Hanna said disdainfully.

"How, when he can't even grow ears straight, in the madness?"

"But he can grow round roots in the madness—and that's what that tree needs, to replace its square roots. The nymph of the tree will be most grateful."

"How do you know all this?" Gary asked.

"This is the future. All things are known."

"Including how we'll find the philter?"

"You will never find the philter."

"And you will never tell the truth about that," he retorted.

She shrugged. "We shall see."

The train pulled into another station. "This is where you get out," Hanna said.

"Suppose we prefer to ride on to another station?"

"You can't. This is the end of the line. You can proceed farther only on the ship of thought."

Gary looked at Gayle, and shrugged. The illusions would be whatever the philter decided they were. And if there were another station, that would probably just be another variant of the same city. "So we'll search in Stone Hence," he agreed grudgingly.

They left the train. The future city spread out around them and towered above them impressively. At the street level there were many fancy shops with lighted displays. Was the philter likely to be in any of them?

He had a bright idea. "Let's see if there are any plumbing shops here," he said to Gayle.

As they looked down the street, they saw an especially bright store with a marquee: PLUMBING GALORE. That was almost too convenient, but still worth checking.

Inside the store were many weird objects. They seemed to relate to water, but their purposes were unclear. "What is this?" Gary asked.

"That's a flush toilet," Hanna said.

"What does it flush?"

She said a dirty word.

After a moment, he realized that the answer had been literal. *That* was what it flushed. Embarrassed, he went on.

They spied a kind of enameled basin with an impossible array of things jammed in it. "What is that?"

"The kitchen sink. Everything is in it except itself."

"What does this shop have in the way of water filters?" he asked, wondering how she would react. Was it possible by some devious rule of mad magic that she would have to show him what he asked for?

She showed him a collection of little meshes and screens. There were hundreds of them. One of these might be the philter—but how would they know it from all the others? And if they spotted the real one, how would they handle it? A demon could not be held in the hand; it would simply fade out and appear elsewhere.

The more he thought about it, the more hopeless his quest seemed. How had the Good Magician expected him to capture a demon?

"You look as if you are realizing that your quest is hopeless," Hanna said smugly.

Then he remembered: she could read his thoughts. That's where she had gotten the image of Hannah Barbarian from. So even if he got a good notion where the philter was, she would know it as soon as he did, and would do something to prevent him from following up.

"You are catching on," Hanna murmured appreciatively.

He sighed. He turned to Gayle. "She knows what I'm thinking. That means the philter knows. So I don't have a chance to surprise it, and if I get close to it, it can move or divert me before I catch it. I don't know what to do."

"But can it read *my* thoughts?" Gayle asked.

"Of course I can," Hanna said.

"Then what am I thinking now?"

"Why should I tell you what you already know?"

"Because I don't think you can read stone thoughts," Gayle said evenly. "You can get into Gary's fleshly head, but my soul and thoughts are secure from you. Prove it isn't so."

Hanna scowled. That was answer enough.

"Then you take the lead," Gary said, relieved. "And if you locate the philter, grab it with stone."

Gayle smiled, showing formidable teeth. "I shall. I think I owe it a reckoning."

"You're fooling yourself," Hanna said. "I call your bluff: find the philter. I'll guide you anywhere you ask."

"Let's take that spaceship building," Gayle said. "I would like to see Alpha Centauria."

"As you wish." Hanna led them from the shop and to the spaceport. Another ship was waiting there.

They took an odd moving stairway up to a door that opened in the side of the ship. Gary was bemused; this just wasn't his idea of a ship, as it had no sails and was standing on its tail end. But he had seen the other one flee from the fire at its tail, so it evidently had strong magic propulsion.

"What kind of stair is this?" Gayle asked as she balanced somewhat nervously on forepaws and hindpaws.

"It is called an escape-later," Hanna said. "Escalator for short. Because it takes more time to get in and out of the ship with it, but is more convenient."

"More convenient than what?" Gary asked.

"Than jumping."

She had a point. It was now a long way down.

Hanna entered the ship, and Gary was about to follow, when there was a noise behind. He turned, startled, and saw Gayle catching at the steps. The esk-later seemed to have lost a step or two, putting her in peril of falling.

Quickly he reached out, catching her by a stone wingtip as her hind feet broke through the stairway. He hauled her in—but her stone weight was much greater than his, and he succeeded only in jerking himself toward her.

"Let go!" she cried. "You'll just hurt yourself too!"

"Not without you," he said. He caught the rail with his free hand and hung on desperately.

Gayle scrambled with all four feet, precariously balanced, but in a moment his pull on her wing enabled her to get more of a grip and haul herself up to secure footing.

"That escalator is intended for human use," Hanna said. "Your great weight must have overstressed it." She did not seem unduly alarmed.

"I must be more careful," Gayle said, somewhat shaken. Gary was shaken too. A fall from this height could have shattered her into a dozen pieces.

The interior of the ship was fairly nice. There were a number of small compartments, and special seats with harnesses. "These are acceleration couches," Hanna explained. "You must strap yourselves in."

"But they don't fit me," Gayle protested.

"That may be a problem," Hanna agreed. "Maybe you will be all right on the deck."

Gary strapped in, and Gayle crouched down. "Now the acceleration will be strong at first, but will ease once the ship attains escape velocity," Hanna said. "Just hang on until it passes." She faded out.

The ship shuddered. Then Gary felt a huge invisible hand press him down so heavily that it was hard to breathe. He gasped and clenched his muscles, fighting to maintain consciousness. Somehow it seemed that the pressure was not merely down but out, as if something wanted to dump him out the window. But he managed to realign, internally, and shore up his constitution. His flesh might be human for the nonce, but his nature was gargoyle, and there was stone in his personality as well as his natural body.

After what probably was not as long as it seemed, the pressure eased, and he was able to function normally again. There was still pressure there, making him weigh perhaps twice what he normally did, but he could handle that readily enough. He looked down—and Gayle was gone.

Alarmed, he looked all around. He saw claw scrape marks on the floor. They streaked back to the rear of the compartment, where the access hole was. And there was Gayle, her teeth locked around the leg of a couch.

Gary remembered how he had felt the push toward the

window. The same force seemed to have affected Gayle. But she had been near the hole rather than the window. Had she slid into the hole, she would have taken a fall with the full power of the downward pressure. That would have been worse than the fall from the esk-later.

He unbuckled himself and went to her, treading slowly and heavily. "I never thought the force would be so strong," he said.

"Neither did I," Gayle said, after prying her teeth from the leg. She, too, could handle this reduced level. "I was lucky to save myself."

Gary looked out the window. Stars, planets, and comets were whizzing by. "We must be traveling very fast," he said.

"And going very far," she agreed.

"Where is Hanna?"

"She must be seeing to one of the other pairs."

"So we're on autopilot now."

"We must be. See, there's a repetitive quality to those stars out there."

"Yes," he agreed. "So maybe we have to talk, while she figures we'll be busy with the extra weight. She probably doesn't realize how tough gargoyles are."

"Talk?"

"I don't think those accidents you have had are coincidental. This is mostly illusion, remember. How can we fall, if we aren't really high up? So why should that esk-later give way under your weight, if it's just a semblance? Weight can't crush an illusion."

"I didn't think of that," Gayle said. "And the way I slid to the hole—yet how could a fall hurt, if it's illusion?"

"But it *could* hurt—if the illusion covers a real pit. I saw Iris dispatch a monster by using illusion to trick it into running into a chasm. Since the philter controls these special illusions, those problems must have been intentional."

"So there really is a pit," she said. "I reacted when I seemed to be falling, but I also realized that it wasn't fully real. Now I'm suspicious that it is." She moved to the access hole in the floor and put a paw in. "There's a void here, all right." She considered half a moment. "But we knew there was a hole here, because we used it to enter this chamber. What about the way the esk-later started to collapse under my weight? You had gone right over the same place."

"Maybe in the real world, there's a pit there, covered by light boards. They supported my weight, but not yours."

She nodded. "I believe you are right. She wouldn't have led us over that spot just by chance. But why would the philter want to get rid of me, and not you?"

"Because it can't get your soul or read your mind. You are of no benefit to it, and may be a danger to it, now that you're looking for it instead of purifying water."

She nodded again. "You are very smart, Gary. But I have to say that I don't know anything about the philter that might help you find it or control it. I never even saw it in all my time in Hinge."

"But it's pretty smart. You must know something or be able to do something that makes you dangerous to it. So even if we don't actually find it here, we have learned something important to the quest."

"Perhaps," she agreed dubiously. "I shall walk very carefully from now on. I hadn't realized how dangerous illusions could be."

"I have noticed another thing," he said. "This is supposed to be the future, with all manner of wondrous things, but we really haven't seen a lot. Just some fancy buildings, a plumbing shop, and this spaceship, which is pretty much like a bedroom chamber. Surely there must be more than this."

"Not if it is limited to the imagination of the philter. It must have drawn notions from your mind about what you thought the future would be like, and animated them. Maybe some notions are from the minds of your companions. So it's just a show to divert you for a while."

"A diversion," he said thoughtfully. "Yes. The philter

doesn't want us to find it, so it is diverting us. I think we won't find it on the centaur world, or any of the others."

"But it is concerned about something I might do," she said. "I wish I knew what."

"Just keep yourself safe until we find out," he said. "Also—"

"Also?"

But Gary was suddenly shy. He couldn't say what was on his mind. But perhaps she suspected.

They returned to their original places and relaxed, waiting for the illusion to get off autopilot. It was comfortable just being quietly together.

14
PAST

I ris watched Gary Gargoyle go. The poor creature was so eager to be with the female gargoyle it was pitiful. But perhaps Gayle would help him, and they would learn something useful. Meanwhile Iris intended to make a serious search, and try to wrap up this mission efficiently. Because she knew how dangerous it could be to remain in the Region of Madness any longer than they had to.

If she could just decide where to look for the demon philter! That was the problem. She knew that this was all illusion, much of it hers and much of it the demon's. She could abolish her own illusion if she chose, but preferred to maintain it until their mission here was done. She could recognize the philter's illusion, and penetrate it by stepping into it, but she couldn't abolish it. But would the philter cover its location with concealing illusion—or have no illusion there, to fool her? She didn't know. Consequently she didn't know where to start. About all she was sure of was that the illusion wasn't lying out in plain sight, because they had done a fair job of checking through the ruins before any illusion was added, and there just hadn't been anything special there. She was sure of that, because of her ability to recognize illusion, whether hers or the demon's. There had been no illusion in the ruins of Hinge until she started it.

Then she reconsidered. The gargoyle's pool—they had seen it, and drunk from its clean water, without being aware of Gayle Goyle on the island in the center. The philter must have concealed it. But how, if not with illusion? Maybe in the demon manner that Mentia had shown, forming a screen around the island. That would not have been illusion, but a thin veil of demon substance masking it. So she could have been fooled by that. The philter hadn't wanted them to know about the gargoyle, though Gayle seemed innocent enough.

"Where are we going, Mother Iris?" Surprise asked brightly. The child had had a good nap, which had been a real relief to the rest of them, and now was ready for action. Iris had long since accepted her designation as mother, because that was the role assigned in the replay of the past, and because she had raised a daughter of her own and remembered the ropes. It was halfway pleasant revisiting the role, and Surprise was a sweet child, apart from her wild power. That wildness had faded, once they realized the limit of her power. Surprise was not a phenomenally powerful Sorceress, but rather a limited temporary Sorceress who would in time be less. The rules of personal talents had not been broken, though they had been stretched somewhat.

"Do you happen to know where to find the philter?" Iris inquired.

"No, Mother," the child said.

"Can you do some magic that might locate it? Such as whirling around and pointing your finger in the correct direction?" That was the talent old Crombie the Soldier had.

"Sure." Surprise spun around and extended one hand.

Iris looked in that direction. "This seems to be toward the pool. We have already been there. But it surely is a suitable place for such a device."

They walked in that direction. They soon came to the edge of the pool. "But it will be difficult to search under the water," Iris said. "Can you move the water out of the way for a while?"

"Sure." Surprise concentrated, and the water humped, jiggled, and formed into a huge doughnut-shaped bubble that floated up out of the pool bed. It hovered there, flexing gently.

Is it safe to go below it?" Iris asked.

"Oh, sure," the child said. "I think."

Iris decided to take that on faith. The child's magic was erratic, but was certainly powerful. She was using it with greater caution and control now, which was also good. If they found the philter, the slight depletion of the child's remaining talents would be justified.

They walked into the basin of the pool. There were pebbles there, and chips of stone, and rock fragments, and pieces of mineral, and some rubble. Also some Mundane coins. How could they have gotten here? They wouldn't have moved themselves, and no one would have thrown them in the pool, because Mundanes were notoriously tightfisted with their money. But no philter. "Maybe it's on the island," Iris said.

They walked onto the island, and into the enclosure. There was the pedestal on which the gargoyle rested, but Gayle Goyle was gone. "She's with Gary," Surprise said.

"Well, at least that means that *she's* not the philter," Iris said, forcing a laugh. She hadn't thought of that until this moment, but the realization was a relief. She understood that the lady gargoyle was a nice creature. It would have been horrible if Surprise had pointed her out as the demon. It might have made sense, because a gargoyle was indeed a variety of filter, and Gayle had been doing that job here.

They kept looking, but the island was bare. There was nothing that looked remotely like a filter.

Then Iris remembered the problem with Crombie's talent: it didn't show how far. They had been wasting time here, when the philter was probably well beyond this place.

They walked on out the other side. The water doughnut still hovered. "You can let the water go now, dear," Iris said.

"Okay." SPLAT! The water sloshed down into its cavity. The splash drenched them both. "Oopsie," Surprise said. "I'll dry us." A barred vent opened in the ground beneath them, and hot air wafted up, lifting their skirts. Iris could feel the drying action.

"That's very nice, dear." Iris said, hastily pressing down her skirt with her hands. Unfortunately the jet of air was so strong that this was mostly ineffective; it was all she could do to keep her panties from showing. It was a good thing there were no men in the vicinity. Then again, maybe that wouldn't be so bad, because she was back in her twenty-three-year-old body. A lot could be accomplished in the way of male motivation by a supposedly accidental exposure of the right material. "But you really should save your talents unless there is pressing need."

"Oh, yes," Surprise said, chagrined.

When they were dry, they walked on in the direction indicated. They came to the train station. There was a train of thought sitting there. It bore a sign saying PAST.

Iris was surprised. "Do you suppose you were pointing to this train?" she asked.

"I guess," the child said.

"I wonder whether the indication is literal or figurative."

"What?"

"Whether the philter is on this train, or whether thinking about the past can tell us where it is."

"Oh. Let's ride the train. It's fun."

Iris shrugged. That seemed to be as good an approach as any.

They boarded the nearest coach and sat together on one of the seats. They looked out the window as the train began to move. Iris knew that this was the work of the philter demon, because it wasn't hers. The train was illusion, of course; they had merely entered a stone enclosure and were now watching screen images beyond it. But she didn't want to spoil the effect for Surprise, who still possessed the invaluable asset of childish wonder. Iris remembered how that had been, eighty-seven years before when she had been that age.

The city of Hinge passed behind them, and they proceeded through attractive countryside. This reminded Iris of the travels of her youth, and the nostalgia pressed in on her, bringing a tear to one eye.

Then they passed a lake with an island shrouded in mist. That reminded her of the misty Isle of Illusion, where she had resided so long, alone. She had had everything her own way, but it had been so lonely. The past was painful.

"This is dull," Surprise said, tiring of the scenery.

"That is perhaps because you have less past than I do," Iris said with mixed emotions.

"Yes, I've been in Xanth only one year," the child agreed. "You've been here for ever and ever. What was it like way way back when you were really as young as you look?"

"Oh, you would not be interested in that."

"Well, it can't be duller than this."

Point made. "I will tell you. But you don't have to listen when you get bored."

"Okay. Maybe I'll just fall asleep."

Iris started speaking, remembering an episode in her distant past: the first time she had been twenty-three years old, and possessed of a far greater store of innocence than she was ever to enjoy thereafter. As she spoke, she seemed to live that life again, with all its early naive feeling.

After she settled on the Isle of Illusion, the isolation and loneliness almost drove her off the edge into madness. She had been so sure she would like it here, with nobody to bother her or object to her constructions of illusion. Here she had things exactly her own way, with a beautiful palace and gardens and fountains and everything. She had strengthened her power and control by practice, going over each aspect repeatedly until she could readily get it exactly right. But somehow, after the fun of crafting it all in wonderful detail, she discovered that the thrill was gone. Instead of creating an ideal residence, she had locked herself into nothingness.

But Iris was a woman of firm resolve. So she did something about it. She gathered herself together with sufficient supplies and went to see the King.

"Please, your majesty," she pleaded after explaining her dissatisfaction. "Give me something to do. Anything. I am a Sorceress, and can surely be useful somewhere."

The Storm King was gracious. "Iris, the only way to find yourself is to lose yourself in the service of others."

"I don't understand. I never did anything for anyone else when I didn't have to."

"Precisely. Therefore, because I am a merciful and not completely dull king I hereby grant your request. I am sending you on a sacrificial underground undercover mission."

Iris was not absolutely sure she liked this. "Under covers I can handle. But there are goblins and things underground."

The Storm King looked at her as if she were a trifle stupid, which seemed to be an accurate assessment. "There is an immoral, illegal, dirty, despicable, revolting, and generally reprehensible slave trade in Xanth," he said. "In fact I don't especially approve of it, and want to shut it down. So I want you to use your powers of illusion to persuade these human cockroaches that although you are an experienced intelligent adult woman of a certain age, you are nevertheless a peach ripe for the picking."

"A peach," Iris repeated, clothing herself with the body of a huge peach.

The King frowned. "Perhaps I did not make myself perfectly clear. I apologize." But he didn't look apologetic. "In other words you will change your aspect to appear young, beautiful, naive, and fresh from the virgin islands."

Oops. Iris had great powers of illusion, but she would never be able to visit those islands. Not after that episode three years before when she had—never mind. "I—"

"The operative word is 'appear,' " he reminded her sternly. "I think your illusion should be adequate to generate such an appearance, challenging as it may be." He frowned. "But I must advise you that this mission is risky. You might lose your life, your love, or your very soul. Sign here." He put a parchment before her.

That seemed like a heavy price to pay for easing loneliness. But she knew that her sacrifice could not be as great as the King feared, because she had no love to lose. So she signed the release form.

There followed some reasonably dull events it was easy to skim over. It was enough to say that in due course her great effort of virginal illusion was successful, and she was captured by pirates and sold to the slavers. She found herself in the company of young women and children, all of whom were stunned by their fate. She was marched with the rest of the luckless captives from the ship's gangplank through the Three Sisters dunes to the Black Heath to the central plaza of a stony city in ruins covered with twisting whispering vines of kudzu. The ancient city appeared to have gray, silvery, stony gargoyles of every known size, shape, and degree of ugliness squatting everywhere. She stared one of the grotesque stone monsters in the snoot, and it required every ounce of her feeble and waning courage not to scream with fear and revulsion. Those eyes of stone seemed to strip away her veils of illusion. Did the monsters know her secret identity?

She saw the dread Blacksmith Anvil in the center of the Black Heath. She had learned that when a slave was sold, he or she was "married over the anvil": new, permanent collars of iron were forged, with metal loops for the chains to connect to. If she were bound in that manner, none of her illusions would free her. But she couldn't escape yet, and not merely because of the manacle on her left wrist that bound her to the others in her miserable group. Be-

cause she had not yet learned the identity of the Master
Slaver. If she identified that man, and told the King, the
man would be taken out and the entire slave industry
would collapse. But if she failed to identify him, slavery
would continue. So her mission was not complete until she
had learned what no other agent of the King had. She was
bound by her mission as much as by the chains.

They marched past a massive stone block. There were
dark stains on it: the remnant of countless beheadings of
slaves who had tried to rebel, or who had been too weak
or lazy to work as hard as they were supposed to, or who
had simply been unlucky. She fancied she could see dents
in the dust where their heads had bounced. "Long live
Xanth," she whispered inaudibly, to squeeze a tiny fragment of a bit of battered courage into her system. Truly,
she thought, vengeance was the heart of justice. She hoped
one day to see the Master Slaver himself stretched across
that terrible block.

They were brought to the steep face of a barren mountain wall where several dark caves showed. They were
separated into chains of four or five and pushed unceremo-
niously inside, two chains to a cave. Ironwood grates were
clanged into place, shutting them in. This was their lodg-
ing for the night.

Iris found dirty straw on the floor, and shaped some of
it into a mattress. She lay on it, sharing it with her
chainmates, who were three girls below Adult Conspiracy
age, and mended their tears as well as she could. She gave
the straw the illusion of soft warm down, and the children
relaxed and slept, not knowing the source of their comfort.
None of them knew the fate they faced on the morrow.

But she was neither beheaded nor sold immediately. It
seemed that she was part of a group that was being held
for a later event. She was not even abused, probably because that would spoil the delicate beauty of her illusion
aspect. The slavers thought she would fetch an excellent
price, if properly marketed, and so they took their time.

And the Master Slaver did not make an appearance. So life proceeded in a halfway or third-way manner for the nonce.

One day she sat with several others at a small, cold, gray stone table in the dark blue shade of a sweet-smelling eucalyptus tree in front of the kitchen cases facing the Black Heath plaza. Iris sat with her chainmate children drinking tsoda popka flavored with the juice of fresh sublime. In reality it was just water, but the children had learned not to reveal or question the illusions that made their lives bearable. Iris never made any obvious illusions, and never made any kind when a slavemaster was near or watching, and no one ever hinted that their lives were anything but drudge. It was a faint conspiracy of silence.

The hot sun was just up, and the day was showing that golden flash of green that Iris enjoyed so much, and if she enhanced it with illusion, any slave who noticed pretended to ignore it. "One day at a time," she whispered to herself. "Take one day at a time." And hope that she got to identify the Master Slaver before any of them were sold.

For although she seemed to be taking her ease, looking around with interest at the red rocks, moody blues, and golden sands of the slave camp, she was far from feeling relaxed or happy. After doing only three weeks of undercover work for the King of Xanth, she knew that if things went wrong it would be undercover work in more than one way. She had seen the slaver men eying her, hoping that some flaw would turn up to make her unsalable so they could take her for themselves. Sometimes they left branches or stones in the path, seemingly by accident, that she might trip on in the dark. A fall could mar her face, dropping her value. Actually it had worked once; she *had* fallen and scraped her cheek. But she covered it with illusion so that they never knew. Now she was careful to make the illusion of a darklight whose radiance could be seen only through the illusion of special contact lenses, so that she could see her way in the darkness.

She was already homesick for the misty Isle of Illusion and the cool green seas that pounded on her sandy beach.

She was also footsore from the original forced march to this hidden slave camp and the constant running around she had to do to serve the slavemasters and keep the children out of trouble. She had traded the lack of company for the lack of comfort. Well, not entirely; she remembered that summer when she had visited Fire Island and been swarmed by fire ants. She had managed to put out the fire with copious wet sand, but had suffered second-degree burns on her feet and first-degree burns on her legs. For weeks she had hobbled along on blistered soles, unable to conceal the pain from herself though of course she covered it with three and a half layers of illusion. Her feet weren't in that much trouble, here in the slave camp, but overall it was about as bad because of the fatigue of the rest of her body and the humiliation of her situation.

She got up to fetch another small drink of water, because illusion could not actually quench her thirst. The children followed in lockstep, because that was the best way to keep the chain from yanking on them. They limped across the black square, using illusion to make the walk seem natural to others, toward the beautiful "Gothic" fountain. She didn't know what kind of creature a Goth was, but it must have been fearsome, because the fountain was lovingly endowed with several unlovable hideous frozen-in-stone gargoyles playing in its golden center. Surely it had required a powerful spell to lock such creatures there.

Beside the fountain a scarred, blue-faced, leather-and-chain, grungy, armored mercenary subhuman male was flirting with a fiery fox-haired feminine feline neohuman creature. She seemed amenable, as she was talking freely and acting very kittenish. Iris had seen her around, and knew her name was Katka. Like all camp followers, Katka, though scantily clad, covered one eye with the black shawl she wore over her hair. This was a very strange thing, and Iris really would have taken note, had she ever been in the mood to think about it. Why should a woman cover her head better than her torso? The slaver, however, seemed satisfied with that mode of dress, and was inspecting it closely.

But Iris' only thought was her wish to jump into that silvery blue cool pool of water and to let the healing streams of liquid spouting from the faucet-mouths of the diamond-eyed, dragon-headed, stone-faced creatures pour over her head, hands, and fiery feet. Unable to resist, she leaned over and splashed water across her face.

"You there!" the mercenary shouted. "That is forbidden!"

Quickly she and the children filled their cups and hurried away. How she wished the Master Slaver would make an appearance, so she could identify him and make her escape and get this entire sordid operation forever shut down. But whether from canniness or indifference, he remained absent.

That night, hot and miserable, Iris moaned in her restless sleep and dreamed a dream:

By the hot and humid noon, in a dale of dragons,
Almost lifeless, a golden arrow in my breast, I lay;
Smoking mirrors rose all around me, and scarlet
Drops of blood ran over my breast and dripped away.

I lay upon the golden burning sands alone.
The sheer precipices of the seven devils made no sound,
The kettenhund (watch-dog) lay panting in the sun,
And I scorched too, near the River of No Return, on the
    ground.

I dreamt I heard an infant crying in the light.
The Demon struck; there in the sand, my lover's body
    lay;
Steam rose from hell's canyon's Oh-No hot springs,
The blood ran cold and down and out of it, and dripped
    away.

She woke, wondering what it meant. She had never been struck by an arrow, especially not a golden one, or had a lover suffering like that. Yet the dream seemed much like a memory. Surely it had special significance.

She heard thunder outside the mouth of the cave. It was raining with appalling violence, and water was coursing down along the floor past her feet and on into the deeper reaches of the mountain. No one knew how far the caves extended, for not even the slavers dared explore them to their end. Only the water dared do that.

It was morning, and now there seemed to be a break in the storm. The children needed to eat. So she led them out. But she was mistaken; in a moment the rain resumed, and to her surprise it was freezing. Sleet battered them, making them hunch low and seek the partial shelter of trees.

She decided to go back to the cave, but it was too late. The storm intensified into a hurricane filled with screaming demons. It drove her to her knees, obliterating her view of the cave entrance and filling her mind with fear. The children cried, but could hardly be heard over the roar of the storm. She reached out, trying to bring them in to her for what scant protection she was able to offer. She realized that Fracto, the evil cloud, must be here, trying to destroy her. Fracto was one of the few things she could not readily befuddle by her illusions. Fracto had no illusions; he was simply destructive.

Blinded and deafened by the terrible storm, Iris went for the only shelter within range: a vulgar thyme tree. It was vulgar not in its appearance or attitude, but in the sense that it was a common, imperfect specimen with little effect on what was near it. Thus Iris and the children were able to huddle by it while suffering only a little distortion of time. It made it seem as if the storm had slowed, with the hailstones angling down at a lazy rate, bouncing slowly on the ground, and rolling in leisurely manner. The howling wind howled in a lower tone, as if tired, and blew the tree's leaves as if they were reluctant to respond.

She knew it was still daytime, but a great darkness was

closing in all around them. Part of it was because of the density of the awful cloud, she knew, but that couldn't account for the rest. The children gazed around fearfully. Even little Surprise seemed daunted. She didn't blame them; the effect was unnerving. She knew she should not have gone out into the storm like this; such weather was never to be trusted. But where was the darkness coming from?

Then she realized that it was because of the thyme tree. It was slowing down the light itself, so that not enough could reach this spot, and that gave the darkness its chance. They would have to get away from the tree if they wanted more light. They couldn't stay here anyway, because the hailstones were piling up around their feet and making their toes deathly cold. This refuge was no refuge.

"Ch-children," Iris said, her teeth chattering. "We m-must go on before we fr-freeze. I will m-make a l-light to lead us to the m-mess hall."

They nodded their little heads, dully. Even the slavery they faced was better than this bone-chilling cold.

Then something halfway good happened. The manacle on Iris' left wrist glazed over, wrinkled, and cracked partly open. The thyme and the cold were stressing it beyond its limit, and it was coming apart.

"Children!" she cried. "The manacles are being unmanned! Maybe we can get them off!"

They drew together in a circle, and pulled on the chain that linked them, and pried with sticks and banged with stones, and bit by bit the manacles came apart. One by one they pried them open and off, slipping their little hands free. They were no longer physically chained to each other.

But they remained socially and practically linked. None of them could survive this storm alone, and the children would surely perish if they escaped the storm and ran into the surrounding wilderness. Iris herself was little better off, because her illusion could not make a material change in her situation.

"Children, we are only half free," she said. "We must get to the mess hall and get warm before we can think about getting away from here. I will make illusion manacles and chains, and you must act as if they are real, until we see a good chance to escape. Do you understand?"

They nodded. They understood all too well. They knew that the chain was only part of what bound them. Otherwise they could have escaped with Iris as a group. They knew how to play the part. They had learned how to survive in this awful situation.

Of course Iris herself didn't want to escape yet, because she had yet to identify the Master Slaver. But maybe he would show up before a good chance to escape with the children turned up.

Iris made a bright illusion lamp and sent it floating ahead. She no longer knew exactly which way the mess hall was, but anywhere was better than here. Then, as an afterthought, she caused the lamp to float down close to the hailstone-covered ground, and brightened it until it shone like a little sun. The ice closest to it melted, giving them a clear path. It was a good thing the hailstones did not realize that the light was illusion.

They followed the light, not much caring where it was going. The storm still raged around them, obscuring everything, but the little ball of light gave them comfort. It floated this way and that as the wind buffeted it, leading them along a tortuous path. It seemed to Iris that they should have reached the mess hall by this time, even after allowing for the curlicues of the route, but she didn't say anything for fear of alarming the children. She didn't dare let them be lost.

Then she spied a dim light ahead. She diminished her illusion light so that the slavers would not see it and forged on toward the real light, the children in her wake. The storm intensified around them as if trying to stop them from getting there. For a moment an icy blast of blown snow air swirled into her lungs and made her breath crystallize within them. She fell to her knees, gasping.

But she had to set an example. She put down her hands and crawled toward the light ahead, slowly drawing near to the huge heavy wooden doors of the building. The children crawled after her.

Then she hesitated. This didn't look like the mess hall. It seemed to be a strange building. But they couldn't stay out here, and her limbs were already too numb to get her to any other place. They would have to gamble on this one.

She repaired her illusion as she struggled to her feet. She made herself resemble a beautiful damsel in distress, and the children looked like cute wee lasses in worse distress. Actually this was all true enough; she merely enhanced their appearances so that anyone answering the door would find them appealing.

She conjured an illusion mirror, and by the light of its reflection adjusted her decolletage to show a bit more bulge of breast and depth of cleavage. Then she clenched her numb fists and jammed them at the doorbell, but couldn't break the ice that froze it. So she tried to beat her knuckles on the door, but they were too numb to make any sound. So she kicked at the door instead, and her lady slipper managed to make a faint feminine tap.

At last the door creaked forward. There was an old maid. "Why it's you, Iris!" the maid said. "What are you doing out there, with your knuckles numb and your cleavage getting iced over?"

"Magpie!" Iris exclaimed. For it seemed to be her old demoness lady-in-waiting maid who had helped raise her before she bloomed somewhat anemically into maidenhood.

"Close enough," the other said. "I was just checking to see how you were doing. You seem to be locked into an interesting memory." She vanished.

Iris tried to figure out exactly what Mentia was doing in her memory, but her chilled mind could not think efficiently enough to figure it out. So she took advantage of the open door to plod on in, with Surprise and the other children following. For that matter, what was Surprise doing here? She hadn't even been delivered until about seven decades later. But it didn't matter, as long as the building offered warmth.

When the children were all in, she pushed the door shut, locking out the dread storm. Immediately her extremities began to lose their chill, and the children looked better too.

But what was this building? Would they be welcome here? Or was this merely the prelude to worse mischief?

She decided to make a wild gamble. "This may be a strange house," she whispered to the children. "Where the slavers don't govern. I'm going to abolish our chains." And the illusion manacles and chains vanished.

There was the sound of feet tramping along the floor of the hall to the door. Iris adjusted her illusory bust line, because that was her best line of defense. A man appeared, wearing a great sword. He paused, gazing at her artful front. "Now that's interesting," he remarked.

Well, it was meant to be. "Kind sir," she said plaintively. "I am a Maiden in Distress, and these are poor waifs in similar state. Will you help us?" She took a deep breath to accent the extent of her maidenly distress.

"Might as well," he said. "I am the Knight Guard, here to protect this house from the ravages of dragons. Do you have anything to do with any dragon?"

"Not if we can help it, bold sir knight," Iris said meekly.

"Then make yourselves useful," he said sardonically. He turned on heel and toe and went back to his dicey card game board court.

Iris hesitated only two-thirds of a moment. "We can be most useful in the kitchen," she told the children. "Besides, there should be food there." So they trooped down the hall, following the smell of baking bread and curdling whey. It led to a large chamber whose entrance bore a sign reading HELL'S KITCHEN. That did not seem encouraging, but what else was there to do but go on in?

They went in. There was a huge fat cook in a white uniform with a hat that looked like a big popover muffin. He turned and saw them. "Get out of here, you rag-muffins," he said. "The meal is not ready. I'm shorthanded." He lifted one arm to show how short his hand was.

"But we came to help," Iris said. "Many little hands make short work."

"In that condition?" he demanded, staring at them, and Iris realized that she had let her illusion slip so that she was no longer a buxom creature with a low dress line and the children were no longer angelic waifs. Instead they were all somewhat cold, grimy stragglers. "Get the bunch of you to that tub and clean up first." He gestured to a monstrous kettle in the fireplace. "I am the Demon Rum; report back to me when you're ready."

Iris looked at the kettle. It was big enough to hold them all inside it at once. A horrible thought came to her. But she suppressed it. "Thank you," she said, quietly restoring her cleavage.

He took a look, which was not surprising; if there happened to be a man alive who would not look when she crafted that particular illusion, he was surely blind. "And eat something," he said. "You look famished." That was a remarkably perceptive observation.

"Thank you," she repeated, deepening her cleavage and leaning forward. "But what should we eat?"

"Eat my hat," he said, and tossed the popover muffin to her. Iris caught it, and found it solid and fraught with assorted berries, with steamy rich pastry between. It was big enough to make a meal for them all.

Iris tore the hat into several delicious pieces and passed them out. The children gobbled theirs down, and Iris herself ate ravenously under the cover of a more ladylike illusion. Of course they all got thoroughly gunked up with dough and cooked berries, but this was the time for it, with a good washing coming up.

The huge kettle was about half full of warm water. It would do. Iris made an inconspicuous illusion screen behind which the children stripped. Then she lifted each up into the kettle and had them start scrubbing themselves and each other. After the last one was in, she went behind the screen, removed her own clothing, crafted an illusion bathing suit, tossed all their clothing into the pot for scrubbing, and climbed in herself. The children were gleefully indulging in a splash and clothing fight, which was getting everything incidentally clean, so she let it be, covering it with an illusion of roiling smoke.

Surprise got into a fit of conjuring, producing things so awful that the other children made passionate choking and retching sounds: fresh vegetables. "It's my curse," she said as she tossed cabbages, squash, broccoli, peas, beans, sweet and sour potatoes, turnips, tomatoes, beets, celery, and other disgusting produce at the others. Soon pieces of vegetable were strewn throughout the water. Iris reflected that this was probably the most enjoyment these children had ever gotten from vegetables.

In due course they and their clothing were pretty clean and the water was ugly dirty. Iris hung the clothing up by the fire to dry and clothed herself and the children in illusory matching olive drab uniforms. It was warm enough in the kitchen so that they were comfortable.

She led them to Demon Rum. "We are ready to work," she announced.

"You have already done the job," he said.

Iris and the children were surprised. "We have?"

"You made the soup."

They remained baffled. "We did?"

"There in the kettle," Rum explained. "Vegetable soup."

They looked back at the kettle, whose fire was now blazing up to heat the water to boiling. "But—" Iris began, thinking of the way they had just washed their dirty bodies in it.

"Flavoring," Rum explained as if reading her mind. "Secret ingredient."

The children nodded, catching on. They would keep the secret. The very notion of tricking unsuspecting folk into eating vegetable soup was hilarious.

Their job done, they mounted the wooden stairs to the servants' quarters on the second floor. There was a nice chamber for them there, with plenty of cushions for sleeping on the floor. Naturally the children got into an enthusiastic pillow fight instead, and soon feathers were flying. They did not stop until no pillows remained intact. Iris, distracted by concerns about exactly where they were and what might be their fate in this mysterious building, did not notice until too late. "Oh!" she cried in horror. "You have destroyed all the cushions!"

Then they heard the tramping of feet coming up the stairs. Iris could do nothing except craft a hasty illusion of pillows the way they had been before the door opened.

There stood the Demon Rum, with all their clothes in his short hands. "You forgot these," he said. "They are now dry." He gazed at the group with mild interest.

Iris realized belatedly that in her concern for the pillows, she had forgotten to maintain their illusions of clothing. All of them were standing naked. "Thank you," she said, taking the bundle and holding it before her in the manner of a shield.

"There is one more task for you," Rum said. "You must remove the feathers so that the cushions can be washed." He blinked as Iris let go of her pillow illusion. "Oh, I see you have already done it. Very good." He gathered up the empty pillowcases and took them away.

Iris resumed breathing. How lucky could they get?

15
LOVE

What happened then?" Surprise asked.

Iris was jolted out of her reverie. "Oh, you wouldn't care to listen to all that," she said, concerned about infringing the Adult Conspiracy. She noticed absently that the train was passing through the city of Hinge again; it must have looped around.

"Oh yes I would!" Surprise said eagerly.

Iris realized that she had made a mistake. All children were eager to get past the Conspiracy, and of course that couldn't be allowed, lest adults lose their power over children. But maybe there wasn't too much forbidden material in the memory, and she could slip by whatever there was with an invisible ellipsis. This was after all a train of thought traveling to the past, so they were bound to explore memories. "Very well," she said with only faint resignation, because the memory was an interesting one.

"Can I be in your memory scene again?"

"But that was long before you were delivered!" Iris protested.

"Sure, but you had children, so I joined them. I promise not to do any messy magic."

At another time, Iris might have been bemused by the anachronism. But if she could be with Surprise now, being physically twenty-three, why not be with the child when she was mentally twenty-three? "Very well," she repeated. After all, memories were best when truly shared.

Iris woke next morning with a feeling of great loss. She knew she had dreamed of her Lost Love once again, the one she had never had in anything other than a dream. With a lingering trace of unease she whispered into her pillow, "Oh, Power that Be, how long must I bear this loneliness?" But there was as usual no answer.

She glanced at the melting none-of-your-beeswax candle-clock and saw that it was still early. She quickly slid out from under her warm down-filled duvet, shivering as her bare feet met the slabs of golden-flecked sandstone and sky-blue turquoise that made up the royal checkerboard pattern of the floor. She hadn't noticed how elegant this chamber was yesterday. Of course the floor had been mostly covered by feathers from the pillow fight, and then they had had to go downstairs to work on another meal in the kitchen, and it had been dark by the time they returned. So this was really her first real chance to examine the chamber in detail. She was impressed. Who could have such a fancy chalet? It could not be far from the slave camp, because though they had gotten lost in the storm, they had blundered only a short time. But she was sure she had never seen anything like this in the vicinity.

The children, exhausted by their labors of kettle and pillow, were sprawled happily amidst their scattered cushions, still asleep. This was a blessing for them, too: to be suddenly well fed and cared for, instead of huddled in a dank dark cave. But Iris had what some might consider to be a suspicious nature; she wondered whether there was some hidden catch in this delight.

She stepped quietly to the lavatory, where there were

wonderful conveniences of sanitation. When she drew back the pretty cotton/linen curtains shrouding the round bathing chamber she could not suppress a gasp of pleasure. There was a steaming bath already prepared. "But this can't be for me!" she breathed, hoping she was wrong.

"Of course it can be, dear," Magpie said, appearing beside her. "I made your favorite lemon verbena-scented bath. You can't expect to endure with a mere vegetable soup bath, now can you?"

"So it *was* you I saw at the door yesterday," Iris said.

"Of course it was, until I got overridden by a more recent memory," Magpie said, helping her into the wonderful bath. "Sometimes I wonder just what adventures you're getting into, in your latter life."

That seemed to make sense of a sort. "But what is this place?" Iris asked as she luxuriated in the scented water. "Why are we being treated so well?"

"I can give you only a partial answer," Magpie said. "The chalet belongs to a young man of noble aspect named Arte Menia. You are being treated well because the cook likes you."

"But the cook doesn't know I am a Sorceress," Iris protested. "And anyway, he's a demon, so he doesn't care about mortal women."

"Now there you are wrong, dear," Magpie said as she scrubbed Iris' back. "Male demons can become quite intrigued by illusion-enhanced mortal women, and female demons can delight in seducing mortal men. Of course this is mostly casual byplay for them, as they seldom form lasting attachments."

"But Magpie, you—"

"I happen to like maidens in distress," the demoness replied. "They can lead interesting lives."

Iris was surprised. She had somehow taken Magpie for granted, before; it hadn't seemed unusual to have a demoness maidservant. "You have served other maidens?"

"Many," Magpie agreed. "Did I ever mention Rose of Roogna?"

"No, you didn't."

"Good. It wouldn't have been proper."

When the bath was done, Iris rose and stood before the full-length mirror. She looked splendid. She knew 999 illusions, give or take a few, so normally used illusions the way artists used their rainbow of colored big hogments or little pigments, to give the viewer sights as beautifully rendered as fine paintings. In fact she regarded herself as an artist with illusions. But right now she didn't need any illusion. For this moment, here in the bathing chamber, Iris saw herself as young, healthy, slender, and with enough non-slenderness to be appealing to whatever man might better not be watching.

"Venus rising from the sea," Magpie murmured appreciatively. "It seems too bad to cover it up." She nevertheless produced a lovely pair of p*nties and br*, and then an ornate robe.

One of the children woke. "You put on what?" Surprise asked.

"Undies," Magpie said quickly. "Now go take your own bath."

That sobered the child in a hurry. But then Surprise had an idea. "Can we have another vegetable fight?"

"*May* we," Magpie said sternly.

"May we?" The other children were waking now.

"Have a fruit fight instead," Magpie suggested, producing several soap bars in the shape of lemons, grapes, apples, cherries, and such. One was even in the form of a small explosive pineapple: the kind that acted just like a real pineapple, but on a harmless scale.

The children gazed at those a bit suspiciously, suspecting that the fruits might be better at cleaning than at splatting. Then Magpie produced soap in the shape of a giant watermelon that would make a horrendous splash and get water all over everything outside the tub, and that decided the children. They grabbed the small soaps and rolled the big one. "Last one in's a rotten eggplant!"

"I will watch them," Magpie said. "You go on to meet Arte Menia now."

"Who?"

"The master of the house. He returned from his long business trip last night, and learned of your presence, so you must make his acquaintance now. It would not be mannerly to remain in his house otherwise."

Indeed it would not; Iris had been brought up to be properly behaved, and this was integral to such behavior. "Where is he?"

"Downstairs in the office foyer. He has some paperwork to catch up on."

So Iris gathered her elegant borrowed robe around her and tripped daintily down the stairs to the office foyer. There was a handsome young man sorting papers. "Excuse me," she said. "I am the Sor—I am Iris." Because some innate caution reminded her to maintain the secret of her identity. "I have been your—I stayed overnight." She wasn't certain whether she counted as guest or scullery maid.

The man stood. He had wavy brown hair and a small butt. "I am glad to meet you, Iris. I am Arte, master of this house. Rum told me you were beautiful, but he understated the case."

Iris blushed, for she was using no illusion at the moment, so was being complimented for her natural appearance. That was a rarity. "Thank you," she said. "Rum has been most kind. The children and I were freezing in the storm, and he gave us food, shelter, and work to do."

"Yes, he's shorthanded," Arte said. His eyes were shades of gray. "But you will not have to work any more. You are obviously a fine lady." He took her hand in his, lifted it, and kissed it. His hand and lips were warm and firm.

Iris felt such a thrill she almost swooned. What a noble man he was! She opened her mouth to say something responsive, but all that emerged was an embarrassing titter.

"You must have breakfast with me," Arte said, drawing

her from the study toward the banquet hall. He seated her across from him with a flourish so that they could look into each other's eyes.

Rum appeared. "What will it be this morning, master?" the demon asked.

"The usual for me, and something that tries to approach the worthiness of the lady for her."

"Very good, sir." Rum vanished.

"But I can fetch my own—" Iris started.

Arte put his firm hand on her trembling one. "I would not care to be deprived of the exquisite pleasure of your company for even a moment, now that I have met you." He smiled, showing his even white teeth and half a dimple. Dazzled, she was afraid she was going to melt, which would be embarrassing.

Rum reappeared with two steaming platters. "A fried dragon egg for you, master, with hedgehog bacon on the side, and a nuclear fruit for the lady." He set them down and disappeared.

Iris looked at the meal. She had never heard of anyone having dragon's eggs for breakfast routinely; they were not the easiest things to come by. Certainly a dragon's egg was considered to be the most manly breakfast available. As for hers—it looked good, being a cluster of flowerlike balls of scintillating circles and ellipses surrounding glowing spheres in the center. But she wasn't sure how to eat it.

"Merely pop it in your mouth," Arte recommended, divining her doubt. He lifted one of the bacon strips, which Iris recognized as deriving from the kind of pig that was made from the leaves of a certain type of hedge that often hogged the best soil of Xanth.

Dubiously, she lifted one of the balls and put it in her mouth. And froze, awed by the experience. Because there was an immediate and extremely potent explosion of taste. It was the most delightful gustatory sensation she had ever experienced. She felt as if she was wafting across a field of roses and being buoyed by the exquisite scents.

After a brief eternity or a very long instant she settled softly back to a semblance of reality. "Oh," she breathed rapturously. "What is it?"

"The fruit of the nuclear plant," Arte said. "The plant detonates when taken from the ground, and the fruit taste explodes when eaten. It is considered a delicacy suitable for a lady, though admittedly unworthy of a lady as lovely and gracious as you."

"But it's by far the best-tasting fruit I've had," she protested. "I've encountered nothing remotely like this before."

"Then you have been eating below your station." He took a bite of his egg.

Iris considered the rest of her plate. The fruits were of different colors, being green, blue, yellow, purple, and polka dot. She had eaten a red one, which had turned out to be rose-flavored. What experience awaited her with the other colors?

She tried a yellow one. This time the explosion carried her into a realm of buttercups brimming with the sweetest, creamiest butter, fragrant vanilla plants, and tangy lemon drops. She would have thought it the finest taste in all Xanth, had she not just experienced the rose flavor. As it was, she gave up trying to make comparisons and just let herself drift through the little slice of paradise.

By the time Arte had finished his most manly egg and Iris had imbibed the last maidenly fruit, she was so pleasantly dizzy that everything seemed clothed in warm fuzz.

"I must show you the premises," Arte said, standing firmly.

Iris tried to stand, but now felt so delicate she almost swooned. Fortunately he caught her in his manly strong arms before she fell. "But I see you are tired," he said. "Let me take you to my room to lie down."

This made such perfect sense that she was more than satisfied to accept his guidance. Soon they were in his private room, which was even fancier than the one she and the children had used. It had an emperor-sized bed that looked wonderfully inviting.

Then he kissed her. This was like nuclear fruit intensified. Her wits exploded into nothingness, and she completed the swoon she had started downstairs.

In a moment, or perhaps two instants, she recovered. She found herself lying on the bed with Arte. Neither of them had any clothing on.

"Oh," she said with a maidenly gasp. "What happened?" For it occurred to her that something might have. She knew that women had a power men lacked: to signal a stork while asleep. Had she been so uncouth as to try that?

"You said something about summoning the stork," he said. "So I removed our clothing. But then it occurred to me that you were not wholly rational, so I waited."

"You mean you—we—didn't—?"

"I apologize if you wished otherwise," he said. "But I remembered that sometimes folk are not in their normal emotional state after eating nuclear fruit."

That was the understatement of the hour! She had been a third of the way freaked out with the pleasure of the fruit. She would have thought that he might take advantage of that state. But it seemed he hadn't. Her body, now that she thought about it, indicated that he hadn't.

She might have been angry if he had. But now that she knew he hadn't, she had the opposite mood. She liked him even better. "Then let's do it now!" she said.

"I thought you'd never ask," he said.

He put his arms around her, and she turned into him for another kiss. They drew close together.

The door crashed open. Several children piled into the room. "There you are!" Surprise cried jubilantly.

Iris barely had time to plunk an illusion blanket over their bare bodies. "Whatever are you up to?" she demanded, not entirely pleased by the intrusion. She suspected that Arte had a similar sentiment.

"We finished our bath and now we're hungry," Surprise

said. "So we came looking for you. Who is that man in bed with you?"

Arte glanced at the illusion blanket. His eyes narrowed significantly. Evidently he was catching on to the nature of her magic. But he did not make an issue of that at the moment. "I am Arte Menia, the master of this house. Who are you?"

"They are the children I was traveling with," Iris said quickly. "They are innocent waifs who mean no harm."

"Then let them get themselves down to the kitchen for their breakfast," Arte said tersely.

Iris drew the illusion blanket closely about her body as she sat up. "Go down to the kitchen; Rum will feed you," she said.

"Okay," Surprise said. The children piled out, slamming the door behind them.

"Now where were we?" Arte inquired, turning to her.

Iris let the blanket dissolve. "We were about to address a stork, I think," she said.

"Yes, I believe you are correct." He paused. "But tell me one thing: how did you make that blanket appear, saving us from a drastic violation of the Adult Conspiracy?"

She had to tell him. "It's my talent. The blanket wasn't real. It's illusion. I—"

"Your talent makes illusion blankets!" he said. "How fortunate for this occasion!"

"Um, yes," she agreed, that bit of caution still clinging to her. "What is your talent?"

"To persuade others of my sincerity," he said.

"Persuasion?" she said, dimly alarmed. "You mean I don't really want to do this, but your magic makes me think I do?"

He laughed. "By no means. I wish I had such a talent, for it would make me far more successful than I am. No, it is merely my sincerity I am persuasive about."

"Isn't that the same thing?"

"It is not. I'll make a demonstration." He looked at her. "We can summon ten storks at once."

Iris laughed. "That's impossible!"

"True. I was unable to persuade you that it was. But do you believe that I would sincerely like to do it?"

She considered. "Yes, I believe you would like to."

"So you believe in my sincerity, not in the impossible. That is the distinction."

She nodded. "Now I understand. You can make me believe in your feeling, but not in the validity of what you may propose."

"Yes. So I can make you believe that I sincerely desire to summon the stork with you, but I can't make you believe that you want to summon the stork with me."

"That's a relief," she said. "Because I do want to do some summoning with you, and I'd hate to think it wasn't a real desire." She lay down again by him, and kissed him.

"I think I have looked all over Xanth for a woman like you," he said dreamily, "and here you show up by chance at my house. I bless the storm that caused you to blunder here." His competent hand ran across her back and down to her—

The door burst open again. There was Surprise. "I finished breakfast," she announced, "and dashed back here so I could see what you were doing."

Iris barely had time to conjure the illusion blanket to get unbare. "We aren't doing anything," she said, frustrated.

"But we would like to be," Arte added.

"Let me see," Surprise said. It was evident that she had some faint suspicion that there might be a Conspiracy thing going on, and like all children, she was insatiably curious about it. She walked into the room and reached for the blanket.

"I really would prefer that you not do that," Arte said.

The child paused. "Oh. Sorry."

Iris realized that Surprise had not distinguished between sincerity and possibility. She hadn't separated his desire from hers. That was fortunate, because if she grabbed for the blanket, it would be something else she got hold of.

But the child wasn't out of incidental mischief. "What's this?" she asked, heading for Arte's pile of clothes.

"Don't touch that!" the man cried, sincerely alarmed. But it seemed that he forgot to use his talent to persuade Surprise of that.

"Don't touch what?" she asked. "This?" She picked up what looked like a miniature fat barrel on a string. It must have fallen out of Arte's pocket when he dumped his clothing down with flattering haste.

"Yes, that!" Arte shouted, reaching for it.

The child backed up just far enough to remain out of his reach. That was another incidental talent all children had. She looked at the trinket. "Why?"

"Because it's mine!" Arte rasped. He lurched off the bed so suddenly that Iris had to make a hasty illusion of a towel wrapped around his middle, lest an awful breach of Conspiracy occur. He grabbed for the object.

Surprise backed up another step. "Say 'please,' " she said, imitating the obnoxious lessons of adults on manners.

"You little &&&&!" Arte said, definitely breaching the Conspiracy. The air wavered in an expanding dirty pattern, appalled, and the stench of brimstone wafted out. "Give it to me!"

Surprise scooted around to the side, leaving him lumbering into the wall. She joined Iris. "Is it fun on the bed?" she asked innocently.

"Well, it was about to be," Iris said. "Please go back to the kitchen, and we will join you there in a while." She did not dare express her reason for wanting privacy.

Arte caromed off the wall, reoriented, and came after Surprise again. "Give it to me!" he repeated mindlessly.

The child ducked and zipped past him, holding her closed fist aloft. But this time he was more alert. He turned on a dimepede that had the misfortune to wander out from under the bed at that moment, and leaped after her. His lunge was so strong that something flew up from the floor and landed on the bed. But Surprise was already going out the door. "Nyaa nyaa," she said, being definitely ill behaved, and slammed the door in his face.

Arte wrenched the door open and plowed after her. Iris watched them go, bemused. This had certainly showed her another side of suave Arte, and not just his hind section, which she had forgotten to cover with illusion. The thing about an illusion towel was that it didn't have to be complete to stay in place; just the front half would do. Why did the man care so much about a stupid ugly little trinket that he would use a forbidden word and chase after a child, clad only in half an illusion? Iris wasn't much concerned about Surprise, who could be uncommonly evasive when she had a mind to be, but about Arte, whose body she had been about to clasp. What could be more compelling to a man than stork summoning? Why hadn't he simply let the child play with it awhile in another room, being distracted until there was a chance to complete their business with the stork?

She looked at the thing that had landed on the bed. It was a sock. Arte had kicked up one of his socks as he charged after Surprise. She picked it up and twisted it into a knot, reflectively. But it smelled, so she stuffed it under the pillow.

Well, it seemed that her liaison was doomed for now. She would speak most firmly to Surprise about that, at a later time. But now there was nothing to do but get up and get dressed, because even if Arte returned soon, the mood had definitely soured. She abolished the illusion blanket—and stared. For there was the trinket under it.

Surprise, with truly cunning mischief, had left the thing here while allowing Arte to chase her all over the castle. He would never get it from her that way, because she no longer had it. And she had done it intentionally, because she had held her little closed fist up in an obvious manner.

Iris was now pretty curious about the trinket herself. She picked it up. It wasn't heavy. It was just the tiny replica of a barrel that might be filled with some kind of spirit. She shook it, listening in case it contained fluid.

Then she rubbed it with her thumb to see if there were any catch that would allow it to open. There must be something valuable inside it.

The cook appeared before her. "Demon Rum reporting, master," he said formally. Then he did a double take. "Mistress, I mean. How did you get the amulet?"

"Amulet?" she asked, surprised. "This barrel trinket?"

"Mistress, you have asked, and I must answer. That is no trinket. It is the miniature barrel I have been cursed to occupy when not in active duty for my master. Er, mistress. I must obey whoever holds it."

Iris' surprise was giving way to appreciation. "You work for Arte—because he commands you with this amulet!"

"True. Now I am yours to command. What is your directive, mistress?"

"Just like that? I just pick it up and rub it, and you are my slave?"

"Even so, mistress."

"So you don't enjoy being chief cook?"

"I don't mind cooking. It's being a slave to a harsh master I can't stand."

"Then why were you so nice to me and the children? We didn't have the amulet."

"You have asked, and I must answer. I was bored, and you had an interesting decolletage, not to mention your powers as Sorceress of Illusion or your mission to capture the Master Slaver. And the children promised much mischief."

"That's not much of an answer," Iris said. "If you recognized me, why didn't you tell Arte?"

"He didn't ask."

It was starting to make sense. "And you are required to obey, not to volunteer. So you let us in and treated us well. But still you had nothing to gain from this, did you?"

"Oh, but I did, mistress. I hoped that you or a child would be my next mistress."

"Why? Isn't one human being as bad as another, as far as you're concerned?"

"Perhaps. But some are more interesting than others, and some are less bothersome to work for. And there is the moral dimension."

"What do you mean? Demons don't care about morals, being soulless."

"Demons differ. I happen to abhor slavery, for an obvious reason."

"That's right!" she said, realizing something else. "You can help me accomplish my mission. Where is the Master Slaver?"

"He is at this moment chasing the child through the kitchen."

"Chasing—" She paused. "Oh, no! You mean—?"

"Yes, mistress. Arte Menia. Didn't you wonder why his house is so close to the slave camp?"

"But he's such a decent man!"

Rum made a peculiar expression. It was as if something was burbling up inside him that would not be restrained. His chest, throat, and head bulged in turn, inflated from within. Was he about to be sick? "Mistress," he gasped. "May I laugh?"

"Laugh? If you wish."

"**Ho ho ho!**" he laughed, the syllables bold-faced. "Decent man! Ho ho ho!"

"But he was being nice to me," she protested, nettled.

"He didn't know you were either slave or spy. He thought you were a lovely lost maiden, and he wanted to summon the stork with you before you learned of his business. Even the meanest man can put on a show for a little while."

She was rapidly coming to believe. "He's responsible for all this misery? He governs the slavemasters? He is the bane of Xanth?"

"Even so, mistress. After you caught on, he would have clapped you in chains and used you to satisfy his lust regardless of your sentiment, until he tired of the sport. Then he would have tossed you to his henchmen for similar treatment. But he liked the illusion, if you will pardon the expression, of decency. A willing maiden is more fun than an unwilling one."

Iris' emotions were mixed. She had hated the Master Slaver by reputation, and her mission was to capture him and destroy his operation. But she had been really intrigued by the suave, handsome, attentive Arte Menia. What was she to do?

She decided that she needed more information. "I never saw you out in the field, or any other demon. Why didn't he use you to round up slaves?"

"I am not a violent demon, mistress. I am no good at nasty stuff. So he finds other uses for me. I keep his house, and I fetch food and supplies, and I move him rapidly from place to place as he goes about his business, but I would faint at the sight of spilled blood."

A faint-hearted demon? "I find this hard to believe."

"Would you believe that I managed to make him believe this, regardless? That it never occurred to him that when he tried to use his talent of persuasion of sincerity on a demon, it bounced back and affected him instead, because it requires a human object? So that I managed to get a relatively soft hitch working for him, instead of being constantly worked?"

Iris nodded. "I think I can believe that. But what am I to do with you? I don't care to keep a demon slave."

"Wrap up your business here, and then turn me over to your Storm King, who will no doubt hide the amulet away safely so that no one else will know it exists. Thus I should have a prolonged rest, which is what I crave. Will you believe that I am a lazy demon?"

"Yes, I will believe that," she said with a smile. "Is there anything else I should know?"

"I thought you would never ask! Arte Menia is returning to this chamber, having failed to catch the child or recover the amulet. His mood is not sanguine."

Iris came to an abrupt decision. "Return to work in the

kitchen, exactly as before, so that no one knows that your master has become a mistress. I will summon you at need." She lay back on the bed.

"Mistress, if I may make a suggestion—" Rum said, looking alarmed.

"Yes?"

"Do not let the amulet leave your person. Because if he should recover it—"

"Understood. I will keep it on me at all times until this is done."

"Thank you." He faded out.

She heard the tramping of angry feet coming down the hall. Quickly she put the amulet to her head, braiding several hanks of her hair over it and through its chain, so that it would not fall free. Then she covered the whole by illusion hair, so that none of the amulet showed. Covered only by her illusion blanket, she awaited Arte.

He burst into the room, disheveled. "That confounded brat!" he exclaimed. He had found a real towel somewhere to wrap around his middle, but it was in danger of falling.

"But what do you care about a mere trinket?" Iris inquired innocently. "We were about to summon the stork." Indeed, she still rather hoped to do so. But first she had to know the truth from his own mouth. She would give him a fair chance to exonerate himself. After all, the demon might have been lying to her, not being truly bound by the amulet. She did not know a great deal about demons, but her mother had cautioned her not to trust them, because they might have Conspiratorial designs on innocent maidens. So her belief in what Rum had told her was less than she had indicated.

"Mere trinket!" he exclaimed. But then a canny look sneaked across his features, and he calmed himself. "True, it is not worth much in any practical sense. But it has sentimental value. My grandfather gave it to me."

"Well, then, I'm sure the child will return it to you in due course. She just likes to make incidental mischief, and loses interest when she can no longer do that."

"I am going to boil that child in—" he started, then reconsidered, forcing a smile. "That is, do you really think so? Perhaps you should ask her to give up this foolish game and return it to me."

Iris shrugged. "Why not?" She let her illusion blanket slip down somewhat beyond the decorous level. "Tell me, Arte, what is the nature of your business?"

"Merchandise," he said. "I handle special merchandise. That is why I must travel so much, to fetch it and to deliver it to the purchasers."

"Really? What sort of merchandise?"

He had the dubious grace to look faintly uncomfortable. "Oh, just items for which there is a market. You wouldn't be interested."

"Yes I would," Iris said, letting her blanket slip another notch.

His eye glimpsed what now showed, and evidently sent a message to another part of his body. "I think we were about to do something interesting, when we were so rudely interrupted," he said, exuding refurbished charm. For some reason Iris found it less conducive than she had before.

"Do you know that there is a slave camp not far from here?" she inquired, intercepting his hand with her own before it reached the region the illusion blanket had recently covered.

Half a shadow crossed his face. "There is?"

"Yes." She saw that he was being evasive, but that didn't necessarily mean that he was a slaver. So she pushed it farther, hoping that he would exonerate himself, because he remained a handsome man. "In fact, I am one of those slaves."

"You are? But you don't wear a slave manacle."

So he knew about those. "The children and I got caught in a storm so cold that our manacles cracked off. Then we came here for shelter. What do you think of that?"

His eyes remained fixed on her front, and his hand, held by hers, quivered as if eager to complete its travel. "I think it's a good thing you found this house. Now let's get on with what we were doing."

Still she demurred. "Aren't you outraged by the situation? People being caught and chained and made slaves against their will?"

"That, too," he agreed. "Now let's just lie down close together and think of storks. Lots of storks."

"In fact," she continued relentlessly, "I am a Sorceress on a secret mission to identify the Master Slaver and destroy his ill operation."

That alarmed him visibly. "A Sorceress! What is your talent?"

"Illusion."

"Oh. Yes. The blanket." But his eyes were calculating now. The news of the slave camp had not surprised or alarmed him, but the news of her nature and mission did. "But illusion isn't real. So maybe I'll just hold you down and get on with the stork, refusing to be distracted by special effects."

"What, against my will?" she inquired, affecting shock.

"Well, it isn't as if I can just let you go, after what you have told me," he said reasonably.

"So you *are* the Master Slaver!"

But he was too canny. "I didn't say that. Come, let's forget about this dialogue and generate some ellipses." He pushed her back on the bed, getting closer to her torso.

How could she get a direct confession from him? She wanted to be absolutely sure, before she took him in. He might be merely a henchman, or a relative.

Perhaps there was a way, though it was risky. She decided to try it.

She let go of his hand and lay back on the pillow behind her. He immediately closed the gap between their bodies. She reached under the pillow. "Oh," she said in feigned surprise. "What's this?"

"If you had ever summoned the stork before, you'd know what it is," he said as he embraced her more closely. He did not seem completely displeased, oddly.

"I mean this thing under the pillow," she said, bringing out an object that looked like a tiny barrel on a chain. "Isn't that the trinket the child took? She must have left it here."

"The amulet!" he exclaimed, snatching it from her hand. "It was here all the time!"

"Amulet?" she asked with all the naivete she could muster. "I thought you said it was just something your grandfather gave you, of sentimental value."

"Some sentiment!" he said. "I'll show you." He drew back and rubbed the barrel.

Demon Rum appeared. "You summoned me, master?"

"Yes. Tie up this spy and leave her naked on the bed, so I can do what I desire with her without any more delay before I throw her away."

"But I thought you were a nice person," Iris said to Arte. "Why should you treat me this way?"

"Nice person!" Arte repeated derisively. "What a foolish girl you are."

Rum approached Iris menacingly. "But I thought you liked me!" she cried to Arte. "You're no better than a slaver!"

"Ho, ho, ho!" he laughed. "I *am* better than a mere slaver. I am the Master Slaver. So know, O foolish Sorceress, that instead of capturing me you have been captured *by* me, and your last act in Xanth will be to satisfy my urge to address the stork. And then I'll have that brat who tried to steal the amulet boiled in beer."

"How can you help him in this?" she asked the demon. "You seemed so nice when you let me into the house yesterday."

"Sorry about this," Rum said as he looped cords about her wrists and ankles and tied her securely down on the bed. "I must obey the one who holds the amulet."

"But how can you mistreat children?" Iris asked Arte.

"I am through listening to your mewling, you pathetic creature. Now shut up or I'll have the demon put tape across your mouth."

"Then I have no choice but to capture you and turn you over to the King," Iris said, coming to her final decision. She had given him every chance, but he had merely confirmed the worst. Her heart ached, because she had really been getting to like him, before learning the truth.

"HO HO HO!" he laughed, harder. "You and who else?" Then, to the demon. "Now go round up those brats and keep them in a safe place until I get new manacles for them." He advanced on her again, the amulet clutched in one hand.

"I think not," the demon said.

Arte paused. "What?"

"You heard me, pee brain," the demon said. "I'm not doing a thing to those children. I like children."

"How dare you!" Arte exclaimed. "Obey, you ludicrous excuse for a foul spirit, or I'll make you do much worse."

"I doubt it, you feculent excuse for a human being. Your days of mischief are over."

Arte turned his head to look at the demon. "You can't say that to me, you crazy spook. I'm your master!"

"Oh yes I can, simpleton. I have a mistress now, and I like her better than I ever liked you."

Arte looked at the amulet, then at Iris. "What's going on here? This isn't in the script."

"As I said," Iris said, "I'm taking you in to the King for justice. Your fell career as a slaver is through."

"When you're all tied up and about to be cruelly ravished? I don't know what's with the demon, but you're about to pay for your arrogance." He lunged for her.

Iris' bonds puffed into smoke as she leaped clear. He landed face first where she had been. She landed on the floor facing him. "Haven't you caught on yet, oaf?" the demon asked with a sneer. "You have been caught in a snare of illusion."

"*What* illusion?" Arte demanded, turning over. "All this witch does is make pretend blankets."

"*I'm* illusion, man cheeks," the demon said. "And so is that amulet."

Arte looked at what he clutched in his hand. It fuzzed out and was revealed as his twisted sock. "What?"

"I have the real amulet," Iris said. She touched her hair, rubbing in the right place.

A second demon appeared. "You summoned me, mistress?" Then he did a double take. "How can there be two of me?"

"Your illusion image has been calling your former master names," Iris said.

"That's an outrage," Rum said. "I demand the right to call him names directly."

"Do so, as you tie him up." Iris went to pick up her clothing.

Rum approached Arte. "You can't touch me!" the man exclaimed, scrambling off the bed.

"Is that so, stink horn breath?" the demon inquired as he conjured stout ropes and looped them around the man. "Mistress, may I dunk him in the boiling soup before hauling him off to the King?"

Iris considered. "I think not. It would spoil the soup."

"All too true," Rum agreed regretfully. "What about the lesser slavers?"

"What would you do with them?" Iris inquired.

"I would give them their heart's desire, which is my very essence."

This set Iris back. She wasn't interested in rewarding the slavers; she wanted to punish them.

"Those lazy bums?" Arte demanded. "Without my harsh discipline, they'd just get blind stinking drunk."

Then she understood. "Yes, give them your essence, Demon Rum," she said. "And tell the slaves to come here to the house for warmth, food, and freedom."

"Done, mistress," Rum said, and vanished.

The door opened. Surprise peeked in. "Oh, goody—you found it!"

"Yes, thank you, dear," Iris said. "How did you know about the amulet?"

"Buttlescutt around the house said there was something.

There had to be, for him to bind the demon cook. So I looked for it in his clothing, but there wasn't time for me to figure it out, so I left it with you while I 'stracted him."

Iris hugged her. "You did exactly right, Surprise. Not only does this enable me to save us, we are putting the slavers out of business."

Soon the slaves started showing up at the house. Rum gave them warm clothing and good hot meals. They were at first fearful, then astonished; most of them had given themselves up to their fate, and not expected any such reprieve. Iris assured them that it was legitimate, and that they could all go home at any time, assisted by the demon.

She and Surprise took a walk outside. The storm had passed and it was halfway warm. There were the slavers, sprawled blissfully across the landscape, half-empty barrels of rum beside them. They were unlikely to recover before the King's men arrived.

"And so it was done, and I had had my adventure and completed my mission," Iris concluded. "The Master Slaver was delivered to the Storm King and never heard of again, and there was no more slavery in Xanth."

"But you shut me out of the good part," Surprise complained. "I wanted to see you summon the stork."

"I know you did, dear, and you know I wouldn't violate the Adult Conspiracy like that, even if I had summoned the stork with that monster."

"Yeah. But the Demon Rum was fun, specially when he started insulting the Master Slaver."

"Yes," Iris agreed somewhat sadly. If only Arte Menia had been as good as he once seemed.

"Did you ever find another romance?"

Ah, the direct questions of children! But it was best to address the painful subject honestly. "Not really," Iris confessed. "Not until Magician Trent, and that was imperfect."

"It was? Why?"

Again that innocent directness. "It was a marriage of convenience. I wanted power and he needed a wife. We didn't love each other. I think he never really forgot his Mundane wife who died."

"But didn't you summon the stork to get Queen Irene?"

"Yes we did, dear. And I came to love Trent. He was exactly the kind of man I needed. But he never really cared for me. Not that I blame him."

"Why not? Aren't you pretty enough?"

"Perhaps I am now. But when I married Trent I was forty-one years old and somewhat dowdy. Of course I enhanced myself with illusion, but he knew the truth. In fact he insisted that I use illusion for all public functions. But he always knew me for what I was, physically and mentally. He never said anything unkind, but he had no passion for me. So the double tragedy of my life was that the man I might have loved turned out to be a slaver, and the one I did love didn't care for me, though I tried to pretend he did."

"But you're young now—and so is he. Why don't you do it now?"

"Do what now?"

"You know—all that stuff I *don't* know. Passion and storks and stuff."

Iris sat amazed. She was young and so was Trent. He was a man who liked beautiful women; she had seen it in her fifty years of marriage to him. He had never acted on it, being a man of scrupulous conscience, but she knew he would have liked to—in fact now would surely still like to—

"You're right, dear. When I return to my husband, knowing all I do now, I shall not let opportunity pass unclasped. Thank you for reminding me of the obvious."

"You're welcome. Hey, see—we're coming into Hinge again."

Iris looked. It was true. They had completed another loop. Apparently the train didn't really go anywhere.

Which meant it had been pointless to use it to search for the philter. They might as well have stayed where they started.

Then, blindingly, she realized that she had after all accomplished part of their mission. She had an excellent intuitive notion where the philter was hiding.

16
DREAM

Hiatus walked through the city, reasonably confident that he wouldn't find the philter. But if he could somehow distract the philter's attention while one of the other parties ran it down, that would be enough. So he tried to look purposeful.

Mentia formed beside him. "Where are we going?" she inquired.

"Anywhere," he said shortly.

"Here comes Desi. Maybe we can ask her."

He tried to laugh, but the joke wasn't funny.

The illusion approached them. She was garbed in an off-the-shoulder blouse and a dress with a short tight skirt. "Why don't you give up this pointlessness and let me distract you?" she inquired winningly.

Hiatus grimaced. "I know you are a mere animation of the philter, and you aren't going to help me find it, so why don't you go away?"

"But I could be so nice to you, if you just let me," she said.

"The only one I want to be nice to me is the real Desiree, not any soulless imitation."

"And if he wanted a fake one he could trust, I'd do it," Mentia said, assuming the form of the dryad.

Hiatus looked from one to the other, disquieted. He couldn't tell them apart. Suppose he thought he was with Mentia, and it was Desi? "I—"

"Good point," Mentia said, resuming her usual form. "I'll pop over and check on the others now. So don't trust her." She faded.

"But—" he protested.

Then he felt the pressure of her invisible hand on his shoulder. Mentia wasn't leaving him; she was merely pretending to, to see what Desi would do. That was reassuring. But he maintained his worried look, so that Desi would not realize. Of course she could read his mind, but maybe she wouldn't do that right now.

"I could help you help her," Desi said.

"Mentia doesn't need any help."

"I was speaking of Desiree. Doesn't she have a problem with her tree?"

"Yes. The madness makes its roots square, and it needs round roots to prosper."

"And your talent is growing round roots."

"My talent is growing ears, eyes, mouths, and noses. But when I try, here in the madness, it messes up."

"Here in the madness, your talent is growing round roots," she repeated. "Which is exactly what the dryad's tree needs."

Hiatus stopped, stunned. "You're right! I can help her tree!"

"And then you will surely have her love, and can remain happily with her ever after. In fact, maybe you should go back to her right now, to get started on your happiness."

"Yes!" Hiatus exclaimed.

Then he felt the invisible hand on his shoulder, cautioning him.

"No," he decided. "Not until Gary's mission here is done."

"You're such a fool," Desi said. "Your dryad's tree will die without your help, and the dryad with it. After you have failed here, what comfort will you have there, when you see the dead tree?"

Her words battered his heart, because he was afraid she was right. But he knew she just wanted to get rid of him, and that might mean that the philter feared he was on course to find it. So he resumed his walk.

"You may then think to take the demoness up on her offer to emulate Desiree for you," Desi continued. "But the moment you leave the Region of Madness, she will revert to form, and be quite irresponsible and crazy. So she won't honor any such deal. You'll be stuck."

He walked on without responding, though again her words seemed mercilessly accurate.

"But you can gain some piece of your desire with me," Desi said. "At least you'll have a notion what it might have been like with the true Desiree."

"You aren't her," he said, though he felt the wicked temptation.

"But you don't need her. Your problem was that you could never find a woman as fair as she is. But now you have; I am exactly as fair as she is. Fairer, in fact, because I emulate your memory of her in her prime."

She was still right. But he knew he couldn't trust her. He kept walking.

"We are approaching the train station," Desi continued, seemingly undismayed. "Perhaps you should take a train."

"I've already taken a train of thought," he said. "That's how we came here."

"True. But these trains go to special places. Your friends are traveling to the future and the past, and not getting anywhere. Maybe you can find a better one."

He was about to reject the notion and turn away from the station. But then it occurred to him that she might be trying another ploy. She had tried to talk him into leaving

Hinge, and it hadn't worked; then she had tried to seduce him again, verbally. Now she could be trying to trick him into denying her a third time—and thus after all failing in his quest of the moment. Because the train might take him to the philter. So he kept walking toward the station.

"In fact there's a train coming in now," Desi said with seeming enthusiasm. That was certainly suspicious.

The sign on the front of the train said DREAM. Was that a distraction, or could the philter be hiding in the dream realm? Hiatus had had some limited experience with big zombie gourds, and knew how weird they were inside. Most gourds could be entered only via their peepholes, leaving the body behind while the spirit ranged through the dream realm. But it was sometimes possible to enter physically, though it was dangerous. What kind of entry would this be, from the madness? The dream realm was already so wild that he could hardly conceive of it becoming moreso. For that matter the madness, beyond this more or less controlled re-creation of the ancient city of Hinge, was pretty crazy too. So this train could be going to the wildest, craziest, maddest realm of all. That daunted him.

Which might be exactly what Desi was trying to do. To cause him to avoid the dreadful prospect. So he ought to go right on into it, and maybe find the philter. This did seem like a suitable prospect; it would naturally hide in the place folks were least likely to want to look.

So he nerved himself and boarded the Dream Train of Thought. He stepped up the steps, entered the coach, and sat down in a seat by a window.

And Desi came with him, sitting beside him. Did that mean she still hoped to divert him, or that she had already succeeded in doing so and wanted to be sure he didn't change his mind? He just didn't know. To make it worse, he hadn't felt Menti's reassuring squeeze for a while. She might really have popped off to see how the other teams were doing. That was fine, of course, but that left him alone with Desi, and he was nervous about that.

"Yes, she's gone, for now," Desi said. "Shall I kiss you first, or show you my panties?"

"Neither, you awful illusion!" he said.

"You'd like both," she said, still accurately. "And I shall be happy to oblige you." She leaned toward him, so that her silken hair brushed his shoulder.

"No!" he cried, pushing her away. His hand passed right through her image without effect. He had forgotten for the moment that she was an illusion, despite addressing her as such. "You're just a manifestation of the philter, who wants to stop us from accomplishing our purpose."

"Of course. But can't we still be friends?"

This struck him as an odd ploy. "Why would you want to be friends?"

"It does get dull, in the course of thousands of years, and I am confined to the Region of Madness. Of course that is growing now, and in time it will govern all Xanth, and I will have everything I may decide to want. But that will take time, and meanwhile it could be entertaining to have a relationship with you."

"Demons get bored?" he asked, surprised.

"When they don't have the company of their own kind."

"Why don't other demons associate with you?" he asked, hoping to learn something useful.

"The madness does odd things to demons, as it does with people," she said. "You may have noticed how Mentia changed. Demons don't really like that, so they avoid it."

"And you can't avoid it?"

"I am a special demon, anchored to my physical component. Since that is in the madness, I can not leave the madness. I have learned to live with it, indeed, to prosper with it. But I am isolated, and that becomes wearing."

Something nagged at the fringe of his attention. "Why are you talking so candidly to me? You concealed your nature before."

"It was not in my interest to reveal my nature, when you were trying to locate and enslave me. Now that you have discovered it on your own, we are entering the next stage: negotiation. It may be that we can do each other some good."

He did not trust this. "We are people with a mission to help Xanth. You are an alien thing with no interest in the welfare of others. What good can we do each other?

"What do you owe Xanth?" she asked, taking the seat opposite him and leaning forward persuasively. Her somewhat exposed front was especially persuasive. Her form was indeed fairer than that of any mortal woman, and she clearly lacked the maidenly restraint of the real Desiree. "What has Xanth ever done for you, other than tantalize you with what you long for but can't have?"

That was difficult to answer. He had not been satisfied with his life. The fact that Desi could read his mind did not change the reality of that blahness that was his life. Xanth had done little for him. Still, there was a matter of principle, and after this mission was done, he could join Desiree Dryad, save her tree, and perhaps win her love. That would make everything worthwhile.

"But you would still be in the Region of Madness," Desi reminded him. "Where I remain. I could destroy her tree at any time, if I chose."

That electrified him; indeed, a few small sparks radiated out from his fingers. If Desiree's tree was lost, Desiree would cease to exist, because she was the essence of her tree. "Then we must capture you, and harness you into the Interface, so you can't do that."

She immediately retreated. "I didn't say I *would*, just that I could. I have no case against the dryad. But I could practically guarantee that you could be with her, by leaving her and you alone. In contrast, if I were limited, and the madness retreated, her tree would be back in un-mad Xanth, and its roots would revert to normal, and she wouldn't need your help. Do you think she would pay you any attention then?"

There was another telling aspect. Hiatus thought he could win Desiree's love if she needed him to maintain her tree, but his chances were next to nil otherwise. He needed to have the madness remain, ironically, in order to have his dream.

But still he didn't trust Desi. "If you remain free, and the madness keeps expanding, you won't need me either, so would have no reason to let me be with Desiree. She and I can be safe from you only if the madness retreats."

"That depends," she said, leaning farther forward, so that the top of her blouse fell away from her bosom, revealing its nicely curving architecture, and it became hard for him to pay full attention to her words. Every breath she took was breathtaking for him. "If you and I had a working association, we might be able to afford to trust each other, and do each other considerable good."

He was amazed. "You are bargaining with me? What could you possibly want of me, other than to let you alone?"

"As I said, it does get dull here, and human company is better than none. I could entertain you considerably, and your entertainment would be my entertainment. Do you believe that?"

"I don't think I do." He hoped that was the right answer. His brain wasn't working very well as long as his eyeballs were glued to her gently heaving bosom. But he knew that what entertained demons was not necessarily what entertained the mortal folk they associated with.

"Then try this: there is a service you could perform for me that I would greatly value. I would do a lot for you in exchange for that service."

Hiatus grew canny, he hoped. "You mean like the service I could do for Desiree's tree, so that she would need me and like me?"

"Yes. If I needed you, I could do an emulation of liking you that you would find persuasive, and certainly enjoyable." She took another breath, more than making her point. "I am a practical entity."

"What service?" he asked flatly. He was learning how

to think a little, though his eyeballs seemed to be heat-sealing themselves in their sockets.

"Moving me."

Hiatus drew a blank. "Doing what?"

"Moving my physical component from one place to another. So that I could travel. Then I would no longer be confined to the Region of Madness, and could extend my influence into normal Xanth immediately."

"But to do that I would have to find you!" he protested. For he remembered that however compelling her twin hemispheres might be, she was not the philter; she was just a projection projected to blind him by cooking his eyeballs.

"Yes. So you can appreciate that I will never allow you to find me unless we have a deal that guarantees your trustworthiness. At present we can not trust each other, but if that changed, we might enable each other to possess our respective dreams."

Hiatus was amazed again. "You can read my mind. You know I don't much like you, however tempting you make your illusion form. And I'm sure you have no feeling at all for me, except irritation at the inconvenience of having to deal with me. How could we ever trust each other?"

"If you knew that only I could guarantee your happiness with Desiree, and I knew that only you could enable me to travel without danger, we would be bound to each other by realistic self-interest. It could be an extremely mutually profitable arrangement."

"But I would be betraying the interest of Xanth," he protested. There was no doubt about it: his eyes had fused in his head, staring at her earnest breast.

"That depends on how you look at it," she said, glancing down as if to make sure her mock hypnogourds were still functioning. "Since in time the madness will expand to cover all Xanth, and my power with it, you would be merely accelerating the speed of the change, not its nature. And you would reap extraordinary benefit yourself. In fact if you wished to have nominal power in Xanth, such as becoming king, it could be arranged. I don't care about that sort of thing; my power is expressed in other ways."

"King?" Hiatus had never thought of such a thing. "No, my talent is not Magician level, and anyway, I'm sort of a nothing person, as my name shows. My sister Lacuna was the same, until she married retroactively. I'm not cut out for greatness. I just want to find happiness with Desiree, and that's all."

"To quote a memory in your mind: some are born to greatness," Desi said earnestly, her breathing deepening. "Some achieve it. Some have it thrust—"

"Hello," Mentia said, appearing. "I hope I'm interrupting something." She eyed Desi's decolletage, which promptly misted over. Then the illusion woman faded out.

"Where were you?" Hiatus asked, trying to crack his eyeballs out of their locked positions. "She was seducing me with wonderful promises."

"And with hot meat, too," the demoness remarked. She peered into his face. "Sure enough, your eyes corroded. Don't you know enough to blink at least once a minute? Here's some lubricating oil." She produced an oilcan and squirted a drop on each eyeball, then massaged his eyelids to spread it around.

His eyes finally ground out of their grooves. It hurt to move them around, but he wanted to get them back to full working order. "She—she offered me a deal," he said.

"What can she offer that I can't offer? I speak theoretically, of course, having no more inherent interest in you than she does."

He considered that. "Actually, probably nothing. But it seemed persuasive at the time."

"Well, that's because you mortal men are constitutionally unable to look and reason simultaneously."

"Oh, I wouldn't say that."

She assumed Desiree's form, with Desi's open blouse. She leaned forward and breathed. "Now reason with me."

"I, uh, duh—" he said, staring.

Her blouse closed itself up. His eyes broke free just before they corroded again. "Point made," he said.

"The other teams are proceeding," she said. "But not finding anything. So I took time to look around myself, but I couldn't locate the philter. It is certainly well hidden."

"But it must be afraid that we can find it," he said, "because it's taking a lot of trouble to interfere with our search."

"Yes. And the ones I think it fears most are Gayle Goyle and you, because it has taken the most trouble to eliminate or subvert you. It ignored Iris and Surprise. So you must have the key to its location."

"If I do, I don't know what it is," he said.

"It may be something you are destined to do or see. Maybe you will just happen to blunder on its hiding place, and it knows that. So it's desperate to divert you or subvert you before that happens."

Hiatus shrugged. "I suppose. But she scared me. She said she could destroy Desiree's tree."

"She lied. How can an illusion hurt a tree?"

"But it's a demon, really. And demons can—"

"Set your foolish mind at ease. I'm a demon. I could hurt a tree. But why would I bother? It would be a lot of work to no purpose. The philter is a demon, but of a different species. Apparently most of its bulk is bound into its physical aspect, and it has very little left over. So it uses a variant of illusion, stretched very thinly, with just a bit of substance to provide the feel of it when necessary. So when she kisses you, only her lips are solid, and when her hand touches you, only the skin of her fingers is tangible. No way could she damage a tree protected by its dryad."

"That's right," he said, appreciating her reasoning. "That lady dog lied to me!"

"That's why I told you not to trust her." She looked out the window. "Say, I think we're getting where we're going."

He followed her gaze. "That looks like a giant gourd!"

"The entry into the dream realm," she agreed. "This is going to be interesting."

"Interesting? Why?"

"Because demons don't dream. I don't know what to anticipate in a dream."

"A dream in madness is frightening," he said. "You demons haven't been missing anything you'd want."

"Well, we'll see." She stood as the train creaked to a halt. "Let's get on with it."

He followed her off the train. A path led directly to the monster gourd. The thing was so big that the train itself could have steamed on into it, but perhaps the train knew better. A sign over its entry said ABANDON HOPE, ALL YE WHO ENTER HERE.

"Is this wise?" he asked nervously.

"If the philter doesn't want us to go here, it's probably where we should go," Mentia said. "Besides, I'm curious."

"You have never had a bad dream delivered by a night mare," he told her.

"Right. I'm sure it's intriguing. Let's head on into Stone Hunch."

He realized that she would have to learn the hard way. She had never dreamed, so had no fear, in just the way small dragons who had never encountered ogres lacked fear. Any human child knew better than to tempt a night mare, but a demon didn't.

They entered the enormous peephole. With a normal gourd the peephole caught the eye of the looker, and would not let it go, much as Desi's exposed bosom had locked Hiatus' own eyes in place. But with a big gourd this effect was minimal, because the whole body was caught in it.

Suddenly they were in a strange room. There was a picture hanging on the wall showing a portrait of a man Hiatus didn't recognize. He glanced away, then back at it—and the portrait had changed. Realizing that he must be mistaken, he looked away, and to it a third time. It had changed again.

There was a window, through which he could see rain pouring down incessantly. He looked away, and to it again, but the rain did not change. But he knew that it had not been raining outside the gourd. More strangeness.

There was a peculiar machine directly in front of him, with a board filled with letters of the alphabet, and a screen right above it. "Oh, no!" he breathed, a shiver of dread running through him. "I recognize that device by reputation. It's Com Pewter, the evil machine who changes reality in his vicinity, so that no one can escape."

"What a weird place," Mentia remarked.

"I think we had better get out of here before Pewter wakes and starts messing with our realities," Hiatus said.

"Oh, pooh," she said. "A stupid machine can't affect a demon."

"I'm not sure of that. I'm leaving." He turned and started back out of the gourd—before realizing that there was a solid wall of the room behind him. The scene had shut him in. "Uh, that is, maybe you can leave," he said.

"Sure." But she remained standing beside him.

"Go!" he said nervously. "Fade out. Pop off. You can warn the others not to enter the gourd."

"I can't," she said, visibly disturbed. "I'm trying to fade, but it's not working."

"I was afraid of that. You're trapped too. We can't get out of this until we figure out how—and it may not be easy. The dream realm doesn't follow ordinary rules."

"You mean this is a dream? Stuck in a stupid room and I can't act like the demoness I am? This isn't fun."

"Bad dreams aren't fun. I tried to warn you."

"Well, then, I'll just bash my way out." She walked to the wall, formed a triple-sized fist, and punched hard.

Her big fist bounced off the wall harmlessly. "Owww!" she cried, jamming the fist into her mouth, which she expanded hugely for the purpose. "Mmmph owmmmmph yowmmmph!"

"What was that?"

She pulled the fist out with a slurpy pop. "That stupid wall hurt me!"

"But demons don't hurt," he reminded her.

She looked at her big hand, which was now turning red and pulsing. "In bad dreams they do, it seems."

"I guess you are now subject to human limitations. Maybe there's another way out."

He turned back to face the picture, window, and evil machine. Pewter remained asleep, fortunately. He took a careful step to the left, avoiding the machine.

A word appeared before him: FLOOR.

Hiatus stared at the word. "I know it's the floor," he said. "Why should I need a word to tell me that?"

Mentia's hand had shrunk back to normal size, though it still looked sore. "Maybe the floor doesn't think much of your intelligence."

Irritated, Hiatus took another step. His foot landed on a rug. Another word appeared: RUG.

He experimented. Whatever he touched evoked a word: PICTURE, WINDOW, DESK, WALL, DOOR. It was really weird. He tried to open the door, but it wouldn't budge.

They discovered that Mentia's motions didn't bring forth the magic words. In fact she wasn't able to have any effect on this set. It ignored her completely, while keeping her trapped within it, to her increasing frustration.

There was an envelope on the desk on which Pewter sat, but he couldn't get it open to learn what writing might be in it. There was also a small piece of paper with some cryptic names and numbers.

There was a sound of ringing from the side. Hiatus looked in that direction, and saw that the sound came from beyond the door to another room. The one he couldn't open.

"Look at the ceiling," Mentia said.

He looked. There were more words. One of them was OPEN. So he reached up and touched that word. It came away in his hand.

He was getting a glimmer of a notion. He carried the glowing white word to the door. Sure enough, when he touched the door with it, the word faded and the door opened. It showed a small chamber with a new door that seemed to lead outside, and another to another chamber. But by this time the ringing had stopped.

Time passed. They explored three rooms of this odd house, including the kitchen, where there was a big white food box that was cold inside and had a sandwich. He ate the sandwich and returned to the second room. The ringing resumed, and he saw that it was coming from some kind of device set on the wall.

"I know what that is," Mentia said. "It's a Mundane phone. I've heard of them. They talk."

"They talk?"

"You use the loose dingus," she explained.

So he took the loose dingus, which dangled a cord which connected to the box. He put it to his ear. "Hi, Dug!" the dingus said.

"I'm not Dug, I'm Hiatus," he said.

"Oh. Sorry. Must be a wrong number."

"Dug?" Mentia said. "Wasn't that the name of that Mundane youth who visited Xanth? My better half was forced to be a prospective Companion, but wasn't chosen. But she never saw the Mundane side of it."

Hiatus had heard of the Game. He realized this could be a source of information that might help him get out. "Maybe not," he said. "Maybe this is the right number but the wrong person. I think I don't belong here."

"Yeah?" the voice said. "Who are you?"

"I'm Hiatus. Who are you?"

"I'm Edsel, Dug's best friend. You say Dug's not there?"

"Edsel," Mentia said. "That's one of the names on that note. So this must be Dug's house."

"Not now," Hiatus said to the dingus. "But maybe he'll be back soon."

"Okay," Edsel said. "Tell him I called." There was a click, and then a buzzing silence.

Hiatus put the dingus back on the device on the wall. At least he had learned something.

In the course of further experiment he learned that Dug's girlfriend Pia had just dumped him, so he made a deal with Edsel: Pia in exchange for Ed's motorcycle. Hiatus had no idea what a motorcycle was, but the deal gave him the chance to try the game of Companions of Xanth, and he thought the game was a better place to be than this weird Mundane dream setting. A flat object arrived at his door, and Mentia figured out how to put it in the computer, because she had had a bit of experience with the real game. The screen formed a picture, and they stepped into that scene.

And found themselves in a cave. But Grundy Golem was also there. He did a double take. "Hiatus! What are you doing here?"

"I'm looking for the philter."

"What are you talking about? Don't you know this is the entry for the Companions of Xanth computer game? It's not for natives." Then the golem saw Mentia. "And what are you doing, Metria? You haven't been selected as a Companion yet."

"I'm not Metria," the demoness said shortly.

"Well, you look exactly like her."

"Have you heard me stumble on a stupid word?"

"No, but—"

"I'm her worser half, Mentia. She did something disgusting, so I split. I'm a little bit crazy."

"You don't seem crazy, either."

"That's because this setting is crazy. I get perversely sane when my surroundings get crazy."

"Well, if you're Hiatus' Companion, get him off this set before a real Player comes."

Mentia became canny. "Just tell us where the philter is, and we'll be gone."

Grundy shook his little head. "I don't know anything about a filter. What's it for?"

"Purifying water," Hiatus said.

"Then it must be out beyond the pail. Look for it there."

"Where's this pail?"

"Out along the enchanted trail." The golem gestured toward a door in the cave, which was now open.

They went out, and followed the trail to Isthmus Village, in whose bay an evil censor ship was anchored. The folk there were grumpy, their dialogue peppered with bleeps. So they headed out into the country—and there was the pail. But when Hiatus went to pick it up, it sailed into the air and flew away toward the horizon.

"What's going on here?" he demanded, feeling as irritable as the villagers.

"Oh, I remember," Mentia said. "You can't accomplish anything until you get beyond the pail. And you have to figure out how to do that. It's one of the challenges of the game."

"So how do I get beyond it?"

"I'm not supposed to tell you that. You have to figure it out for yourself."

"But I'm not playing this stupid game!" Hiatus said. "I'm just trying to find the philter."

"That's right; I forgot." She looked thoughtful. "Maybe I can ask the pail."

"You can talk to the pail?"

"Yes. But it's an arrogant thing and won't help."

"Then why ask it anything?"

"Because I can be obnoxious, when I really try."

Hiatus didn't understand her logic, but didn't protest. They walked on along the path until they caught up to the pail again. Then Hiatus waited while Mentia floated up to it.

"Listen, pailface," she said. "I'm a crazy demoness, and the only thing I have better to do than bug you is find the philter. Since we don't know where the philter is, I think I'll just bug you forever."

"You can't bug me, you nuisance," the pail said. "You can't pick me up, and your stupid-looking friend there doesn't know how to get beyond me, so ha-ha-ha in your face."

"It's not my face you'll be meeting," Mentia said. "You can't move away because of me, because I'm not the Player, so you have to remain there for it." She adjusted her dress.

"For what?" the pail asked derisively. "You going to kiss my pot, demoness?"

"Not exactly." She lifted her hem as she stood beside the bucket.

"You going to show me your panties? You can't freak me out, demoness, because I'm not a man."

"We shall see." She hoisted up her skirt and squatted over the pail. Hiatus clapped his hands to his face, just barely in time to avoid seeing her panties.

"Hey!" the pail cried, alarmed. "You can't do that!"

"I can't? I'm going to make a good effort, though." There was the sound of panties coming down.

"AEEEEE!" the pail screamed. "All right, stop this asinine display. I'll tell you how to find the philter."

"I don't know," she said. "I think I'd rather see what it takes to fill you to overflowing."

"Enough of this crap!" the pail cried desperately. "You're a demoness! The philter is a demon. You know how to fetch a demon."

She paused. "Why so I do," she agreed. "Demons can be conjured. Very well, I'll spare you my effort, reluctantly." She straightened up and let her clothing re-form around her.

Hiatus walked up to her—and immediately the pail sailed up and away. That didn't matter. "We can conjure the philter?" he asked.

"Yes, any demon can be conjured. You just have to know its true name."

"So what's the philter's true name?"

She shrugged. "I never knew the philter personally. The

true name is a demon's most private thing. Maybe one of the other parties will have learned it."

Hiatus nodded. "I think we have accomplished something. Let's get out of here and rejoin the others."

She looked around. "I'll be glad to. How do you get out of a dream?"

He remembered that demons didn't dream, so she wouldn't know. Actually he wasn't too sure himself. Usually his dreams ended when he woke. But how could he wake from this one? "Sometimes a dream gets scary, and the fright wakes the dreamer," he said. "Since I'm the mortal here, I must be the dreamer; if I wake, we should both be out of it."

"Shall I make a face like this to frighten you?" she asked, taking her hands and stretching her face into a grotesque shape.

"No, I know who you are, so I'm not frightened."

"Maybe if I show you my panties." She reached for the hem of her skirt.

"No, don't do that! It might freak me out, but maybe not wake me."

"How about jumping off a high cliff?"

"No, that would kill me."

"In a dream?"

He reconsidered. "That's right—falling in a dream scares you awake without killing you. Very well, let's go jump off a cliff."

They walked on until they found a cliff beside the path. It dropped off into a crevice of a valley. "Does that scare you?" Mentia asked.

"It sure does!" He backed away from the brink. "I don't think I have the nerve to jump."

"No problem." She wrapped her arms around him, lifted him, and flung him over the brink.

"AEEEEE!" he screamed as he plummeted.

"Interesting," the demoness remarked, appearing beside him. "That's exactly what the pail said when it viewed my pale posterior."

"But the pail wasn't about to die of fright," he gasped, trying to grab on to her to slow his fall.

She eluded him. "No, it was about to die of disgust. I told you I could be obnoxious when I tried."

"Agreed!" He grabbed for her again, but his clutching hands passed right through her image without contact.

The rocky ground was rushing up at him. Hiatus savored one more instant of utter terror, then landed—

And found himself sitting on the ground near the palace of the city of Hinge. He was awake, unharmed.

"It worked!" Mentia said, pleased. "We must do that again sometimes. Dreams are fun."

17

HARNESS

Gary and Gayle rode the train of thought back to thestation at Hinge. When they got off they found Hiatus and Mentia waiting for them. A train was arriving from the other direction, and soon Iris and Surprise joined them. They all walked slowly back to the palace, comparing notes. It seemed that one couple had gone to the past, but this had been merely a matter of reminiscing. Another had gone into the dream realm. Gary and Gayle had of course visited the future. None had found the philter.

"But the philter seemed determined to kill Gayle," Gary said. "We finally turned our ship around and came back, because it was too dangerous and we weren't learning anything."

The demoness Mentia nodded. "It is clear that Gayle knows something we need."

"I don't know what that would be," Gayle protested. "I have been nowhere for three thousand years."

"And Desi tried to seduce me from the mission," Hiatus said. "Physically and emotionally. She offered me everything—Desiree, the kingship of Xanth, whatever I might desire. She even showed me her—" He stopped, overcome by delicacy. Actually, Gary had a fair suspicion what Desi might have shown him, based on what Hanna had done. The philter seemed to be getting desperate.

"So you, too, must know something important," Iris said.

"Or have been about to find it out," Mentia said. "As I believe we did."

"We, too, may have learned something," Iris said. "But not enough."

They entered the palace. "Let's discuss this," Mentia said. "I think we may have learned more than we thought."

Desi appeared. "Oh, you must be very tired after your long journeys," she said solicitously. "And hungry. We have beds and banquet waiting."

"Now I'm sure of it," Mentia said with satisfaction. "Ignore her and proceed with the discussion. What do you know, Iris?"

"I think I have figured out where the philter is," Iris said.

"That won't do you any good," Desi said. "It is only an object physically, and won't do a thing for you."

"Where is it?" Gary asked.

"In the center of the magic," Iris said. "The very center. That's why the trains of thought all circle around; they can't go beyond the philter's range. And I think it needs the very strongest magic to craft its powerful illusions and effects. It's not inherently strong; it is buoyed by that intense field, making it a super demon. It must be in the center of the focus circle."

"But that's where I was," Gayle protested. "Surely you don't think that I—"

"No, dear," Iris said. "You are no demon; Mentia would have known if you were. And you are no illusion; I would have known. And you *are* a gargoyle: Gary knows. As a group we are uniquely qualified to assess your nature, perhaps by no coincidence. You are beautifully innocent. But your location is also that of the philter. I strongly suspect it has been hiding in the tiles beneath you for three thousand years."

"Beneath me!" Gayle cried, amazed. "I suppose it could be true, for I talked with its illusions often. But I never suspected it could be that close!"

"This is ludicrous," Desi said. "Even if you found the philter, you wouldn't be able to affect it. You don't have the—"

"The what?" Mentia asked alertly.

"Nothing."

"What did you find out, Mentia?" Gary asked.

"That we can conjure the philter," the demoness said evenly. "It's a demon."

"You can't summon the philter," Desi said. "The philter can't move."

"I said conjure, not summon," Mentia said. "That is, to exert power over it. We can conjure it into the Interface. We merely need to be close enough to it for our conjuration to have full effect—and we need to know its real name."

"Why, I know that," Gayle said. "It's—"

There was a deafening blast of sound, drowning her out. Then Mentia assumed the shape of a great golden blob, and the noise faded.

"What did you do?" Gary asked, surprised.

"She became a blob of golden silence," Iris said. "She's neutralizing Desi, who had become an obstructive noise. Gayle, you were saying—?"

"Its name is Fil," Gayle said. "Fil Philter. I remember that from when they were first working on the Interface. I didn't realize that was important."

"But the philter knew it was important!" Gary said. "That's why it was trying to kill you, when you started associating with me."

"So now we have the whole of it," Iris said. "We know how to right the wrong of three thousand years ago, and reverse the spread of madness, and free the gargoyles. We have simply to go to the center of the magic circle, and conjure Fil into the Interface, and our quest will be done."

"Then let's do it!" Gary said.

Mentia reappeared in her usual form. "That may not be easy," she said. "Desi is gone for the moment, and so is her noise, but the philter as it is presently enhanced by the madness magic is one powerful demon, much stronger than I am, and it is determined not to let us conjure it into the Interface. It tried to distract us from learning its secrets, and now it will distract us from acting."

"But now that we know where it is and what to do, it won't be able to stop us," Gary said.

Iris shook her head. "The philter has powerful illusions. Those will be difficult to get past."

"But we'll know they are illusions," Gary said. "So we'll just have to feel our way forward, and not fall in any holes."

"Illusions supported by demon powers," Mentia said soberly. "I agree: that's a potent combination. We had better organize carefully."

"Now I can recognize and perhaps counter some of the illusions," Iris said. "Surprise may be able to lend me support when I need it. But the demonic aspects—"

"I will be able to identify," Mentia said. "And to counter to a degree, if I don't face the full brunt. Hiatus can help me. That means that the gargoyles will have to be our guides when we get preoccupied with illusions and demonics."

"We can do that," Gayle agreed. "I know the way."

"But—" Gary said, still not seeing what all the fuss was about.

"Let's go," Iris said grimly. "Before the philter has any more time to organize its defense."

"And there's still something missing," Mentia added. "Something we need. Desi's not the smartest of illusions, and she almost let it slip. But we don't know what it is."

"Maybe we can find it," Iris said. "By traveling in a

zigzag pattern and keeping alert for anything out of the ordinary."

"Everything's out of the ordinary, here in the madness!" Hiatus protested.

"True," Mentia said. "But there may be something different, even so. If we can catch it, it may give us the final key to victory."

This seemed nonsensical to Gary, but he realized that there was no point in arguing. Either they would find that mysterious thing, or they wouldn't.

So they left the palace. Gayle led the way, with Gary close beside her. And suddenly he realized why they were taking it so seriously.

The city of Hinge had completely changed. It was now a plain, covered by a ripple on the ground. It was pretty in its way. But he knew that if the philter could change the semblance of the city into that of a plain, it could do other visions too, and that could be real mischief.

Surprise screamed. Then Gary saw a terrible bug stalking her. It was a nickelpede—the insect whose pincers gouged out coin-sized chunks of flesh. There was another nickelpede behind it, and others coming toward the rest of them. In fact the entire ground was covered with them; that was what made the ripple effect. Gary realized that though his natural form was immune to them, his human form was vulnerable. It was impossible to cross this region.

"Illusion," Iris said tersely. "Ignore them."

"Nuh-uh," Mentia said. "Some may be real, hidden among the illusions."

Iris winced. "You're right. What a devious ploy! I'll burn them."

Devious indeed! Suppose they had nerved themselves and waded through the illusion swarm, only to be chomped by the few real ones they hadn't recognized?

"You can't just wipe out the illusions?" he asked Iris with faint hope.

"No, I can't. I can abolish only my own illusions, not

someone else's. That has never been a problem before, because all illusions were mine. This is a new and difficult situation."

Then her fire started. An illusion lightning bolt came down, casting off several fiery washers and a nut, and flames spread out from the scorched region. The illusion nickelpedes squeaked and chittered as they caught fire. They fled the blaze, and in the process spread it much faster than it spread itself.

"So illusion fire burns illusion insects," Hiatus murmured, impressed.

"Yes," Iris said. "I can't abolish the enemy effects, but the philter can't abolish mine either, and where they meet, nature takes its course."

A clear path was opening, where the fire had cleared the nickelpedes. They started to walk along it. But then Gary saw a nickelpede that hadn't been scorched. That was one of the few real ones.

The creature scooted toward them. But Gayle bounded forward and stepped on it with her massive stone foot. The thing was flattened into the ground, and stirred no more.

But already a new menace was forming. There was a mountain in the distance, and down that mountain flowed a large river, and the river was spreading out and flooding the plain. That was depriving the fire of its base, and it was hissing and flickering out.

They moved on, cautiously, knowing that illusion could cover a pit in the ground. Gary banged into something, and realized it was one of the huge hinged stones, covered by the illusion of nothingness. He and Gayle tapped the ground ahead with their toes, making sure it was solid.

But the water kept rising. It came up around their ankles, so that their feet could not be seen under its brown swirl. There could be more nickelpedes concealed under that, ready to chomp them. It wasn't safe to proceed.

Then Iris made an illusion causeway. It seemed to rise up just above the level of the water, so that they could see their feet again. The river couldn't made the water rise faster than the causeway crossed it, because it required a lot more illusion water to fill the plain than illusion sand to make the causeway.

Until the storm started. "That looks like Fracto," Iris muttered.

So it did. There was a huge fuzzy face on the surface of the cloud, with bulging cheeks and angry moist eyes. The mouth opened and lightning shot out, followed by a freezing gust of wind. "What's Fracto doing in an illusion?" Surprise asked.

"Wherever there is ill to be winded, Fracto is there," Mentia explained. "He doesn't care where it is. He has a nose for mischief like none other."

The wind struck the surface of the water and stirred up waves. The waves became huge, and reared up to pound against the causeway. In a moment they had breached it, knocking big holes in it. The water surged through, eating at the remaining edges, carrying the sand away.

"I can fix that," Mentia said. She dissolved, and reformed into two towers girt by many thin cords, supporting a planking. It was a suspension bridge across the first big gap in the causeway.

Gary set foot on it, and it was solid because the demoness did not use illusion; she used her own substance, which could become as hard as she wished it to be, for a while. So he crossed, and the others after him. Gayle walked beside it, because her weight would be a special burden, and she had no fear of nickelpedes anyway.

There was a pained squeak. Gayle lifted a forefoot from the surging water. There was a nickelpede attached to a toe. It evidently had suffered a broken tooth. It fell limply into the water without a splash. Gary almost, but not quite, felt a bit of sympathy for it.

But while they were on the middle of the bridge span, something huge appeared in the water. It looked like the fabled Mundane creature, a whale, so big nobody could believe it. It forged onward ever onward toward the bridge, threatening to bash it down. It was illusion, of course, yet it looked so real that Gary spooked. He ran on to the solid section of causeway ahead, while cursing himself for his foolishness.

The whale crashed into the nearer bridge tower—and the tower began to tip over. The whale *was* real!

Surprise screamed. Gary reversed course and ran back onto the tipping bridge to save her. He caught her just as she slid off into the water. But then he fell into the water himself. There was no help for it; he just had to run through it as well as he could. It was only waist deep, and illusion, so he really was running, though it looked like deep wading.

There was pain in one foot. A nickelpede! No, in half an instant he realized that it was just an ordinary bruise; he had kicked a hidden rock. He made it to the island section of the causeway, carrying Surprise.

The moment they were safe, he set her down and turned back to see what else was happening. The bridge was down and dissolving, but part of it was forming into a giant rubber band whose end was around Iris. The band contracted, almost catapulting Iris to the island. Mentia had saved her.

But Hiatus was floundering in the water. "Oh, I want to use my magic to help him!" Surprise said.

"Don't you dare," Iris told the child. "You need to save your magic for the conjuration."

So that was why Surprise had been so meek, magically. It made sense. She still had powerful and varied magic, but she might need all of it when they came to the final reckoning with the demon philter. So she was exercising painful restraint, and in the process learning the way of control. She would surely be a much better child when she returned to her family.

Then Hiatus rose in the water, looking startled. "It's got me!" he cried.

The rubber band opened a mouth. "You fool, that's Gayle Goyle!" it called.

Hiatus looked down at the sleek stone shoulder beneath him. "Oh. Thanks." He looked somewhat sheepish.

Now the sun came out, huger and hotter than it ever was in regular Xanth. Gary realized that it, too, was probably illusion. It blasted down on the water, making it so hot it boiled and evaporated in a hurry. The intense radiation didn't bother Gary, but of course he wasn't illusion. They watched as their island grew, because of the receding water. Soon the plain was bare again. If there were any nickelpedes remaining, they were probably seasick by this time.

Now Gary thought of something. "How did an illusion whale knock over a real bridge?"

Mentia reappeared in her usual form. "The philter is a demon, remember. It has demonly powers. Not a lot of physical strength, because its real body is elsewhere, but it can become solid in some instances. So it made just the top of the whale solid, and it pushed against the top of the tower, and the magic of leverage made it fall."

Gary was now satisfied: the philter was a formidable opponent, with its combination of illusion and substance. A lot of one and a little of the other, but they did the job.

But as the plain reappeared, so did another threat. It looked as if a rug were sliding slowly across it. But the rug grew as it got closer, and Gary saw that it was actually an enormous herd of animals. They were stampeding directly toward the erstwhile island.

"Buff low," Mentia said, looking at the oncoming mass. "If they run over us, we'll all be buffed low."

"No, they're illusion," Iris said.

Then her counterillusion formed: another fire. It swept across the plain toward the buffs, looking very hot. The animals saw it and spooked. In a moment they were milling around, trying to reverse course. But the ones behind were still surging forward, not yet aware of the danger.

It didn't matter. The rampaging herd had been halted, and it was possible to make some progress toward the magic circle.

But now a new class of illusions formed. The surroundings became pleasant, with trees and a castle ahead. "Why that's Castle Roogna," Iris remarked, surprised.

"The philter can read our minds," Hiatus reminded her. "Anything that any of us remembers, it can make appear."

"And all of it is dangerous," Mentia said. "Because of the real threats it covers."

"I am well aware of that," Iris said somewhat sharply. "I'm just trying to figure out the nature of this ploy. Why should the philter present us with something unthreatening?"

"We were countering the threats," Gary said. "So now it's trying another approach."

"Or merely trying to guide us in the direction it wants," Mentia said. "And away from what it doesn't want us to find. Remember, there may be something we are looking for, besides the philter itself."

A figure appeared before the castle. It walked toward them. It seemed to be a young woman, carrying something heavy. "And that's Electra, my grandson's wife," Iris said. "A wonderful girl."

"What's she carrying?" Surprise asked.

"I am not clear on that," Iris said. "It's all illusion, anyway."

They waited while the woman approached. Gary saw that she was not especially imposing or beautiful, but she seemed like a nice person. Her hair was bound in a practical braid, and she wore blue jeans.

"She doesn't look like a princess," Surprise said.

Iris smiled. "She never acted like one, either. She was always rather scrawny. Had I been in charge of things, I would have had Prince Dolph marry Princess Nada Naga, an outstanding creature. But Electra's doing the job, and now I know I was mistaken. Her magic talent of electricity is far from Sorceress level, but she makes up for it by being very nice and reliable. She gave me twin grandchildren, Dawn and Eve; the stork brought them NoRemember Two. I wouldn't change her for any other."

Electra came to stand before them, bearing her object. It was black, with red and white knobs on the top. "Can someone help me carry my battery?" she asked. "I have charged it up, but it's very heavy."

"Why, sure, Princess," Hiatus said, starting to step forward.

"Nuh-uh," Mentia said, extending an arm to restrain him. "There's demon substance in that battery."

"You won't take my battery?" Electra asked, looking extremely innocent.

"You're an enemy illusion," Iris said grimly. "We don't trust you."

"Then you must accept the other thing I have for you," Electra said, setting down the battery. "Assault." And she sprouted fangs and pounced on Surprise.

But Gayle moved more swiftly, leaping to intercept her. The gargoyle knocked the woman to the side, so that the child was never touched. The image of Electra dissolved into an irritated cloud.

"Gee, thanks," Surprise said, curiously unconcerned. Maybe she thought the attack had been another harmless illusion. She stepped forward to investigate the battery.

Mentia formed into a bright metal shield and jumped between the child and the battery. And the battery exploded. Shards of metal flew out, some bouncing off the shield. One struck Gary, but it didn't hurt him, being illusion. But it was clear that there was substance in the ones that struck the shield, because it clanged loudly with their impact.

Iris kneeled down before Surprise. "Are you all right, dear?" she asked.

"Sure." But now the child looked shaken. "Why did that nice lady try to hurt me?"

"Because you are evidently now the leading threat to the freedom of the philter," Mentia said, reforming from the shield. "The rest of us were threats when we were figuring out how to locate and control it, but now we know how to do that, so we no longer matter to it. We will need your magic for the actual conjuration, so it seeks to destroy you first."

"How do you know that?" Gary asked, surprised.

"Because the philter is a cold, logical demon without a lot of direct physical substance or energy to waste. It wouldn't attack her physically unless it feared her."

The others nodded. The demoness had proved to be the most sensible of them all, again.

"We shall have to be specially protective toward her," Iris said.

"I will carry her," Gayle said. She lay down before the child, and Surprise climbed up onto the stone back and grabbed on to the stone fur. "This is fun!" she announced. "A gargle ride!"

"A gargle ride," Gary agreed, though he winced internally. They had to keep the child safe, and happy as well, if they could manage it.

Already something new was developing. A group of creatures was advancing from the castle. "Centaurs!" Iris said. "Beware their expert archery."

"But if the arrows are illusion—" Gary began.

"Whatever flies at Surprise won't be," Mentia said. "Any more than the fragments of the battery that flew at her were."

"Then we had better take evasive action," Gary said, appreciating the point. "But it's hard to flee when we can't see the real terrain."

"I can't abolish the philter's illusion, but I can recognize it," Iris said. "There's an avenue through the city, that way." She pointed to the thickest section of the orchard surrounding the castle. "We can run along that with fair safety."

"And it looks completely impassable," Mentia said. "Suggesting that that's the way the philter least wants us to go."

They were still searching for they knew not what. Gary remained doubtful, but had no better alternative to suggest, so he kept his mouth shut. In this Region of Madness, maybe the maddest notions were appropriate.

So Gary ran, trusting her perception, and the others followed him. It looked as if he were heading directly into a thicket of needle cacti, but there was nothing there. It reminded him of Desiree's magic path, invisible to those not on it. But this one remained invisible while they were on it.

However, the centaurs changed course to pursue. Several nocked arrows to their bows as they galloped within range. Mentia formed into another shield, this one with legs, and ran directly behind Gayle and Surprise, protecting them. But at the rate the centaurs were overhauling them, they'd soon get around that.

"We can't outrun those illusions," Hiatus said, puffing.

"There's a real hinged stone column here," Iris gasped, pointing to the left. "Hide behind that."

Gary swerved into what looked like a mud puddle, and glanced off the side of the stone column. Ouch! But he found the corner of it, and gestured to the others. They whipped around it and clustered behind its protection, the illusion-invisible stone at their backs.

Mentia formed into a metallic tube with wheels. "What's that?" Gary asked.

"A cannon," a mouth on the tube said. "When the centaurs appear, touch this flame to my rear." A thin torch appeared.

Gary took the torch. When the centaurs slued around the corner, he touched the flame to the back of the cannon. There was a muffled boom, and smoke flew out of the mouth. A big ball plowed through the centaurs, knocking them down.

"So that's what a cannon is," Hiatus said, impressed.

The remaining centaurs took positions behind other stone hinges. The stones looked like trees, but Iris identified them for what they were. The cannon would not reach the centaurs beyond those columns.

"But neither can their arrows reach us," Gary said with some satisfaction.

Then an arrow sailed around the corner, just missing him. It struck a projection of stone and fell with a death rattle.

"One of those centaurs can shoot around corners," Hiatus said, awed.

"These special effects in madness are stretching my imagination," Mentia said, resuming her usual shape and squeezing her ballooning head back together. But stretch marks remained on her forehead.

More arrows squealed around the corner, striking all around them. Only one was real, and that one struck Gayle's shoulder and was shattered. But it remained nervous business, because the arrows appeared so swiftly that they could not tell which ones were real until after they struck. One of them passed right through Iris' nose—and though that one was illusory, it did have some effect.

"Oh, I'm losing my wits!" Iris cried, as a shower of whitish glowing blips sprayed out from her head. "I'm just not used to taking my own medicine!" She grabbed ineffectively for the blips.

"I'll help," Surprise said eagerly. She crossed her eyes. The wits expanded to building block size, and lay tumbled about, their glow now suffusing the area. "Oops—that worked wrong."

"Wait—we can use those as they are," Mentia said. "Stack them up before us to make a safe mental haven." She grabbed a big wit and set it on the ground before Surprise.

Gary picked up another wit and set it beside the first, and Hiatus joined in. Soon they had formed a wall as high as they were, and the arrows could no longer get through.

"But why are some of these brighter than others?" Hiatus asked, pointing to the uneven glowing of the wall.

Gary shrugged. "Some are dim wits."

"Thank you so much," Iris said caustically.

"I have a more serious question," Mentia said. "Why

did Surprise's talent misfire? She was trying to collect the wits, and instead she made them large."

"She's a child," Gary said. "She doesn't have perfect control yet."

"Yes I do," Surprise said. "Except when we first got into the madness, but now I allow for that. Something messed me up."

"Are you sure, dear?" Iris asked. She had recovered her wits. They weren't in her head, but they were right before her and well organized into the wall, so she seemed to be all right now. "Couldn't you have gotten confused in the excitement?"

"No," the child said with certainty. "Something interfered."

"The philter?" Mentia asked. "If it can change your magic, we have more of a challenge than we thought."

"No, it can read my mind but it can't change it—or my talent," Surprise said.

"We don't need to hassle the child about something unimportant," Hiatus said. "She's doing her best."

"You don't believe me," Surprise said accusingly.

"It's not that," Hiatus said, taken aback. "It's just that—"

"You think I'm too young to know what's what!"

"Please, dear, don't get fussed up," Iris said, alarmed.

"And you do too! You all think I'm confused."

"Well, you *are* young," Gary said. "But that's no disparagement."

"Well, I'll show you!" Surprise flared. "I'll make myself old!"

"No, don't waste your magic!" Mentia cried. But her voice of reason was too late.

Surprise crossed her eyes. Suddenly she was a grown woman. Fortunately her clothing had grown along with her. She was now an attractive lady of perhaps thirty, though she looked unfinished in some undefined way. "I am now adult," she said. "I apologize for my erstwhile childishness. But I assure you that some force outside myself or the philter distorted my prior effort of magic. I had intended to draw the wits magnetically into my hands, and instead they expanded and solidified."

"Oh, you are lovely, but you need a finishing touch," Iris said. She reached into a pocket and brought something out.

"What is that?" Surprise asked.

"Makeup. It's a secret illusion girls use that boys don't know about. It makes girls who are too young look older, and women who are too old look younger." She touched Surprise's mature face with powder and sticks of color, and sure enough, soon the woman came into better focus.

The others exchanged most of a glance. Surprise did seem to be a credible witness. "What do you suppose caused that distortion?" Mentia inquired.

"I have no idea. But I can orient on it, if you wish."

"Perhaps you should, as it may be important for us to know what is influencing us."

Then Gary realized what Mentia was after. That mysterious thing they might need to complete their job, that the philter was trying to hide from them: they might be near it. But the demoness was being cautious, lest this be merely a false lead made by the philter.

Surprise crossed her eyes, exactly as she had in childhood. "Why it's a cache of reverse wood in powder form!" she said, surprised. "Someone long ago mixed a potion consisting of equal parts magic dust and ground reverse wood and sealed it in a jar. After three thousand years or so the seal is beginning to leak, so it affected the exercise of my talent. It did not reverse it, merely distorted it, because the potion has odd magical properties."

"Why would someone make such a potion?" Mentia asked, a demonly light of excitement showing in her eyes.

"I conjecture that it is for some specialized purpose," Surprise replied.

A new barrage of arrows came. These ones glowed. One stuck in the end of the wits wall, setting fire to it. "Incendiaries," Iris said, alarmed. "At my wits' end."

Gayle went out beyond the wall, came at it from the other side, caught the shaft of the arrow in her stone teeth, and jerked it out. The burning stopped.

Flares went off. The sky beyond the wall lit up with fancy silent explosions of light. There were beautiful red, blue, green, and yellow streaks across the sky.

"Can you lead us to that jar?" Mentia asked. "Or tell me exactly where it is, so I can fetch it?"

"I can take you there," Surprise said.

"But you shouldn't waste your magic on some stupid potion," Hiatus protested.

"I think this may be important," Mentia said. "Look at how the philter is trying to distract us from it."

Hiatus nodded. "Point made. It doesn't want us to have that jar."

"We'll hold the fort here," Gary said. "You two fetch that jar."

The flares became so bright and dense that the entire landscape and sky were intolerably bright. Now there was noise, a kind of roaring moaning, as of a fierce north wind with its toe stuck in a grinder. The philter was certainly alarmed—or wanted them to think it was.

Mentia formed herself into an impervious transparent sheet. She wrapped herself around Surprise. Surprise walked around the stone hinge and disappeared into the seeming forest.

"Let's distract the philter, if we can," Hiatus said. He patted the ground with his hand, feeling for things to throw. He evidently found something, though it was invisible because of the overlay of illusion.

Gary and Iris did the same, and Gayle sniffed the ground. Soon they found a number of throwable stones. They heaved these out toward the source of the fireworks. Gary doubted that this would have much effect, but in one and a half moments there was a crash, and a section of the sky went blank. Apparently they had scored on a source of illusion.

Then the color faded. There was a clucking sound, and a squat bird walked toward the wall.

"What's that?" Hiatus asked.

"It looks like a hen," Iris said.

"Do hens have scales?" Gayle asked.

There was something familiar about it. Gary focused his memory, trying to place the creature. Then he had it: "That's a drag-hen!" he exclaimed. "Stay away from it!"

"Why?" Hiatus asked.

Then the hen opened her beak. A jet of flame shot out and splashed against the wall.

"Now I know why," Hiatus said.

Fortunately the wall was solid and most of the henfire was illusory, so not much got through.

Mentia and Surprise returned. Surprise was holding a glassy jar about a quarter full of a gray powder. "The lid was loose," she said. "I screwed it tight, so there's no more leakage. But I thought we'd never get through to it; the illusions were horrendous."

"So the philter really didn't want us getting that jar," Gary said.

"It really didn't," Mentia agreed. "But all it had was illusion and a smattering of substance, and those weren't enough to stop us."

"But we still don't know why it fears the jar."

"I can divine that," Surprise said.

"I think you should," Mentia said. "Then you should return to your natural age. We wouldn't want you to get stuck in this age."

"That would be horrible," Surprise agreed. She crossed her eyes, then looked surprised. "They used this for the original conjuration of the Interface! It's the main ingredient. It allows the conjuration to change the nature of existing magic."

"You mean—?" Mentia asked, her eyes growing so large she looked like an insect.

"Yes. It will enable us to bind the philter into the Interface without otherwise disturbing it. It should all have been used up before, so they threw the jar away. They didn't realize that it wasn't empty. That some was left over, which should have been used to harness the philter."

"But why—"

"Because the philter made an illusion that the jar was empty. To conceal the fact that it had avoided incorporation in the Interface. They thought they had done the job properly. When they let go of the jar, the philter covered it with illusion so that it could not be found again, so the error could not be corrected. And it got itself a three-thousand-year rest—at Xanth's expense."

"And now we shall end that rest," Gary said.

Surprise crossed her eyes. Suddenly she was small again. But the makeup remaining on her face made her look uncannily mature.

"You did well, dear," Iris said.

The child clouded up. "But I used up more of my magic. I won't ever be able to do those things again." A tear fell from her eye.

"In a good cause," Iris said soothingly. "Now, if you can transform my wits back so I can have them again—"

"Oh. Yes. I can do that, now that the jar's sealed." The child crossed her eyes, and the wit-blocks dissolved into whitish specs that zipped back into Iris' head.

"That feels so much better," Iris said gratefully. "I shall try not to lose them again."

They plowed on through the massed illusions, countering them one by one and two by two and three by three. When an army of ogres tromped toward them, Iris made an army of giants to oppose them. The result was a battle so horrible to watch that they quickly fled its carnage. When flying dragons appeared, Iris made land dragons to counter them, with more awful battle. When foul harpies flew in, dropping their explosive eggs, foul goblins with slingshots came to strike those eggs with stones and explode them before they were dropped. All manner of monsters were met by all manner of other monsters, and annihilation was continuous.

They followed a hi-way, the low road, and a bye-way, saying hello to the first, cheer up to the second, and farewell to the third. When a giant appeared with a BB gun that fired stinging B's from a B-have at them, they countered with an AA gun that Aced out the B's.

They came at last to the null magic circle. Here the effects diminished, but they knew that the worst was to come. For they would have to brave the philter in the very heart of the strongest, maddest magic of all.

Gary was surprised to see that it was now night. The rock stars were out: bright stones in the sky, rocking with the music of the spheres and cubes.

They waded and swam through the pool and reached the central island. There there was light, as the great central cone of intense magic fed down to bathe what they now knew was the philter's hiding place in some of Xanth's most powerful magic. It shimmered with seeming malignancy. It was mentally and physically daunting.

"But I can help you handle it," Gayle said. "I'm used to its intensity. Just grab hold of my fur."

They did so, and it did help. They moved as a group inside the enclosure to the pedestal where the gargoyle had squatted for three thousand years. It was empty, of course, but now shimmered with the hint of an illusion.

In a moment the illusion became more than a hint. The copy of the warrior maiden Hannah appeared. "So you think you have won!" she spat at them. The spit made weird contortions in the air before landing in the channel around the pedestal. "But you don't have the nerve to harness me!"

Mentia turned to Surprise. "We can support you, but you are the one who must actually take and hold the philter. Can you handle it?"

The child looked stricken. "I can do the magic I need. But nerve isn't magic, is it?"

"No, dear," Iris said. "It is a quality of character."

"I'm too young to have such character," Surprise said, a tear forming at one eye or the other.

"I have learned to use my messed-up magic in a new way," Hiatus said. "Maybe you can use yours in a new way too, to get what you need."

"Gee, I can? How?"

"Well, can you orient on what you need, as you did to find the jar of potion?"

"No, I can't do any magic twice."

"But you can do similar magic. Suppose you could make things become visible, so—"

"Sure." Surprise crossed her eyes.

Suddenly the chamber was littered with things. Gary looked around, trying to figure out what they were. It looked like so much garbage.

"Talents!" Mentia said. "Those are individual talents made visible!"

"She has the talent of seeing the talent of others," Iris said. "In fact, she's given that talent to all of us."

"Sorry," Surprise said. "The magic is so strong here that it turned out a whole lot stronger than I expected."

"And of seeing talents as individual entities," Hiatus said. "See—you look like an illusion, Iris."

"And you look like a cluster of twisted roots," Iris retorted. "But you do have a point. Gary looks like a horrendous stone gargoyle surrounded by pure water."

"You're beautiful," Gayle told Gary.

"But we must not be diverted from our need," Mentia said sensibly. "I would love to collect all these talents and figure out what each one is. This one, for example." She picked up a little ball of whirling whatevers—and puffed into psychedelic smoke. Gary felt seasick, watching it, and he saw Surprise getting wild. Even Gayle seemed quite nervous. Hiatus was waving his arms in some insane pattern.

"Don't do that," Iris snapped. "You're driving us crazy."

The ball dropped to the ground. Mentia's usual shape reformed. "That was the talent: that of driving people crazy."

"What are all these loose talents doing here?" Hiatus asked, bewildered.

Mentia got sensible again. "This is just about the most powerful magic in Xanth, because of the focus," she said. "When people fade out of the scene, it may be that their talents are left without hosts. So they must drift toward the strong magic. Magic surely attracts magic. So they collect here."

"That does make sense," Iris said. "But it doesn't solve our problem. We need nerve for Surprise."

"Maybe a variant," Gary said. "Make qualities of character visible."

"Sure," Surprise said, crossing her eyes.

The talents faded. New things appeared, just about as oddly scattered. There were chunks of stone, splotches of mud, puddles of goo, portions of anatomy, chips of wood, and things that might have resembled squished insects if examined sickeningly close. These were qualities of character?

"Some folk have strong backbone," Mentia remarked, gazing at a fragment of human spine. "Some don't." She looked at some goo. "But where's some nerve?"

"Let me see," the child said. She looked around. "Ah—there's what I need."

Gary looked. He saw a bit of string at the edge of the channel. He picked it up. "This? It's just lying around."

"That's nothing." Hanna said derisively. "Pay it no attention."

"But look what it says," Surprise said.

He looked. The side of the string was printed with the word NERVE. That was what Hanna had said the child lacked. It seemed that it resembled a talent.

So he took it to the child. She laid it on her little arm, and it sank in. "Now I have plenty of nerve," she said confidently.

"Curses, foiled again," Hanna muttered.

"I think she is giving up too easily," Gayle murmured.

Gary had to agree. The philter was as slippery and deceptive as any demon.

"So now at last we are ready to harness the philter," Iris said. "As I understand it, from our vision of the original conjuration of the Interface, Surprise must use her magic to pick up the demon, and the rest of us must speak the words of the conjuration. Then we add the potion in the jar—"

"I don't remember the words," Hiatus said. "And anyway, the philter's vision couldn't be trusted to show that part right. How do we know the real words?"

"He's right," Mentia said. "When you conjure a demon, you must have the ritual down perfectly, or it will turn on you and destroy you. That's why Hanna is being so submissive; she's expecting us to blunder ahead, thinking we are ready, when we're not. There must be a spellbook or something that tells how to do it."

"This is going on forever," Iris exclaimed.

"It has been three thousand years," Gayle pointed out. "It will be another three thousand years, if we don't do it right."

"Point made," Mentia said. "Surprise, can you do magic that will make whatever we need to do the conjuration appear? So we won't miss anything important?"

"Sure." The eyes crossed.

Nothing changed.

"Um—" Iris began.

"I did it, really I did," Surprise said.

"But the philter is covering it over with illusion," Mentia said, catching on. "Iris, if you can penetrate the illusion—"

"Yes." Iris's eyes assumed a faraway look. She turned around in a circle. "Yes," she repeated. "They are glowing, under heaped layers of illusion. A little book, and a—a tangle of straps."

"Straps?" Mentia asked. "What do straps have to do with harnessing the philter?" Then she did a double take. "A harness! We need a harness! Of course. Most demons are conjured for spot purposes, but this one we mean to bind into the Interface. A magic harness will hold it there."

"Where are the book and harness?" Gary asked.

"Not far away," Iris said. "The original folk must have dropped them after they thought the job was done, and they've never been touched since." She walked to the edge of the chamber, plunged her hand into the seeming wall, and came up with a book bound by a strap. Then she went to the other side and reached up toward the ceiling, bringing down that tangle of straps from some masked alcove. "Now we have it all. We can do the job."

Hiatus took the book and opened it. He read the instructions aloud. They were surprisingly simple. They had merely to take the philter, put the harness on it, pour the potion over it, and speak the words "Fil enter Interface— recompile." Then put the philter in a safe place and depart.

"Gary must speak the words," Mentia said. "It's his mission."

"Why, anyone could do this," Hiatus said, looking up. "Why did the Good Magician send us?"

"Not anyone could do it," Mentia said. "We needed you to find our way, Hiatus; you asked Desiree, who directed us to Jethro Giant, who directed us here. We needed Iris to counter the formidable illusions. We needed Gary to read the story in the old stones. And Gayle to give us the philter's true name. And me to counter the demonly aspects. And Surprise to do all the kinds of magic we needed along the way—and will need now, to pick up an unwilling demon. We are the only ones who can do this."

Suddenly it was all making sense. "Then let's do it," Gary said. "If the philter is in this formation, I can find it." He touched the stone, reading it. "There's a crevice here, and it's artificial." He felt around the stone pedestal, and found a loose panel. He opened it, and there in a deep cubby was a flat disk, a ring with mesh across it.

They peered in at it. "That's it?" Hiatus asked. "That tea strainer?"

Hanna appeared. "Of course not," she said severely.

"The philter is a huge mass of unfathomable complications, buried way too deep in the stone for you to ever reach. This is just a decoy."

"Obviously that's it," Gary said with a smile.

"And it is a demon," Mentia said. "It will burn anyone who touches it unprotected. Surprise, make your hands invulnerable and take it out."

The child crossed her eyes. Her hands glowed. The philter assumed the form of a nickelpede, daunting her. Then she exerted her nerve and reached into the cubby and brought out the little object. It seemed like such a nonentity, after the phenomenal displays they had braved to reach it.

Hiatus took the harness and brought it to the philter. There was a hiss, and he snatched his fingers away; it had burned him. So Surprise took it with her free hand and set it over the philter, and the straps enclosed it and drew themselves tight. "Ooh," Hanna said, looking pained.

Then Gary stood before the harnessed philter. He took the jar of potion and unscrewed the top.

Hanna glared at him. "If you pour that potion, I'll destroy you," she said fiercely. Gleams of dangerous light radiated from her eyes.

Gary was daunted. But he reminded himself that this had to be a bluff. He continued to unscrew the lid.

Hanna became a basilisk. She leaped for him, forcing him to meet her gaze. Gary was terrified, not sure whether that baleful glance would turn him to stone in human form, ruining his future with Gayle. But he forced his shaking arm to pour the powder over the harnessed philter.

Hanna reappeared in her usual human female guise. "Then see this!" she cried, hoisting up her skirt.

But Gary had steeled himself against that freakout. "Fil," he said.

"No!" Hanna cried, in evident anguish.

"Enter," Gary said.

"You are destroying me!" Hanna said, looking distraught.

"Interface," Gary said, feeling guilty despite his knowledge that she was a mere illusion crafted to appeal to him.

"I beg of you," she said. "Anything you want! Riches, power, fair women—"

He was about to retort that he was a gargoyle, who needed nothing of those things. But he realized that this was another trap. He couldn't say anything except the words of the conjuration, or it would be spoiled, and might not be repeatable. The philter was still full of tricks.

"Recompile," he said.

Hanna faded into smoke, with a heartrendingly despairing wail. The scene dissolved into a blinding flare of light. Then there was an image of darkness pierced by pinpoints of light. One of these expanded until it became a big bright ball, and near it was a small dark ball, and on the dark ball was a map of Xanth with a crown set on it. This was the mineral kingdom, Gary realized. From that map sprouted a tree, and the tree wore a crown and from it trees like it spread, covering all Xanth. This was the plant kingdom. Then an animal appeared, a seeming composite of all animals, and it wore a crown, and from it many types of other animals spread out, filling niches between the trees. This was the animal kingdom. Finally the human folk came on the scene, and made their villages, and from them spread out all the crossbreds, and then the stone city of Hinge appeared, and from it came two invisible curtains: the Interface outside, and the limit of madness inside, and it was done.

The scenes faded. The six people were left amidst the ruins of Hinge, standing on a weathered island in the middle of a tired pool, with barrenness all around. Their vision of madness was done. Yet somehow Gary did not feel exhilarated. The philter had been a rogue demon, selfish and sometimes dangerous, but it had put up a considerable battle and almost defeated them. It had shown them a significant aspect of the phenomenal history of Xanth. Hanna and Desi—had they really been no more than mindless fig-

ments? Now all the philter's illusions were gone. He
wished it could have been otherwise.

"Put it back in the cubby, and let's go home," Mentia
said. "We are finished here."

Gayle sniffed the water. "It's pure," she said. "The geis
of the gargoyle has been lifted."

"That means that we are free to do whatever we want,"
Gary said, exchanging a significant glance with her. He
was starting to feel better. "When I regain my true form."

"Yes," she said demurely.

18
RETURN

They returned the way they had come, wending their way through the barrens of Hinge to the forest. Gary kept looking around, hoping to glimpse one more glimpse of the magnificence that was the bygone folding city, but that wonderful image was gone.

"The philter may have been a selfish demon," Iris said, "but it did craft a lovely vision."

"I'm almost sorry we had to harness it," Hiatus said. "It had a lot of personality, for a simple object."

"It was a demon among demons," Mentia said. "I can admire it, now that I'm not fighting it."

The others nodded agreement. They had done what they had to do, but the fruit of their victory seemed dull. Gary was relieved to know that he was not the only one to feel some respect for their vanquished and harnessed opponent.

They followed Jethro's footprints until they reached the fallen giant. He was now sitting up. "I think you must have accomplished something," he said. "The madness feels different."

"It is being confined," Mentia explained. "It will retreat slowly to its former boundary, and remain there."

"That is good news," the giant said. "Any day now I shall heave myself the rest of the way up and try to blunder back to Xanth proper."

They wished him well and went on.

Next they came to Desiree Dryad and her tree. The two were still in sad state, but she looked more cheerful than before.

Hiatus approached her. "I can help your tree," he said.

"I know."

"You know?"

"I had this weird dream of you, being in the middle of a strange ancient city," she said. "And in my dream I called myself Desi, and I—" She paused, looking modestly pained. "I think you are a nicer person than I thought before, steadfast and true, and if you would like to remain here—"

"First let me mend your tree," he said. He bent to its base, and concentrated, and round roots sprouted, displacing the square ones. Almost immediately the tree brightened, its leaves uncurling and turning green. The roots were performing.

As the tree recovered, so did Desiree. She went rapidly from haggard to plain to radiant. By the time Hiatus straightened up from his exertion of magic, she was the very loveliest of ladies. And as he turned to face her, she stepped into his embrace and kissed him. Little red hearts flew out and dissolved, making the scene around them rose-colored.

"Hiatus has his reward," Mentia said. "And I think he likes it as well as anything the philter offered him."

The others agreed. They walked on, knowing that they would not be missed.

They found Richard and Janet, and explained that the madness would be retreating, but it would take time. The two were reassured. "And I think Hiatus and Desiree will marry," Iris said wisely. "I am sure they will want you to visit."

They passed Castle Zombie and informed Millie the Ghost of her son's success. Millie was duly gratified.

In due course they reached the golem household. Surprise immediately reverted to golem size and leaped into the embrace of her mother.

"But is she—?" Grundy inquired cautiously.

Iris looked sober. "I know this will come as a regret to you, but Surprise discovered that she can perform each magic talent only once. She is determined not to waste any more magic. So she will be very restrained. In fact, she is apt to become a distressingly normal child, except in emergencies."

Grundy considered. "No more wild magic? No more out-of-control effects? That is a regret." But somehow he did not seem unhappy.

Rapunzel grew to normal human size and brought the child to them in turn. Surprise gave them each a tiny hug. "Thanks for the great adventure," she told Gary. "We must do it again sometime." Then she dissolved into a naughty titter. She was definitely normal.

"That reminds me," Iris said. "Surprise will tell you a fantastic tale that you will find almost impossible to believe. But you must make the effort, for it is true."

They made their way to the Brain Coral's Pool, promising the figgle nothing but giving it a fig at the end. As they approached the pool, Magician Trent came out to meet them.

"When I was twenty-three the first time, my romance was bad," Iris said. She looked very determined and feminine and appealing, which was odd because she was using no illusion at all. She had evidently come to a significant decision. "This time I'm going to make it good." And she put her arms around Trent and shoved him into the pool. They sank together without a splash, kissing as they disappeared.

"Ah, the follies of youth," Mentia remarked. "It's a

good thing that we who are many centuries old aren't like that." But she looked somewhat wistful.

"Are you really that dissatisfied with the situation of your better half?" Gary inquired.

"After seeing how much you living folk enjoy romance, I'm beginning to wonder," the demoness confessed.

"Why not go back and try it, then?" Gayle asked.

Mentia shrugged, her shoulders passing along the length of her body in her old, slightly crazy, way. "Maybe I will. But look, you illustrious animals—if you ever go out on another mad adventure—"

"We'll be sure to invite you along," Gary said.

"Thank you." The demoness vanished.

Magician Trent emerged from the pool. His hair was disheveled and there were kisses all over his face. "I don't think I properly appreciated my wife before," he remarked. "Youth is intriguing. I discover a new horizon of emotion and experience ahead, and am most interested in exploring its avenues. But there is something I have to do first." He gestured, and suddenly Gary had his natural body back. He was a gargoyle again.

"Oh, at last!" Gayle cried. "Now we can do it."

"Now we can do it," Gary agreed. There was no need to discuss what it was; some things were inherent. "Thank you, Magician Trent!"

"Have a nice time," the Magician said, as a female hand emerged from the water to haul him back under. "I'm sure *I* will."

Gary and Gayle made their way to Castle Roogna, a place neither of them had seen before. On the way they encountered a militant woman. "You! Gargoyle!" the woman cried. "I have a score to settle with you!"

It was Hannah Barbarian. Was it possible that—?

"I had the weirdest wildest dream, surely brought by a night mare with the croup," Hannah said. "You were in manform, and I—ugh!"

It was possible. "I'm sure you could never be a seductive handmaiden," Gary said.

"You had better believe it! Nothing like that could ever happen." She marched off. Then she paused, as if thinking of something, but Gary and Gayle were already bounding on their way.

In due course they reached Castle Roogna. There was Princess Electra coming out to meet them. Gary knew it was her, because she wore blue jeans and braids and looked innocently unprincessly. "You'll never believe what I dreamed!" she said.

"We believe," Gary and Gayle said together.

"But I would never do that in real life. I don't even have a battery to charge."

"Of course not."

"And according to the magic tapestry, Xanth has been saved from madness and the geis of the gargoyle has been abated."

"Yes," Gary agreed.

"And Wira sent a message from the Good Magician," Electra continued. "We have your places ready." She paused. "But do you really—I mean it seems like such inadequate repayment for such heroic service."

"It's what we want," Gary reassured her.

And so Gary Gar and Gayle Goyle took their places, and settled blissfully in for the next century. On parallel corners of the roof of Castle Roogna, spouting pure rainwater to the ground. The position of ultimate honor for gargoyles.

AUTHOR'S NOTE

Stories of Xanth normally move swiftly; I wrote *Vale of the Vole* in six and a half weeks. But *Gargoyle* took me almost nine months. What happened? Well, I had other projects going, whose timing was harder to control, so I fitted Xanth in around them. Thus I started it in Dismember 1992, wrote 10,000 words, then broke to edit the simplified version of the first Xanth novel, *A Spell for Chameleon*. That reading of *Spell* was surprisingly influential, because it reminded me of a number of things about Xanth I had forgotten, and I realized that there were some serious discrepancies between this and later Xanth. Thus came to be the need for fixing them, as was accomplished in this novel. Then I got into research for, and writing of, my continuing GEODYSSEY novel, *Shame of Man*, my major project of this time. Then I worked on the collaborative eco-horror novel with Cliff Pickover, *Spider Legs*. It wasn't until Apull 1993 that I returned to *Gargoyle*—for another 500 words, before I had to read another manuscript, and do more work on GEODYSSEY. In Mayhem I came back to Xanth for another 7,000 words, before going into another collaboration, this time a fantasy of medieval India with Alfred Tella, *The Willing Spirit*. In Je-June I returned for another 30,000 words of Xanth, and continued in Jewel-Lye for another 46,000, and went on to finish it in AwGhost with another 20,000. So it was mostly written in that later stage. I hope to write the next one in more of a single piece. I did edit it in one swell foop, in AwGhost 1993, to gain a better sense of the whole, and believe it is a unified novel.

During the intermittent course of this novel something significant with respect to Xanth happened: Lester del Rey died. He was the editor with whom Xanth started, and he helped shape it. Surely he had been exposed to the magic Edit Ore, which transforms ordinary folk into hard-headed editors. He became the model for grumpy Good Magician Humfrey, just as his wife Judy Lynn del Rey became an aspect of the indomitable Gorgon. She even sent in puns, like Gorgonzola cheese. I made the Humfrey/Gorgon wedding day the same as the del Rey wedding date, in the Xanth Calendar. My wife and I and our two daughters, then teenagers, met them and liked them; we had quite a time at the American Booksellers' Association convention in Dallas in 1983. Everything was great. But then the contrary magic of irony entered the picture, making things happen opposite to the way they should. Judy Lynn died tragically three years later, and things fell apart, and that glad season came to an end. As it happened, there came a point where I was no longer willing to work with the kind of instructions the Good Magician gave, and so I took Xanth elsewhere, but the debt it owes to Lester can not be denied. I had the Good Magician disappear for several novels, because of the awkwardness of no longer working with Lester, but Xanth needed him, and in due course Humfrey returned. As I said in my private writeup of my experience with Lester and Judy Lynn del Rey: they were giants, well deserving of the respect their critics never gave them in life, and I think their like will not be seen again. Just as there are no others in Xanth like Humfrey and the Gorgon. I couldn't save their lives in Mundania, though I owe more to them than perhaps to any other editor and publisher, but at least I can recognize them in Xanth. Their magic put Xanth on the bestseller map.

Another thing happened in this period of writing: I found a long-lost song. This was "The Girl in the Wood" or "Remember Me," which I had heard once in 1956 and never again. I had mentioned it in an Author's Note, and two of my readers responded. I followed up, and discovered two versions of it, one by Jimmie Rodgers and one by Frankie Laine. I listened to them so often that I memorized both versions—and of course the song became part of this novel. Thus the background on Hiatus and Desiree in Chapter 5. My thanks to Kim Diaz and Moira Currie, who found that song for me.

I'm still trying to discourage puns and talents and other notions from readers, but the readers keep sending them anyway. So this time there are about one and three quarters slews of credits, and I still have dozens of notions left over. I have mostly caught up with the list through 1992, but about fifty remain to be used another time. Here, at any rate, in one huge mass, are the ones used this time, roughly in order of their appearance:

Ein Stein—Jim Loy; Pay Dirt—Claud L. Medearis; Mint Plant—Carol Jacob; Dogs in Xanth—Beatrice Taylor; Wolf puns—Andy Wolf; Underwear wolves—Eric Hafner; Hannah Barbarian—Mike Hafner; Hurry Canes—Heather Scott, Scott Stancliff; Tea Pea, Fountain Pen—Carlos Blake; Control of Fire, twins whose magic together is stronger—Matt Markovina; Quartz holding water—E Jeremy Parish; Rain Check—Jeffrey Ku; 20,000 Leagues Under the Sea—Thomas Hanana; Naia Naiad, talent lying around—Natasha Droza; Talent of recovering things from the Void—Jonathan Hicks; Stanley Steamer's birthday—Dor Casses' sister; Nose stuck in a book—Tirtzah Hoffman; Industree—Clair Litton; Harpychord—Ron Urwongse; Talent of conjuring things from Mundania—Cinnamon Kelly; Rock and Roll—Charles Gattuso;

Pop Rocks music—Michelle Lahue; Hybiscuits, mushroom—Nuri Parker; Finger and toe matoes—Gillian Rose; Toiletree—Mirav Hoffman; Limbbow—Nichole Adkins; Chairman—Dor Casses; Arm chair, Wits as building blocks for a safe mental haven—Holly Hunt; Coat of arms—Juliana Boiarsky, Josh Frankel; Board meeting—Christian Kipp; Can't be found talent—France Bauduin; Talent of changing into any human crossbreed—Gillian Rose; Talent of dehydrating—Tamara Lynn Bailey; Talent of changing self to object of same mass—David Raines; Talent of turning any material to any other material—Jonathan B Tsur; Talent of making things invisible—Jenny MacDonell; Cereal killer—Stephanie Erb; Transform animate creature to inanimate—Dawn McClain; Talent of changing hair color and quality—France Bauduin; Maize puzzle—Julie Grimes; Zombie gourd snakebite restoring Zora Zombie—Peggy Curiel; Change one fruit to another—Alexander Livingstone; Talent of control of weather—Kathie Burch; Sex change—Sonny Giannola; Talent of becoming intangible at will—Najam (Morningstar) Mughal; Talent of adapting oneself: arms into wings, etc.—Jonathan Carter; Talent of turning water to healing elixir—Mark Stillwell; Engine Ear—Charles Gattuso; Talent of stregthening oneself: muscles, sight, hearing—Dawn McClain; Talent of drawing figures that come alive without changing—Julie Brady; Deaf-o-dils—Nuri Parker; Rabbit's-foot ferns hopping—Melissa Martz; Dentist who dents—J. Michael Major, DDS; Steel wool from metal sheep—Colleen Sentance; Ironweed—Ben Smith; Souls of shoes—Jeremy Hayes; Rationale for two souls—Jeffry Ku; Passion Vines—Ben Smith; Animate the inanimate, such as a chair—Matthew Peddinghaus; Pun-kin Pie, Honeycombs—Robert Ruthart; Poke-a-nose Mountains—Tirtzah and Shira Hoffman; Rock pictures—WG Bliss; Train of Thought—Juliana Boiarsky, Cinnamon Kelly; Sun House, Screen, Blocks, Glasses, Water Hole—Joey Hendry, Ben Smith; Punching Bag—Stephen and Alan Belsky; Talent of seeing through another person's eyes—Aimee Amodio;

Talent of switching places with others—N. Landau, K. Reiter, France Bauduin; Rug Bee—Tirtzah Hoffman; Future Xanth (though this copped out)—Kevin Wildrick; Sorceress Iris' distant past—Barbara Hay Hummel; A child's curse: conjuring vegetables—anonymous; Nuclear Plant, Hedge Hog—Ravi Kanodia; Assault and Battery—Jeff Sligh; Talent of shooting around corners—Julian Beardwell; Stretch marks from stretched imagination—Heather Scott; Talent of changing one's own age—Caroline Webb; Powdered reverse wood mixed with magic dust—Tommy Keogh; Drag-hen—Jason Walton; Date of the delivery of Dawn and Eve, Makeup—Paula Jean Blum; Hi-way, bye-way, low road—Donald Marte; BB gun—David Miller; Rock Stars—Eric Cole, Anne Wooster; Seeing the talents of others—Katy Robinson; Talents as individual entities—Matt Gillmore; Talent of driving folk crazy—Anita Tong; Plant and animal kingdoms—Mark DeRose; Edit Ore—Rachel Ali; Irony—Brian Horstman.

I repeat: I have puns overflowing the barrel, so there is no need for readers to send in more. I realize that won't stop some of you, but maybe the news that it takes me several years to use some of them will.

For those of you who fear that this is the last Xanth novel: relax. Xanth is an open series, continuing indefinitely, as long as the readers like it and the critics hate it. I am pondering a number of interesting future notions.

Those interested in sampling my Newsletter or ordering the Anthony titles local stores don't carry may call troll free 1-800 HI PIERS.

PIERS ANTHONY
THE GRANDE MASTER

☐	53114-0	ANTHONOLOGY	$3.50 Canada $3.95
☐	53098-5	BUT WHAT OF EARTH?	$4.95 Canada $5.95
☐	50915-3	CHIMAERA'S COPPER	$4.95 Canada $5.95
☐	51384-3	DRAGON'S GOLD	$3.95 Canada $4.95
☐	51916-7	THE ESP WORM with Robert E. Margroff	$3.95 Canada $4.95
☐	52088-2	GHOST	$3.99 Canada $4.99
☐	51348-7	HASAN	$3.99 Canada $4.99
☐	51982-5	MOUVAR'S MAGIC with Robert E. Margroff	$4.99 Canada $5.99
☐	51177-8	ORC'S OPAL with Robert E. Margroff	$4.99 Canada $5.99

MORE FROM THE GRANDE MASTER PIERS ANTHONY

FANTASY BESTSELLERS
FROM TOR

☐ 52261-3 BORDERLANDS $4.99
edited by Terri Windling & Lark Alan Arnold Canada $5.99

☐ 50943-9 THE DRAGON KNIGHT $5.99
Gordon R. Dickson Canada $6.99

☐ 51371-1 THE DRAGON REBORN $5.99
Robert Jordan Canada $6.99

☐ 52003-3 ELSEWHERE $3.99
Will Shetterly Canada $4.99

☐ 55409-4 THE GRAIL OF HEARTS $4.99
Susan Schwartz Canada $5.99

☐ 52114-5 JINX HIGH $4.99
Mercedes Lackey Canada $5.99

☐ 50896-3 MAIRELON THE MAGICIAN $3.99
Patricia C. Wrede Canada $4.99

☐ 50689-8 THE PHOENIX GUARDS $4.99
Steven Brust Canada $5.99

☐ 51373-8 THE SHADOW RISING $5.99
Robert Jordan (Coming in October '93) Canada $6.99

Buy them at your local bookstore or use this handy coupon:
Clip and mail this page with your order.

Publishers Book and Audio Mailing Service
P.O. Box 120159, Staten Island, NY 10312-0004

Please send me the book(s) I have checked above. I am enclosing $ _____
(Please add $1.50 for the first book, and $.50 for each additional book to cover postage and
handling. Send check or money order only— no CODs.)

Name _____

Address _____

City _____ State / Zip _____

Please allow six weeks for delivery. Prices subject to change without notice.

MORE BESTSELLING
FANTASY FROM TOR

☐ 50392-9   DRAGON SEASON $4.99
        Michael Cassutt   Canada $5.99

☐ 51716-4   THE FOREVER KING $5.99
        Warren Murphy and Ellen Kushner   Canada $6.99

☐ 50360-0   GRYPHON'S EYRIE $3.95
        Andre Norton & A.C. Crispin   Canada $4.95

☐ 52248-6   THE LITTLE COUNTRY $5.99
        Charles de Lint   Canada $6.99

☐ 50518-2   THE MAGIC OF RECLUCE $4.99
        L.E. Modesitt, Jr.   Canada $5.99

☐ 50249-3   SISTER LIGHT, SISTER DARK $3.95
        Jane Yolen   Canada $4.95

☐ 55815-4   SOLDIER OF THE MIST $3.95
        Gene Wolfe   Canada $4.95

☐ 51112-3   STREET MAGIC $3.99
        Michael Reaves   Canada $4.99

☐ 51445-9   THOMAS THE RHYMER $3.99
        Ellen Kushner   Canada $4.99

Buy them at your local bookstore or use this handy coupon:
Clip and mail this page with your order.

Publishers Book and Audio Mailing Service
P.O. Box 120159, Staten Island, NY 10312-0004

Please send me the book(s) I have checked above. I am enclosing $ _____
(Please add $1.50 for the first book, and $.50 for each additional book to cover postage and
handling. Send check or money order only—no CODs.)

Name _____

Address _____

City _____ State / Zip _____

allow six weeks for delivery. Prices subject to change without notice.